# The
# CRIDER CHRONICLES

Anderson Gentry

Cover Design by Hanna Al-Shear

CRIMSON
DRAGON
PUBLISHING

Copyright © Anderson Gentry 2022, 2005

Printed in the United Sates of America

Second Edition, Revised

ISBN 978-1-944644-33-8
E-pub ISBN 978-1-944644-34-5

Science Fiction: Action & Adventure
Alien Contact
Military

All rights reserved. This book or any portion thereof may not be reproduced or used in any manner whatsoever without the express written permission of the publisher except for the use of brief quotations in a book review.

This is a work of fiction. Names, characters, businesses, places, events, locales, and incidents are either the products of the author's imagination or used in a fictitious manner. Any resemblance to actual persons, living or dead, or actual events is purely coincidental.

Swash for section break Assortment vector created by www.freepik.com
https://www.freepik.com/vectors/assortment

Crimson Dragon Publishing
Willow, Alaska
https://crimsondragonpublishing.com

# Contents

The
# CRIDER CHRONICLES

# Prologue

**Earth, 2130**

*The history of the First Confederation in fact goes back almost a hundred years prior to the formal beginning of the Confederate government. In 2130, a young French-English scientist named Hiram Eugene Gellar was working at the Institut National de Physique Nucléaire et de Physique des Particules in France. The Institut was doing pioneering work in anti-matter and string/counterstring physics, but it took the imagination and creative urge of young Gellar to take the work to the next level.*

*Gellar inhabited an Earth in transition, eighty years after the Third World War. The United States remained the planet's primary power, having retained an almost two-century primacy in economic and military might. Sub-Saharan Africa had been devastated by brush wars and plague, China's population was recovering from the Chinese Civil War, and Russia was once again emerging as an economic power following huge oil and power metal finds in Siberia.*

*Europe was in many ways still recovering from the Third World War, but France – now a state in the European*

*Community – was becoming a center of physics research, mostly aimed at exploring alternative energy sources for a world rapidly running short of resources.*

*Gellar's invention would very quickly change everything.*

*—Morris/Handel, "A History of the First Galactic Confederacy," University Publications, 2804CE*

Following are selected excerpts from Morris/Handel, "A History of the First Galactic Confederacy," University Publications, 2804CE, and selected news media from the Pre-Galactic Era.

**Morris/Handel: 2041-2044, the Third World War**

While the international tensions that led up to the Third World War are generally accepted to have begun with the destruction of the World Trade Center in New York City on September 11, 2001, the base causes of the conflict began long before. Decades of instability in the oil-rich Persian Gulf nations along with a persistent religious fanaticism rooted in the area had given rise to a number of extremist/terror groups dedicated to spreading chaos through the region and, early in the twenty-first century, around the world.

Following the September 11th attack, the United States – by then Earth's only major military power – reacted swiftly, invading and crushing the southwest Asian nation of Afghanistan. Afghanistan's ruling Taliban government had provided resources and refuge to the group behind the September 11th attacks. The overthrow of the Taliban followed two years later by the overthrow of Iraq's dictator, Saddam Hussein, started a democratization trend in the Middle East that spread to Saudi Arabia and Syria in the next forty years. Democratization did not, however, spread past those four nations until after the Third World War.

July 14, 2041 saw another major terrorist attack, this time in Paris. The Bastille Day bombing attacks killed over 4,800 Parisians, and destroyed the Eiffel Tower and the Arc de Triumph, along with several newer buildings and landmarks. The European Union, then a reluctant partner in the West's attempts to democratize the Middle East, promptly voted to authorize sending EU forces to Iran, the nation that sponsored the Bastille Day attacks. August 14th, 2041, when elements of the US 1st Marine Division, 82nd Airborne Division, and the EU's First Parachute Division landed in Iran, is generally accepted as the first day of the Third World War.

**Transcribed from Fox News International webcast, December 9th, 2044:**

"Thank you, Lisa. It's an exciting moment here in Brussels, where the leaders of the Allied Powers are gathered along with the leaders of the defeated Central Alliance, to sign this historic treaty. Details of the treaty have not yet been released, but one source confirms that one clause stipulates free, open, internationally monitored elections in the Central Alliance nations are to take place within one year. Just entering the hall now, we can see the President of the European Union, the President of the Russian Republic, and the President of the United States…"

## Morris/Handel: Peebles Mining Corporation, Earth

The Third World War drained not only the defeated Central Alliance, but also the victorious Allied Powers. While Earth's population was still increasing in the developed and developing nations, ongoing brush wars and plague in Africa and the aftermath of the war in the Middle East had rendered much of those regions uninhabitable, and their resources inaccessible. Ever-expanding technology, however, was making new sources for vital materials economically feasible for the first time.

At least three private corporations were involved in the first wave of exploration into the Sol system. Peebles Mining Corporation was the largest of these. Peebles financed almost one-half of the first International Orbital Station and shipyard, and from there, and their bases on Luna, ran mining operations to Mars, the asteroid belt, and as far out as the Jovian satellites.

The key to the economic feasibility of off-planet mining lay in Peebles' construction of the first of Earth's five Skyhooks. The Quito Skyhook was a carbon-fiber tower, based on a mountain in the Andes and tethered to a captured asteroid in geosynchronous orbit. The Skyhook Station enabled Peebles' huge mining ships to offload their cargoes into barges that descended to low Earth orbit. The barges then docked at the Station, where refined ores and mineral products were lowered to the surface by magnetic freight car.

But still Earth's population continued to grow, and advancing technology made the demand for resources ever greater. By the beginning of the twenty-second century, Earth's demand for mineral resources was fast approaching a crisis level.

**Associated Press, Denver, Colorado, USA, September 23, 2136**

A privately owned spaceship, designed here in Denver and built in great secrecy in a closed dock on the International Orbital Station, now promises to change the way humanity looks at the universe.

The *Lever de Soleil* departed the Station fourteen days ago, and was observed accelerating at an unprecedented rate; Luna City Tracking and Traffic control reported that the ship was accelerating at a logarithmic rate.

"It was impossible – at least we thought it was impossible," said Andrea Martins, the senior Duty Controller at Luna City, who was on watch at the time. "No known drive system can accelerate a big ship like that

– not chemical rockets, not ion drives, not reaction motors. And there was almost no drive signature. We didn't have any idea what was happening."

The world found out what was happening this morning, when the *Lever de Soleil* returned to the International Orbital Station from the Alpha Centauri system. The crew of the ship brought back petabytes of data from the Alpha system that revealed the existence of three rocky planets in the habitable zone. While all three planets are barren and sterile, one of them shows signs of great mineral resources.

The question is now one of economics. Will Gellar Systems Enterprises, the *Lever De Soleil*'s builders, be producing more ships? Or will the design be licensed to other shipbuilders?

In either case, the entire economic picture of the Sol system has just been irretrievably altered.

## Morris/Handel: Gellar Star Drive

If one man can be named as having had the most significant effect on human history in the modern era, that man would be Hiram Eugene Gellar, inventor of the Gellar Star Drive. The Gellar Drive made interstellar flight not only possible but also practical and launched mankind on its greatest era of exploration and discovery. The stage was now set for humanity's expansion into what was to be the first Galactic culture.

Book One

# Forest

# Earth

In the year 2136 CE, Hiram Eugene Gellar invented a mass-drive engine capable of tremendous power. The prototype Gellar Star Drive was a massive affair, combining thirty-meter-wide scoop with a mass converter tunnel. Gellar built his pioneering starship around his mass tunnel, and christened it the Lever de Soleil. The Gellar Drive not only generated tremendous power, its' negative-energy drive field enabled ships to penetrate the subspace field barrier, resulting in trans-light speeds. Indeed, the nature of the mass-tunnel drive was such that a large ship could attain higher speeds than a small one.

Gellar's first ship was a private yacht, and it was in the *Lever de Soleil* that the first interstellar jump was made by Gellar and his partner Edda Jean Fauvier. In 2138, they left Earth orbit for the Alpha Centauri system, returning fourteen days after their departure to report two rocky planets, supporting no life but holding a rich variety of mineral resources.

The Peebles Mining Company Inc. subsequently purchased the patent to the Gellar Star Drive for the record sum of 2.1 billion dollars. Gellar and Fauvier were married and retired to an estate in the south of France.

Within five years, the entire face of human life changed. Peebles swiftly re-organized as the Off-World Mining & Exploration, Ltd. and built the first commercially owned and operated Skyhook in Peru, providing an inexpensive transport of raw materials to low Earth orbit. From this base, a floating space-dock was built in high orbit. In this first major space-bound naval architectural platform was built the StarShip *Blue Giant*, a colossal mining and exploration ship built around a two-kilometer-long Gellar Star Drive tunnel.

The SS *Blue Giant* left Earth orbit late in 2165, with a crew of 16,000, 48 mining shuttles and a thousand tons of specialized mining equipment, bound for the Alpha system. Two other major mining ships and four smaller exploration craft were already under construction.

But the sensation caused by the ability to mine planets in other systems was quickly eclipsed. In 2167, the SS *Demeter*, an OWME exploration ship, discovered the first habitable world orbiting Tau Ceti. The planet, later named Caliban, was a temperate world of oceans and continents, forests and mountains, with gravity slightly higher than Earth's and a variety of native flora and fauna. The *Demeter* returned to Earth with the exciting news, and OWME Ltd. quickly began construction of colonization ships. Within three years, four more habitable planets were discovered. The next great phase in Man's evolution had begun.

One of the first thirteen worlds to be settled was Forest. While Forest lacked mineral wealth, colonists were attracted to the mild climate and rich soil. OWME intended Forest to be an agricultural world, and began recruiting farmers, hunters, and pioneers to settle what promised to be a difficult new home – Forest's flora and fauna being strikingly similar to Earth's Jurassic period.

But the difficulty only began there, as it was on Forest that humanity first encountered the hostile, militaristic Grugell Empire.

*—Morris/Handel, "A History of the First Galactic Confederacy," University Publications, 2804CE*

# One

*Far better it is to dare mighty things, to win glorious triumphs even though checkered by failure, than to rank with those poor spirits who neither enjoy nor suffer much because they live in the gray twilight that knows neither victory nor defeat.*

—*Theodore Roosevelt, President of the United States, 1901-1909*

**October, on a trail in the Salmon River Mountains near Challis, Idaho.**

The last few golden aspen leaves were clattering in the breeze as Michael Crider and his hunter-client climbed through the grove on their way to a high drainage. The Idaho sun was bright, but the air chilly and, at 3500 meters altitude, very thin. Mike was used to both, his lungs and muscles hardened by a life in the mountains. He paused, looking back and wishing the same were true of his client, an overweight security consultant from Atlanta who'd had an urge to try elk hunting. The heavy, balding man was struggling to reach the small bench where Mike waited.

"Just another kilometer or so," Mike assured the red-faced, wheezing man, "and we'll break out into the big drainage I told you about. It levels out some up there, and that's where we'll find the elk."

The client, Jeff Davies, pulled a drab green handkerchief from his pocket and dabbed the sheen of sweat from his forehead. "Steep," he puffed. He managed a grin at Mike. "Y'all aren't even breathin' hard. Must be great to be young."

"Well, Mr. Davies, I live up here. Makes a difference." Mike couldn't help taking a liking to the man, out-of-shape as he was. "We can rest here for a few minutes, but we'll want to be up in that drainage before very much longer. There's been a bull in there about an hour before sunset most days I've been up in here."

"You mean to say y'all walk up here every blessed day?"

"Well, not every day. Only three or four times a week."

"Your Dad said it'd be hell keepin' up with you."

"Who do you think showed me this place?" Mike grinned. "Dad could walk the legs off a mountain goat." He turned to squint at the sun. "We've got another hour or so to cover that last klick. We'll take it kind of easy, Mr. Davies."

"Well, Ah sure do appreciate ya'll not tryin' to kill me," Davies replied. He unzipped his bright orange jacket and adjusted the sling of his expensive Hooper Super Magnetic rifle, settling the weight of the eight-pound piece more comfortably on his shoulder.

"So, boy, where are your folks, anyway?"

"Dad decided to check into some land in Africa, and Mom went along for the ride. Getting pretty crowded around here," he pointed back down towards the rapidly growing city of Challis, "and Dad heard that the big plagues and the war over there left an awful lot of land empty. Hard to find a quiet place anymore, you know?"

"Don't Ah know it," Davies answered. "They'll be takin' the semi-ballistic, then? Rough way to travel, but fast." Mike nodded.

Semi-ballistic intercontinental flights were fairly new. The ship itself was deceptively simple. Each SB was a passenger compartment grafted to the front of what was, for all purposes, a huge ballistic missile. Following a rocket-powered launch and ascent to the very edges of the atmosphere, folding wings deployed for a controlled but unpowered plummet to the destination. The New York – Nairobi semi made the trip in an hour and thirty minutes, providing fast passage for any passengers that could stand the six-gee takeoff.

The hunters turned to stroll up the rest of the slope at a more leisurely pace.

As he hiked, Mike represented an almost lost picture of the Old West. Tall and rangy, a large gray Stetson perched on his head, a gray and black flannel shirt, leather vest, jeans and lug-soled boots, Mike was an authentic character of a type that was all-too quickly disappearing. As he was guiding today and not hunting, he was armed only with a wickedly sharp skinning knife – Davies had seen him shave hair with it – and, most fascinating, an ancient Colt .45 caliber single-action revolver that had to be three hundred years old, hung low in a leather holster secured with a hammer loop. Mike's face was hard, angular, his eyes blue as a mountain lake, his close-cropped hair the pale blonde of winter hay. Even now, at eighteen, the corners of his eyes showed the crows-feet placed there by a hundred bright sunny afternoons.

He moved with a brisk economy; a hunter born. Mike had killed his first deer at age ten, his first elk at thirteen. He was not a creature of the growing cities, but rather of the disappearing wilderness, and like a wolf or grizzly bear, he chafed under the pressure of the expanding urban areas. Mike liked nothing better than roaming the mountains, on foot or on horseback, with only a bedroll, a rifle, and a minimal set of camping equipment. Many a summer, he'd spent weeks on end in the wildest reaches of the Salmon River Range in just this fashion. Every year though, the wild places grew fewer, the houses and condos grew thicker, the whistle of skimmers louder. Mike was a child of the wilderness, and his wilderness was shrinking by the year.

The last kilometer was covered slowly. The sun was still a hand's breadth from the mountainside to the west when they arrived at a huge, open basin. Mike was pleased to see that Mr. Davies had almost caught his breath.

"Quiet, now," Mike whispered. "We'll sneak along this tree line to the right and find a spot up on that little rise to watch from."

Davies nodded as he unslung his rifle to carry it in at port arms. Mike was surprised to learn that the heavy man could move quietly through the firs and spruce that edged the drainage. He said as much, and Davies smiled. "Well, Ah may not be as young and tough in these blasted mountains as y'all, boy, but Ah have been huntin' deer in Alabama swampland since long before y'all was born."

Mike chuckled. "Well, sir, you'll do fine then. Here's our spot."

Davies eased himself to a sitting position, extended the bipod from the fore-end of the Hooper, checked the batteries, and took a glance through the scope. He looked up at Mike and nodded.

The two hunters sat for over an hour, while the shadows lengthened and the air grew chillier. Chipmunks frolicked in the leaves around them. Once, a gray jay glided to perch on Davies' boot tip, drawing a smile from both men.

Then, the elk were there.

"Look," Mike hissed, pointing. On the far side of the drainage, some three hundred and fifty meters distant, two cow elk nosed slowly into the open, nibbling on the lush grass as they went. Two more cows and a yearling appeared a few moments later.

"The bull will be the last one out," Mike whispered from just behind Davies. "Get ready, he'll come out behind the cows. The rut's been over for a month, but he's still hanging with the cow herd."

Davies raised the butt of his rifle to his shoulder but kept his finger off the trigger. He touched a stud on the wrist of the plastic stock with his thumb. There was a barely audible whine as capacitors charged.

Mike raised his battered old binoculars to scan the far tree line. "There," he whispered, "Right there, just to the left of that big cow with the split ear, he's a big five-by-five."

The bull was just inside the tree line, edging with agonizing slowness into the open. Davies lowered his head to the stock, sighting now through his riflescope. "Ah got him," he whispered back. "Hey, he's a dandy."

The seconds passed like hours, as the bull examined the clearing meticulously. Finally, he took a step into the open.

Davies placed the crosshairs just behind the bull's front leg and pressed the trigger. The Hooper Super discharged with a loud crack, the firing electrets sending a magnetic pulse down the super-conducting barrel, driving a plastic-coated steel projectile at over 1500 meters per second out of the rifle's muzzle. Struck in the chest by the hyper-velocity projectile, the bull staggered a few paces and dropped. The cows scattered, barking in alarm, back into the trees.

"Good shot," Mike applauded as Davies let out an exultant whoop. He carefully cleared his rifle before picking it up to sprint across the drainage to the downed bull.

Mike walked along behind, enjoying the moment. *At least this guy sprung for the retrieval droid*, he reminded himself. *All we've got to do is dress it out.*

It was almost completely dark when the bull was field-dressed, but that didn't matter to the retrieval droids. Davies fished the beacon out of his pack and pressed the activation stud. A small red light on the top of the oblong metal box began flashing.

"Well, boy, that bull's a dandy."

"He sure is, Mr. Davies."

"Ah sure hope I'm gonna be able to get a head mount of him listed to take on my ship."

Mike raised an eyebrow in an unspoken question.

"Ah'm goin' off-Earth, boy. Took a job as a security chief with Off-World Mining and Exploration. This here's mah last Earthside vacation, and Ah sure do appreciate y'all makin' it a memorable one."

"I'm glad to do it, Mr. Davies. You know where you're headed yet?"

Davies shook his head. "Nope. Depends on where they need me when the departure date pops up, six weeks from now. Ah'm sorta hoping for Caliban, it's at least part-way civilized, but Ah reckon Ah'll get posted to some pioneer backwater. Well, the money's good, anyway. You ever thought about headin' out there?" He gestured at the stars that were now twinkling overhead.

"No, not really. Dad and Mom would never go for it, and I'd hate to leave them here, never see my folks again. Besides, I like it here. If it just wasn't getting so crowded, though…" His comment trailed off as the whine of the droid swelled out of the east. Within moments, the large, flat silver platform glided in over the trees and settled into the grass a few feet from the downed bull.

Five minutes later, the bull has been manhandled onto the platform and tied down. Davies went to the front of the droid's cargo platform and flipped up two plastic seats. "Sit down, boy, and buckle up. We might just as well ride as walk on down there in the dark, wouldn't you say?"

"Sure thing, Mr. Davies," Mike grinned. If it were his own elk, he'd have to backpack the quarters out in the dark by himself. It was illegal to use artificial conveyances to pursue game, but once the game was taken, any hunter that could afford to do so was welcome to use a droid to take his game and himself out of the woods. Mike wasn't one of the ones who could afford retrieval droid service.

The four-hour hike they'd made since lunch was replaced by a fifteen-minute flight back to where Davies' expensive Cross skimmer was parked at the trailhead. As soon as he and Mike hopped off, Davies pressed another stud on the beacon, and the droid obediently rose back above the trees and headed off for the meat processing shop in Challis.

A red light was blinking on the skimmer's dash when they climbed inside. "Humph. Message. Don't they know Ah'm on a vacation?" Davies grumped. He picked a handset off the dash, punched three buttons, and listened for a moment. He turned to Mike with a curious expression.

"It's for you, boy," he said. "It's the Sheriff's office."


**Sheriff Gordon Lichter's office, Challis**


"But I thought those things were supposed to be so safe!" Mike was in shock.

"They are, son, they are," the Sheriff tried to console the boy. "I know it doesn't do you any good hearing that now, but they are. You know nothing is a hundred percent. This one apparently had a liquid oxygen leak right at the top of the launch burn, and she went up over the north Atlantic. I'm sorry son, but lots of people lost family on that semi. If it's any comfort, nobody on that ship had time to know anything was wrong. She went up that fast."

Mike slumped in the chair, staring at the wall in disbelief. His parents were gone, vanished in a puff of flame at the edge of space. He was alone, orphaned at eighteen. He had no other family. What would he do now?

"All right," he announced, getting to his feet. He used his sleeve to wipe his eyes dry and braced himself in a taciturn tradition that went back as far as the history of the West. "I'm going home." He placed his gray Stetson squarely on his head and strode out into the night.

# Two

**Armstrong City, Luna**

"Andrea, don't just stand there. The checked bags have gone on ahead. There's no turning back now. Jenny, have you got your stuff? Let's go!"

Paul Aggruder was more than ready to leave the Moon's gypsum mining colony. Three years they had spent living in a dusty pressure dome. Three years of Paul's life gone, driving an ore skimmer from the mine site to the processing stations. Three years in a pressure suit for ten hours a day, four days a week. Three years of the whole family spending two hours a day on an exercise bike in the Centrifuge, keeping their bones and muscles up in the Moon's low gravity.

His wife and daughter were less enthusiastic.

"Daddy, the shuttle doesn't leave for two hours. It only takes five minutes to walk to the station. What's the rush?" Jenny was sixteen, and well into the throes of teenage smart-aleck-ness. She dropped her bag on the floor and plopped down on the Couch. The furniture came with the house, which was leased from the mining company.

"Don't you want to get good seats on the shuttle? It's going to be our last look at the Moon. Last look at Earth, for that matter. Don't you want to get a window seat?" Paul teased.

"Paul, relax. Jenny's right. There's no rush to go leave a nice, civilized, established colony to run off and pioneer some new wilderness planet that's just opened up."

The decision to immigrate to the new world of Forest had been hotly contested in the Aggruder household.

"Now, Andrea, let's not start that up again. We talked it over a hundred times. Why stay in some dusty, dry-bones lunar pressure dome, paying rent to a mining company for three rooms and a parking stall, when there's a whole planet out there for the taking?"

"Yes, a whole planet. A whole, uninhabited, undeveloped, howling wilderness, just waiting for us to take our teenage daughter out God knows where to start a dirt farm." Andrea Aggruder threw herself down on the couch next to her daughter.

Paul threw up his hands. "Andrea, I've told you, I can't stay here any longer, breathing recycled air, eating recycled food, drinking recycled water. I need to get out where there's some fresh air! Don't you? Wouldn't you like to get some fresh food for once?"

"I would!" Jenny piped in. Her mother gave her a stern, be-silent look.

"Yes, Paul, you know I do. I just don't see why you can't try for a spot on Caliban, or Corinthia, or one of the planets that's been open a while. They need farmers, too. Why pick some wilderness like Forest?"

Paul grabbed his wife's shoulders, dragging her protesting off the couch and swinging her around the room. "It's an opportunity, baby! We're going to be settlers, just like on Earth in the old days!" He grabbed her waist with one hand, took her left hand in his right, and began dancing her around the room, singing:

*In a cavern, in a pressure suit, excavating for a mine,*
*Dwelt a wore out gypsum miner, and his daughter*
*Clementine.*

*Oh my darling,*
*Oh my darling,*
*Oh my darling, Clementine,*
*Thou art lost and gone forever, dreadful sorry,*
*Clementine!*

On the couch, Jennifer collapsed in laughter. Andrea pushed her husband away, feigning a cross look. She turned away to hide the smile she couldn't quite suppress.

"Paul Aggruder, you really are certifiable."

"My Dad's a freak," Jenny giggled. Paul Aggruder stood in the middle of the tiny living room, arms akimbo, and regarded his daughter sternly. "Well, come on, Clementine, if you don't want to end up in a pressure suit excavating gypsum like your poor old freak Dad, you'd best grab your stuff!"

Andrea Aggruder picked up her overnight bag and suitcase. "Well, we might as well wait at the station."

"Let's go!" Jenny agreed.

The family gathered bag and baggage, and left their leased house for the last time.

The five-minute walk to the shuttle station was extended to fifteen, as it happened. Paul and Andrea Aggruder were a well-liked couple, and with shift change a half-hour away, the dusty streets of the Armstrong City pressure dome were crowded with people. Repeated goodbyes had Andrea and Jennifer both red-eyed and tear-streaked by the time they arrived at the shuttle station.

After presenting their tickets, the Aggruders were ushered into the departure lounge. The family went to the window to get a look at their ride off the Moon.

Outside the dome, the battered white lunar shuttle *Perigee* sat on its landing pads in the gray lunar dust. Pressure-suited maintenance techs scurried about with fuel lines and baggage carts, raising little puffs of dust with every step.

"That's one thing I sure won't miss about this place," Andrea pointed at the techs. "That horrible gray dust that gets all over everything. Even in the dome, that stuff gets everywhere."

"Yecch." Jenny agreed.

To the left, a door swung open and a bored-looking forty-ish woman stepped out. "All passengers bound for OWME ship *Hidalgo* to Forest, gather your stuff and follow me."

The Aggruder family obediently picked up their bags and followed the woman to the shuttle. Ten months from now, they'd be on Forest, starting a new life.

# Three

**Two years later: Challis**

A light snow was falling as Mike guided his aged Ford into Challis, the large flakes reflecting the lights of the growing town, striking stars where skimmer headlights struck through the tiny falling crystals. Sparkles of light reflected from the snowbanks along either side of the roadway.

November in central Idaho was always cold, always snowy, but Mike was used to both. A lifetime spent in the mountains had hardened his body to physical discomfort. Another kind of discomfort assailed Mike this evening though, the sight of another set of condominiums rising on the outskirts of what was rapidly becoming a booming young city.

Challis was fast approaching half a million residents. Mike's family had left central Colorado for the Snake River valley two generations before, his paternal grandfather seeking to escape the vast metropolis that had consumed the Front Range. Now a vast city stood along the front of the Rockies, with Cheyenne at the north, Pueblo at the south, and Denver at its heart. Nor was there much escape to the west--the Las Vegas metropolitan area was gobbling millions of acres of desert, and in Utah the Salt Lake City metro area had climbed high into the Wasatch Range.

Mike's father had watched the spread of humanity's urbanization creep into Montana and southern Idaho, and had fled the increasingly crowded Snake River valley for the mountainous center of Idaho. Now, in Mike's generation, even the tiny mountain communities of the Sawtooth, Salmon River, Clearwater and Lost River Mountains were filling up with people.

People, people, everywhere people. Mike's parents were gone. Mike was left alone now, twenty years old, and heir to a small cabin on ten acres of land in the Salmon River range. He hunted an elk every fall for meat, but the elk herds were dwindling, pushed into tighter and tighter habitats every year by encroaching humanity. The few acceptable fishing streams left were packed, spring summer and fall, with dozens of anglers along every bank, swinging expensive fly-fishing tackle in the hopes of dragging in a forlorn ten-inch brook trout. Mike's chosen lifestyle was growing more impossible by the year.

Parking his old Ford skimmer pickup near the Country Market, Mike headed for the vast store, his list of required canned goods clutched in one callused hand.

He walked up to the cavernous entrance, looking left and right. The checkout lines were long and unruly, as usual. More people came to Challis every year. A new ski resort was in the works, which promised to bring more people still to the area. The crowding was driving Mike to distraction. A solution, though, was not immediately forthcoming.

Or so he thought.

Following his parent's death, he'd investigated Africa; doubts about remaining pockets of plague as well as wandering bandit tribes had dissuaded him. Alaska was out, filling up as it was with millions attracted by ready employment at the vast oil fields. Siberia was under development, millions of Russians and Chinese pouring into the mineral and oil-rich region. Mike was feeling increasingly hemmed in.

He hadn't considered emigrating off world.

The entryway to the giant supermarket was wide open, a forced air curtain holding back the early winter chill. Just inside the entryway was a large bulletin board, covered with announcements; used skimmers for sale, hunting and fishing leases, calves and feeder pigs, moving sales, and so on. This evening there was something new, a large, colorful poster in the middle of the board:

FOREST

OFF-WORLD MINING & EXPLORATION, LTD. SEEKING

COLONISTS

TO SETTLE AND DEVELOP THE EXCITING NEW TYPE II

WORLD

FOREST

GRAVITY, ATMOSPHERE WITHIN 3% EARTH NORMAL

61% OCEANIC, 39% LANDMASS, HEAVILY FORESTED,

MOUNTAINOUS, APPROXIMATES EARTH CLIMATE IN

MID JURASSIC ERA, NATIVE WILDLIFE PLENTIFUL

COLONY REQUIRES:

PIONEERS

FARMERS

CIVIL AND COMMERCIAL DEVELOPERS

CIVIL ENGINEERS

FORMER MILITARY PREFERRED,

COMBAT VETERANS IDEAL

SETTLERS LEAVING JAN 1ST ON COLONIZATION SHIP

*MAYFLOWER*, KILIMANJARO SKYHOOK

APPLY NOW, E-MAIL FORESTSETTLERS@OWME.COM

OR APPLY IN PERSON, OWME HEADQUARTERS,

ONE OFF-WORLD PLAZA, DENVER, 52140-6582-5215.

*Wow*, Mike thought to himself. *Pioneering a new planet? I wonder how the hunting is.* The image of his hunting client from two years ago, Mr. Davies, swam back into this mind suddenly.

"Ah'm goin' off-Earth, boy. Took a job as a security chief with Off-World Mining and Exploration."

A voice behind him interrupted his perusal.

"If I were thirty years younger, boy, I'd go myself!"

Mike turned to greet the speaker. "Otto, you old devil, I'm surprised you aren't going anyway!" Otto Greentree was an old friend of Mike's family, a skinny, white-bearded hermit who lived in a cabin a few miles from Mike's home. At age 79, Otto still lived alone, still hunted deer and elk every fall, and still tramped the mountains all year around. Seeing him in town at all was a surprise, much less on a snowy evening. Mike grinned at the old hermit. "What brings you into town on a night like this, old man?"

Otto shook his head, frowning. "This cold snap, boy, it plays hell with my arthritis. I caught a ride down with Joe Steen in his skimmer, I had to get my pain medicine."

Mike cocked a thumb at the poster. "You really mean what you said? You think this would be a good deal?"

The old man squinted at the poster. "Well, boy, says here that they especially want military and combat vets, so I reckon there's some dangerous game there. On the other hand, they want hunters and farmers, so it's pioneering. Think of that, boy! You'd be out there like Jim Bridger, only better. This ain't no new country, it's a whole new world! Do I think it's a good idea?" Otto gestured around, at the huge supermarket, the crowded parking lot, and the teeming skimmers on the road out front. "Hell, yeah, I think it's a good idea. If they'd let someone my age on the spaceship, I'd be signing up today."

"I'm sort of tempted myself," Mike admitted.

"Let's go in and get a sandwich, boy." Otto offered, pointing at the deli section of the supermarket. "You'll be more than tempted when I get through with you!"

In a few moments, the two were seated with sandwiches and soft drinks. Otto had dropped his old leather daypack on the floor next to his chair, and now he rummaged in it a moment before fixing Mike with a basilisk eye.

"Now, boy, what do you suppose I got here?"

"A skunk pelt?" Mike offered. He was surprised to see Otto produce a dog-eared copy of *Jane's Habitable Planets*, the benchmark listing of all known Type I and II worlds. "I been thinking about leaving Earth some time now," Otto confessed. "All these people. Well, never was a planet I was interested in, 'til this one, and I'm too damned old now – nobody over 55 gets on an OWME starship for any reason."

Flipping open the large, cloth-bound volume, Otto found a certain page and spun the book over to Mike:

### Forest

Planet specifics: Type II, gravity .98 Earth normal, atmospheric ratios nitrogen 74%, oxygen 22%, CO2 .03%. Climate is temperate, with mean temperatures averaging 4-5% warmer than Earth. Land surface 61% ocean, 39% land. Continental landmasses include two large in northern hemisphere, two large in southern hemisphere, and one small at northern magnetic pole. Various volcanic islands and archipelagos are found in the southern oceans.

Flora and Fauna: Initial orbital surveys by Off-World Mining & Exploration, Ltd completed June 2199.

Majority of continental landmasses heavily wooded, mountainous in many areas. Predominant flora includes trees resembling Earth conifers, some large tree ferns. Undergrowth is sparse in forests, lush on the few plains. Plant life has not yet evolved to the level of flowering species. Various herbivorous animal species include large grazing animals found in forested areas and edge habitats, and many arboreal species. One large predator possibly dangerous to Man, a bipedal birdlike carnivore, 18 meters in length, 6 meters in height. Flora and fauna in general approximate Earth during the late Jurassic period.

Colonization considerations: Heavily forested nature of planet promises to make agriculture difficult without extensive terraforming. Presence of possibly dangerous indigenous life requires well-armed and equipped colonists. Further, Forest lies on the outer edge of explored space; it is unknown what possible other intelligent species may lie beyond the boundary.

Mike snapped the book shut. "I guess nobody'd landed there yet when this book was printed?"

"Nope." Otto grunted. "But last summer, I guided a fella on a fishing trip who was a surveyor for OWME. He was tellin' me that OWME has over a thousand people on Forest now. He was there to help set up the initial landing point and the town around it; they're calling it Settlement. Original, huh?" he grinned, revealing tobacco-stained teeth. "Anyway, there are people starting to push out into the woods there. OWME is looking to start farming the place. I guess most Earth crops grow like gangbusters there. He says these big bird-things – 'rocs,' they call 'em, after some mythical bird-beast – are right dangerous, and big as a tyrannosaurus; but there aren't very many of 'em."

"Figured that right off," Mike said. "A predator that big, it stands to reason it would need a big territory. That means not too many of them around."

"Best part is," Otto continued, "this fella tells me the hunting is unbelievable. The settlers there now are mostly dirt-crop farmers, and they need some good marksmen to bring meat into the villages. Boy, they've got a critter like a squirrel that weighs a good forty pounds. They've got these funny-looking two-legged sort of cow-looking things, only with a crest of gray and brown feathers on their heads; critters are bigger than a moose, and seems they travel in herds."

"Like the buffalo here in the old days," Mike reflected.

"Yep, you know it, boy; only Man's a smarter animal now than we was then. People are only hunting them to feed the colony; the feathers are valuable, I guess, but the Company's only taking what animals they need to feed their construction crews and settlers. Now; you got a girl here?"

Mike shook his head. His lifestyle was too secluded to attract many girls, and in any case, most of the young people in the area were leaving for the bright lights and fast times of Denver or Las Vegas. The couple of potential girlfriends he'd known in his teenage years had been deterred by Mike's frequent absences to wander some distant stretch of wilderness.

"Well, that settles it then, don't it?" Otto pointed out. "Not much keeping you here, is there? Like I said, boy, I'd be heading there myself if I could."

"No mention of any intelligent life, there," Mike noted.

"Ain't been any other intelligent races found yet, and OWME's on a dozen planets, with orbital charting done for another twenty."

Mike considered the old man's description. There didn't seem to be much future in staying on Earth, unless he wanted to end up living in a city condo with a few thousand other people within spitting distance. Maybe, he thought, maybe this is what I've been looking for.

"Go, boy," Otto urged, leaning across the table. "Get out now, while you can. Don't wait until you're an old man too! Don't get stuck here!"

In the aisle just outside the deli seating area, the bustling throng of people pinged on Mike's consciousness. The sight of the condos going up on the edge of town sprang to mind, unbidden.

*It might be the best thing going*, he thought. "OK, old man, you've sold me. I'll e-mail the company tomorrow and see if they need a good mountain boy."

Otto grinned again. "Good decision, boy. I'll admit I'm envious, but it's a good deal for you. Imagine it – a whole new world!"

"A whole new world," Mike echoed. "A whole new life. Well, there's nothing keeping me here. Not anymore."

# Four

**Forest**

"OK, Jenny, just like I told you. Sight on that chunk of wood."

Jenny Aggruder hauled the ancient Remington to her shoulder, still unused to the nine-pound weight of the old Magnum rifle. She lined up the sights as her father instructed her, placing the front sight blade in the notch of the rear sight, and placing her target – a large chip of wood placed on a stump a hundred meters away – atop the front sight blade.

"OK, honey, now take a deep breath. Let it out. Take another in, let it half-way out, and *squeeeeze!*"

The Remington discharged with a roar. The .338 Magnum bullet hit the wood chip a centimeter to the left of center, blasting it into fragments.

"Good shot!" Paul Aggruder exulted. "Andrea, this girl's a natural!"

"As long as we can all eat. Wood chips don't stew up very well, Paul."

"I bought six boxes of cartridges, honey. Jenny needs to learn to shoot. You should too, you know."

"I'm perfectly content to let you do the hunting, Paul."

"This thing kicks, Daddy."

"You get used to it," Paul assured his daughter.

On their arrival a year and three months earlier, Paul Aggruder had paid for the use of a retrieval droid to transport the family to the limit of its range – about fifty kilometers – and then they'd walked another ten klicks north.

On their second day of walking, carrying everything they owned, they'd stumbled on a beautiful setting. A small fern meadow nestled in a semi-circle of huge pines, with a tiny creek wandering along at one side.

Now, fifteen months later, a three-room cabin nestled in the semi-circle of trees, surrounded by four fields planted in corn, sorghum and vegetables. The Aggruders settled quickly into the life of a frontier family.

A bandy-legged little man carrying a bulging pack and an enormous 20mm semi-automatic Krupp cannon had visited them once, six months earlier. Their sole visitor to date, he'd spoken almost no English, but had cheerfully accepted an invitation to supper, during which he'd grinned from ear to ear and answered every question with a cheerful, "*Da! Da!*"

"He doesn't look Russian," Andrea Aggruder quietly observed to her husband.

"Sure is a cheery little fellow, isn't he?" Paul replied.

The funny little man spent the night snoring in the ferns against the cabin's rear wall. In the morning he'd bowed, grinning happily, in front of Andrea and Jenny, hugged Paul and kissed him on both cheeks, and inquired, "Logger? Logger?"

"What's he mean, Daddy?"

"Remember the briefings, honey?" Paul answered his daughter. "Loggers are those great big, armor-plated critters that live on the savannahs east of here. I guess this fellow wants to hunt them. That would explain the cannon."

He nodded at the little hunter, pointing east. "Loggers that way," he'd stated, slowly and clearly. The little man burst out laughing, hugged Paul again, cried out *"Dosvidanyia!"* and walked off to the east, the morning sun on his back.

"Well, there goes about the happiest man I ever met," Paul observed.

Life was good out on the edge of nowhere, even Andrea had admitted. Jenny's education proceeded by a hyper-wave terminal purchased at the sprawling Mercantile in the main town of Settlement. The family had little by way of income, but they ate well, between the grain and truck crops from their four fields and the occasional boser Paul killed with the ancient Remington, also purchased at the Company store in Settlement.

The evenings were peaceful, the days long and hot but satisfying. There was one issue, though, that worried the elder Aggruders.

"Paul," Andrea Aggruder whispered to her husband late one night as they lay on their mattress of ferns. "Do you think we've done the right thing, bringing Jenny all this way out here?"

"What do you mean? I thought you liked it out here!"

"I do, Paul, but that's not what I mean. Jenny's almost eighteen, Paul. We've seen one other person the whole time we've been here, and he was at least our age, and he didn't even speak English! Paul, Jenny's a healthy young girl. She's going to want to meet someone, sooner or later."

"Well, I don't think we'll be able to afford to send her back to Earth to go to Harvard, honey. Hey, this is a growing colony, you know. More people are coming in all the time. When Jenny's ready, she'll probably want to get a job in Settlement, and live in the Company dorms there."

"Oh, Paul, I don't want her taking up with some grubby service droid repairman in Settlement."

"You'd rather she married some ragged-assed dirt farmer, eh?" Paul chuckled.

"Oh, you hush. You know what I mean, Paul."

"Look at it this way, honey. What would her prospects have been in Armstrong City?"

An image of the grubby, dusty Lunar mining colony popped into Andrea's head.

"Remember what it was like there? The gangs of punks wandering around in the passageways? The dust all over everything? The drug problem? Andrea, leaving there was the best thing we ever did."

"I suppose so," Andrea answered. "I just worry about Jenny, Paul. I hope she finds a good husband when the right time comes. At least," she hugged Paul hard, "at least as good as the one I found."

"She will, honey. She has her mother's good taste in men!"

# Five

**Six weeks later - Africa, the Kilimanjaro Skyhook**

Mike found himself in a huge, glass walled building at the foot of Kenya's Mount Kilimanjaro, waiting in a line for the tube to the summit. Throngs of people milled about; lines formed here and there to no noticeable end. The huge structure echoed with random snatches of conversation, barked orders, and wailing children. Mike longed for the quiet, cool mountains.

The African midday sunshine beat in through the glass, combined with the milling bodies to turn the giant building into an oven. Mike pulled a red bandanna from his pocket, tipping up his big gray Stetson to wipe sweat from his forehead. A little girl clutching the hand of an elderly matron grinned at him, taking in his Western outfit and big hat. He returned the smile.

The semi-ballistic trip had been an ordeal. The crowded magnetic shuttle from Denver to New York had been bad enough, and negotiating the congested streets of New York worse still. Mike had only found breathing room once, when out of curiosity he'd climbed the fire stairs to the top of the Freedom Center. The tower was still an impressive sight, even if it had been long since eclipsed as Earth's tallest structures. Mike read a plaque on the rooftop observation tower which described how the current tower, sixteen stories taller than the originals, had been rebuilt after the first pair had been destroyed by terrorists way back in 2001, an act that had eventually led up to the Third World War.

But the semi-ballistic trip was the worst of all. Strapped into an acceleration seat, Mike had fidgeted uncomfortably until the ships boosters fired. After that he was too preoccupied trying to breathe against the six-gee drag.

At the top of the climb, Mike's weight suddenly went from six times normal to nothing as the blast stopped and the ship went into free-fall. Mike wasn't the only passenger reaching for the plastic 'barf bags' as the ship nosed over to dive for Nairobi. The whole ordeal was finally ended by a jarring impact with the six-mile, concrete runway in Nairobi, following which the passengers were discharged into the blasting hot sunshine of Kenya.

At least all that was behind him now. He stole a glance at this travel tickets and agenda; the ship was supposedly the OWME Colonization Ship *Mayflower,* an appropriate name to be sure. The boarding papers gave a description of the ship:

> OWME operates four Colonization Ships. Our newest, the C.S. *Mayflower,* is our most modern as well as the largest. With a crew of 225, the *Mayflower* can carry 10,000 colonists, their personal effects, and supplies to set up a colony self-sufficient for one year.

> All four OWME Colonization Ships are using the state-of-the art Gellar Star Drive, which utilizes interstellar matter to power a mass converter. The Gellar Drive is capable of propelling even the largest ships at many times the speed of light. OWME has utilized this new technology to place colonists on no fewer than ten new worlds.

Passengers on the *Mayflower* will find ample accommodations, many entertainment opportunities, and complete educational preparation for their embarkation on their new home.

OWME welcomes you to the exciting new era of colonization!

On the glass wall, high above the milling throngs, a large sign beckoned, "*Mayflower*," Mike joined the queue forming under the sign.

The cabin had been sold to a wealthy lawyer from Salt Lake City who wanted a vacation getaway. The proceeds, rather more than Mike expected, had gone towards his passage and purchase of the recommended pioneering supplies. He even had a small stake left over.

The cavernous tube station was surprisingly crowded. As Mike wondered if all these people were bound for the *Mayflower* and Forest; he failed to notice he had arrived at the counter. A barked question, "You there, in the big hat! You for the *Mayflower* or the New Bedford?"

"*Mayflower*," Mike replied, intimidated.

The gnome like figure in the green OWME shirt pointed. "Up the escalator on the left, turn right, ten people to a capsule. Wait your turn, you've got two days to board before the ship leaves. Your baggage checked?" Mike nodded. "Good; you got any pharms, weapons, live plants or animals?"

"Uh, no. I mean, yes. I've got my rifle and revolver, but they're in my checked baggage. None of the other stuff."

"Good. That's fine. Here's your boarding pass; get going."

Another strange experience. Clutching his one allowable carry-on bag, Mike rode the escalator to the next level, and joined another line under a red neon sign reading, "*Mayflower*." This line moved swiftly. In a matter of moments, he was being strapped in a clear plastic capsule for the ride to the summit. A middle-aged woman sat across from him, a Bible clutched in her hands. She smiled at Mike's pale face. "First time in a capsule?" she guessed. Mike nodded. "You'll be fine," she assured him. Mike politely tuned her out as she began to prattle on about "Jesus this, Jesus that." The religious were something of a disappearing breed on Earth these days; it had been a while since Mike had run into one.

The capsule ride wasn't bad at all. The pod accelerated smoothly, rising in its clear plastic tube. Mike was treated to the spectacular scenery of Kenya stretching out below. *Maybe Africa wouldn't have been such a bad idea*, he mused. The capsule reached the summit in about an hour, moving into another crowded, glass-walled building, this one round, perched on the very peak of Africa's most famous mountain. Mike was now treated to the sight of an impossible thing; a five-hundred-meter-wide hexagonal column, rising from the center of the round building, disappearing, inconceivably, into the sky. At each of the six sides, a track climbed this incredible beanstalk. As Mike watched, a shiny silver bus shot out of the building, racing upwards on the track for the unseen space docks above.

This was the Kilimanjaro Skyhook, a mighty carbon-fiber tower that sprang from the mountaintop all the way to well past the atmosphere. The space dock at the top was actually in geosyn-chronous orbit, tethered by the tower to the mountain below. A sister skyhook sprang from a mountain in the Andes and another in the Himalayas. Earth's three Skyhooks were the only means, now, of leaving the planet.

It turned out that the building inside was hexagonal as well. Each capsule tube delivered travelers to the section where the bus to their ship waited. Mike joined a growing throng in the waiting room.

He used the time to examine the people around him, assuming correctly that many of these would be fellow colonists bound for Forest. Mostly young people, mostly single, but with a smattering of young couples. A surprising number of young children in tow as well; Mike wondered about the wisdom of bringing young children to a new and possibly hostile world.

A chime sounded, and an electronic voice intoned, "Skyhook Bus Two for CS *Mayflower*, bound for Forest, Caliban and Corinthia, boarding now. Please make your way to a boarding port." Mike joined the obedient throng.

The ride to the low-orbit dock took two hours, during which Mike dozed, ignoring the movies playing on a screen at the front (upper) wall of the passenger compartment. At the top, Mike was handed another surprise; the passengers left the Skyhook bus, only to be herded onto a small orbital shuttle, a gray, vaguely bug-like contraption with *CS* Mayflower *Boarding Shuttle Four* printed on the side. An attendant noticed Mike's puzzled expression.

"You didn't think a ship the size of the *Mayflower* could come right down to the Skyhook's boarding platform, did you cowboy?" she chuckled. "This is low Earth orbit, fella. Only small transports and shuttles down here. You'll get on *Mayflower* in about another, oh, six hours."

Four hours into this penultimate journey, Mike finally saw the ship on which he would spend the next ten months, bound for Forest.

A vast, pale-gray cylinder stretched out, almost three kilometers long by a kilometer wide. An outer portion rotated, slowly, clockwise around a stationary inner cylinder; this would provide a sense of gravity for passengers on the trip. At the front of the ship, a titanic scoop stood ready to gather grit, rocks, dust, stray matter, interstellar gases, all grist for the ship's interstellar mill. At the rear, an equally huge maw glowed a faint orange. The *Mayflower's* massive, powerful Gellar Star Drive was already warmed up for departure.

Three hours later, Mike was shown to the quarters he would share for the next ten months with three other single men. Four bunks lined one wall, a small bathroom to one side, four lockers, a small refrigeration unit. Two desks and chairs, a couch, and a view screen for video completed the bachelor's quarters. The whole steel-gray room was only about ten meters by six.

Fortunately, Mike's roommates were congenial people. Albert and Jim Morrison were farmers, heading to Forest to homestead a truck farm. Jeffery Adams was bound for a computer-networking job on Caliban, and would be alone in the cabin for the second leg of the trip. Once Mike discovered it was possible to roam freely in the vast greenhouse areas mid-way down each section of the giant, rotating cylinder, time passed fairly quickly.

Classes began the next day; flora and fauna of Forest, the layout and amenities of the one large town, Settlement, and the three smaller villages already established. Mike paid close attention to the classes on the local wildlife, edible plants, climate, and economic value of the various species; this, now, would be his livelihood. Mike would quite literally be hunting to survive. Any cash he'd need would come from game he could provide the colony for provisioning.

# Six

**Forest, the Aggruder homestead**

"Daddy!"

Jenny's urgent hiss stopped Paul Aggruder dead in the cabin doorway.

"What is it, Jenny-pie?"

"There's a roc coming this way, Daddy! Get inside and shut the door!"

Paul did so, quietly latching the plank door. He walked to the east-facing window Jenny was watching from.

The dinosaur-sized predator was strolling slowly in from the fern prairies to the east. It's massive, eagle-like head turned slowly from side to side as it walked, showing its razor-sharp meter-long beak.

"Amazing how quiet they are, isn't it?" Paul whispered. "Jenny, go get your Mom, both of you get down on our bedroom floor and lie still. I'll keep an eye on our friend here."

Jenny complied quickly. The drill was well rehearsed by now. This was the fifth time a roc had sauntered past the cabin, following the little creek as it looked for the bosers that formed the great bird's habitual prey.

Paul Aggruder watched as the massive predator strode towards the house, walking almost silently on its wide, spreading, three-toed taloned feet. The roc was a big male, with a wide crest of scarlet feathers on the back of his head.

*I should have bought the big Parks rifle the Company recommended*, Paul thought to himself. *If only that terminal for Jenny's cyber-school hadn't been so expensive!*

The roc walked up to the edge of the planted fields and lowered his head, peering curiously at the disturbed ground. Uttering a series of small squawks, it followed the edge of the cornfield for a few meters, and then raised its massive head to look directly at the cabin.

"Oh, shit!" Paul lowered himself slowly, quietly to the floor, and scuttled backwards away from the window, crawling under the rough table he'd made from planks.

A heavy sound of breathing grew slowly louder as the roc walked up to the tiny house, lowering its head finally to peer in the window with one eye. Paul crouched behind a table leg, trying to remain perfectly still as his heart hammered in his chest. A fetid smell of rotting meat wafted into the room from the great carnivore's breath.

A groan from the cabin wall startled Paul. The roc had placed its huge beak on the wall and was pushing, gently. The boards creaked and groaned as the massive bird leaned on the wall.

Then, suddenly, the vast predator seemed to lose interest. Turning swiftly on one great, taloned foot, it raised its head and strode swiftly away to the west.

Paul scuttled to the west-facing window and watched as the giant bird disappeared finally over a rise two kilometers away.

"You can come out now – it's gone," he called.

"What are you going to do if one of those things walks in when you're out in the field, Paul?"

"Run for the trees! They're too big to get around in the woods."

Andrea Aggruder gave her husband a skeptical look.

"Well, maybe I should start keeping my rifle closer at hand."

"You might as well throw spitballs," Andrea snapped. "That one was as big as a tyrannosaurus, Paul!"

"OK, I'll start digging another field, Andrea. I should be able to plant enough to trade for one of the big Parks doubles. Those are supposed to be able to handle a roc, OK? That's all we can do for now." Paul Aggruder went to his wife, laying one arm around her shoulders. "Honey, that's only the fifth one in over a year. There aren't that many of them around."

"Well, I'll feel better when you get a bigger rifle."

"See why I'm teaching Jenny to shoot?" Paul chided his wife.

# Seven

**A small planet 165 light years from Forest**

"Clomonastik," the Governor called. "Come in, old friend. I've got good news for you."

Clomonastik III was an up-and-coming officer in the Grugell Imperial Navy. The Grugell were a heavily militaristic society, and ruthlessness was rewarded and encouraged. In that and all other respects Clomonastik was a model Grugell officer, recently promoted to the rank of Group Commander, and he was ripe for an Occupation Group command.

As he strode into the Governor's office, he projected the ideal image that young Grugell officers strove to achieve. His bearing was cold and efficient. He was tall and thin, as was the Grugell ideal, his hair and eyes jet black, his skin stark white, the result of a millennium of ruthless eugenics on the part of a succession of autocratic Emperors. The Grugell Royal House had long been fanatical about "genetic purity," the result of which had been the elimination of any racial or ethnic variation among the Grugell.

"Sir!" Clomonastik barked, coming to attention in front of Governor Bortattisk IX's high, polished black desk. The Governor was an old friend of Clomonastik's family, and had been an effective patron for the young officer.

"Sit down," the Governor ordered. Clomonastik complied, sweeping his black cloak to the side. He perched himself on the high stool in front of the Governor's desk, adjusting his uniform carefully. Clomonastik wore the standard issue – a tight, high-collared black tunic, black leggings, polished black boots, and the ubiquitous floor-length black cloak. He flicked a barely visible speck of lint from his boot top. The Grugell were almost universally fastidious, and Clomonastik was no exception.

"Well, Clomonastik, I'm pleased to tell you that I have orders for you, from the Imperium."

"Yes, sir?"

"Yes. You've been ordered to take command of an Occupation Group forming now at our Navy base at Gigatos City. We've charted a new planet – habitable, but only just. It's a high-gravity world, but rich in mineral and herbal resources. It's on the edge of our space, Clomonastik, an exposed post."

"Exposed, sir? We are alone in the Galaxy, sir."

"We *thought*, Clomonastik. We *thought* we were alone in the Galaxy." The Governor grinned, revealing pointed, serrated white teeth behind thin, jet-black lips. He raised one hand, pointing a black-clawed finger at the younger officer. "We have explored less than one star system in a million, you know. It would have been arrogant of us to assume we were the only intelligent race in the universe."

"Sir." Clomonastik offered no retort. His patron's friendly demeanor was misleading. Bortattisk IX was not to be underestimated. He'd had underlings disintegrated for minor insubordination.

"And, we've now discovered otherwise. A scout ship sent to the new planet detected a settled area on the surface, and an orbiting ship departed into subspace within a short time of their arrival. They left the area undetected."

"A settled area, sir? As in a town of some sort?" Clomonastik scratched his pointed chin with one claw. "That would indicate an intelligent race indeed, sir."

"Yes, not to mention the orbiting ship." The Governor stood up, walking around his desk to pace the office floor. "The Navy has sent its newest construct to the planet to conduct an orbital survey. Are you familiar with the cloaking technology that has been tested?"

"No, sir, I'm not."

"Well, it's been placed on one of our newest frigates. This technology warps electromagnetic radiation around its energy field, which has the effect of rendering a cloaked ship undetectable by any means we've been able to devise."

"Clever indeed, sir."

"Yes, but your Occupation Group ships won't be so equipped, I'm sorry to say."

"Yes, sir."

"You'll be tasked to occupy that planet, Clomonastik. You'll be given twice the normal complement of troops, and an enhanced orbital power station. The Emperor has personally stated his confidence in you, Clomonastik. You understand what that means? The consequences of a failure?"

"Yes sir," Clomonastik replied. His cold, hard bearing spoke eloquently of his confidence.

"At any rate, you'll take command of the Group in three days. This new frigate has been sent to scout the planet and conduct an orbital survey. You should have that report before you're ready to take the Occupation Group out."

"Yes sir." At the Governor's waved dismissal, Clomonastik took his leave.

Born of a fiercely militaristic and wholly authoritarian society, Clomonastik was the result of a thousand millennia of Grugell evolution. As he left the Governor's office, pondering his role in the Emperor's relentless agenda of expansion, a snippet of his Crèche-school instruction came back to him:

The glorious history of the Grugell race began with
the rise from the dust of a species of fierce predators in
the deserts of Planet Grugell's largest continent. The
fierce intelligence of these proto-Grugell led the development of weapons, the genesis of the technology
that would one day dominate the stars. Rising quickly
to the top of the hierarchy of life on their world, our
ancestors quickly used their superior abilities to either
destroy or subjugate all other life forms on the planet.
With the evolutionary advent of the modern Grugell,
our ancestors spread to conquer the entire world in a
matter of a few hundred years.

Following that period was a long period of racial and
nationalistic warfare, lasting for many thousands of
years. Technology advanced rapidly during this time,
driven by conflict, until battles were fought at the very
edge of space itself.

This period of warfare ended with the glorious rise
to power of the first Emperor, Traskellid I, known as
Traskellid the Ruthless.

Emperor Traskellid began the glorious campaign to
eliminate the racial and national variations that led to
the violent wars. During this same period, Traskellid
and his successor Traskellid II began the search for
other habitable worlds. The vision of the Traskellids
was that the Grugell should expand into other star
systems, and that vision was to be realized when the
light barrier was penetrated late in the reign of Traskellid II.

The expansion of the Grugell Empire extends to the present day. The Grugell remain the only intelligent life forms in the known Galaxy, and as our Empire grows, the destiny of the Grugell is plain: to rule over a Galaxy that is home to only the Grugell Empire.

The irony of that last portion wasn't lost on Clomonastik. His Occupation would be the first to confront another intelligent, space-faring species. For Clomonastik personally, this assignment would mean either Empire-wide eminence and a Governorship, or disintegration. There was no other alternative.

It was the chance of a lifetime – in the event of failure, it would be the end of his life. Clomonastik knew and accepted the cost of failure, as did all in the Grugell Navy.

He hurried down the corridor towards his office. He had a tremendous amount of work to do before he assumed his new Command.

# Eight

**The CS *Mayflower*, in transit**

Four months into the trip, Mike found himself seated at dinner with one of the ship's engineers, who tried to explain at length how the ship's Gellar drive used a negative energy drive field that actually acted on the mass of the ship itself. This, according to the tech, made it easier to drive a huge ship at a greater speed than a small one.

Mike went away shaking his head. Animals, trees and rifles Mike understood; the intricacies of interstellar drives, he'd leave to others.

Six uneventful, boring months after that, as the four young men played a thousandth round of nickel poker at the table in their cabin, a tone sounded, followed by an electronic voice:

"Ship has entered orbit. Ship has entered orbit. Passengers for Forest will prepare to disembark beginning tomorrow morning at 0800. Ship's navigation viewer display of the planet is now available on your view screens."

Mike and the two young farmers jumped for the viewer. Jim flipped the screen's power toggle, and a view of an Earthlike planet materialized on the panel, their first view of the planet Forest.

Two large emerald-green continents were in view, as the colonizing ship drifted over the northern hemisphere. Mike saw a faint tracing of white at the pole, and faint signs of mountains in the center of the larger continent; puffs and strings of white marked Earthlike temperate weather patterns. All in all, the planet looked far more ordinary than Mike would have imagined.

Since only about fifty people were debarking for Forest, Mike's debarkation number came up quickly. Early the next morning, ship's time, he found himself in a shuttle bound for Settlement, the OWME Company's port city and main colony base. Surrounded by his light baggage, Mike endured the hammering, bouncing ride down the gravity well, arriving finally in front of a large wooden building, which sat on a wide concrete apron that perched on a stupendous concrete flat intended for landing cargo ships. One such cargo ship was departing as Mike stepped off the boarding shuttle. He watched in amazement as the giant disk, a full three hundred meters across and fifty meters tall, rose on four pillars of gray-white smoke from a pad a kilometer or so away. In orbit, it would re-dock with its Gellar tunnel and navigation module to jump into subspace, bound for Earth.

Immigration checks and medical exams occupied the better part of a day, including a hot and uncomfortable UV bombardment to eliminate Earthly microorganisms from Mike's skin. The treatment left him feeling mildly sunburned and itching all over. Immediately following the UV, he had to take a shower that smelled evilly of chemicals. This, at least, washed away the white powder of oxidized epidermis the UV bath had left on his body, and a clear-water shower afterwards removed the chemical smell. Finally, he was given some strange medicinal cocktail to drink, and received four air-hypo injections, two in each shoulder. He could now emerge from the quarantine area sterilized, with no bio-load of microbes to spread on a new planet. There was one drawback, as the Med Tech informed him: "You'll have the trots for a few days until your intestinal fauna sorts itself out."

Finally, Mike was directed to a room labeled '*Occupational interviews and placement*,' which was, apparently, the last step. Inside the door a skinny, balding man sat at a desk, flipping idly through a sheaf of paper. He didn't look up when Mike entered, instead simply motioning with a pen to the chair in front of his desk. Mike sat down, and after a few moments, the interviewer spoke.

"Name?" he demanded.

"Michael Crider."

"Middle name?"

"Don't have one."

More shuffling of papers. "Ah. Here you are. You signed on to be a pioneer and hunter?"

"Yes, that's me."

The balding man fixed Mike with a gimlet eye. "You do realize pioneers don't receive a salary? You earn cash for any meat, skins or feathers you bring in for sale. Other than that, you're responsible for your own food and shelter, got that?"

Mike bristled a little at that. "That's why I signed up!"

The interviewer chuckled suddenly. "Don't get your back up, sonny; I just wanted to make that plain. We got all these gomers coming in here looking for a paycheck, every day I see people complaining when they're expected to be self-sufficient. Hell, if they wanted a handout, they should have stayed on Earth. But if you can hunt and handle yourself in the woods, I expect you'll do all right. Two tips. First, don't hang around Settlement. The hunting around here's pretty picked over by the company troops and the townies. Also, watch out for the rocs, they're no joke. Have you got the rifle the Company recommended?"

"Yeah, I got the Parks double."

"Good; you'll need it. We've got 15mm ammo here in the company store. It's heavy stuff, but you'll find the Parks is a damn fine piece. You can trade for ammunition and supplies. The Company will credit you a fixed rate per pound for the various species. Here's a chart that gives the rate. Extra paid for salable skins or plumage. Or you can sell meat and skins outright to the other colonists for cash, but you're better off dealing with the Company. This here's a pretty cash-poor colony. There are only a little less than four thousand people here on the planet, three thousand of 'em right here in Settlement. The feathers and such have markets elsewhere, but the food we can use right here. You're one of," he consulted a large binder stuffed with paper, "eighteen hunter-pioneers we've got now."

A stamp on Mike's paperwork: DISPOSITIONED. "All right, cowboy, out through that door and collect your gear. Good luck." The skinny, balding man returned to his papers, ignoring Mike's departure. He found his gear directly outside, a large frame backpack stuffed with clothing and gear, his small carry-on from the *Mayflower*, and a long, heavy case containing his rifle. In front of him was a door marked *Exit*.

This was it. Gathering his gear, Mike strode out the door into the bustle of a Settlement afternoon.

The very air was strangely different, smelling oddly of an alien world. A hot, orange-yellow sun beat down on the bare red soil outside the door; a few skimmers rode lightly on the company street just ahead.

It took him a moment to notice that there was no grass. A few odd-looking forbs grew along the building, but otherwise the earth underfoot was bare, red hardpan. Past the last buildings Mike could see a wall of huge green trees that looked much like the familiar pines and spruce of Idaho. In the northern distance, a range of mountains stood watch over the landscape, but there were no snowcapped peaks here; the green continued unbroken all the way to the top. A large, sluggish river meandered by the town on the east.

Mike accosted a passerby. "Where can I buy some maps and a few supplies?" The frowning, middle-aged woman pointed at a warehouse-like structure up the street that bore a large, crudely painted sign: 'OWME Mercantile.'

A wide and varied display of merchandise was inside, some of which Mike needed for his already bulging backpack. A clerk informed Mike that most of the pioneers and farmers were settling the area to the south, so Mike picked up several good maps of the land to the north. His Earth compass seemed to work alright; the helpful clerk assured him it would be fine. Two more boxes of ammo for his 15mm Parks double rifle, one hi-ex and one solids, and (much to his surprise) a box of shells for his grandfather's old .45, now holstered once again low on Mike's hip in an equally ancient leather holster and gun belt rig. He also invested in a few provisions, including two large packages of something called 'Boser jerky.' Out of curiosity, Mike sampled a bite; the leathery stuff tasted faintly like a cross between turkey and beef. A locater beacon for Settlement's provisioning droids was expensive, but essential. Most of Forest's game was too large for a single person to move easily, and a field-dressed carcass would be picked up and credited to Mike's account when marked by the beacon.

Looking over the dehydrated foods, Mike bumped into a grizzled, broad-shouldered man who was busily selecting packets of dried vegetables.

"*Observez votre étape, garcon!*" the older man snapped. "Watch you' step, eh?"

Mike noted the thick Cajun accent. "Sorry," he apologized. The older man nodded, scowling, and went on selecting packets.

An hour was spent in the mercantile, tramping around on the rough-hewn plank floor, selecting this item and that, and then

Mike was ready to leave. In his pockets were tickets for a skimmer bus to Outskirts, a tiny village twenty kilometers to the north. Past that was, according to the maps, nothing but empty forest all the way up to the approaches to the three-kilometer high New Pyrenees Mountains. The bus ride, up a red-dirt track following the river, took only ten minutes, the giant conifers whipping past at a frightening rate.

Outskirts was indeed a tiny concern. Four houses, a Company warehouse and a miniature version of the Mercantile back at Settlement made up the whole place.

Beyond that, was the endless forest.

Mike hopped from the bus, nodded his thanks to the driver, shouldered his pack and strode off into the trees. This would be his world now, his new home planet, and he would face it on his terms as he had preferred to on the planet he left; rifle in hand, alone, a man in the wilderness. Two small boys paused in their roughhousing to watch Mike's tall, rangy form topped by the large gray Stetson, heading into the woods.

"I bet the rocs'll get him in a week!" the smaller of the two dirty-faced urchins giggled.

"A day!" the other challenged, and they began their play-fighting anew. Behind them, the shifting shadows of the trees swallowed the young man's form.

# Nine

**Six months later, forty kilometers north of Outskirts**

A drop of sweat dripped in Mike's eye, stinging. He didn't dare move to wipe it away. Fifty yards in front of him at the edge of a meadow carpeted with giant ferns, a tyrannosaur-sized roc fed on a three-day old boser carcass. He'd been stalking for over an hour, and the moment was at hand.

The roc was a good-sized one, a full six meters high at the withers, maybe seventeen meters long. He still hadn't gotten used to what was, by Earth standards, a pretty strange-looking beast. A male roc like the one before him stood on two strong, pillar-like legs with three-toed, clawed feet. A heavy, robust body covered in a hairy/feathery coat ended in a long, whip-like tail at one end, and a two-meter-long head with a razor-sharp hooked beak at the other. No front limbs were visible, having been reduced to a few residual bones deep in the chest. This male also sported the usual crest of meter-long, bright crimson plumes on his head.

He waited, hidden behind the bole of a massive conifer until the roc dipped his head to wrench loose another chunk of flesh. Then, slowly, ever so slowly, raised his Parks double rifle. The right barrel had a hi-explosive penetrator round loaded. When the sights came to rest on the roc's chest, Mike carefully moved the selector to fire the right barrel and squeezed off his shot.

A thunderous *BOOM* roared through the forest. Mike rode out the recoil as the 15mm double rifle slammed back, the barrels rising past 45 degrees. The hi-ex round performed perfectly, slamming deep into the roc's chest. A dull *thump* announced the warhead's detonation, wrecking the great predator's hearts and lungs and severing both spinal cords. With a squawk of surprise and shock, the great birdlike beast fell to one side, kicking.

With a grin, he grabbed his dressing knife and strode forward. The plumes this male roc sported would bring him a premium. Before he started dressing the giant carcass, he activated his locater beacon. A provisioning droid would take at least an hour to get there, and he would have the carcass ready by then.

The past six months had been the best of Mike's adult life. The one close call he'd had, with a large female roc, had been close enough to be exciting but not close enough to be terrifying. The roc had been herding two horse-sized chicks, and he hadn't wanted to get too close. He'd killed four of the giant predators, and a dozen or so of the smaller, herbivorous bosers. This, and the one trip he'd made back into Outskirts, had kept him in supplies and food.

The boser that formed the roc's habitual food source didn't look any less outlandish. Only slightly smaller than a roc at fifteen meters long, bosers were herd-dwelling herbivores with a coat of brown-gray feathers, two stout legs, smaller arms used for stuffing branches into a turtle-like beak, and a short, thick tail. A fantastic frill of stiff dun-gray quills formed a crest behind a boser's head, larger on the males than on the females; males also sported a small, sharp horn on the nose.

The truly gigantic, ill-tempered loggers were another herbivorous species, which roamed in small family groups instead of large herds. They stayed in the large open woodlands to the east of his usual haunts. He had seen two of them cropping trees a month earlier when he'd explored towards the east.

While the Mercantile listed loggers as a valuable species, he doubted even his big Parks double could handle the giants. Rocs, he'd been told, detoured far out of their way to avoid the armored beasts. A logger could easily measure twenty-five meters nose to tail, and with a short tail at that. They massed an average of twenty-five metric tons. But size alone wasn't what made the loggers formidable. Beginning with a foreshortened, turtle-like beak that could snap a meter-thick pine trunk in half, continuing onto a short, thick neck with a projecting frill of spines, a heavy torso covered in chitin armor, and a short thick flattened tail with razor-edged chitin plates that transformed the tail into the natural equivalent of a broadsword; every inch of the logger was a walking weapon. Unlike the other large animals of Forest, they supported their bulk on all fours. Their front legs were longer, bearing me-ter-long claws protected by their knuckle-walking gait. The rear legs were shorter, thicker, column like, with short thick claws. The two he had watched were braced up on their hind legs, leaning back on their thick tails, using the long clawed front legs to pull down trees to easy browsing reach. He had watched the giants, fascinated, for half an hour before slipping silently away.

A cave in an overhanging cliff was now Mike's home camp. A week's work with axe and pack saw had provided rough but comfortable furniture. Roaming the woods for weeks at a time, he reveled in the warm climate, the clean air, the giant trees, and the plentiful game.

Finishing his field-dressing job, he sat back to wait for the provisioning droid. This roc would go back intact. He had plenty of jerked meat, and he found roc meat unappealing.

Twenty minutes later, the robotic hauler swooped in from the south. Powered by a tiny fusion reactor, the provisioning variant of the standard OWME heavy-service droid resembled a weird, flying dump truck. A camera eye scanned the ground beneath, settling finally on the downed roc. The droid came into hover at treetop height above the huge carcass. Three robotic arms unfolded, latched onto the roc's legs and neck, and retracted, pulling the carcass into the cargo bay. The robotic voice boomed out, startling him as it always did:

ROC, MALE, PLUMES RATED 2-A. 6 METRIC TONS, PAID AT STANDARD RATE, 1,200 CREDITS. 500-CREDIT BONUS FOR PLUMAGE. FUNDS DEPOSITED IN SETTLEMENT BANK ACCOUNT, M. CRIDER, 485957991303.

*A good day's work,* he thought to himself. In his solitary lifestyle, entire weeks went by in which he never heard the sound of his own voice, but he found that strangely satisfying.

Suppertime was coming on. The sun was sinking in the eastern sky. He had almost gotten used to the sun's moving in the wrong direction across the sky, but not quite. Chewing a bit of jerked boser meat, Mike decided to hike on another kilometer or two before making camp.

At least the walking was easy in this stretch of woods. The last week had been spent exploring a large valley between two ranges of mountains, a few miles west of his home cave. The river that had cut the great valley sprawled out across the valley floor, creating a wide, flat floodplain heavily forested with giant conifers. Under the great trees the forest floor was mostly bare, but meadows of giant ferns grew as high as his waist. In the fern meadows, bosers grazed, and there the rocs hunted them. Since his day's hunting had been successful, he headed back into the depths of the forest.

Lowering beams of sunlight struck spears of yellow down through the branches. A bevy of small, weird, flying creatures fluttered away as Mike looked for a good campsite. He didn't know what the little fluttering things were called, but at roughly the size of an Earth chicken, they weren't bad eating. Mike had a few shot shells for his 15mm Parks rifle, which made a moderately effective close-range shotgun when so equipped, although the rifled barrels tended to scatter the pattern of fine iron birdshot somewhat.

Tonight's menu, though, consisted of boser jerky and cold water from a stream just ahead. A large pine (he hadn't learned if there was a local name for the various trees, and so had fallen in the habit of thinking of them as the Earth tree they most resembled) leaned over the stream from a short way up the bank, shading a thick stand of ferns. A leaning tree made a good shelter, and the ferns would make a soft bed. Rocs weren't a worry, as they were strictly daytime hunters. They seldom came this far into the deep woods either. Sheer size made it necessary for them to stay in the open spaces. As long as he was up and alert by sunrise, there was no worry about sleeping in the open.

The light was fading quickly now. He tromped down the ferns under the tree bole into a soft bed before dropping his backpack. His light bedroll was slung on the frame. He untied the bedding and spread the blankets out on the bed of ferns. After filling his canteens at the stream, he kindled a small fire and reclined on his bedroll, chewing another bite of boser jerky, and pondered his next day's adventure.

*I've been over this country pretty good*, Mike reflected, looking over his map. *I wonder how the hunting is closer into the mountains? There have only been a couple little farms out here, but I wonder if there's anyone at all up that way. Not much shows on these maps.*

The sun had slipped below the horizon now, so Mike fished a small popup light from his pack to continue his map reconnaissance.

*Country opens up some over northeast,* he noted to himself. *Might be more big stuff over that way; bosers like the fern meadows. Company's paying good for boser meat. I could use some more jerky, too.* He examined the intervening terrain closely. *Not too rough a walk; looks like about twenty kilometers before you start to hit the open spots. A river to cross, but doesn't look like a big one. Have to watch out for loggers, that's the kind of country they like, too.*

*I'll start out tomorrow. Figure a week to have a good scout through that country, and then back to the cave. If the hunting's really good, I can always move base camp up that way for a while.*

With that decided, he shut off his light, kicked off his boots, and closed his eyes. The forest's night creepers and crawlers chattered and snapped in the darkness, forming a familiar evening chorus he had come to expect as he dropped off to sleep.

Morning came, as always, a little too soon. Mike opened his eyes and sat up, yawning. He startled suddenly in the gathering morning light. A few feet away, one of Forest's strange little arboreal herbivores sat watching him.

The dun-gray squirrel-like animal was about the size of an elongated Labrador retriever. Short-legged, rough-haired, the odd-looking animal had a long tail with a fringe of feathers extending to each side; long plumes on the animal's legs combined with the tail to make the climbers fairly effective gliders over short distances, usually from tree to tree. He had seen a stuffed example of this critter in the store in Outskirts. The storekeeper informed him the creatures were called grilfens, prompting him to comment that whoever was naming Forest's wildlife needed to grow a better imagination. They were common creatures in the deep forest, but he hadn't seen one this close before.

"Hey!" he barked suddenly at the animal. The grilfen cocked its head, staring. *This one hasn't seen a human before*, he decided.

The creature sat back on its hind legs, threw back its head, and squawked "Hey!" in a remarkably good imitation of his voice.

Mike was unable to keep from laughing out loud. He wasn't surprised when the grilfen imitated his laugh, too, before bounding away and scurrying into the nearest tree. The elongated gray mimic poked its head around the bole once to steal one last glance at the unfamiliar creature lying under the leaning pine, barked "Hey!" once more, and scurried off up the massive tree trunk.

*Well, that was unexpected. Funny start to the day.* He hadn't laughed out loud in quite a while; it felt good.

This morning he took time to kindle a tiny fire and cook a hot breakfast, dipping into his tiny supply of concentrates from his last trip to Outskirts. The dehydrated foods weren't bad, and his hunting success gave him more than sufficient funds to indulge himself. After breakfast, it was only the work of moments to pack his gear, and he was off for new horizons once more.

He moved quickly, traveling, not hunting. Four hours and sixteen kilometers later, the day had grown hot, he had grown sweaty in spite of having had to wade a hip-deep river, and as the map had predicted, the country had opened up some. Fern meadows now broke up the forest fairly regularly. He had encountered three herds of peacefully grazing bosers and detoured around one prowling female roc, whose attentions were luckily focused on the bosers. The fluttering chicken-like flyers of the deep woods had been replaced by a larger variety in this more open country, a birdlike thing that looked for all the world like the familiar sage grouse of Idaho. The walking was hot in the sunshine of the open areas, so Mike was glad for the shade of his old gray Stetson.

It was then that he crested a small knoll and saw the ruins of a family's home.

Somehow, someone had gotten passage all the way up here, and built a small cabin on the edge of the woods bordering a large fern prairie. Four fields were cleared out of the ferns, but no crops would grow there this year. The cabin and one small outbuilding were wrecked, a tiny hydrogen-powered tractor was lying on its side, and the area was covered with unmistakable three-toed, clawed footprints.

A roc. A big one.

Mike instinctively checked the load in his Parks. Removing the shotshell from the left barrel, he replaced it with a hi-ex round. Both barrels were now ready for dangerous game. After examining the area carefully and seeing no sign of the roc, Mike sprinted for the ruins of the cabin.

A few feet from what was now a pile of scrap lumber, he came upon a man's lower leg, severed neatly just below the knee, the pant leg and farmer's boot still intact. He fought to keep his stomach contents down; the leg had obviously been sliced off by the razor-edge of a roc's beak. There was no sign of any other remains.

A groan caught his attention; someone was still alive in the wreckage of the cabin! Mike fell to the pile of wood, digging with his hands, throwing beams and siding to the side; slowly, he grew closer to the pained whimpers. A final beam with several large planks attached was flipped to the side, and Mike found the lone survivor.

It was a girl Mike's age or a little younger, unconscious. Mike pried one last board off her legs, and gently pulled her to a sitting position. Clad in a brown, one-piece jumper of some sort, the girl was slightly built, tiny-boned and slim, no taller than most twelve-year olds. Her heart-shaped face was bloody on one side, but unmistakably pretty, framed by short, curly blonde hair, matted now with blood and dust.

"Miss?" he asked, shaking her shoulders slightly. "Miss? Can you hear me?"

A scream in the near distance, a roc. He knew the great predators habitually returned to kill sites, although he couldn't imagine why it would return here, there was nothing left to eat.

*Nothing but us,* he thought. With one hand, he reached out and grabbed the barrels of the Parks double, pulling it closer. With the other, he supported the girl, calling to her more urgently. "Miss? Wake up! We've got to get out of here!"

The roc screamed again, closer now.

The girl's china-blue eyes fluttered open. "Mom? Dad?" she groaned.

"Miss, your Dad is dead. I don't know about your Mom. We've got to get out of here, Miss! The roc is coming back. We've got to get back into the trees!"

"No!" the girl blurted, disoriented. "I've got to find my Mom and Dad!" She struggled out of his grasp, attempting to stand but falling to one side.

"Not now!" Mike pleaded, but it was too late. The roc crested the ridge, coming in from the open prairie. It saw the two young people instantly.

The roc could strike quickly, but it had a hundred meters to cover, and Mike was a fast and accomplished shot. He stood, raising the Parks rifle just as the roc charged. The sights swung onto the roc's chest with practiced ease, and Mike touched off the left barrel.

A thunderous *BOOM* sent the barrels skyward. The girl fell prone, screaming. Mike dragged the barrels down, sighting again on the charging predator. The familiar faint *whump* sounded as the charge detonated in the roc's chest. The giant bird-beast staggered but came on.

*Not good enough*, Mike thought. *Aim for the spines*. He sighted again, carefully, higher up on the chest, nearer the neck. *BOOM! Whump!* The roc stumbled, one leg went out from under it, and the great predator spun to the ground, raising a cloud of dust. One last kick and the beast lay still.

"Damn," Mike breathed. His heart was hammering as though he'd just run a hard mile uphill. He broke the rifle, removed the spent rounds, and dunked two fresh high-ex rounds in the barrels. The roc might have a mate.

The girl! Mike dropped to his knees beside her. She was awake, but only just, her eyes glazed, her breath fast and shallow.

"Miss!" Mike pleaded. Her eyes focused, slowly, coming finally to meet Mike's.

"What's your name?" he asked.

"Jenny," the girl groaned. "Jenny Aggruder."

"Jenny, I need you to help me, here. Was there anyone else here beside you and your folks? Is there anyone else around, Jenny?"

She was crying now. "No, just Mom, Dad and me…I saw the roc get Mom. She was in the garden when the roc came out of the trees. She never even saw it. I was in the house. I saw Dad running for the shed to get his gun. The roc ran right over the top of the house, and it fell down on top of me.

"I don't remember anything after that. It got Dad, too, didn't it?" Overcome, she collapsed, sobbing.

"Listen, Jenny, I can't help your folks now, but I've got to get you out of here. It's not safe to stay out on the plains too long. We've got a little time now that this roc is dead, but we need to move away from here soon."

"I know," Jenny sobbed. "I know."

"Listen, my name's Mike, Mike Crider," he told her, trying to sound reassuring. "I'll get you back to Outskirts, you can get a skimmer-bus there back to Settlement."

"What am I supposed to do in Settlement?" Jenny cried, tears streaming down her face. "I don't have any money! Dad wanted to homestead and farm, that's why we came clear up here. He hasn't sold any crops. We just barely raised what we could eat!"

"I know, Jenny, I know, but you can't stay here!"

She clutched at his arm suddenly. "Take me with you?" she begged. "I can keep up! You're a pioneer, aren't you? I'm a good shot!"

Mike frowned. For the moment, he didn't see any real alternative. He'd seen the brothel in Settlement, legal on OWME planets, and with no money, the girl would have little choice but that. *No,* Mike thought, *she's too young to be a camp doxie. I can't let her do that. Damn.*

"OK," he conceded, "I guess you should come with me for now. Get what stuff you can find. We've got to get moving."

Together they dug through the ruins, uncovering a trunk containing Jenny's clothing. In the shed, Mike found a leather knapsack and, more important, an ancient, battered Remington 700 rifle. Mike checked the chamber; the rifle magazine was full but the chamber empty. A moment's scrounging uncovered five boxes of .338 Winchester Magnum ammunition. He examined the weapon with a critical eye. The old rifle's stock was dented and scarred, and the bluing faded, but the arm seemed to be in good working order. It had obviously been well cared for, old as it was. Gathering his finds, Mike walked back to the wrecked cabin.

After changing into a blue cotton work shirt and knee-length brown shorts over stout work boots, Jenny had gathered what belongings she could find to take with her. Essential clothing, an extra pair of boots, a lantern, two books, and a small pile of what she thought of as "girl stuff," a hairbrush, a tiny mirror, some soap, and two towels. She had a floppy brown leather hat, her short blonde hair spilled out in curls under the brim. She'd washed her face and hands, and looked much more composed now, in spite of the bandage on her temple.

Mike handed Jenny the knapsack and held up the old Remington.

"Can you shoot this?" he asked.

Jenny took the rifle, chambered a round. "See that jar?" she asked, inclining her head towards an empty glass jar on the ground. Mike nodded. "Throw it in the air, far as you can."

Mike picked up the jar, wound up and shagged it towards the far tree line. Jenny shouldered the ancient rifle, followed the arc of the glass jar, and touched off one shot. The jar shattered into a thousand fragments in midair.

"Daddy taught me to shoot. The kick doesn't even bother me anymore." Jenny's eyes were red, and her face was still tear-stained, but a stubborn pride shone through now.

Mike couldn't help grinning. "That'll do," he assured her.

"I guess it wouldn't have been much good against the roc, anyway, would it?" Jenny asked, regarding the antique arm with a grimace.

"Well, they're awfully big. That's a hell of an elk rifle where I come from on Earth, but here on Forest, it's a popgun. That's OK, popguns have their uses, too, and I bet your Dad got plenty of eating meat with this one, didn't he?"

Jenny nodded, tears streaming anew.

"Well, as good as you can shoot, you'll get plenty of eating meat for us, too, and you've seen that I can handle a roc, as long as I see him coming," Mike assured her, patting the heavy Parks double. "But the best way to handle rocs is to stay out of their way, and that means staying in the woods."

"You've killed rocs before, right?" she demanded. "You did that too well not to have."

"Yeah, I've killed a few. But only when I've been able to set up the stalk just right and catch them from a tree line. They're too big to come into the woods much, and I only shoot from a tree line. They're too big to take chances with, and that's why we've got to get out of here now."

Nodding her assent at last, Jenny bent to stuff her belongings in the leather knapsack. In a moment, they were on their way.

"So where do you come from? On Earth, I mean," Jenny asked as they retreated into the safety of the deep forest.

"Challis, Idaho." Mike replied. "Well, near there, anyway. I had a place up in the Salmon River Mountains. I grew up there, inherited the place after my Ma and Pa died."

"Why'd you leave?" Jenny lengthened her stride to catch up with Mike.

"Too many people, I guess. Condos going up all over. How about you? Where did you come here from?"

"We came from Armstrong City."

"The Moon, huh?"

"Yeah. Daddy grew up on a corn farm in Iowa. He took a mining job in Armstrong, but gypsum mining wasn't his thing, I guess. He wanted to get back to farming, and not hydroponics farming in a pressure dome, either. One day he saw an OWME poster for Forest, and off we went, three days after my sixteenth birthday." Jenny used one hand to pantomime a lunar shuttle blasting from the surface.

"We've been here two years now." That, Mike figured, would make Jenny right around nineteen, when you figured in transit time. Two years younger than he was, more or less.

"I've been here six months," Mike offered. "My folks have been dead three years now. Remember the semi-ballistic that went up over the Atlantic a few years back? Liquid oxygen leak?" Jenny nodded. "Well, they were on it. Pa was fixing to look at some land in Africa."

"I'm sorry," Jenny offered.

"S'alright," Mike assured her. "I stayed in the place outside Challis for a while. But shoot, it was just more people all the time. The hunting was about gone, the deer and elk are almost finished. No place for wildlife on Earth anymore."

"I guess we're both the same, then," Jenny said, looking down at her boot tips as she walked. "We're both orphans. We both lost our homes."

Mike hadn't thought of it in those terms before.

"I guess you're right," he answered, "but my home is wherever I am, now. As long as I've got enough to eat, a place to sleep and a good rifle," he patted the Parks double, "I'm at home."

"That's OK for a pioneer," Jenny said, "but what about when you get older? You can't live in the open and dodge rocs forever."

"Cross that bridge when I come to it," Mike demurred.

They walked throughout the remainder of the morning, stopping finally in a tiny glen in the deep woods, along a tiny trickle of a stream. Mike filled his canteen cup with the ice-cold water, and brought the drink to Jenny where she lay, exhausted, in the ferns.

"Here, have a drink," he offered, holding out the cup. Jenny took the cup and drank thirstily. One good thing about this planet was the water. Back in Idaho, Mike would have boiled the water first. There was no Giardia on Forest. In fact, no hostile pathogens had been found at all, according to the briefings.

"I'm tired," Jenny confessed. "I thought all the farm work had me in shape. I guess not in enough shape to be a pioneer."

"You're doing fine," Mike assured her. "You know, we're pretty deep in the woods, I think we'll make camp here. It's a little past mid-day, so we can rest up the rest of the afternoon, lounge around a little, and think about what to do next."

"That sounds good to me."

"Hungry?" Mike asked, holding out a strip of jerked boser meat. She seized the tidbit, tearing at it with even, white teeth.

"What is this?" she asked around a mouthful.

"Boser jerky. Made it myself. They aren't bad eating at all, but they're better fresh. If we keep on north, we'll hit some open country; I'll see if I can bring one down, and I'll chop off a back strap before we send the carcass back. I wouldn't mind a bit of fresh meat, would you?"

"I guess not!"

Mike smiled.

Jenny suddenly dug into her backpack. Pausing in her search, she looked up at Mike where he sat in the ferns. "Close your eyes!" she ordered. Mike complied.

A small, hard object landed in his lap; he picked it up, opening his eyes.

"A Nutty Crunch Bar?" he exclaimed. He couldn't have been more surprised if she'd pulled out a folding video monitor and a series of movie disks. "I love these things!"

They shared the sweet. "That's the only one I found, so enjoy it. Daddy got a box of them on the one trip he made into Outskirts."

"This almost feels like a picnic," Mike grunted contentedly. He leaned back on his elbows, squinting up at the sun from under the brim of his gray Stetson. "I'm exhausted." Jenny lay back in the ferns.

"You know," she reflected, "It's like it's been ten years since the roc came in. It was only this morning. I guess it hasn't sunk in yet."

Mike nodded; he wasn't quite sure what to say. A moment later he looked over, Jenny was asleep.

*Exhausted,* he told himself. *OK, Mike, you're not on your own anymore. What are you going to do now?* Jenny was undeniably pretty, her heart-shaped face was peaceful in sleep now, with only a slight frown furrowing her brow. She'd tied the ends of the blue cotton shirt up above her waist in the heat of the day, and now as she slept, her bare, flat little stomach rose and fell gently with her breathing. He felt a slight physical reaction but pushed it away. *She's in no condition to be thinking about that,* he reminded himself harshly. Standing up suddenly, he grabbed the Parks and went to sit by the stream bank. He'd keep an eye out until dark fell.

Jenny awoke towards evening, just as the shadows were lengthening. She sat up, stretching her arms and yawning. A few feet away, Mike squatted next to a tiny, smokeless fire, stirring something in a tiny folding metal pot.

"What have you got there?" she asked, walking up behind him.

He looked around, grinned. "A little boser jerky, stewed in creek water, with a few dehydrated vegetables tossed in. Doesn't make a bad stew. Feeling better? You slept a good while."

"My legs are sore, but I'll be alright. Where are we going from here?"

The 'we' wasn't lost on Mike. They were partners now.

"Well, look here," he replied, drawing her attention to an unfolded map lying in the ferns next to him. "We're right about here," he explained, pointing. "Now as we go north, we cross these open areas I told you about, and then back into heavy woods again right at the foot of the New Pyrenees Mountains. I was thinking of going up in there a while. I know mountains better than any other kind of country."

"How long will that take?"

"Well, from what I understand, we're getting into the dry season now, and things will get hotter. No rain for six months or so, and the fern prairies will pretty much dry up. I had figured on staying up in there most of the dry season, it'd be cooler if nothing else."

"Sounds good to me. It's not like I've got any other plans," Jenny answered, a little downcast now. She sat down across the fire from Mike. "How long till supper? It smells good."

"Should be ready now. Here," he handed her a small stainless-steel bowl and spoon. Retrieving the pot from the coals, he dished her up a portion. He only had one bowl, and so ate directly from the pot himself with a spoon he'd whittled from a piece of dry wood while Jenny slept.

"It's good," Jenny said around a mouthful. Mike nodded.

After they ate, Jenny insisted on taking the few dishes to the tiny stream to clean them. "You cooked, I'll clean up," she pointed out. "It's only fair." The darkness was gathering when she finished.

The fire was burned down to a faint bed of glowing coals. Mike kicked some dirt over them. Jenny asked, "Won't we want a fire going? For animals?"

"Well, back home I would have," he explained, "but the only predators here big enough to hurt you are only active in daylight. I haven't kept a fire at night since I've been here. It's sure warm enough without one." He retrieved his bedroll from the backpack and was a bit surprised when Jenny came to spread her blankets beside his.

"I'd feel better if you were close by, if it's OK with you." Mike nodded assent and proceeded to pull his boots off. He tossed his Stetson with practiced skill to the top of his backpack where it sat a meter or so away, and lay down, sighing. Jenny silently wrapped up in her blanket beside him.

The night gathered around them, punctuated as always by the chittering and scrambling sounds of Forest's nocturnal creepers and crawlers. Mike lay awake, listening; he always enjoyed the sounds of the woods at night, whether on Earth or here on Forest.

After a few moments, he became aware of another, less familiar sound. Jenny was crying, softly, in her blankets. Her sobbing was barely audible, but Mike had a hunter's ears.

"Jenny," he asked gently, reaching one hand to touch her shoulder. "Are you all right?"

She turned suddenly, throwing the blanket off and burying her face in Mike's chest. She clutched him with both arms, crying fiercely now. "I was just standing there looking out the cabin window," she sobbed, "and the roc just burst out of the trees and ran Mom down. It grabbed her up and she was just *gone*, just like that; there just wasn't anything I could *do*! I heard Dad yell; he'd been out in the field on the other side of the house. He ran for the shed, I could hear him running, but the roc saw him, and it just ran right over the house. Its foot came right through the wall, just missed me, and the whole thing fell down. I guess that's when it got Dad, too."

Mike wrapped his arms around Jenny and hugged her hard, speaking urgently. "Jenny, if you hadn't stayed in the house, it would have just eaten you, too!" he reminded her. "Your parents would have wanted you to stay alive, Jenny. And I promise you, I'll make sure that you are OK, you hear? I'll take care of you, Jenny. Your folks are gone, but you aren't alone, you hear me?" He felt her nod, even as she cried against his chest.

She cried for a good while; Mike guessed half an hour or more. Finally, the storm passed. She lay quietly at last, her head on his chest as he lay on his back on the blankets.

"I'm sorry," she apologized.

"Hey, you needed to do that," Mike reassured her. "You need to feel bad before you can feel better."

She raised her head, looking into Mike's eyes; her face was framed, faintly, against the starlight that drifted through the trees.

"If it wasn't for you, I wouldn't be feeling anything. I'd be dead, too. I'd be dead without you."

"Lucky I came along just then, huh?" Mike added, trying to lighten the moment.

"Yes… Very lucky, for me." She raised herself up on her elbows, squinting at Mike in the faint gleam of starlight.

Mike felt himself falling into her eyes for a moment. Jenny had loosened her clothes for sleeping, and as she leaned forward her cotton work shirt gapped open, revealing a glimpse at the feminine curves within. A violent physical reaction seized Mike, forcing him to tear his gaze away from her with an effort.

"We'd better try to get some sleep," he husked. "Lot of ground to cover tomorrow."

Jenny nodded, smiling a small, secret smile. She wiped her eyes again, lay back, and was asleep again in a few moments.

*I sure wasn't counting on this*, he thought, watching again her sleeping form. The night passed with agonizing slowness. The western sky was beginning to show pale traces of dawn before he finally fell asleep.

# Ten

**A Grugell frigate, in high orbit over Forest**

On a terse order from the Commander, a small silver ship disengaged its cloaking device. Swimming into visibility, the frigate consisted of a bright, mirror-finished silver pod trailing two glowing yellow orbs on shining silver metal arcs. The ship's crew immediately began running a series of sensor scans.

The Commander sat in his lounge chair on the bridge, awaiting input from his crew. Two years earlier, the initial scout ships had detected signs of intelligent activity around this planet, which was charted for occupation. The scouts had withdrawn, and this new frigate had been hastily put together, the first of a new class of armed ships. The flower of their technology, this ship incorporated a device that warped light around the ship itself, rendering it undetectable by visual and infrared scans. But the effect was two-way. In order to make scans of the planet, they had to drop the cloaking field.

"Sir, our scans are complete," the Assistant Commander reported. The Commander waved an impatient hand. His assistant held up a printout in one stick-thin, snow-white hand. His black claws ticked over sheet after sheet as he summarized the data.

"Get to the point. Where are these aliens located on the planet?"

"Sir, there is one settlement centrally located on the larger continent in the northern hemisphere. There are several smaller colonies within a short distance. No other signs of alien life anywhere else. It is as we suspected, sir, this is an early colonization in progress."

The Commander smiled, parting thin black lips to reveal twin rows of pointed, serrated teeth. "Good. They will not have detected us. The Occupation Group can land on the planet in an uninhabited area, build up their forces, and destroy the aliens in their own time."

"And all the better it should be left to the Occupation Group, sir," his Assistant Commander sniffed. "The gravity on that planet is half again Grugell normal."

"That's why we chose Fleet duty," the Commander replied.

He turned to his Navigation staff. "Re-engage the cloaking device. Take us back to base. I have a report to prepare for the Emperor."

A moment later, the silvery ship shimmered, wavered, and disappeared.

# Eleven

**The foothills, two weeks later**

"Want a drink?"

Jenny accepted the offered canteen and drank thirstily. "We'll have to find a stream pretty quick," she noted. "About out of water."

Mike pointed. "I expect we'll find one up ahead – see that line of trees across the ferns? Stay sharp, this still looks like roc country up here." He opened the big Parks double for the fifth time that morning, checking the loads in both barrels were high-explosive penetrators. Jenny adjusted her grip on the old Remington she carried at port arms.

The two young pioneers were heading due north, crossing a five-kilometer-wide fern prairie on the approaches to the mountains. Two rocs, apparently a mated pair, had just passed by them half a kilometer away, heading south. They had slowed to look over the two humans, but in the end had turned and went on their way. Mike watched them go from where he crouched on a small rise, staring at the giant predators over the barrels of the Parks as Jenny hid in the ferns a few meters away.

"I guess we're too small for them to bother with when there's bosers in the area," Jenny had observed.

Mike nodded agreement. "Or maybe they've already eaten today. Either way, let's get the hell off this open ground. We should be able to make it into the trees on those hills by evening."

Mike set off again in the long, ground-devouring stride he'd used since he was twelve. Jenny matched his pace easily now. Two weeks on the march had toughened her. Even though she only came up to Mike's chin, she had no trouble keeping up with him now.

"Think we'll be in those mountains in the next day or so?"

"I reckon," Mike replied.

"What are we going to do when we get there?" The look in Jenny's eyes held another, unspoken question. Mike suddenly found reason to look at the opposite horizon.

"Hunt, scout around, see what there is up there. Wander around. Set up a base camp of some sort."

Jenny moved the old Remington, loosening its sling to hang it over her right shoulder. "We should be able to build a cabin up there. These trees they have here, one or two makes a house."

"Maybe. I've got an axe, bow saw and an adze back at my base camp. If we like it up there, I'll make a trip back down for the rest of my stuff."

Jenny smiled her secret smile again.

Their relationship had been an odd one from the moment of the rescue. While Jenny had felt an understandable rush of gratitude for this taciturn young man who'd saved her life, that feeling had deepened into something more. Respect and admiration for the young hunter had progressed into a more profound affection. She was certain Mike had similar feelings for her, judging from the way his face reddened if she smiled at him in a certain way.

But she didn't know quite how to take the next step, and she wasn't sure why he hadn't tried. She didn't know that Mike didn't know how, either.

His tendency to wander the woods for weeks at a time had deterred the normal girlfriends that a teenage boy acquires during his formative years. While his peers were chasing girls, dating, and learning the ins and outs of relationships with the opposite sex, Mike had been wandering the dark timber, high mountain meadows and alpine tundra of the Salmon River range. His solitary lifestyle had been, and was, an eminently satisfactory one, but it had left Mike with one glaring social handicap.

He'd never had a girlfriend, not even casually.

Now, he found himself spending his days *and nights* with an attractive girl two years younger than himself, and he wasn't sure how to handle it.

He stole a glance at Jenny as she hiked along beside him. *She's the prettiest girl I've ever seen*, he thought, an all-too-familiar feeling of frustration rising in him again. She wore a short, blue denim skirt and a black t-shirt in the hot sunshine. Her legs were browned by the sun and tight-muscled by their many days of walking. As was her habit during the heat of the day, she'd gathered the ends of her big black v-neck t-shirt together, leaving her stomach bare. A hint of cleavage showed at the dip in the neckline. The small wound on her temple was healed now, leaving only a tiny scar on side of her pretty, heart-shaped face. Her blonde curls bobbed under the brim of the floppy leather hat as she walked.

Mike ground his teeth together.

They reached the trees an hour later, and there as Mike had predicted was a small brook bubbling over a rocky streambed. They drank their fill of the sparkling clear water, refilled canteens and rested in the shade of the pines for an hour.

"We've only got about half a klick before we hit trees again. We can cross that in a few minutes, then we'll be climbing into those hills. You ready for a few days of climbing into those mountains?"

Jenny rolled over onto her back, chewing reflectively on a stick of boser jerky. "Oh, I'm ready for it. Think we'll find a place up there to settle down for a while?"

Mike nodded. "I'd like to find a nice site before the rainy season starts. We'll want to have a good shelter before then."

Jenny rolled back to her side again, her movement releasing a burst of peppery fragrance from the ferns she lay on. She reached over for Mike's hand. He jumped, but Jenny pried his hand away from the map he was looking over and curled her fingers around his.

"How'd you get this scar on your finger?"

"Uh," Mike stammered, "a skinning knife, when I was twelve. Dressing a deer."

"Oh." Jenny looked up at Mike. His face was burning red. *He doesn't know how to react*, she realized. "You killed a deer when you were only twelve?" Better to steer him onto familiar ground.

"It was my third. Got my first one at ten. First elk at thirteen, first bear at sixteen." Mike took a deep breath. The velvet-soft touch of Jenny's fingers on his was exquisite agony.

"No wonder you wanted to be a pioneer."

"We should probably get moving. I'd like to find a good spot to overnight before it gets dark," Mike suggested. Jenny nodded her agreement, letting go of his hand to stand up. Mike's fingers burned where she had touched them as he slowly got to his feet to gather his pack and rifle.

Late afternoon found them on a wooded bench halfway up a hillside. A tiny brook trickled into a pool on the lower edge of the bench, while a stand of ferns promised a soft bed on the upper. Mike kindled a small fire to boil water for their customary evening stew of jerked boser meat.

"Haven't seen any roc sign since we left the open country," Jenny said.

Mike nodded. "They don't come into woods like this. Too big."

The darkness was gathering around them, accompanied by the usual chirping and chattering of the nocturnal creatures of the woods. Their meal and cleanup finished, the young pilgrims spread their bedrolls out side by side as they had done the previous fourteen nights. Mike kicked off his boots and politely averted his face as Jenny removed boots and denim skirt, covering herself at last with a blanket. They lay silently side-by-side, watching as the stars began to wink on in the darkening sky.

"Mike," Jenny began, "There's something we should talk about."

"What's that?" Mike asked, suddenly nervous again.

Jenny rolled over closer to Mike, propping herself up on her elbows to look down into his face.

"You saved my life the first day we met, Mike. I owe you my life, but there's something more to you and me than that, isn't there?"

Mike nodded. "Yes, I think so."

"To tell you the truth, Michael No-Middle-Name Crider, I'm pretty sure I'm falling in love with you. I'm pretty sure you're falling in love with me, too."

Mike managed a nod. "Yes, I am… I've never… I mean, all my life I've been kind of a loner, and…"

Jenny laid a soft finger on his lips to hush him. "I know. But it's not really complicated, Mike. Being in love is the main thing. We can work out the details as we go, don't you think?"

Jenny leaned forward suddenly, kissing Mike gently on the mouth.

Mike froze. He wasn't sure how to react, but Jenny was. She drew back a moment, almost reflectively; then, decisively, forcefully, she rolled over on Mike, straddling his waist, and leaned down to kiss him fiercely. He wrapped his arms around her slim body, pulled her close and returned the kiss for all he was worth.

The largest of Forest's three moons rose to cast a silver light over the scene. Jenny broke away from the kiss now, and sat upright, still straddling his middle. Slowly, she pulled the black t-shirt over her head and tossed it aside. Her breasts were small, high and round. She reached for Mike, coaxing him upright, guiding his mouth to her nipple.

They were aware of nothing else for some time. The hardships of the journey, the deaths of Jenny's family, all the rigors of the past weeks gave way to the imperative of their youth, of their bodies, of the drive to survive. They loved each other frantically, driving away the specter of death with the most basic reaffirmation of life, collapsing at last to sleep in each other's arms. The three Moons of Forest watched over the young lovers until dawn.

# Twelve

**One year later: just outside the Forest system**

"Sir, we are about to enter the system's space," a minor functionary from the ship's crew conveyed the information to Clomonastik in his tiny office.

"Good. Inform the Task Group Commander that we will proceed directly to high orbit. If no alien ships are detected about the planet, we will deploy the power station satellite and begin landing operations immediately."

"As you command, sir."

# Thirteen

**A meadow high in the New Pyrenees**

Forest's orange-yellow sun rose in the west, striking light into the mountains, peeling back the shadows of the night. On a west-facing slope, facing the morning sunshine was a tiny cabin built of hewn logs.

Mike had built the cabin right in a tree line, overlooking a high meadow. The big ferns of the lower meadows and prairies didn't grow up here in the mountains, just low, ground-hugging broad-leafed forbs. The trees were different, too. While the trees up here were similar to Earth conifers, as below, these pine and spruce look-alikes were smaller, more densely packed, with shorter, lighter green needles.

The local fauna included the ubiquitous grilfens, a creature much like a boser but only half the size, which traveled in small family groups instead of large herds, and small flyers the size of quail. Best of all, the rocs didn't seem to come this high. The only local predators were small, arboreal creatures that looked something like a feathered pine marten, and a larger, catlike creature about the size of an Earthly leopard. Cautious creatures, they gave Mike and Jenny a wide berth.

Mike was in the meadow in front of the cabin, practicing with a new weapon. A small local tree proved to have a tight, close-grained wood suitable for crafting into an old-fashioned longbow and arrows. He had crafted a few arrowheads from a flint-like stone, and over the past few weeks had become an accomplished archer.

Drawing his bow, he sighted over the wooden arrow at a leather bag tied to a stump. He made his shot; the arrow *thumped* into the target, only a centimeter or so from four others. With a self-satisfied smile, he tipped his old, slightly beaten-up gray Stetson back on his head. Out here, ammunition for their two rifles was precious. The archery tackle would greatly extend their provisioning capability. Other than rifle ammo, they had everything they needed. The few provisions and supplies Mike had left in his old cave home, he'd retrieved on one three-day trek down and back, while Jenny had put their new cabin in order.

The rough door of the cabin swung open, and Jenny stepped out. Her pale blonde hair was longer now, hanging almost to mid-back. She kept it plaited into two long braids, which hung down either side of her pretty, heart-shaped face. She wore a simple dress of tanned leather, a one-piece, sleeveless affair that ended just above her knees. A U-shaped neckline revealed the upper curve of her firm, high breasts. She padded towards Mike on tiny bare feet.

Jenny had made the dress herself, from tanned skins provided by her pioneer "husband," as she put it. While no legal authority had sanctioned the relationship, after a year together the two young lovers were as married as two hearts could be.

She had made his leather vest, leggings, breechclout and moccasins as well. The only clothing he wore now from before was a blue cotton shirt faded by repeated washings in the stream a hundred meters from the house. While Jenny had fashioned a new floppy leather hat for herself, Mike insisted on retaining his battered old gray Stetson. Out of habit, his grandfather's ancient .45 still rode at Mike's hip whenever he went outdoors. His hair was longer now, too, and he'd grown what he told Jenny was a "Zapata" mustache, although he used a small skinning knife honed to deadly sharpness to keep his beard shaved off.

Jenny had been experimenting, trying to grind flour from nuts gathered from the pines around the meadow. Smiling as she padded up to Mike, she had one hand behind her back. "Close your eyes," she said, smiling mischievously.

"I bet it's a Nutty Crunch Bar!" Mike teased, eyes closed. She reached for his hand, placing something warm and fragrant in his palm.

He opened his eyes. "Bread!"

"Well, sort of. I finally found the trick to grinding pine-nut flour. It even rises a little bit, without yeast or anything, if you just leave it in a cool place for a while." She stood on tiptoe to kiss Mike's cheek. "The stone oven you made works perfectly, too. Try it!"

The small loaf was delicious, nutty, and slightly doughy on the inside with a crisp, tasty crust. Eyes wide, Mike nodded enthusiastically. "Good!" he exclaimed, spewing out a few tiny crumbs.

A few meters away, in the trees, the familiar mimicking voice of a grilfen piped, "Good!" Jenny giggled.

Mike swallowed. "It's your little friend again."

Jenny called to the tree line, "Bongo!"

A grilfen's pale-dun face poked around a tree trunk, three meters off the ground. "Bongo!" it piped. The squirrel-like Bongo dropped to the ground, advancing cautiously towards the two.

"I know what you want, Bongo, don't I?" Jenny asked.

"Don't I?" Bongo replied, cocking his head to one side.

She reached into a pocket in her dress, extracted a handful of pine nuts. "Here you are, Bongo!" she called, holding her hand out.

"Bongo?" The grilfen approached, cautiously, to within three meters, but would come no closer. "Bongo?" it asked again. Giggling, Jenny tossed the handful of seeds a meter away, and she and Mike backed away a little to let the grilfen claim his breakfast. Leaping forward, Bongo used his agile front paws to stuff his mouth full of the pine nuts before bouncing back into the trees. "Bon-o!" it called back, voice muffled by pine nuts.

Mike retrieved his arrows and the two walked slowly back to the cabin, with his arm over her slim shoulders and her arm tight around his waist. As they walked, she leaned against him, pressing her hip and the side of one breast against him, moving rhythmically together. The effect on Mike was devastating, aggravated by her habit of wearing nothing at all under the thin, soft leather dress. He moved his arm closer about her shoulders, his hand wandering down the neckline of her dress, playing gently with one taut breast, teasing until he felt the nipple perk up in his hand. Jenny giggled, rubbing catlike against him. Mike began to have a strong physical reaction. He looked forward to getting back to the cabin. Breakfast, it seemed, was to be followed by a warm, amorous dessert.

In the distance, slowly growing louder was an odd whine. Mike stopped in mid-stride.

"Do you hear that?"

"Yeah, I hear it – a skimmer or a droid from Settlement or Outskirts, maybe?"

"I've never seen anyone else this far out. The provisioning droids don't come up this far, remember? My beacon doesn't even reach this far. Remember the time we tried it?"

Jenny nodded. "It must be somebody in a skimmer or something, then."

"Funny sounding skimmer," Mike replied, frowning. "It's getting closer. Let's get back in the trees, until we see what's what."

From the tree line, they watched as the craft came over the trees, hovering for a moment over the meadow before drifting off to the south. The flying vehicle was bright silver, spidery, with a small oval central pod between four long, thin silver arcs, each with a brightly gleaming orb at the end. The central pod was about six meters wide by ten long, Mike figured. The silver arcs stretched out perhaps ten meters on either side. Suddenly cautious, Mike and Jenny hid themselves in a waist-high clump of woody brush just inside the tree line.

"I've never seen anything like that before," Jenny whispered.

Mike nodded. "It's not an OWME ship or any kind of droid I've ever seen," he agreed.

The strange flying machine hovered, drifting slowly, aimlessly over the meadow for a few moments, finally coming to a stop over the cabin. A series of tiny lights blinked underneath the central orb, and then, finally, the weird-looking ship drifted away up the ridgeline above the meadow.

"Let's get in the house," Mike whispered urgently. "I've got a bad feeling about this."

They darted into the cabin. Jenny crouched down beneath a window, pulling back the leather curtains. "It's still moving away, Mike," she reported.

Mike went to the shelf on the far wall where his old frame pack stood next to Jenny's battered leather knapsack. "Keep an eye on it, baby," he said. For some reason, the strange ship had him spooked.

His carefully maintained Parks double and Jenny's antique Remington hung on pegs on the wall. Mike took them down, checked the actions, and grabbed all the ammo they had, loaded both rifles and stuffed the ammo boxes in his pack. He took the Remington .338 to Jenny where she kept watch. "Here, take this."

She took the rifle, eyes wide. "You think its trouble?"

"Honey, I don't know what I think," he said, bending to kiss her, "All I know is that this thing is giving me the creeps. Nothing wrong with being ready, is there?"

Jenny shook her head, turning her attention back to the meadow.

Mike went back to their stores, loading his backpack quickly with extra clothes, dried meat, leather bags of pine nuts, canteens. He grabbed his locater beacon, useless as it was, and stripped their bed of blankets for bedrolls. He paused a moment, looking at the bed he'd fashioned from saplings, the mattress of soft leather filled with leaves. There had been many happy wrestling matches on this bed he'd made, giggling, scratching, passionate catfights ending in an explosive, joyous release.

But something was out there, now; something he hadn't expected, and wasn't sure how to deal with. All his instincts were screaming "flight," at him, and a lifetime spent in the wilderness had taught Mike to trust his instincts.

"Come on, baby, this way," he called to Jenny as he pulled open the shutters on the window above the bed. This window faced the trees, away from the meadow.

"Mike!" There was a note of panic in her voice now. "It's coming back this way!" A bound took her across the cabin. Mike tossed both packs out the window, took Jenny's rifle and helped her out. He passed her both rifles, and then, remembering suddenly, passed out his longbow and quiver of arrows. Then he climbed out himself. They shouldered their packs, checked their rifles; Mike loaded a hi-ex and a solid in the two barrels of the Parks as Jenny chambered a round in the ancient .338 Magnum.

"Let's head back into the trees a way, scout along back this way. We'll get a couple hundred meters away, find a spot to hide and see what this thing is up to."

Jenny nodded and took a moment leaning against the cabin wall to tug on her own knee-high moccasins before they headed for cover.

Behind them, the whine of the weird spider-like craft grew louder as it settled a hundred meters to the front of the cabin. Hurrying along through the trees, the two came to another high clump of woody brush and crouched down to watch.

The ship dropped down, down, to the ground cover that carpeted the meadow; the four glowing orbs touched the ground, dimming to reveal dull gray metal. The craft was larger than it had looked from below; as the two young lovers watched from the brush, a panel slid open in the side of the central orb, dropping down to form a ramp to the ground. Two incredible figures emerged.

"Mike!" Jenny whispered urgently.

"I know, Hon," he assured her, wrapping one arm tight around her. "I know – they aren't human, whatever they are."

The two aliens were twice as tall as Mike, but stick-thin. Their arms and legs looked no thicker than the shaft of one of Mike's arrows. Mike watched them, moving nothing but his eyes with a hunter's practiced stealth, as they walked a few paces away from their ship. As they walked, they kept up a steady stream of conversation in a strange, high-pitched, flowing, oddly musical tongue. They wore jet-black uniforms, polished black boots, and hooded black capes; beneath the hoods, their faces were snow-white, narrow. They had an almost-human face; two jet-black, lidless eyes glittered under a high, gleaming white forehead. No noses of any kind were visible, but they had narrow mouths with thin, black lips that contrasted sharply against the stark white faces. Their hands were long-fingered, white, with claws instead of nails on the fingertips.

"Geez," Mike whispered, "they're really aliens. They really are."

"What are they doing? Why are they here?" Jenny asked, somewhat rhetorically.

Mike shook his head. "I don't know, but I'm not taking any chances. We don't know if they're friendly or not and we sure can't go up and ask them. Listen to that chatter," he whispered.

One of the aliens raised something to his mouth and spoke into it. Almost immediately, three more ships, identical to the first, appeared from the west. Two of them landed within meters of the first, while the third hovered overhead.

A gray head appeared from behind a tree. "Bongo!" Jenny hissed, fear in her voice. "Get out of here!" Bongo let out a string of mimicking calls, imitating the alien's speech.

The two tall, skinny figures looked at each other for a moment. One of them raised a small, rod like object, pointed it and a flash of green light shot from the weapon and crashed into the tree. As bark chips flew everywhere, Mike and Jenny saw Bongo drop from the tree and flee for the deep forest. The two aliens grinned at each other, showing evenly spaced, pointed white teeth against black gums. "You bastards," Mike muttered.

"Mike," Jenny hissed, close to panicking, "Let's get out of here!"

"Wait, honey, just hold on for a few minutes," he whispered back, "If we panic and run, they're sure to hear us. You stay here, I'm going to scoot ahead a few meters, see if I can get a better look." He raised his head a little to get his bearings, but never got the chance to move.

One of the aliens was speaking into the little object in his hand again, gesturing with the other towards the cabin. The hovering ship slipped in closer and from the central orb, a beam of white light lanced out suddenly, playing against the side of the house; it settled, finally on the front door.

Then the hovering ship spat out a jade-green bolt that shot down the white guide beam and slammed into the cabin, blasting it into splinters. Flaming wreckage fell hundreds of meters away. Mike grabbed Jenny, pressing her to the ground as a shock wave rolled the earth sickeningly under them. In a moment of rage, Mike made the biggest misjudgment of his life.

"You son of a bitch!" Mike roared, coming to his feet, Parks rifle rising to his shoulder; with sure instinct, he laid the sights on the central orb of the hovering ship and fired the hi-ex round at the alien craft. The exploding 15mm round may as well have been a spitball, the ship was shielded. With a shower of sparks, the round glanced off the invisible force shield surrounding the ship, exploding in mid-air a hundred meters above the orb.

*OK, that was a wasted shot*, Mike thought, instinctively switching his aim. The alien with the communicator was waving a hand in Mike's direction and shouting. The white guide beam from the hovering craft flickered towards him. Ignoring it, Mike took careful aim and shot the shouting alien in the head. The tall, angular head exploded in a spray of black and white with the impact of the huge 15mm solid. The second alien raised his hand, and a jade-green bolt missed Mike's head by half a meter. Mike broke the Parks open, reaching for two fresh rounds, thinking, *I'm not gonna make it* as another green bolt shot past, closer this time.

A loud *BANG* erupted to his left, and the second alien slammed to the ground clutching his chest. Jenny stepped forward, chambering another round in her Remington.

"Got you!" she spat.

Mike reached down, grabbed Jenny's arm, and almost before the thought could form, they were running, back into the thick forest, making for a narrow ravine formed by their tiny stream where it dropped down to a wide, open valley three kilometers away. Mike knew of several deep caves towards the bottom of the ravine. If they could make it that far, the caves would make an ideal place to hide until nightfall.

Jenny fought back tears as she ran, having just witnessed the loss of a second home. But this time, the man she loved so desperately was not in the stomach of an alien beast but running beside her, dunking fresh rounds in the twin barrels of his monstrous rifle, encouraging her, "Come on, baby, down the ravine, we'll get into the caves at the bottom, they'll never find us in there."

Mike gave himself a couple of mental kicks as they ran. *If we had stayed hidden, they would have thought they'd killed us! Why did I shoot at that ship?*

The hovering ship followed them only a few hundred meters, sending a few jade-green, explosive energy bolts down to impact harmlessly on the forest floor, before suddenly rising up and racing ahead. Mike and Jenny could hear the whining drivers increasing in pitch as the ship shot ahead, screaming down the side of the mountain. They stopped for a moment under a giant pine to catch their breath. At least none of the other ships, or any dismounted aliens, seemed to be following them. So far, anyway.

Mike caught Jenny up, hugging her ferociously; then he held her at arms' length, his hands on her quaking shoulders.

"Ok, baby, here's the deal. We're in a tight spot, but we've got the edge; we know this country, those gomers don't. They know we're dangerous. We already got two of them, so now they'll be careful. We should be able to run faster than they can hunt. We'll get down the slope into those caves, wait for nightfall, and move from there."

"Where will we go, Mike?" Jenny wasn't shrinking away from the challenge. With her father's ancient Remington in hand and blood in her eye, she was ready to avenge the destruction of her home, knowing even so that the only rational tactic was to run, as far and fast as they could.

"Baby, we've got to get back to Outskirts, and then to Settlement," he told her. "We've got to let the Company know about this. You saw how they blew up our house! They don't want anyone to know they're here, and they're willing to kill us or anyone else to keep them from telling anyone. We've got to let someone know so they can get some security troops out, get some folks up for a militia or something."

Jenny nodded, still breathing hard. She grabbed Mike suddenly, kissed him once, hard. "I love you, Mike," she breathed, leaning against him for a moment.

"I love you too, honey," he replied, hugging her to him. "Now, let's get out of here!"

They slipped into the ravine a kilometer downhill, creeping carefully down the steep side to the bottom. At the floor of the narrow canyon a tiny stream trickled over thick boulders, brushy trees grew from the sides combining with the larger pines on the sides to almost completely enclose the ravine from overhead observation. Moving slowly now, they made their way down the streambed in silence. Once or twice, they heard the screaming drivers of the alien ships overhead, following the ravine. There was only one possible conclusion to be drawn from this.

"They're hunting us," Mike told Jenny as they paused to refill their canteens from the trickling stream. "Let's just keep our heads. We've got to get to the bottom of the ravine. I don't think they can see down through these trees, so let's just watch out for the open areas. We'll have to cross those fast."

An hour later, they rounded a small bend in the ravine, close to the bottom. Before them, the ravine opened up as the ground leveled out, forming a large, fern-covered meadow. The brush just a hundred meters ahead hid the cave Mike intended to hide in, but there was an obstacle in the way.

Two of the tall, thin aliens stood at the edge of the meadow, fifty meters away. Back-to-back, they each held one of the rod-like energy weapons. Their heads swiveled as they scanned the trees around them for the fugitives.

"Look," Jenny whispered, pointing.

Mike followed her pointing finger. A grilfen was laid across a branch, watching the aliens silently. "There's another one," Mike pointed out another grilfen in the trees a few meters from the first.

Over the course of a few minutes, they spotted no fewer than five of the elongated animals crouched in the trees, watching the aliens silently.

Mike laid a hand on Jenny's arm. "Listen, baby, I've got an idea. We don't want to make any more noise than we can help, but we've got to get past those two." He laid down his Parks rifle, picking up his longbow and quiver, slinging the latter across his back. "I'm going to creep just a little closer. I'm going to try something. You cover me from here with your Remington, if either one of them starts shooting in my direction, plug him."

Jenny nodded. "Be careful!" she added.

Mike grinned at her. "Hey," he assured her, "I've played this game longer than they have!"

He managed to sneak up to the cover of a pine tree thirty meters from the weird pair. Tipping his head away from them and back, he muffled his voice with one hand and barked, "Hey! You!"

The two aliens spun as one, weapons pointed, but neither saw a target. Mike hid behind the trunk. As he expected, the grilfens took up the chorus, a round of "Hey! You!" echoed from five points in the trees.

The two guards spun again, firing bolts of green now into the trees. Mike saw one grilfen duck a jade bolt, leaping to glide to another tree. Then, when the aliens were distracted, he made his move. He nocked one of his flint-tipped arrows, took a deep breath, and moved.

Stepping from behind the tree, Mike quickly assessed the shot. One of the aliens had its back turned to him, the other stood facing just to Mike's left; he had his weapon raised, aiming at a bounding grilfen in the trees above. *You first*, Mike thought. He raised his longbow, coming to full draw just as the arrowhead came to rest on the alien's chest, forming a perfect sight picture. Attracted by the motion, the sticklike figure looked Mike's way, but before he could react, Mike loosed his arrow. The shaft sailed across the meadow, landing with a wet thud in the alien's skinny chest.

The alien soldier spun in a half-turn and started to fall, but Mike ignored him. He knew a fatal shot when he saw one. His right hand shot back over his shoulder, grabbing another arrow, nocking it even as the other alien made a half-turn to look at his companion. Before the second enemy could assess what was happening, Mike's second arrow shot across the gap, penetrating one glittering black eye and slamming through the alien's brain. The skinny form dropped in a tangle of arms and legs.

"Jenny!" Mike called urgently.

"Jenny!" the grilfens echoed from the treetops. A moment later, Jenny had sprinted to Mike's side. Together they inspected the two fallen alien soldiers.

They looked even stranger close-up, scrawny, sticklike, snow-white skin contrasting weirdly with jet-black hair, lips, eyes. "Let's get these two hidden in the brush," Jenny offered, as she began to drag one of the almost weightless forms into a stand of woody brush.

"Get their cloaks," Mike suggested. After a moment's examination, they flung the weird, unfamiliar weapons as far as they could into the woods. Returning to the meadow, Mike kicked some dirt over the two pools of sticky, black blood. Then, the young couple finally made for the hidden caves.

They spent the balance of the day hidden deep in the cave, guided back to a small chamber by the light of a tiny battery lamp from Mike's pack. At intervals, they heard the sounds of an alien ship passing overhead. At one point, just before sunset, a ship landed in the meadow. Mike crept to the mouth of the cave long enough to see three aliens recover the corpses of the two Mike had killed. After a prolonged, chattered argument, they loaded their dead aboard their craft and shot off down the valley. Mike slipped back to the tiny chamber in the rock where Jenny waited.

"Good thing they can't track worth a damn," he told her. "It'll be dark in another half hour or so. They'll be looking for us downstream, so I figure we ought to get out, climb the ravine wall on this side and take off south. There's a big open valley to cross, but we'll do it right after the moons set. Once we get past that, it's heavy woods for a way. When we get to the prairies, we'll decide which way to go then." Jenny nodded agreement and crept into Mike's arms. The two held each other tight for thirty minutes, until Mike announced, "It's time we got going, honey."

In the darkness, they slowly climbed out of the ravine, emerging onto a reasonably level stretch of pitch-dark forest. Mike consulted his compass, got a bearing, and they headed slowly off south.

At least the walking was easy and quiet. The foothills were reasonably gentle, as they dropped lower in elevation the trees grew larger, returning to the high-canopied giants that left no light for undergrowth; underfoot was a quiet, soft bed of needles. Mike checked his compass every hundred meters or so, to help keep their bearings in the darkness. In the distance, they heard the regular passage of the silvery, spidery ships of the alien invaders. Twice, they dove to the ground and lay flat as alien ships screamed overhead within a hundred meters. The message was perfectly clear. They were still being hunted.

Just after midnight, they paused at the edge of a large fern prairie. "We've got to wait until the moons go down," Mike observed, pointing to the open area that was bathed in silvery light from two of Forest's three moons. At the edge of the meadow, a colossal old pine had fallen, and the bole of its trunk had rotted out inside, leaving a hollow log with a space almost two meters wide inside; the two climbed inside, turning inside so they could lie down on their stomachs and keep watch over the meadow. From the sounds of things, the hunting ships had moved off to the east a little, concentrating on the forest in that direction.

"Good thing they don't seem to have infrared or anything like that," Jenny said, yawning. They were both desperately fighting exhaustion now.

"They don't seem to be very good at this, do they?" Something about that was nagging at Mike's subconscious, but in his exhausted state he couldn't quite put a finger on it. He was still trying to pin the evasive thought down when he dropped off to sleep.

He woke slowly, grunting at the pain of Jenny's finger poking him frantically in the ribs. How could he get any sleep with that going on? His eyes cracked open a minute amount, in response to the finger poking and Jenny's insistent, "Mike! Mike! Wake up! It's morning!"

*Morning?* The thought burned his brain like a brand, bringing him immediately awake. He tipped his head up, peering out from under his Stetson. The fern prairie in front of them was bathed in brilliant morning sunlight. A kilometer or so away, a female roc led two three-meter-long chicks along the edge of the woods, angling carefully towards a herd of twenty or so grazing bosers.

"Shit!"

"What are we going to do now?" Jenny asked. She had her old Remington at the ready, barrel pointing out the opening of the hollow log. Mike grabbed the barrels of his Parks double, bringing it up to where he could use it quickly if necessary.

"Well, for the moment, we'll stay right here. At least until that roc moves off a little farther. Let's listen for a while; I don't hear any of those ships, do you?"

Jenny shook her head. "I don't hear anything."

Mike fisted the sleep from his eyes, rubbed one hand over the stubble on his chin. "At least we got some sleep. You just wake up?"

"Yes, I woke up and first thing I saw was sunlight. I almost jumped right out of our little hidey-hole, here."

Mike almost laughed out loud. "Well, let's not do that until our friend there gets into that boser herd," he said, motioning towards the roc. As they watched, the roc turned, wagged her head at the two chicks. They crouched in the ferns as Mama stalked closer to the herd of grazing bosers.

*You have to admire something that big that can be sneaky,* Mike thought. The roc stalked along a line of trees to within a couple hundred meters of the herd, and then, all at once, the great predator sprang into action. She charged silently, each stride covering ten or twelve meters, huge, three-clawed feet eating up the ground. She was within fifty meters before the first boser saw her. The herd broke up, scattering in every direction and bellowing in terror, but the roc closed in mercilessly. One boser showed a moment's indecisiveness, turning first one way, then the other, and then back. Before it decided which way to flee, the roc closed in, leaping high in the air and slamming the beast to the ground with both clawed feet. The roc's feet clenched, driving huge talons deep into the screaming boser. The huge bird leaned down then, and used her razor-edged beak to snap through the boser's spines just behind its frill of feathers. As soon as the boser's twitching ceased, the great predator stood up and stretched her neck out; she opened her huge beak and let out a piercing, ringing shriek. The victory cry was still ringing from the hills as the two chicks joined the mother in tearing the carcass apart.

"Wow," Jenny exclaimed, somewhat breathlessly.

"Well, at least we can go now; they won't be paying any attention to anything but their food for quite a while." After a final listen for alien ships, they crawled out of the log and stretched their stiff limbs. Mike shot another compass reading. Pointing, he said, "that way," and they hurried across the open meadow into the trees on the far side.

"We'll stay in the heavy trees," Mike began, and then suddenly grabbed Jenny's arm, yanking her to a stop.

"Wha?" she began; he silenced her emphatically, with one finger on her lips.

He inclined his head towards a narrow depression in the trees fifty or sixty meters ahead, two aliens were there, each with a strange little vehicle. The couple dove for the cover of a tree trunk.

The two aliens were standing, looking off to Mike and Jenny's left. As they talked, one of them fiddled with some sort of instrument. Their rides resembled nothing more than a round platform with a domed underside; a tall t-handle on one end was obviously the control. The two platforms sat, like a skimmer, a few inches off the ground. *They must use a presser field like a skimmer does*, Mike told himself. A clump of knee-high ferns was a few meters away. The two humans moved cautiously in that direction, dropping into the meager cover unobserved.

Whatever the two alien scouts were doing, they were taking their time about it. Mike managed to squirm to a position where he could see them through the ferns. The one holding the instrument was waving it, slowly, back and forth, all the while examining some kind of readout on its upper surface.

"Get ready, baby, this might be trouble," Mike hissed, "I think that's some kind of a scanner they've got there." Jenny moaned, softly, in fear, but she brought her old Remington around to the ready, even as Mike got into a good prone position behind the Parks double.

Whatever the two were scanning for, though, it wasn't people. After a few tense minutes, they put the object away, mounted their platforms, and flew away to the west. Their mounts made an odd, buzzing noise, as though the domed enclosure beneath the platforms the aliens stood on were filled with a lot of angry black hornets.

With a sigh of relief, the two young humans hugged each other hard, and set off into the forest again.

They stopped at mid-day, at another large hollow log into which they crawled and napped until nightfall. Taking care not to wake Jenny, Mike crawled from the log at dusk, listening carefully to the normal, uneventful sounds of the nighttime. Pulling a map from his backpack, he sat down with his tiny penlight to try to place their location.

Jenny crawled from the log, yawning, as Mike frowned down at the map. "What is it?" she asked.

"Well, I'm not sure," he admitted. He indicated a point on the map, "We're about here, see, and we need to get through these prairies and over these hills here," pointing again, "To get back to Outskirts, here."

"Problem is crossing these open areas?"

"You betcha, sweetie. They've got transport, we don't. We can cross at night, which ought to help us keep away from the rocs, but I'm more worried about them than the rocs. Rocs I can handle. These things are sure to be looking for us. They've got to know where the major human settlements are, and I'm sure they're going to figure out we're heading that way."

"And you think they probably have some way to see at night? Infrared or something?"

"We'd be crazy to think otherwise, baby. They're at least as advanced as we are, and even the Company security troops have night vision goggles."

"So, what do you think we should do?" Jenny wanted to know.

"Maybe swing over here to the east, but there we've got a big river to cross. No, I guess we'll just keep on south. We'll cross open areas at night, and count on being able to hear any of their ships or those buzzing platform things."

They set out just as the first of Forest's three moons rose over the horizon, casting a pale light through the woods and over the intermittent fern meadows. Twice they ducked into heavy cover at the buzzing sound of alien flying platforms, and once for one of the spidery ships as it floated slowly along, playing a white guide beam for its blaster along the ground. Towards morning, Mike killed a little feathery flyer with his longbow, and as the sun rose, they kindled a tiny fire under a huge, branching "spruce" to roast the grouse-like creature. A small pond glittered in a tiny glen nearby, and after they ate, Jenny produced a bar of soap and a towel from her pack.

"You, my dear man, need a bath," she informed Mike, "and since there's just one bar of soap, I'll clean up our supper mess – or breakfast, I'm not sure which – while you go over to that little pond and wash. There's a clean shirt, breechclout and leggings there by the big tree. I'll go when you get back."

Mike nodded, they hadn't heard an alien ship in a couple of hours, and Jenny had her old Remington close at hand. A chance to clean up was very welcome.

A few moments later, he returned to their tiny fire, hair dripping. The bath had helped, he actually felt distantly human. Jenny winked at him, taking the bar of soap, picked up another towel and a second leather dress similar to the one she'd worn during their flight from the mountain cabin, now badly soiled and sweat-stained. She pulled off her moccasins and, dimpling at Mike, padded off to the little pond.

Mike unrolled their bedding after kicking off his moccasins and removing his leather leggings he lay back on the blankets with his head propped up on his hands. *Not a bad place to spend the day*, he thought, *big trees all around, a hillside behind us, water close by. If we take turns sleeping, we'll hear anything or anyone coming in time to bug out.* Immediately after that thought, he dozed off.

He awoke with a start as something light landed on his chest. He opened his eyes to see Jenny's clean dress lying across his chest. A giggle turned his attention upwards to where she stood next to him, pale-blonde hair wet, her tanned, naked body glowing in the morning sun. "I didn't feel like getting dressed just yet," she announced. She dropped to her knees beside him, taking his hand and placing it on her breast. "Maybe I'll feel like getting dressed a little later. It's a little warm for leather clothes down here, isn't it?" She lay down on the blankets next to Mike, one hand busily teas-ing in an area best calculated to produce an immediate response.

Rolling over, Mike kissed her slowly, lingering, his hands wandering over her minnow-slim body. Jenny pulled his head down to her breasts, groaning as he took one nipple in his mouth. She reached down, grabbing his old cotton shirt, drawing it off it over his head and pulling his head back to her breasts. Under his leggings, Mike wore a breechclout, a millennia-old design borrowed from the Shoshone Indians of Mike's original mountain home. Jenny's quick fingers found the thong, and a flip of her wrist discarded the clout.

Mike let one hand wander slowly downward, over Jenny's flat little stomach. He moved his palm indolently in a tiny circle, reminded for a moment of her sleeping form the day he'd rescued her from the wreckage of her parent's farmhouse. Jenny moaned softly, opening her legs as Mike's hand wandered lower, over the downy patch of soft blonde hair; she arched against him suddenly with a small cry of pleasure.

Jenny rocked her hips slowly. Then, with a cry, she grabbed Mike's shoulders, rolling him on his back. Smiling, her eyes hooded, she climbed on him straddling his hips, guiding him into her as she let herself down, slowly, her moist warmth enclosing him. She moved slowly, agonizingly, back and forth; arching her back, catlike in her passion. Mike held her hips, gently, letting her move as she wanted. After a few moments, her movements grew faster, almost frenzied. She dropped down on Mike's chest, hips working against him. Mike moved with her now, faster and faster, until both of them exploded together.

Jenny hugged Mike, lying on his chest, beads of sweat coating both their bodies. He kissed her gently, grinning. "And here we are, being chased through a howling wilderness by murderous aliens from who knows where, and all you've got on your mind is making whoopee?"

"After all we've been through, don't you think that as long as we're alive, we should live? Doesn't that mean grabbing any opportunities that come by?"

"Can't argue with that," he replied.

She insisted on taking first watch, sitting upright against the bole of the tree with her antique Remington in her lap as Mike slept. Waking at noon, Mike felt like new, refreshed by more than the bath and sleep. After a kiss, hug and a few minute's' whispered endearances, Mike sat up with his monstrous Parks double across his knees while Jenny curled up to sleep. Faint whines in the distance warned him to stay alert, but the aliens seemed to be searching in the wrong direction.

Jenny woke as the shadows were beginning to grow long. The two breakfasted on what remained of the grouse, a handful of pine nuts, and water from Mike's canteen. They set off south just after dark, surrounded by a glow of contentment.

That day was to be the last pleasant interval on their journey.

# Fourteen

**The mountain meadow**

Clomonastik stepped off the landing craft carefully, adjusting his balance to the high gravity. The planet positively pulled at him, his weight half again what he was accustomed to.

"Sir, the two aliens are fleeing south," his Assistant Commander reported.

"Yes," he answered. "Station two of the scout ships at altitude in front of their expected route. Send as many troops as you can spare, out on scooters to patrol to the south. These aliens will no doubt try to reach their fellows in that colony."

"Yes sir. We'll have two hundred troops landed in the next rotation."

Clomonastik reached out to tap his Assistant Commander on the shoulder. "Tell them to take them alive, if possible, but to kill them if they must."

"As you command, sir."

The hunt was on.

**In the forest, thirty kilometers farther south**

Mike and Jenny crossed a good-sized fern meadow just after midnight. Mike had scouted the edge of the open area, finding nothing. They'd lain in the brush for ten minutes, listening for any sign of whining or buzzing conveyances. Hearing nothing, they had jogged across the kilometer-wide opening, disappearing into the trees on the south side.

**Meanwhile, fifteen kilometers overhead**

"Subcommander, I have them." A Grugell scanner technician pointed at his screen. The Subcommander in charge of the ship took a look at the tiny figures darting across a clearing far below, and turned to send a message. The spidery scout ship slipped slowly from a hover to float farther south towards another opening in the trees.

**In the forest**

Two hours after crossing the clearing, Mike began to grow worried. Something was nagging at him, and it took him a while to figure it out. When the realization hit him, it came like a hammer-blow between the eyes.

"Honey," he whispered to Jenny, "We've got to pick up the pace some. Something's following us."

"What? How do you know?"

"Listen," he pointed out, "hear all the creepie-crawlies chirping and squeaking all around? They usually just stop as we pass by, and then pick right up behind us. Now listen behind us."

She paused, listening hard; there was a silent zone in the woods they'd just passed through.

"Oh, no, Mike, how close do you think they are?"

"Not too far, if they're disturbing the night critters close enough to hear. They're pretty good at moving in the dark, too, or I'd have heard them by now."

A hundred meters to their rear, two Grugell scouts approached slowly, their flying platforms turned down to minimum power to damp out the buzzing. This held their speed down to a little more than a fast walk but eliminated the sounds of booted feet in forest litter. The mounted scouts, guided by low-light scanners, floated over the forest floor in silence, and now they picked up the images of their quarry in the trees ahead. They exchanged a glance and a nod, turned up the power, and accelerated after their prey.

The buzzing sound swelled up suddenly in Mike's ear. It was too late to run; he could hear the alien craft buzzing in fast now; they'd have to make a stand here. "Mike!" Jenny screamed, a note of panic in her voice.

Mike fought back the urge to flee. "Jenny! Hit the ground and stay down!" he shouted and prepared himself to face the enemy.

Buzzing madly now, the first of the platforms shot out of the darkness, a fiercely grinning alien standing behind the t-handle. He drove directly at Mike, apparently intending to run him down. Mike had other plans, however. As the alien drove at him, he stood his ground, diving aside at the last minute. He hit the ground on his side, and as the platform buzzed past a few centimeters over his head, he struck out with the heavy barrels of the Parks double, snapping both the alien's legs just below the knee. Howling in agony, the stick-thin monster fell one way, his flying scooter the other. The platform coasted to a stop a few feet away. Mike rolled once, bounded to his feet, and ran to the screeching alien. As he ran, he drew his razor-edged skinning knife. The alien was lying in a clump of ferns, clutching his legs. The swipe of the knife nearly decapitated him, spraying Mike with black ichor and ending the screams.

The familiar buzzing rose again. The second pursuer had overshot Jenny and was screaming back in for another try. A scream came from the ferns, as the platform-bound alien brushed the back of Jenny's dress. She pressed herself harder into the forest floor.

The Parks rifle lay on the ground back where it had fallen. In a moment, Mike pounced on it. In the slight trace of moonlight filtering down through the trees, Mike saw the second attacker rounding a tree, turning for another pass. Now it held one of the rod-shaped weapons in its clawed hand, aiming at the spot where Jenny lay on the ground.

"*NO!*" Mike shouted, throwing the Parks to his shoulder. The flying invader moved in and out of patches of moonlight, the shot would be almost impossible, a fleeting glimpse in the silver light. Mike squeezed off his shot.

The Park's roar split the night wide. When Mike recovered from the recoil, he saw the second attacker spinning around, clutching one shoulder where the giant 15mm solid had shattered it. Regaining control of his flying platform with one hand, he made off clumsily to the north.

"Jenny!" Mike shouted, running for her face down prone form on the forest floor. Dropping to his knees beside her, he grabbed her shoulder and flipped her over. Her eyes were closed, her breathing shallow. "Jenny!" he shouted, tears streaming down his face. Her eyes snapped open, and crying in fear and relief, she threw her arms around his neck.

They held each other for a moment, soaking up comfort from the contact. "We've got to get out of here," Mike said, a sense of urgency consuming him. "One of them got away. I hit him good, but he might get back to tell the others. We've got to get out of here."

Gathering their wits, they looked around a moment to get their bearings. Mike pointed, "This way," but before he could take a step, Jenny grabbed his arm.

"Wait a minute," she said, "What about that thing?" She was pointing at the flying platform belonging to the dead alien.

They examined the vehicle with Mike's penlight. The thing was eminently simple in design. A twist throttle on one side of the t-handle, a dead-man switch affair that had to be held open to move the platform. The t-handle moved forward and back and side-to-side to steer the strange vehicle. Mike guided it cautiously around the area for a moment to get a feel for the controls, finally floating back to where Jenny stood watching. He stepped off, picking up his great Parks double and slinging it even as Jenny slung her old Remington. He kissed her once, murmuring, "What would I ever do without you?" He stepped back on the platform. Jenny stepped on behind him, wrapping her arms tightly around his waist. He gradually opened the machine's throttle; the buzzing sound rose beneath their feet as the contraption slowly acceler- ated. He kept the pace to the equivalent of a hard run, at which speed the buzzing was present but not excessively loud. Taking a bearing, they headed south on their captured alien machine, buzzing into the night.

# Fifteen

**The mountain meadow**

Clomonastik left his hastily assembled temporary Head-quarters shack when a shout came up from the perimeter guards. A critically wounded Grugell scooter troop limped his damaged machine into his group's headquarters. He collapsed at the feet of his commander, but not before relating details of the encounter. Clomonastik sent a message out to the hunting troops once again, a tracking device in the stolen machine remotely activated, and several more units diverted to the chase.

"I want those aliens found," he ordered the pursuers. "Alive, if possible," he reinforced his original command. "If we can take prisoners, they may have useful information."

"Sir," his Assistant Commander asked, "How will we communicate with them? They are aliens, they won't speak Grugell."

"Then we'll teach them, Apportamattid. If they can't be taught, time enough to kill them later. But," he lectured the younger officer, "A prudent Commander never squanders possible sources of information."

Clomonastik's motivations were more personal than that. These aliens, primitive as they seemed on the surface, had space-faring technology. They no doubt had developed in different areas than the Grugell, and that could be of vast use to the Empire.

He intended to be the first to tap this trove of new technological knowledge, knowledge he intended to retain personally to use to his own advantage.

*This*, Clomonastik told himself smugly, *will be the beginning of a truly great career.*

# Sixteen

**The Grugell base camp**

Clomonastik was less than pleased with the progress his forces had made thus far. It was nearing the end of the second night the two aliens had been on the loose, and his troops hadn't caught them yet. Worse, he'd suffered losses. Losses were hard to explain.

The Grugell Empire richly rewarded successful Occupation Group Commanders. He was sure to be appointed Governor if he established a Grugell foothold on this planet. Usually, the occupation of a new planet was a simple matter of landing a few troops, dealing with any dangerous life forms, and setting up an occupation base. Grugell itself was dangerously overcrowded, and the fourteen planets of the burgeoning Empire were expanding rapidly. The planet-hungry Grugell Empire needed room to grow, and Clomonastik was enough of a student of history to know that an Empire, to survive, must grow.

But this troublesome planet was different. On this planet the Grugell occupation encountered something they'd never found on any planet before. This planet had inhabitants, intelligent creatures not unlike themselves, with space-faring technology. The Occupation under Clomonastik had specific orders directly from the Emperor, and the Emperor's orders were simple: destroy the inhabitants and occupy the planet.

The plan concocted by Clomonastik's operations staff was perfect. Land in an uninhabited area, establish a base camp, and land sufficient troops to attack the one city they'd detected. The plan had begun to unravel before the first ship had touched down. A scout ship commander had chosen a touchdown point in a meadow, and when he'd detected a habitation, he'd simply ordered it destroyed instead of finding a new location.

Well, that Subcommander had paid the price for that error. The two creatures hadn't been in their dwelling, and when the scout ship had blasted the structure, one of them used some sort of projectile weapon to blast the idiot's head off. If the creature hadn't done so Clomonastik would have killed the erring Subcommander himself, but now that the deed was done, they could hardly let the killers escape. Besides, it wouldn't do at all to have them warning their fellows. So, now Clomonastik was obliged to send a considerable force after the two refugees, who had already killed three more troops and seriously injured a fourth.

From his seat in a camp chair at the rear of his hastily constructed field shelter, Clomonastik motioned to his Assistant Commander, who was examining a map tacked to the wall near the door.

"Are they still headed south on the stolen scooter?"

"Sir, they are. As you commanded, there have been five other teams and one scout ship dispatched in pursuit."

Clomonastik frowned. He was uncomfortable in the heavy gravity of this planet. That fact didn't do anything to improve his mood.

"Sit down, Apportamattid, and tell me why we haven't captured or killed these two yet."

Apportamattid seated himself gratefully, the heavy gravity was telling on him as well. It would be some time before they all acclimated. "Sir," he began, "The creatures we are pursuing are demonstrating a great knowledge of the terrain, and considerable skill with their weapons. They are also quite willing to kill to escape capture. This, sir, is a dangerous combination." Apportamattid leaned back in the camp chair, crossing his legs and adjusting his black trousers. He paused to flick a bit of foreign matter from his leg. Even among the fastidious Grugell, Apportamattid IX was considered something of a dandy.

"Continue," Clomonastik ordered.

"Sir, the issue we face here is one of limited resources. These two have already killed three troops and wounded another. We have only the first landing party of five hundred troops, and the number of scooters and scout craft we have are limited as well. To be certain, it is important to achieve surprise if we are to destroy the alien's base city and the few outlying bases without suffering serious losses, but we must ask ourselves, 'How likely are these two to reach their base, to sound an alarm, to be believed?' It is unlikely they will escape the forces we've sent after them, particularly since they've made the mistake of stealing one of our scooters. We can now track their progress. If they are successful in reaching the city, we must consider the probability that these two are outcasts at best, criminals at worst; why else, sir, would they be living in a hovel in the wilderness? And with that being the likely case, who would believe them when they claim to have been attacked by intelligent creatures from another planet? When, sir, have the Grugell ever encountered another intelligent race? Would we believe a Grugell criminal who returned from exile with such a story?

"Sir, that being so, I propose that we send no further troops in pursuit. The scooter troops and the scout ship should find them. If they fail, we face no significant risks."

He made sense, Clomonastik had to admit. He'd chosen his second-in-command well.

"Still," the Group Commander pointed out, "We should ensure they do their best to succeed. Wouldn't you agree? Pass on a message, there will be a 10,000-gnok reward for the team who bring in the fugitives alive. 5,000 gnok if they only bring the heads. Also, pass on that there will be, harsh, yes, *harsh* penalties for any who have them and let them escape."

"I agree, sir, of course. To that end, I suggest we have the one scout ship assigned to the mission orbit at high altitude over the charted location of the stolen scooter. As you know, sir, the scouts we are using were fitted with the latest high-resolution passive visual scanners; the scouts can use them to keep watch for the creatures. They can remain above unaided visual range, and when they detect the two creatures – as you may rest assured, they will – they can guide our troops in on foot for the capture."

"On foot?"

"Indeed yes, sir. These creatures have proven their skill at evading pursuit, and at detecting our troops. We must assume that they are familiar with the sounds of our scooters and the scout ships, as well. By approaching on foot, our troops will sound like another forest creature, if they notice the sound at all."

"Yes, excellent," Clomonastik agreed. "See that the orders are given, exactly so."

"As you wish, Commander." Apportamattid stood up, bowed, and left.

Clomonastik sat back, relaxed now even in the heavy gravity. He'd have his Governorship yet.

# Seventeen

**Deep in the forest, early the next morning**

The fugitives stopped to take a short break near a small stream that trickled down a hillside. The alien transport (neither Mike nor Jenny had come up with a name for the thing yet) sat a few feet from the pair, floating a few inches above the needles that carpeted the forest floor. Mike leaned back against the bole of a huge tree with Jenny's head on his shoulder.

"We should get back on the trail, baby," he told her. She didn't answer; she was staring intently at the flying contraption. "What is it?" Mike asked.

"See that?" she pointed. On the underside of the craft, a small yellow light was shining softly. "Did you notice that before?"

"No, but I couldn't tell you if I looked under there before. Did you?"

Jenny shook her head. "You suppose they can track this thing?"

"Oh, shit," Mike exclaimed. "I hadn't thought of that."

"Should we leave it here?"

"Speed or stealth? Let's go for stealth. Leave it here."

They had to find a place to lie up for the day, but it seemed prudent to put some distance between themselves and the suspect conveyance. Following the stream up the hill, they came to a narrow ravine near the top. At one point, a large rock had fallen across the top of the gorge, providing overhead cover. They crawled underneath, finding a fairly flat, dry spot alongside the trickle of water where they could both lay down comfortably. This time, Mike took first watch.

It was mid-morning when he heard the now-familiar buzzing sound. He crawled out the back of the rock overhang and leaned over the top of the flat boulder, poking the barrels of the Parks rifle out in front, he had an idea what was up.

Two aliens mounted on flying platforms circled the area twice appearing and disappearing in the trees. They finally raced in on the glen where they'd left the alien craft, now half a kilometer away from Mike's perch. Mike followed them in with his gun barrels, but held his fire when they disappeared into the trees. Several faint shouts, angry-sounding, drifted up the hill, and then the two re-appeared, with the stolen platform tethered between theirs. They dragged their find off to the north, still arguing, with shouts and vigorous hand-gestures.

Mike dropped back down under the boulder to find Jenny sitting up, rubbing sleep from her eyes. "What was it?" she asked.

"You were right, baby; two of them just came and took our ride. They must have been following it. They beamed right in on where we left the thing. At least it bought us some time and distance."

He couldn't have been more wrong.

Fifteen thousand meters overhead, the Grugell scout ship had noted Mike's brief appearance on top of the flat boulder. A message was sent, and three pairs of patrollers abandoned their scooters and set off for the spot, guided by the floating observers high above.

Jenny was on her watch when the faint swishing sounds distracted her. *An animal?* she wondered. The faint sounds came and went, came and went. Mike snored softly, laid against the rock wall under the boulder. Jenny poked her head out from under the flat rock's lower edge.

Four of the aliens were approaching on foot, only twenty meters away. The rock walls of their hiding place had muffled the sounds of approach.

"Mike!" she hissed, ducking back under the rock.

A shout came up from their stalkers; she'd been seen. "Mike!" she shouted now, close to panic. Mike came surging awake, grabbing for the Parks, but it was too late.

Another pair of aliens had crept in from above them. Mike caught a flash of motion from the corner of his eye, looking up to see one of the rod-like weapons aimed directly at his face. The alien grinned viciously at him and fired. A green flash. Mike saw nothing more after that.

## The Grugell base camp

"Sir!" Apportamattid burst into the command hut. "Sir, our foot patrol reports both creatures captured. They are stunned but unharmed."

"Fine, fine. Excellent work. Pass on my compliments to the commander of the pursuit mission, and have the aliens brought here." Clomonastik smiled contentedly. That loose end was nicely tied up now.

# Eighteen

**The ravine.**

Mike awoke face down on the ground. His full consciousness returned slowly. He tried to regain his senses by shaking his aching head. He tried moving, no luck. His arms and legs were bound with some sort of cord. *Jenny!* He looked around, turning his head as far as his prone position would allow. He sighed in relief, Jenny was likewise tied up next to him, her eyes closed but her breath coming regularly.

Two of the aliens had appeared on flying platforms, these two larger, with space for three or four people to stand. A meter-high railing surrounded the flat surface on these larger machines but for a meter-wide gap at the rear. This, obviously, was to be their conveyance to wherever they were being taken. Their rifles, packs and Mike's longbow were already loaded on one of the contraptions.

A pair of the scrawny things approached Mike, chattering weirdly. He closed his eyes, feigning unconsciousness. They grabbed his arms and dragged him towards the platform that held their equipment, it took four of them to load him aboard. *No great shakes physically*, he told himself. *Skinny as they are, that's no surprise.* He risked a glimpse through slitted eyes; Jenny was being loaded on the other contrivance. One alien climbed on each platform. Mike noted that they had to step over the cargo to reach the controls. *You made one big mistake, Gomer*, he thought to himself grimly. *And you sure are gonna pay for it.*

A bump under his right hip was the mistake. The aliens had seen the effects of Mike's Parks double and the longbow, but they hadn't recognized his grandfather's antique .45 as a weapon. The old Colt Single Action Army still rested in its leather holster on Mike's hip, held securely by the hammer loop.

One of the creatures standing by made a chattered comment to the one driving Mike's platform. With a sniggering laugh, he tossed Mike's Stetson on the platform next to the Parks double. The drivers of the two cargo haulers chattered a reply before twisting their throttles, spinning their vehicles in place and heading off north.

The trees whipped past at a sickening rate. Mike gritted his teeth as he pulled against his bonds. The aliens' physical limitations were reflected in their hog-tying job. He wrenched his wrists back and forth, back and forth; the cords loosened, stretched. His skin burned and bled, but he finally worked a little slack in his bonds.

Jenny's captor buzzed along beside them. Mike risked turning his head enough to see his driver. The alien's attention was focused on the trees ahead. *Good*, he thought, *keep looking that way.* He'd gotten one wrist free now, and used the free hand to pull the loose cords off the other. He reached down, feeling for his holster and knife sheathe. Not only was the Colt in place, his skinning knife was there as well. *Sloppy, boys, sloppy!* He turned slowly, gradually, moving with practiced stealth, until he lay on his side facing the alien piloting the platform. *OK, here we go…*

His hand snaked down to the holster. Years of watching old cowboy movies had inspired him to spend many an afternoon practicing quick-draws with the old Colt, and it paid off now. He rolled and rose swiftly to one knee, cocking the revolver with his thumb. The classic triple-click of the old single-action went unheard over the buzzing of the vehicle, but what came next did not. Time seemed to creep now, as Mike's arm slowly, slowly, extended, towards the alien's head, the Colt at the end; a sight picture slowly resolved, the front blade nestled in the rear notch. A voice from the distant past, his grandfather, telling him, "focus on the front sight." The platform bucked and rocked, forcing Mike to grab for support, but the ancient Colt had been designed three hundred years earlier to be easily and accurately fired in one hand, from horseback. The old gun was up to the task. The front sight blade finally came to rest on the back of the aliens' head, and Mike squeezed the narrow trigger.

The Colt discharged with a boom, blowing away the top of the aliens' head in a spatter of black blood and white bone. The platform immediately slowed as the alien's body dropped to the flat surface. Mike rolled off through the gap in the railing at the rear of the cargo area, dropping into the pine needles and litter on the forest floor. Rolling as he hit, he snagged the skinning knife in his left hand and slashed the bonds on his ankles. A buzzing sound faded away through the trees, the platform driver carrying Jenny was fleeing.

"No!" Mike shouted as he leaped for the platform he'd just rolled off of. Kicking the driver's body off into the ferns, he grabbed for the controls, revving whatever passed for a motor in the thing and racing after the fleeing captor who bore his Jenny off to an unknowable fate.

The alien driving the platform ahead was far more skilled than Mike. He ducked and dodged through the trees, sideslipping and racing through every open area. Mike couldn't shoot from his bouncing platform without taking a chance of hitting Jenny.

They came to a wide-open fern prairie, and Mike whooped with glee, opening the throttle up wide, he'd stand a better chance now. The alien was looking over his shoulder now, but it wasn't fear that registered on his face; he was grinning, showing fine, white pointed teeth. He shouted something into a small device held in his free hand, and Mike's platform suddenly lost power, coasting to a stop in the middle of the kilometer-wide clearing. He leaped from the platform and ran a few yards after the fleeing alien, bracing the Colt in both hands. No good – there simply wasn't a clear shot. The alien captor raced away, disappearing in the trees even as Mike roared in rage. The image of Jenny's inert form still hog-tied on the back of the speeding platform burned itself indelibly into his mind.

For the briefest of moments Mike felt like shouting with rage. But he'd always favored actions over words, and it was action that would get Jenny out of wherever she was being taken. Mike had a pretty good idea where that would be.

He listened for a moment more to the alien craft buzzing off to the north, and then sprang into action. It was certain more invaders would be along in moments, the one that had escaped was sure to have been in contact with his fellows. Mike ran to the craft he'd appropriated, leaping to the controls with one bound.

No good, the controls were dead. He'd figured as much. Grabbing both backpacks, the rifles and longbow, Mike sprinted for the nearest spot with good cover. An hour later, he'd gone six kilometers northwest into the shelter of an enormous outcrop of rock that covered most of a hill. The rock was riddled with caves like a giant Swiss cheese, and caves made for good cover. He needed a safe place to cache some of the equipment, to think, to plan.

A small, dry cave camouflaged by brush made a good hiding place for the moment. *I'll need to get moving pretty quickly. I can't imagine what they want us for, but I bet it ain't good*, he thought. He picked and sorted through the gear, taking only what he needed to travel light and fast. Jenny's leather knapsack would hold all he needed, and would be much lighter and less cumbersome than his big frame pack. Two packages of boser jerky, twenty rounds of hi-ex and ten solids for the Parks, forty rounds for his .45, all went in the pack. In with them went one blanket and a clean shirt. His Colt and skinning knife were still belted on his right hip. He hung his half-meter dressing knife on the left side. His tiny compass and a minute pair of binoculars hung around his neck.

Stealing a peek out the cave entrance, Mike noted the direction and length of the shadows. It was an hour or two past midday. He sat down to wait for nightfall and, in the meantime, tended his weapons. The Parks was broken down and cleaned meticulously; likewise, the ancient Colt. Both knives were honed to deadly sharpness, tested by shaving a bit of hair from his forearm. He inspected his longbow as well; the braided sinew bowstring was tight and sound, the wood clean and undamaged, all his arrows were in place in the quiver and unharmed by the tussle with his former captors.

Dusk was coming on by the time all this was finished. Chewing on a bit of jerky, Mike looked carefully from the cave entrance, listened for ships or flying platforms, and satisfied himself that the coast was clear. He set out north, just as the night creatures began their chorus. Somewhere ahead, in the mountains, laid an idyllic meadow that once held a cabin shared by a young couple in love. Now, Mike was certain, an alien invasion force was headquartered in the vicinity. There, he would find his love. Somehow, he'd get her out, if it took all the skills and woodcraft at his command to do so, one man against an invading army.

And he was sure it would.

# Nineteen

**Next morning, the Grugell base camp**

Clomonastik regarded the captive with some distaste. Odd-looking creatures, these aliens were. This one was awake now, but still tied, and regarded him with a distinctly hostile gaze, hate positively glittered in its eyes. It was lying on its side in the back of the command hut. Clomonastik had only just arrived from his personal quarters to find the thing had been brought in during the night. The capturing officers had been duly awarded half of the reward offer, and dispatched to find the other one. Apparently, it had killed a transport technician. The things were nothing if not resourceful.

"So, what manner of creature are you?" he asked it, somewhat rhetorically. The thing really was hideous. Its skin was an odd, pinkish color, its hair a hideous pale yellow. The creature was short, less than half the height of a typical Grugell, but massively muscled. "It wouldn't do to have you get loose, would it?" he asked it. "No doubt you'd cause all sort of trouble in my base camp." The creature obviously was native to a high-gravity planet like this one.

The creature made an odd, strangely musical series of sounds, not at all like the clipped, precise Grugell language. Still, it communicated verbally, that was a start. He pulled up a stool and seated himself in front of the thing.

Pointing at his chest, he slowly enunciated, "Clo-mon-a-stik."

The creature looked puzzled. He repeated his name, tapping his chest for emphasis. "Clo-mon-a-stik."

Suddenly the creature's eyes, opened wide, and it repeated the syllables in its guttural voice: "Clo-mon-a-stik. Clomonastik." Followed by a burst of unintelligible gibberish.

They were getting somewhere now. Clomonastik pointed at his chest, repeating his name again, and then pointed at the creature. Its eyes widened in comprehension again, and it spoke. Clomonastik did his best to repeat what was apparently the thing's name; "Jen-nycrider?" It nodded its head up and down, repeating the syllables. "Jennycrider!" he burst out, laughing. Well, they knew each other's names, now. That was a start.

For her part, Jenny was more than a little confused. This thing, whose name was apparently Clomonastik, was trying to communicate with her. Up until now, every one of the aliens she'd seen had been trying to kill her.

Of course, she was still hog-tied and lying on the dirt floor of some sort of hut. When Clomonastik had opened the door to come in, she'd seen outside long enough to at least know where she was--just outside were the familiar trees that bordered her and Mike's adopted home meadow in the mountain. The aliens had set up shop in her front yard. As much as this angered her, there were greater issues concerning her.

*Where is Mike now? What happened to him?*

Jenny knew Mike had been right beside her when the stun charge had hit, and figured he'd been knocked down too. Then again, they knew he'd killed several of their friends. Had they just killed Mike outright? Was he being held somewhere nearby? Had he escaped?

The alien was chattering at her in its weird tongue again. "Gru-gell," it said, motioning to itself and then all around at the building and, Jenny supposed, the camp around them. She thought she understood the gesture.

"Grugell," she repeated, rolling her head at the sounds of a group walking past outside. The alien laughed again, and pointed at her, then made the sweeping, inclusive motion again. "Human," she told him. It leaned over closer, jet-black eyes glittering like marbles. "Hu-man? Human." It sat back, apparently satisfied for the moment.

There was a clattering noise on the outside of the building's metal wall, lasting a minute or so, and then another alien came in. This one was carrying some sort of…

…*No*, she thought, *it couldn't be*…

But it was, most definitely some sort of collar.

Clomonastik chattered at the second alien, who chattered back.

"Ah, Apportamattid; the confinement collar. Good. The leads are attached to the outside wall?"

"Yes, sir, as you ordered. The creature will not be able to leave the building without receiving a considerable stun charge."

"It has a name, Apportamattid, and its name is Jennycrider. Let's show it how the collar works. The field is turned on?"

"Yes, sir, and full strength. These creatures are strong. The other one apparently broke free by breaking the cargo tie-down cord it was tied with."

"Very well, but all the same, a full stun charge will knock one down."

Clomonastik walked to the doorway, extending the collar through the open door. A blinding flash of electricity snapped across the open inside of the collar.

He turned back to face the alien. "See, Jennycrider? You can't go outside with this on," Clomonastik explained. He handed the collar to Apportamattid, with an order: "Put this on it, and remove its bonds. Have we any food left from the morning meal?"

"Yes, sir"

"Very well, bring food and water."

"Sir?" Apportamattid was a little confused.

"It talks, Apportamattid," Clomonastik explained. "If we can communicate with it, we may be able to learn much. If it is, as you say, an outcast for some reason, treating it decently may well convince it to talk more freely. We can always," he pointed out, "dispose of it later."

Jenny flinched as the second alien – 'Apportamattid,' the first one called it – fastened the collar around her neck, and then untied the cords holding her wrists and ankles. She sat up, rubbing the circulation back into hands and feet. The message was clear, as clear as the skies past the open door, Clomonastik had showed how any attempt to leave would earn her a nasty shock. Apporta-mattid left, and Clomonastik busied himself at a desk on the other side of the room.

Jenny stood up, somewhat unsteadily. A chair of sorts was nearby. She seated herself gingerly on the flimsy-looking thing, but it held her weight.

*So,* she thought, *they are called Grugell – the Grugell. This one, Clomonastik, seems to be in charge. He sure barked enough orders at the other one, Apport – Apportamattid. Why is he trying to talk with me? What does he want?*

*Where is Mike?*

Clomonastik looked around once, saw her seated on the chair. He grinned his pointed-tooth grin at her and returned to his work. After a few more minutes, Apportamattid returned with a dish of some kind of stewed meat, and a cup of water. He set the dishes down on a small table near where Jenny sat, and after looking reflectively at her for a moment, picked up both dishes, taking a small bite of the stew and a sip of the water before setting both down again.

*He's showing me they're OK to eat, she thought. Stupid! Why would they bother poisoning me when they could just shoot me?*

Well, she was hungry, and needed to keep her strength up. The stew wasn't at all bad, and the water was very welcome. The inevitable need followed, but was easily solved by a peek behind some sort of screen that stood in the corner. A privy of sorts stood there, and was close enough to human dimensions to allow easy use. Fortunately, Clomonastik seemed to feel she was no threat wandering loose in the small building, and since she clearly couldn't leave, attacking him would serve no purpose anyway.

She had little to do but wait.

**Several kilometers to the south**

Traveling light and fast, Mike had covered almost half of the distance back to the mountain meadow in the first night. After grabbing a two-hour nap under an overhanging bank, he'd set off again, risking daylight travel to make time. He ate up the distance in a long, loping pace, a pace his mountain-hardened legs could keep up for hours if necessary.

It was necessary now.

He was certain he was still being hunted, but the aliens must have assumed he'd continue on south. There had been no scout ships, no flying platforms, and no foot troops since he'd killed the platform driver the previous day.

A large fern prairie loomed ahead now, a good two and a half kilometers across. Mike paused, checked carefully for aliens and rocs, and set off at a run. As he crested the slight rise in the center of the open ground, he saw a female roc with a single chick a kilometer or so off, both raised their heads from where they lay comfortably in the ferns. They watched him but made no move. A half-eaten boser carcass lay between them, they'd be no trouble. At least, not until the food was gone. Relieved, he jogged on into the trees, angling now up the first of several heavily forested hogbacks that would take him to the meadow. If all went well, he'd get there about nightfall. He carried the Parks in his right hand, his longbow was slung across his back, his Colt holstered low for a fast draw. When the time came, he'd be ready.

It was late afternoon when he came on the first alien outpost. He'd slowed his rate of travel, slipping now like a wraith through the woods, using skills developed over a lifetime of stalking wary, wily elk, deer and bear. Before cresting a ridge, he'd crawled to a low point and poked his head over, scanning the area ahead with his binoculars. *There. Two of them. They're guards*, he realized, *I was right, their camp is up there. That's where my Jenny is.*

He couldn't afford to be detected. Killing these two, personally satisfying though it might be, would no doubt cause some alarm. They no doubt were required to check in at intervals; he'd let them continue to do so. The night would be falling soon, and darkness was his friend. He bared his teeth in a snarl of rage. "You messed with the wrong guy, you bastards," he whispered to himself, "And it's going to cost you."

A clutter of rain clouds was scudding in from the east, out of the setting sun. The wind was freshening, bringing with it the smell of rain. *Perfect*, Mike thought. Rain made things quiet. The first big drops came down just as the woods were growing dark. Mike dropped below his ridgeline vantage point for a moment, thinking.

He'd been planning stalks all his life. This wouldn't be any harder than sneaking into an elk herd, past a dozen or so alert cows for a shot at the herd bull. *Probably easier*, he told himself. *These things sure don't have an elk's sense of smell.*

By the time the light was completely gone, the rain had settled into a thin drizzle that would likely last all night. He slipped over the ridge, angling well off the spot where he'd seen the two guards, and then looping in behind them. He watched them from fifty meters away for a while. The two had moved closer together, and were huddled miserably under their black cloaks, chattering to each other. *Good, they don't like a chilly rain. I don't mind it at all.*

Slipping away from the guards, he crept into a ravine that led to the high meadow. Mike knew this stretch of woods intimately. The ravine would take him to the edge of the meadow, about eighty meters from where the cabin had stood. The rain dripped off his Stetson. The big hat kept his head dry, but the cold water dripping from the rear of the brim fell on his back. He ignored it; he'd be warm enough soon. It was an easy hour-long stalk, by-passing one other pair of guards, he came to the lower edge of the meadow.

There were several buildings in the clearing now, and four of the spidery ships parked a few meters away. A dozen or so of the flying platforms floated just outside the largest building, tethered to a railing to keep them from drifting. One of them was a big cargo platform.

He lay in cover for a while, watching and thinking. A thought occurred to him, if Jenny was in the camp, there might be a way to let her know he was nearby.

In better times, he had confided in Jenny that one thing he missed about his Idaho mountain home was the nocturnal singing of coyotes. He'd learned to imitate the yapping howls quite well and could get the local song-dogs howling in reply whenever they were in the vicinity of his Salmon River Range cabin. The two of them had hit on a compromise here. The mimicking grilfens were still active at dusk, and they copied Mike's yaps and howls with characteristic accuracy. It had been a fun and nostalgic game for the young lovers.

But grilfens weren't active at night. Better still, the invading aliens wouldn't be familiar with all the local wildlife yet. They wouldn't know they were hearing the song of a nocturnal predator from a world hundreds of light years away. If Jenny had been brought here, as he suspected, she'd know he was coming for her. He tipped back his head and pealed out a series of yapping howls.

**The Grugell base camp**

In Clomonastik's headquarters, the language lessons continued. Jenny was seated uncomfortably on a stool built for a Grugell. Clomonastik relaxed on a larger chair in front of her, with a variety of objects. Apportamattid stood behind him, watching curiously.

He held up a cup, shaking it to splash the water inside. "Water," he intoned in the Grugell tongue, it sounded like a squeaking rat to Jenny.

She approximated the sound as best she could, then pointed and said "Water," in English.

Clomonastik repeated, "Wa-ter? Water." He was smart, Jenny realized.

Just then, from outside, came the unmistakable howl of a coyote.

Clomonastik and Apportamattid looked towards the door. "Sir, have you heard that animal before?"

"A night hunting beast of some sort, I suppose," Clomonastik shrugged. "Nothing of consequence Apportamattid, just some animal. We have guards out if it gets too curious."

Jenny sat up straight suddenly, trying to conceal the leap her heart had just taken. Thinking furiously, she motioned to the cup Clomonastik held. "Water?" she asked in Grugell. She pantomimed drinking.

"See that? It's asking for water," Clomonastik pointed out. "It's talking to us!" He handed Jennycrider the cup, watching as she drank thirstily. It held out the empty cup, making an inquiring noise.

"More? More water?" Jenny asked in English. Clomonastik chattered something to Apportamattid, who retrieved a bottle from the desk next to the door. The bottle only held a trickle.

"Apportamattid," Clomonastik ordered, "Go to the field kitchen and bring another bottle of water. We're getting somewhere now."

"As you command, sir." He took the empty bottle and stepped outside.

As the door opened, Jenny leaned around Clomonastik and stole a look outside. She could see nothing but drizzling rain and the distant tree line, barely visible in the darkness. She knew she hadn't imagined the coyote call. Mike was out there somewhere. She had to find some way to let him know where she was.

Mike was indeed out there, only fifty yards away from the door, wriggling prone through the ferns. He saw a brief glow of interior light from an opened door, and peeked through the fronds to see one of the aliens open a door to a small building. It stepped outside, and in the brief moment before the door closed Mike caught sight of a familiar moccasined foot, and the side of a familiar face peering around another alien seated facing her. Jenny!

He was inside the double ring of guards, and there was almost no activity in the compound. The aliens were all apparently indoors, out of the drizzling rain. The one that had left the building Jenny was held in had walked off towards a larger building a few meters closer to the cabin site. It went inside and the door slammed shut behind it. Mike seized the moment and sprinted for the side of Jenny's prison. He threw himself prone just around the corner from the door, on the side of the building that faced the trees.

The rain continued to drizzle down. Mike lay still for a moment, shielded from casual observation by a tall clump of ferns. He listened intently to sounds from the interior; one of the aliens was chattering unintelligibly, and from time-to-time Jenny's soft voice would reply. She sounded calm and unhurt; so far, anyway.

*I'll wait a few minutes*, Mike reflected, *in case that one that walked off comes back.* Sure enough, moments later the door slammed, and two alien voices chattered away at each other inside.

He crawled around to the rear of the shed, looking for a way to have a peek inside; sure enough, these aliens put windows in their buildings like anyone else. Trouble was that the window was eye-level for one of them, which meant he had to stand on his tiptoes to even peek over the bottom ledge. He did so regardless, first removing his rain-darkened Stetson and leaning so that only one eye peeped over.

Jenny was seated facing one alien, who was holding up – what, a light of some kind? Yes, he was holding up a globular thing that emitted a beam of light when squeezed. A flashlight. The second invader was standing behind the seated one; Mike had the impression that the first one was the boss.

The seated alien played the light beam on the floor between itself and Jenny, repeating a word over and over. Jenny slowly repeated the chittering word back to him.

*It's trying to talk to her*, Mike realized with some surprise. Then a realization: *It wants to interrogate her.*

Time to move. He crawled around to the corner by the door and lay there for several minutes, watching. There seemed to be no roving patrols, nobody was wandering around the compound. Satisfied that they wouldn't be interrupted, Mike slowly got up, slid to the door, and stood next to it, listening. The voices inside went on unchanged.

*Now or never, boy,* Mike told himself. He took a look at the door. It didn't look like much, just a thin metal panel with a cheap-looking latch. Raising one long leg, Mike gripped the Parks tightly by the stock and fore-end, barrels held high, and kicked the door open.

The door gave way, slamming into the interior, hinges and latch shattered. Mike took one long step inside, Parks raised. The standing alien let out a squawk, reaching for something attached to his belt. One of the rod-like weapons! Mike acted faster, ramming the Parks double forward, smashing the alien in the forehead with both muzzles. It dropped as though pole-axed, black blood flowing from a cut in the snow-white skin.

The seated alien tried to leap aside, but Jenny grabbed him by one arm and swung him around, pulling him fully upright and stomping one tiny foot down hard on the thing's instep. Bones crunched, and the alien sank to the floor with a groan of agony. Before he could regain his wits, Mike relieved him of his holstered rod-weapon, tossing it to the side. He stood then, and as the alien's eyes fluttered open, Mike shoved the twin barrels of the Parks down on the creature's mouth. The thing looked up at him, glittering black eyes wide. Mike placed one finger over his own lips in an easily understood gesture: *Keep quiet.* He glanced over to the other alien, but it was either dead or out cold.

Only then did he look to Jenny, who was standing a meter away, face radiant. "I knew it was you!" she burst out, leaping to kiss him. "I knew you were out there when I heard the coyote call!"

"Good idea, huh?" he replied, returning the kiss with a quick one of his own. "But now that I'm here, what do we do with these two?"

Jenny went to the alien Mike had pole-axed with the Parks. "It's alive," she reported, "but I bet it'll be out for a while."

"Good," Mike snorted. He grinned evilly down at the second alien, who stared at him now almost reflectively.

"That one you're covering there is called Clomonastik, he seems to be the big boss around here. This one's Apportamattid, he's Clomonastik's second banana. They're either called Grugell, or they're from a place called Grugell, I'm not sure which. They've been trying to speak with me for hours."

"Didn't tell you why they're here, did they?"

"No, but that's obvious, isn't it?"

Mike had to admit that it was. "Yeah, sure enough. They want the planet, and I imagine they want to kick us off. That's why they made their base way up here in the hills away from anywhere the security troops or the provisioning droids go."

"So, what do we do now?" Jenny wanted to know.

"Get out of here. Think Gomer there can help us?"

"Not until he gets this collar off me," Jenny growled. Mike hadn't noticed the smooth, black metal collar around Jenny's slim neck.

"What is it?" he asked.

"If I go through that door with this on, I get a hell of a jolt – probably would knock me flat." She turned to the alien, who was still prone under the blue-steel stare of the Parks double. "Clomonastik!" she barked at him. "Get this off me!" She pointed to the collar, gesturing unmistakably.

Clomonastik got to his feet slowly, as Mike covered him with the Park's cannon-like barrels every inch of the way. He sidled over to Jenny, glancing sideways at Mike and holding his empty hands up, palms forward, in what Mike correctly assumed was a gesture of peaceable intent. He fiddled with the collar for a moment, and then dropped it to the floor.

"You know, baby," Mike offered, "Clomonastik here can help us. I bet he can fly us out of here on one of those big platform things. If it stops, or anything funny happens, he gets a 15mm solid in the ear. If not, we take him back to Settlement with us, let the Company figure out just who the heck he is."

"I guess we could give it a try. We've got to get out of here somehow."

He nudged Clomonastik with the Park's twin muzzles. With one hand, he pantomimed twisting the controls of a flying platform, and pointed at Clomonastik, at Jenny, and then at himself.

"You're going to get us out of here, pal," he informed the alien, somewhat rhetorically.

Clomonastik was indeed an intelligent Grugell. You didn't get to be an Occupation Commander by being stupid. It was obvious what the creatures wanted, to be flown out of here on a scooter. The worst part of it was that it just might work. The camp was shut down for the night, the guards on the two perimeter duty lists would probably be hiding from this wretched rain, and with Apportamattid apparently knocked out cold, nobody would notice his absence until morning. Clomonastik's one mistake had been in ordering minimal security, and that mistake was about to cost him his Governorship.

The larger creature prodded him with its weapon again. There was nothing else for it; his choices were obviously to comply or be killed outright.

Well, Governor or no Governor, Clomonastik was one who valued his own life rather highly. Besides, something might come up that he could turn to his advantage. He nodded agreement and made for the door; the parked scooters were right around the corner.

They followed the alien outside into the rain. It led them to where Mike had seen the flying platforms parked. Mike motioned him towards the one large cargo carrier version, and the three got on board.

Jenny seated herself on the wet, somewhat slippery surface, wrapping one arm around a post for the railing. Mike handed her the Parks, and drawing his Colt, stood immediately behind Clomonastik. He motioned off to the south. "Get going," he told the alien commander.

Clomonastik looked back at him once and complied. The platform buzzed only slightly as the alien, apparently realizing his life depended on stealth at this point, guided the craft slowly out of the camp and into the trees.

They evaded the guards easily by slipping through gaps in the coverage Mike had passed through earlier, moving at the pace of a slow walk. The machine was almost noiseless at that pace, and the dripping water more than covered the slight buzzing sound. Once Mike figured they were clear, Mike motioned Clomonastik to stop, ordered it to sit on the platform opposite Jenny, and took over the controls himself while Jenny covered the alien with Mike's Colt. He bent on some more speed and aimed for the rock outcrop where he'd stashed their gear. It took about two hours to reach the cache, by which time fatigue was hammering Mike hard. *We've got to keep moving at least until morning,* he told himself, *we won't get any longer than that, and they'll be tracking us.* It was the work of moments to retrieve their gear and load it aboard. The rain had stopped, yet low clouds were scudding across the sky, breaking occasionally to allow glimpses of Forest's three moons. Water still dripped from the trees, but otherwise the woods were silent, the usual nighttime creepers and crawlers apparently silenced by the wet.

"OK, let's get to disappearing," he announced, climbing aboard once more. He turned to Jenny before grabbing the controls. "I'm gonna see how fast this thing goes. I'm going to have to sleep before long, but we need some serious distance between us and them. Hang on, now!"

He was rapidly gaining skill in handling the platform. He aimed it south again and wrenched the throttle open. Buzzing madly, the contraption leaped like a spurred horse and raced off.

They raced at a reckless pace through the trees, Mike kept the machine opened up as far as he could, canting and dodging through the woods. They came at last to a series of open areas. Mike remembered one fern prairie from his map studies, it ran almost ten kilometers north to south and forty east to west. He aimed the machine in that direction, covering the distance in about three more hours.

He stopped on the edge of the clearing.

"Jenny, I've got to get some sleep. There's a length of rope in my backpack. Let's tie Clomo here up to a tree and crash out for a while."

Morning was at least three more hours off. Jenny looked up at Mike, eyes red and swollen from exhaustion. "Sounds OK to me. I'm wiped out. How long do you think before they start looking for our friend here?"

"We've got a five-hour head start, and I figure it will likely be morning before they start looking. That means eight hours. Still, I've got that little alarm clock in my pack. We'll get about four hours and head on out just after sunrise. That ought to get us into Settlement by the end of the day, as fast as this thing goes."

They lashed Clomonastik to a stout pine, arms and legs securely trussed with the nylon rope from Mike's pack. Jenny laid out bedrolls while Mike checked his knots one last time and then they lay down, wrapped their arms around each other, and fell almost instantly asleep.

Clomonastik was almost as exhausted as they appeared to be, the Grugell required sleep in a similar daily ration to humans, and the events of this night had been telling on him as well. But the scene before him was intriguing.

*They're lying there like that, wrapped around each other*, he thought. *That's out of affection. They're mates! Of course! That's why the big one came after the small one!*

He scrutinized them with new intuition now. The Grugell were similarly sexually dimorphic, with male and female genders. This gave Clomonastik a frame of reference. *The smaller, rounder one, that's the female*, he thought, *and the larger more muscular one is the male. Amazing!*

*Maybe I can use this to my advantage*, he reflected. *Many a Grugell male has taken a stupid risk to protect one of his females. Perhaps these 'hu-mans' are much the same.*

Fatigue claimed him then, and he dozed for some time. He awoke to feel a tugging motion. The male human was using some sort of blade to cut through his bonds, while the female – Jennycrider – held another of the noisy projectile weapons aimed at his chest.

Once his bonds were cut, the male human jerked Clomonastik roughly to his feet. Rubbing his cramped wrists, Clomonastik regarded the scowling human impassively. *Well, it worked with the female*, he thought; *why not try to start with the male?* He tapped his chest, repeating his name, "Clomonastik." Pointing then at the female, he stated, "Jennycrider." The male's eyes opened wide at that. Then, with what he hoped was a questioning look, he pointed at the male.

Mike turned to Jenny, a grin splitting his face from ear to ear. "Baby, you told him your name was Jenny Crider?"

"Honey, just because we haven't stood up in front of a Magistrate and signed a paper doesn't make us any less married. You're the only family I have now, aren't you?"

Mike nodded, still grinning. "Well, maybe we'll have to take care of that when we get to Settlement, huh?" Jenny dimpled at him. She had referred to him as her 'husband' before, but hearing her use his surname was better than any ceremony. Shaking his head, he turned back to Clomonastik, who was obviously a bit confused and waiting for a reply. "Mike Crider," he answered the alien, tapping his own chest.

"Mikecrider?" Clomonastik repeated, then pointed at Jenny. "Jennycrider," and then, pointing back at Mike, "Mikecrider?" Then, he spat out a few chattered syllables in his own language, ending by looking intently in Jenny's direction.

"He's asking for water," Jenny told Mike.

Mike picked up a canteen and tossed it to the alien, who unscrewed the top and drank thirstily. He went to hand the canteen back, but Mike motioned for him to keep it. "I guess we got us a prisoner, huh?" he asked Jenny, somewhat rhetorically. "Now we've got to feed and water the bastard."

Clomonastik was thinking furiously. *Their names end with the same sound. They're either mates or siblings and they don't act like siblings. I've got to think of some way to take advantage of this.* Nothing, unfortunately, came to mind. The creatures had grabbed him with no time to leave a clue of any sort, no chance to secret away a weapon or tracking beacon, no clues left behind but the unconscious Apportamattid and a missing cargo scooter. For the time being, he had little choice but to do what he was told, and there was little doubt as to where they were headed. The Occupation's first orbital survey had detected one fairly small city south of their current location, and Clomonastik was sure that was where the humans would want to take him.

He wasn't wrong in that assessment.

Mike prodded Clomonastik, motioning him towards the cargo platform. Clomonastik boarded the craft obediently, encouraged by Jenny's rifle muzzle, which varied no more than a centimeter from the center of his chest. The alien seated himself as before on one side of the platform, Jenny took the other, while Mike stood at the controls. He twisted the throttle and they set off, following the tree line east for the moment. "They'll be expecting us to go south," he explained, "so we'll head east for a few kilometers. Maybe that will throw them off a little."

From her seat on the platform, Jenny regarded Clomonastik coldly. This creature had given an order, she was certain now, to have her and Mike either captured or killed. She wasn't sure what would happen to them all in the end, but her mind was made up then and there, *if we are going to be re-captured*, she thought to herself, *it won't be before I put a bullet through his chest.*

They carefully skirted around a sight Mike hadn't seen before and had wondered about. A female roc, seated on what was obviously a nest of piled branches and debris. The heaped, two-meter-high nest was placed in the shade of a huge, overhanging pine at the edge of the clearing, and the roc appeared to be dozing as she sat on the nest, as Mike correctly assumed, brooding eggs. *Amazing,* Mike thought, *the thing's got to be fifteen meters long, and you could easily walk right up on it without noticing. Especially if you weren't paying attention to what you were doing. A moment's slip on the plains here, and you can be history.* He filed the observation away in his hunter's mind. Opening the throttle a little wider, he sped them on east.

The morning sun was warm on Mike's back as they sped east. It was pleasant after the chilly rain the night before. All the colors were bright, the yellow-gold and green fern fronds in the opening, the darker green of the pines to Mike's left, the flashes of brown and gray from deeper in the trees, bark and branches. Then Mike noted a flash of light, oddly, from the front, above the trees to the left.

Suddenly cautious, Mike took his hand off the t-handle. The flying platform slowed suddenly. The flash showed again, above the trees, some hundred meters to their left front. *A flash of light?* Mike wondered. *A reflection?*

*A reflection off of what?*

A sudden mental image pounded into Mike's mind as though driven through his forehead with a spike, an image of one of the Grugell's flying spider-ships, gleaming polished silver. He shouted, "Hang on!"

Yanking the t-handle to the right, he twisted the throttle around full. The platform spun neatly and accelerated hard, a buzzing roar rising as Mike drove it back west at full throttle.

# Twenty

**Overhead**

In the Grugell scout ship, Apportamattid shouted in triumph, pounding the pilot on the shoulder. He leaned forward over the pilot's head as he sat in the control station, shouting, "There they are! There's the Commander! Dive, dive on them, get them!"

The pilot, startled by the sudden outburst, could only reply, "As you command, sir!" and then he dove his screaming scout ship directly at the fleeing fugitives.

Apportamattid had seen his main chance with the Commander's disappearance, obviously as a captive of the humans. With Clomonastik dead or disgraced by capture and rescue, his second-in-command would be well placed to take over the Occupation, and the eventual Governorship. Either way, Apportamattid saw a promotion coming, and revenge on the creature responsible for the painful knot on his forehead in the bargain. And so he'd taken only one pilot and a squad of troops commanded by a leader he trusted, and informed no one else in the camp of the events of the previous night. The morning was shaping up remarkably well.

## On the ground

Mike sped the craft back the way they'd came, as Jenny and Clomonastik held on for their lives. A bolt of green fire blasted out from the ship pursuing them. Some instinct forced Mike to dodge to the left, to the right, and to the left again. The first green bolt exploded harmlessly to one side, followed by two more. Showers of dirt and rock rained down on the craft. Mike made for the northern tree line, but the sight of a huge overhanging pine stopped him. *Yes*, he thought, *it just might work. If it doesn't, we're no worse off.* He angled the platform directly for the pine, holding the throttle open wide. Behind them, the silver spider-ship dropped lower, picking up speed, gaining on them rapidly.

## Immediately behind

"Hit them! Ram them! Crush them against the ground!" Apportamattid was shouting at the scout ship pilot. The pilot was shocked, but he had no choice but to comply. Grugell discipline was harsh and unforgiving.

## On the ground

Mike side-slipped again, dodging from side to side. The ship had stopped shooting at them, but it was gaining at an alarming rate. Mike stole a glance over his shoulder, and then ahead, figuring angles and speeds. *Going to be close*, he predicted. Ahead, the roc's giant, eagle-like head raised slowly, eyes open and slowly, sleepily focusing on the approaching objects--one small and closing fast, another, much larger one just behind. Startled, it clambered to its feet, shaking its head threateningly and screech-ing a warning.

"MIKE!" Jenny screamed at the sight of the roc.

"I KNOW, BABY, JUST HANG ON!" he roared back, driving directly at the great predator.

Clomonastik clung to the railing in panic. *Was this human intending to kill them all?*

Behind them the spider-ship dropped lower, until its main central pod was ripping the tops of the ferns. A squad of troops in the passenger compartment waited for orders, but in the meantime, they had no view out the front port. Both Apporta-mattid and the pilot were focused on the fleeing scooter, until a movement caught the pilot's eye, something impossibly huge was towering up, actually above them, as they drove towards the trees…

Mike yanked the t-handle this way and that, slipping the platform between the roc's legs, dodging through and out, and back into the trees even as the great beak snapped downwards at them, missing Mike's head by centimeters. The great bird-thing turned its attention forward again, the larger threat was screaming in on its nest now.

The pilot screamed. It was too late to turn, too late to stop. They were going to hit the unspeakable monster. Belatedly, Apportamattid looked up, and saw Death approaching. He was, for once, speechless, managing only to mutter a single Grugell obscenity.

The roc roared in rage, leaping forward, grabbing one of the thin silver spider legs in its great beak. The strut severed as the predator's razor-keen beak sheared through the metal. Out of control, the scout ship slammed into the ferns. The roc screeched as it leaped again, landing on two of the remaining struts, snap-ping them off. She slammed one meter-wide, taloned foot down on the central orb and used her beak to rip a long strip of metal clear, exposing the passenger compartment and cockpit below.

Fifty meters into the trees Mike slowed the platform to a stop. They watched as the roc proceeded to rip the ship apart. At intervals the giant bird would extract a screaming, stick-thin figure from the wreckage, tossing them into the air or slamming them against the ground before gulping them down whole. Clomonastik clung to the railing, weak-kneed from pain and fright. The rocs' giant beak had ripped one sleeve off of his uniform jacket as they'd passed underneath, and the pain started to hit him now as the black blood flowed from a ten-centimeter gash on his shoulder.

Jenny noticed the wound and reached for her daypack. "Mike, get us out of here," she called. Spinning the platform around again, he aimed them south through the trees. Jenny motioned for Clomonastik to sit down, her earlier animosity largely forgotten now as she extracted her first-aid kit and began to clean and bandage Clomonastik's wound.

This last act shattered Clomonastik as none of the previous two day's events had. *I ordered these hu-mans captured or killed,* he thought. *I was going to order this Jennycrider killed once I'd had a chance to question her. Were they prisoners on a Grugell mission, they'd be shot and discarded the moment they became a liability, but not only have they kept me alive, they've given me a water bottle and now the female cares for my wound?*

*What manner of creatures are these?*

Jenny answered the question for him, even though the alien didn't understand her words. "This, Clomonastik," she informed him wryly, "is what being human is all about." The alien cocked his head at her, wincing as she dabbed antiseptic on the gash. Jenny couldn't help thinking he'd somehow gotten the gist of the statement. At the controls, Mike glanced back once, then turned his attention back to the woods ahead, smiling.

# Twenty-One

**Outskirts, at sunset**

Mary Lenell was just walking back from Outskirt's tiny mercantile towards the cabin on the north end of town that she shared with her security officer husband when she heard the buzzing sound. She looked up from the red dust of the road to see, emerging from the trees to the north, one of the strangest things she'd ever witnessed.

A buzzing silver-gray platform, two meters wide, floated out of the trees. At the front, both hands on a tall t-handle, stood a tall, thin man with a huge mustache, a big gray hat like she had only seen in old Western movies, dressed in leather vest, leggings and moccasins. On the platform behind him was a petite blonde girl who sat on a bulging backpack, holding a rifle on…

She screamed for her husband Walter, who was in their small house trying to fix their leaky kitchen sink drain.

Minutes later, the platform floated to a stop next to Mary and her security officer husband, who stood with his pistol held loosely in one hand, pointed at the ground. Behind him in the open door of their small house, two small boys watched, wide-eyed. The man at the controls reached up and tugged downward on the brim of his huge hat.

"Ma'am," he asked politely, "Sir, would either of you know where I can find a Company security troop?"

"I'm a security officer," Walter informed him.

The young man smiled broadly. "You better take us to your boss, Officer. This here's a long story."

"I bet it is," Security Officer First Class Walter Lenell admitted, staring over Mike's shoulder at the skinny, weird form of Clomonastik hunched on the alien scooter. "Can you give me a thumbnail?"

"Yeah, there's a whole piss-pot full of these things," Mike pointed at Clomonastik, "landing up in the New Pyrenees. They blasted the hell out of our cabin the minute they showed up, and they've been trying to kill us ever since. This one here seems to be the boss. I brought him along out of their main camp, figured he'd be a nice safe-passage. My guess is they'll be coming here before long."

"You'd both better come along with me, and bring…whatever that thing is. I'll call a skimmer to come down from Settlement. The Colonel's going to want to talk to you both." Officer Lenell turned to his wife. "Mary, honey, would you run in the house and bring me my duty belt? I'm going to have to go to work for a while, I guess. There goes my weekend off," he grumped.

"Weekend?" Jenny exclaimed. "What day is it?"

Officer Lenell stared at the young couple, finally noticing their hand-made clothing of boser leather. "It's Saturday. How long have you kids been out there in the woods?"

Mike and Jenny traded a look and laughed. "Right around a year and a half for me, and Jenny here a year or so longer, before her folks got killed by a roc. I guess we don't have much use for calendars up there."

Thirty minutes later, a large black skimmer with the blazon of OWME Security on the side settled to a stop in front of Officer Lenell's small house. A large, heavy-set man strode out of the troop bay door at the rear. Mike looked, and a jolt of recognition shot through him.

"Mr. Davies!"

"Well, Ah'll be damned." OWME Security Forces Colonel Jeff Davies, Commander of Security Forces, Forest, strode up to Mike with his hand outstretched. "Ah'm damn glad to see you, boy!"

Mike grabbed Colonel Davies' hand and shook it enthusiastically. "Jenny, I guided the Colonel here on an elk hunting trip what, two years before I left Earth."

Jenny stepped around Mike, smiling prettily. "Pleased to meet you, Colonel." Davies blushed a little.

"Pleased to meet you, Miss. You got yourself a fine young man, there. And Ah've still got fond memories of that elk hunting trip, boy, Ah tell you what! That elk head is a-hangin' on the wall in my office back in Settlement right now, as it happens." He turned to stare at Clomonastik, who was now standing nearby, guarded by two more security troops from the skimmer. "Well, now, boy, I wonder just where the hell y'all came from."

"As far as we can tell, he's the big boss." Mike said.

"Well, there's gonna be a second banana up there, and if these things are really planning to come down here looking for a fight, then Ah imagine their timetable just got kicked up a ways. Kids, Ah'd like y'all to come with me. We've got an invasion to get ready for."

# Twenty-Two

**The Grugell base camp, that evening**

Second Assistant Commander Dispotratik XII has waited long enough for the report, and was in a foul humor when it finally arrived. The young Subcommander that had found the Assistant Commander's ship stood nervously fidgeting in front of him now.

"Well, get on with it. Make your report."

"Sir," the Subcommander piped, his voice shaking slightly. "As you know, we found the wreckage of Assistant Commander Apportamattid's ship in a clearing to the south. Sir, the ship had been torn apart and scattered. There were signs of some sort of large animal – a very large animal, sir – in the area. There were no survivors we could detect, and there was no sign of Group Commander Clomonastik."

"Very well. You are dismissed, Subcommander. See to your troops, have them ready for movement in the morning."

"Sir!" The Subcommander spun on one boot heel and gratefully departed. Dispotratik turned to the communications technician on watch at a panel in the rear of the building.

"Send a message to the Fleet, to be relayed to the Emperor. Message follows: 'Group Commander Clomonastik III and Assistant Commander Apportamattid IX missing and presumed killed in a scout ship crash following contact with unknown native life form. I am assuming Group Command, this date, Second Assistant Commander Dispotratik XII, Grugell Imperial Navy,' and so on." He stood up to pace the floor of the Headquarters shack. "Send that immediately."

"Sir!"

"We will have to step up the tempo of our operations, I'm afraid," Dispotratik turned to the two other officers in the room, each of whom commanded a unit of scooter troops. "Send patrols to the south as far as the river. Establish a patrol using the river as the southern border. We will mass our forces on this side of the river and strike south at the aliens when our troops are fully prepared. Dismissed!"

Dispotratik smiled inwardly at the rich opportunity fate had placed before him. *Group Commander Dispotratik*, he savored the words silently. *Governor Dispotratik. How obliging of the Group Commander and Assistant Commander to get themselves killed so fortuitously!*

**Settlement, three days later**

A sudden rush of activity had seized the normally sleepy town of Settlement. Security troops and skimmers rushed this way and that, and every droid and flying transport available was pressed into service to retrieve every pioneer and hunter that could be located. To his lasting surprise, Mike found himself deputized at the rank of Lieutenant and placed in charge of a squad of five other hunter/pioneers. Jenny had volunteered to join Settlement's defenders, and while the Company's few engineers and scant store of heavy equipment prepared a palisade around the main part of the town, Jenny was engaged in teaching rifle marksmanship to

the town's merchants and housewives. Anyone who could handle a
rifle would be on the palisades in the event of attack.

"Your scouts will be doing recon work to the forward of our
main positions north of Outskirts, probably a few raids, some
hit-and-run," Mike was informed by OWME Security Major
Adam Wells, who was to conduct a mission briefing for his group.
"We don't have uniforms or weapons to go around, so you'll have
to use your own arms. The Mercantile will supply you all with all
the ammo and supplies you need."

Mike met his team of scouts for the first time at their first
mission briefing in a small classroom in the OWME Security HQ.
They proved to be a varied lot.

Beauregard Rousseau was the oldest at 47, a rough-featured,
squint-eyed Cajun swamp hunter from Lake Charles, Louisiana.
He was tall, broad-shouldered, with huge hands like grapples and
a perpetual frown glowering from a thin black beard heavily shot
with gray. Rousseau had been on Forest the longest, four years,
and had made a specialty of hunting the huge river delta a hundred kilometers south of Settlement where the big river emptied
into the Central Ocean. Rousseau carried a 15mm Parks double
identical to Mike's.

"Hey, I know you," Mike said on first meeting the Cajun. "The
Mercantile, the day I got here – you were buying *dehydrates!*"

*"Eh? Don' remember you, boy."* *The Cajun regarded Mike coldly.*

Originally hailing from the taiga of eastern Siberia, Yuri Pyak
was a madly happy Nenets tribesman. A short, bandy-legged,
wiry little gnome of a man, he nonetheless carried a monstrous
Krupp 20mm semi-auto, cradling the fifteen-kilogram bulk of the
four-shot cannon casually in his crossed arms. His 36-year-old
face was deeply wrinkled but constantly split with a wide grin.
With sign language and a weird combination of broken English
and cackled Russian, he managed to get across the message that

he hunted the giant loggers of the northeastern fern prairies. Any further questions were met with a grinning series of shrugs and a repeated "*Nyet, nyet!*"

Thomas Quiet Water was a Cheyenne from southern Colorado, a tall, stately figure who appeared silently at the muster carrying an old leather knapsack and an even older Lazzeroni 10.57mm Meteor rifle. He greeted the others with a silent, grave nod before seating himself cross-legged on the floor.

"We don't even know how he knew to come in," the Major whispered in Mike's ear. "As far as I know, nobody's heard him speak more than a word or two. He just showed up and signed the volunteer roster yesterday afternoon." Thomas was 29, and the unassuming holder of Forest's top gun rating for the steady stream of boser and roc carcasses dispatched to Settlement's processing plant from the open country to the southwest.

Mike was less impressed with Edward and Albert Greene, identical twins from Wales who boasted of a history "on safari" all over Earth. Mike was skeptical. They were the only scouts who weren't employed as hunter/pioneers, having instead paid private passage to Forest to speculate in some sort of "private business" the exact nature of which was somewhat vague. The Greene twins were thin, ferret-like men with shifty eyes and loud, strident voices, always ready with a boast. They arrived with well-worn backpacks, though, and identical 12.5mm Belgian FN bolt-action rifles. *Maybe they hunt better than they look*, Mike reassured his nagging doubts.

He was acutely aware that he was the youngest of the group by several years, and judging from Rousseau's scowl, at least one squad member resented his appointment as their commander.

Finally, everyone was seated, so Major Wells began the briefing.

"Ok, troops, we've got a mission for you already, as it happens."
He turned to uncover a large map of the area north of Outskirts,
along the river – which had recently been named, "Settlement
River," showing a slight lack of imagination on the part of
OWME's Cartography Division.

"The Grugell base camp is too far away for us to hit directly.
We don't have enough transport to move enough people up that
way, it's too far to go on foot with a large force, and we don't have
enough men of fighting age in any case. So, we're going to have to
let them come to us, and choose the time and place for any fights
on our own terms."

"So we just gon' sit here an' wait, *est-ce que c'est il?*" Rousseau
snorted.

"No," Major Wells corrected, "We're not. We're going to
harass them every step of the way in, and you six are going to
figure in on that action. But first, we've got to know when they're
coming in."

He pointed at a wide bend in the Settlement River about
twenty kilometers north of Outskirts. "The river turns west here
for a few klicks. There's some high ground on the south bank right
here," he pointed at a forested hill overlooking the river, "and from
there, you command a piece of real estate that covers most of the
direct route down from the New Pyrenees."

"But you can't see much through those trees," Mike pointed
out.

"We've got something for that, actually," Wells replied as a tall,
gangly man with a shock of unkempt black hair and wire-rimmed
glasses entered the room. "Men, this here is Doctor Gerald Richfield, and he's going to explain this little gizmo he's put together
for us."

"*Ah, ceci devrait être bon,*" Rousseau muttered. Yuri Pyak smiled
broadly, clapping his hands together once.

"Good morning," Richfield greeted them. His voice was strong and clear, practiced from several years of lecturing college students on Caliban before signing on to the Forest project for a change of pace.

"You already know the problem. The Grugell are somewhere up to the north, and they're going to be heading this way soon. Problem is, in these thick forests we might not see them coming until they're right on top of us. Since we can't let them gain the advantage of surprise, we've had to come up with a way to detect them in the trees." He held up a small black cylinder with a blinking red light at one end.

"This is a multi-spectrum motion detector and visual sensor. We've built three of them, and that's all there's going to be. I had to use some specialized parts cannibalized from some of the few pieces of geological survey gear we've got here. They don't have enough range to transmit to us here in Settlement from that high ground south of the river bend, so we have to have a small relay device placed halfway in between. The relay device is about the size of a wheelbarrow, and with a bit of luck we'll have it in place using a modified provisioning droid no later than tomorrow."

"So, I suppose we're going to place the three sensors?"

"Yes," Major Wells replied to Mike's query. "And remain in the area and in contact with us here. We've got a handful of tight-beam burst transmitters that should reach Settlement from there, and hopefully these Grugell won't be able to pick them up. You'll be on the sharp end of the stick, men, and we'll have to react fast to decide how best to get in the first few licks before they get as far as the town."

"So, we to be de 'xpendable cannon fodder, *droite*?" Rousseau wanted to know.

"No! Nobody in this deal is expendable. Let's get that straight right now," Wells snapped. "There's less than four thousand people on this planet. We can't afford to lose even one settler if we're going to hang on to this planet. Personally, I kind of like it here. I intend to bring my family in from Earth next year, and I'll be damned if I let a bunch of stick-men from wherever the hell they come from chase us off this rock."

One or the other of the Greene twins piped up. "So, mate, what are we to do up there all by ourselves? Chuck pinecones at these lads?"

"No, you're to observe, avoid contact, report anything you see, and await further instructions. Clear?"

"It's clear to me, sir," Mike interjected. "How soon can we leave?"

"The detectors are ready now. We'll be placing the relay tomorrow," Richfield offered, looking at Major Wells.

"Can you men be ready to go at first light?"

Mike looked around at the men – his men – that he was expected to lead into harm's way.

"Tomorrow morning, then?" he asked.

"*Da! Da!*" Pyak burst out. Mike laughed. The Greene twins looked at each other, back at Mike, and agreed. Thomas Quiet Water nodded once and turned to look out the window.

Rousseau stood up. "*Pourquoi attente?*" he agreed. "Le's go'on, den, and get dis t'ing done."

"OK, let's see you all back here an hour before first light, then," Major Wells announced. The six men filed out silently.

With that decided, Mike went looking for Jenny.

The streets of Settlement rattled with activity. Earth-moving and logging equipment raised clouds of red dust, people bustled everywhere, and in the near distance Mike heard the repeated bangs of a number of people at rifle practice. He headed in that direction.

He found the rifle practice under way at a rough 100-meter range hammered out of a small meadow by a large earthmoving machine. The red dirt was a scar in the green ferns where the great blade of the machine had piled it up into a berm, against which targets were placed. A row of people, mostly women, lay prone on pieces of carpet at the opposite end. Mike spotted Jenny standing some ways behind the firing line and walked over to her.

"How's this going, babe?" he asked after receiving a quick peck on the cheek.

"Not bad." She nodded towards the firing line. "Most of them at least had a rifle to bring, and most of them have at least fired a few shots at some point. I guess most of the people here get out looking for some fresh meat once in a while."

"That's not too surprising. The equipment list for most of the occupations included a rifle of some kind." Mike observed. He put an arm around Jenny, drawing her away from the firing line. "Honey," he began, "I'm going to be gone for a few days." Jenny looked at him evenly. "They want me to take five men up to put out some electronic listening posts up on the river north of here."

"The other five are pioneers, too, I suppose?"

Mike nodded. "All but two, they're merchants of some sort but they claim to have done a lot of hunting."

Jenny turned to face Mike, looking up into his eyes. "It will be dangerous, won't it?"

"Yeah, but not near as dangerous as running through the woods with a bunch of those things breathing down our necks, and not near as dangerous as sitting up behind a log on the palisade waiting for those things to come screaming down out of the sky in those spider-looking flyers. Don't worry, baby, we'll be safe. This is one hell of a great group going out there. Couple of them are twice my age, easy."

"But you're in charge?" Jenny's pride was obvious.

"Well, I guess that elk hunt stuck in old Colonel Davies's mind."

"Well, I'm proud of you. We'll be breaking for lunch in an hour, so if you want to wait around for a while, I'll take you back to that tiny little shack they gave us and I'll show you just how proud."

Mike smiled. Jenny's attitude was infectious. "Well, I'll tell you what. I've got to go over the Mercantile to arrange for some supplies, so I'll go do that and meet you back at the room in an hour. Then I'll be free for the rest of the day. How's that?"

Jenny smiled her agreement and gave Mike a quick hug and a warm, wet kiss before returning to her marksmanship students.

# Twenty-Three

**Early the next morning, two kilometers north of Outskirts**

"*Pourriez-vous faire plus de bruit?*" Beauregard Rousseau turned
to shoot a whispered snarl at one of the Greene twins who had
just stumbled over a branch, falling to one knee with a loud grunt.
"Boy, you gon' ghost us. You need be careful, boy, ol' Rousseau, I
ain' gon' be ambushed by these *chiens petits* 'cause a' you, eh?"

Whichever Greene twin it was glared back at the Cajun.
"Worry about your own feet, old man."

A few meters ahead at the head of the column, Mike looked
back briefly. He shook his head. The Greene twins weren't working
out well. Behind him, Yuri Pyak had abandoned his usual happy
grin for a doubtful look. He turned spaniel eyes on Mike and
shrugged.

The six men were filtering silently through the woods towards
the big bend in the river. They had been on the trail since an
hour before sunrise. Mike and Yuri Pyak were taking turns on
point, with Beauregard Rousseau and the Greenes spaced out
at three-meter intervals. Thomas Quiet Water floated ahead as
a scout, drifting through the woods like a puff of smoke in the
breeze. Even the cynical Rousseau was impressed with the young
Cheyenne's movement skills – on one of the Indian's sudden
appearances, Mike heard the Cajun breathe, "*Ce garçon, il peut
bouger comme un fantôme!*"

*"Il est-il bon, n'est-il pas?"* Mike whispered back, eliciting a surprised stare from the Cajun.

*And there I thought that two years of high school French would never amount to anything,* Mike told himself in a moment of wry amusement.

He planned to cover the twenty kilometers to the river bend by late afternoon, get the sensors placed before dusk, and find a good hiding spot from which to keep an eye and ear out for the Grugell. So far, things were going according to plan. They'd been overflown once, by a provisioning droid out of Settlement carrying a squat black cylinder in its robotic arms – the relay.

It was late afternoon when Mike heard the first familiar whining buzz. He held up one hand, fist clenched. The scouts stopped instantly.

Mike stood, eyes half closed, listening hard. The buzzing wasn't getting any louder, and seemed to be moving left to right. He motioned for Rousseau to come forward.

"I reckon that's the river just ahead," he whispered. "You hear that?"

*"Oui, je pense ainsi* – I t'ink so, yeah," Rousseau agreed.

The Greenes and Yuri Pyak gathered around. "That's one of their flying platform things," Mike explained. "You all saw that one I brought in from the mountains, right?"

Pyak grinned, not understanding. The others nodded agreement.

"I bet they're running a patrol over the river."

Thomas Quiet Water appeared suddenly, startling the group. "Two," he whispered, slicing one palm in front of his chest like a flat object scudding along a surface.

"How far is dis' river, eh?" Rousseau hissed.

The Cheyenne held up two fingers. "Two hundred meters?" Mike whispered. Quiet Water nodded.

The buzzing faded in the distance.

"OK, here's what we should do," Mike announced. "Let's get up close to the riverbank, lay low for a while, and get a feel for how often they run the river. There should be time between patrols for us to get these little sensors placed in the big trees on this bank. Then we can back off, find a decent spot for a base camp, and figure out how we'll keep watches."

"Sounds good to me, mate," the Greene twins chorused. Rousseau nodded, frowning.

Yuri Pyak, grinning as always, let out a burst of Russian, shook his head, and laboriously intoned, "*Da*, we watch river? Yuri watch, uh, watch, first watch?"

"OK, Yuri, you can take first watch with me." Mike had taken a liking to the madly cheerful little Nenets hunter from the start. "Edward and Albert, you can take a watch together, and Thomas and Beauregard, will you take the third watch?" Mike had noted the Cajun's respect for the Indian's woodcraft. It was the only outward sign of respect he'd shown anyone.

The second Grugell patrol came just at nightfall, a little over two hours after they'd heard the previous run. Two Grugell mounted on flying platforms buzzed straight down the middle of the river, heads turning from side to side scanning the banks but not noticing the scouts dug into a heavy patch of ferns.

"Dem boys, dey don' see so good, eh?" Rousseau chuckled. "Here we be, Gru-gell! *Ici*!"

"Let's get these sensors placed," Mike said.

Yuri Pyak took one sensor, Thomas Quiet Water another, and Mike the third. The sensors were to be placed a kilometer apart. After a few moments whispered conversation, Mike ran one klick upstream, Pyak placed his in a large tree on the spot, and Thomas Quiet Water went a klick downstream. The sensors were in place and the group settled into a base camp before midnight.

Once their rough camp was established, Mike took the opportunity to call in to Settlement. To his surprise, Colonel Davies himself was on the other end of the comm linkup.

"Well, boy, how y'all getting' along out there?" the Colonel's drawl tinned from the little hand-held unit.

"We're all OK, Colonel. The sensors are in. We put them up in some big trees, all about a klick apart. We've seen two alien patrols; they're running about every two hours straight down the river."

"Good, that might mean they're a-getting lazy. How many each trip?"

"Two, both times, each on one of those little platform things," Mike replied.

"Good! Ah reckon they'll make their move before long. You boys hang in out there, son, you hear? Ah don't expect we'll keep you out there too much longer. Our tech boys here are workin' on some other things. Ah'll be back to you around sunrise."

"OK, sir. We'll be here." Mike shut the communicator off and motioned to Yuri Pyak. "Let's go get a spot where we can see the river, Yuri. We've got first watch."

Mike and Yuri passed their four hours uneventfully. One Grugell patrol buzzed down the river midway through their shift. Other than that, the river flowed peacefully, and the usual night-time creatures chattered and buzzed in the undergrowth.

That all changed when the Greene twins took the second shift.

Mike sat bolt upright suddenly, awakened from a fitful sleep. *A shot!* The thought burst into his brain. The unmistakable sounds of shouting, human voices, English accents.

The Greenes.

Another shot sounded accompanied by more shouting, curses this time. Mike was already up and running through the pitch-dark woods, his big Parks double held at the ready. Somewhere towards the river, he heard the unmistakable crack of a Grugell energy weapon. A flash of green light illuminated the trees in front of him. Then another.

More running footsteps sounded to his right, then a crash as the runner tripped in the darkness and fell hard. The snapped "*Ces idiots, ils nous obtiendront tout détruits!*" told him it was Rousseau.

Thomas Quiet Water appeared, making eye contact with Mike for moment. "Two, on skimmers," he shouted before disappearing into the darkness, running for the river. A green bolt crashed through the treetops over Mike's head.

Mike arrived at the riverbank forty meters from the lookout point where the Greenes were supposed to be. He could barely see in the faint light from the two moons that were up, but he could see enough. A Grugell flying platform was looping away towards the far bank, with one alien at the controls. If there was a second alien craft, Mike couldn't see it.

Another shot sounded from the lookout point. The platform pivoted and swung back, unleashing a green energy bolt from a pod attached to the base of the control handle. A scream came from the bank where the bolt hit, sending showers of sparks into the air.

Mike risked a shout. "Beauregard! Tom! Yuri! Where are you?"

"*Ici*! Right 'ere, boy!" the Cajun shouted, somewhere off to Mike's right. Thomas appeared to Mike's left, waving one hand at Mike from a few meters down the bank. A moment later Yuri Pyak crashed through the riverbank growth to Mike's side.

The Grugell flying platform had looped away again, crossing right to left in front of the scouts, its driver craning to seek out the source of the shouts. He turned in suddenly, driving at Mike's position. A green bolt shot past, fired blindly, crashing into the trees on Mike's left.

"Yuri!" Mike shouted, pointing.

Pyak didn't need any further instruction. He leaped to the edge of the riverbank, dropping into a prone position and sighting down the barrel of his massive Krupp semi-auto. The cannon roared once, twice, belching a two-meter tongue of flame into the night. Both shots hit, the first blasting the alien driver backwards off the platform in a shower of black blood and white bone, the second impacting on the weapon pod and detonating it in a thundering flash.

"Over here!" a shout from one of the Greenes. "We're hurt! Good God, man, we're both hurt!"

Mike ran for the lookout point, white ghosts from the explosion dancing in his vision. The others ran with him. Across the river, a familiar whine was growing louder.

"That's one of their big flyers," Mike shouted, "We've got to get out of here!"

A dead alien lay by an upturned platform in the shallow water by the bank. One of the Greenes – Edward, it turned out – was messily and obviously dead, his chest shattered and scorched, still smoking from the energy weapon bolt that ended his life. Albert Greene was hunched a meter away, thrashing around and screeching his agony, holding one shattered leg.

"*Il ne va nulle part*," Rousseau observed unsympathetically, looking down at Edward Greene. Thomas Quiet Water knelt by Albert.

"You can't walk. Hold still. Look at this," he ordered the surviving twin, and held up his left hand. When Albert Greene reflexively looked up at his hand, the Cheyenne sliced his right into the Englishman's temple, knocking him instantly unconscious. He looked up to meet Mike and Yuri's shocked expressions.

"Now he doesn't hurt. Now we can carry him."

Nobody argued as Thomas slung Albert Greene over his shoulder. "Back to the camp, get our gear," Mike ordered.

"They gon' be huntin' us now, boy," Rousseau snapped. "What we gon' do? *Courir ou se battre?*"

"Hear that?" Mike snarled back, pointing across the river. "That's one of their flying ships, probably with a bunch of troops aboard. One of those things blasted my cabin into splinters with one shot. You want to hang around and see it for yourself?" They ran for their gear.

## A Grugell Scout-ship, circling over the river

"There they are," the ship's pilot said to his co-pilot, pointing at five red dots on the scanner display. "We'll land on the riverbank, drop the troops, and cover them from above when they pursue."

He stabbed one claw down on a toggle and barked into a wand microphone on the control panel in front of him.

"Prepare to disembark. Set all weapons on full power. There will be five aliens to your front as you disembark. Kill them all."

The ship swooped like a diving hawk, disgorging ten armed troops on the riverbank. They fanned out and, as one, trotted into the trees.

## The scout's camp

Albert Greene was still unconscious, groaning slightly where Thomas Quiet Water had dropped him unceremoniously on his bedroll. The four uninjured scouts frantically grabbed gear, stuffing bedding and equipment into packs one-handed while clutching weapons on the other.

"Quiet! Listen!" Mike hissed. The whining of the alien ships' driver had changed, dropping and then rising again. "What are they doing?"

"On the riverbank," Thomas whispered, "Eight, nine, ten, ten of them, coming this way."

The whine of the ship increased, passing somewhere overhead in the dark.

"Damn," Rousseau hissed. "Ever' body should be getting' down, I t'ink we gon' 'ave a fight 'ere."

A green energy bolt slammed into a tree a foot from Yuri Pyak, showering him with splinters. He let out a yelp, diving for the ground. The other scouts followed suit.

Another bolt flashed overhead, ripping through the ferns between Mike and Rousseau.

"We gon' need some 'elp, here, boy!" Rousseau shouted. "Dese t'ings maybe got low-light gear, eh? Dey can see us, but we can' see dem!" He rose to one knee, firing his big Parks at a shape barely glimpsed through a gap in the ferns. The high-ex round hit a small tree and detonated, sending the conifer crashing harmlessly to the ground. The shot drew a volley of return fire. Rousseau yelped as a bolt grazed his shoulder.

*Help*, Mike thought frantically. *Where are we going to get any help?*

"Behind you!" Thomas Quiet Water's imperative hiss cut into him. Mike rolled to his right as a green bolt struck the ferns where he'd been lying. Dimly he heard Thomas' old Lazzeroni roar once in reply, drawing a thin screech from out in the woods.

"They be all 'round us!" Rousseau shouted.

Mike dug in his pack suddenly. A hard, square object in the bottom of his pack hit his hand; he grabbed it and pulled it out.

It was his provisioning droid beacon. *I hope they're still turned on*, he thought, pressing the stud. The tiny red light winked on, indicating the unit was transmitting. *About forty klicks, it'll take fifteen minutes or so.*

Another volley of green bolts raked the ground in the midst of the group. Albert Greene sat up suddenly, screeching in pain – an energy bolt had neatly severed his left arm at the elbow.

Mike caught a glimpse of a shadowy, stick-thin figure moving between two trees. He raised his Parks and fired, bisecting the figure with a flash of flame from the 15mm high-ex round. He fired the other barrel at another half-seen form, missing that round. He dropped the Parks and drew his Colt.

A screeching whine from overhead drew his attention. The alien scout ship came in low overhead, drivers screaming. A white guide beam lanced downward, illuminating Yuri Pyak where he crouched in a fern thicket.

Yuri looked up once. The aliens were fast, but Yuri was a fraction of a second faster. He threw himself backwards, raising the Krupp cannon, sighting on the source of the white guide beam that flickered after him. He fired once, twice, three times. A shower of sparks blasted off the craft where each of the first two shots hit. The third hit the energy weapon projector just as it was about to fire, disintegrated the ship in a flash of green-white light. The thunder of the explosion flattened all of the human scouts into the ferns, the blast rippling through their insides with a sickening feeling. Shards and chunks of metal pattered on the ground all around.

An eerie silence followed. Mike crawled to where Beauregard Rousseau lay staring into the darkness. "You OK?" he whispered.

"I s'pose I gon' live, boy, but dis shoulder be burnt pretty good."

"Can you shoot?"

"'Ell, yes!"

Mike grinned in the darkness. "You'll do, Beauregard, you'll do." The Cajun merely snorted in reply as Mike low-crawled off towards the little Siberian's hiding place.

Mike found the Nenets tribesman calmly stuffing five-inch-long shells into the massive Krupp cannon he wielded so deftly. "Yuri, now I see how you can hunt loggers with that big thing!" he whispered.

Yuri smiled as broadly as a child at a birthday party, and replied, "Logger, *da! BOOM!*" Chuckling to himself, he tucked the last cannon shell into his weapon, worked the enormous bolt to chamber a round, and rolled over to a good prone firing position.

Thomas Quiet Water was crouched next to Albert Greene, who was moaning in agony.

"He needs a doctor," Mike observed. Thomas nodded. He was staring fixedly off into the trees. "What is it?" Mike asked. Thomas held up two fingers, and then pointed straight ahead into the trees.

"Stay here," the Cheyenne whispered. He drew a half-meter long, razor-edged knife from his boot and faded silently into the pitch-black forest.

Mike knelt next to Albert Greene. A faint smell of burnt meat rose from the severed arm, making Mike's stomach lurch. The Englishman's eyes rolled open once, passing over Mike without recognition before closing again as he fell off into a faint.

*At least he's not bleeding too much.*

The thought was interrupted by a thin, reedy squawk from the trees. A green bolt shot twenty or thirty meters out, lancing left-to-right, striking a tree.

Silence.

A faint sound of footsteps drifted slowly closer. Mike slowly crept backwards into a patch of high ferns.

Somewhere, out in the night, a twig cracked.

"Dat won' be dat Injun boy," the hiss from behind him almost made Mike jump out of his boots. "Dat boy move like *Une bouffée de fumée*." Rousseau raised himself just enough to see over Mike's shoulder. "Dey be *les monsters* comin' in, I t'ink." Mike nodded.

A faint shape took form, sticklike against the darkness. The faint moonlight filtering in through the tree branches shone dimly on a snow-white, pinched face. Another alien appeared behind the second, then a third a few meters to the left. At least the aliens didn't seem to have any sort of low-light gear; their eyes were uncovered.

"Dis ain't good," Rousseau whispered.

"Take the one on the left," Mike barely breathed the words. "I'll get the one on the right."

"An' de one in de' back?"

Before Mike could reply, a horrible sound split the night. It was the screech of a banshee, a bubbling, horrendous outpouring of sound. Mike felt his bowels tighten suddenly as a dim shape leaped from a tree behind the two aliens in front of him, screeching to wake the dead.

It was the Cheyenne, Thomas Quiet Water, wielding his field-dressing knife.

He almost decapitated the rearmost alien with a backhanded swipe, but the knife wedged in bone and was pulled from Thomas's hand. He didn't hesitate, even as the second alien spun, pointing his weapon. The Indian stepped inside the arc of the Grugell soldier's swing, grabbing the arm and snapping it like a dry branch, continuing through in a fluid movement, grabbing the alien by the neck with his left hand and squeezing work-hardened fingers closed to the crackle of snapping bones. The alien fell in a heap.

The third Grugell fired a bolt of green fire, but too high. He didn't get another chance. Mike's Colt spoke with authority, striking the alien's shoulder, sending him spinning into the under-growth.

"Damn," Rousseau muttered.

Yuri Pyak crawled in a moment later, eyes questioning. "It be all over now, *ami*," Rousseau assured him.

Thomas Quiet Water had calmly knelt beside the first fallen alien, worked his knife free and was wiping the blade clean on the black Grugell tunic. "Four, maybe five more," he reminded the others.

"We have to stay put," Mike informed them. "I set off my provisioning droid beacon. If the droids are still working, we should hear it coming any minute."

"If we still alive in any minute, eh?"

A series of green bolts crisscrossed the air over their heads, forcing the scouts to crush themselves face down in the ferns. A lance of green flame brushed Mike's temple ever so slightly, making his head explode with pain. He raised his head, catching a glimpse of a rake-thin form in the darkness. He fired twice with his old Colt to no avail.

"They're all around us," he gritted the words out through teeth clenched against the pain.

"Two, five meters, in front," Thomas Quiet Water whispered. "Two more behind us. Don't know about any others."

"Roll to your left," Mike told him, "I'll go right. Make some noise. I bet they'll come right up the middle. Yuri, Beauregard, take 'em when they come in."

"*Oui, je les ai.*"

Mike heard a faint whine, slowly growing louder, approaching from the south. The provisioning droid was on its way in.

"Ready, *go!*"

Mike rolled as fast as he could to the right, hearing the crashing of fern fronds under his body matched by more crashing as Thomas Quiet Water rolled the other way. He rolled three meters and stopped, gasping in pain from the burn on his temple. Two bolts of green shot overhead, aimed at nothing in particular. The woods fell silent again.

*They aren't going to fall for it*, Mike thought.

A few more seconds crept past. Then, the faintest sound of a cautious footstep in the ferns, to Mike's left front. Another a few meters to the rear. The aliens were approaching, cautiously, scanning the woods for their enemy.

One of them paused, dimly illuminated in the faint moonlight filtering through the pines. His head was angled upwards, listening carefully to a steady whine, slowly growing louder, approaching from the south. From the river, a faint buzzing slowly grew louder. Reinforcements were on the way to the beleaguered Grugell troops.

Beauregard Rousseau struck upwards from the ferns suddenly, rearing up behind the Grugell and sinking a large skinning knife into the alien's chest. Another Grugell soldier appeared suddenly, aiming his energy weapon at the Cajun, only to have his arm snapped by the huge barrel of Yuri Pyak's Krupp cannon. Pyak continued the swing, shifting his grip on the huge gun, pivoting it on the action as the stock swung around to smash into the alien's head. The Grugell soldier's skull collapsed with a sickening crunch, and he fell into the undergrowth.

The night was split now with the whining drivers of the provisioning droid. Mike scrambled for his beacon, flipped open the top cover, and hit a large red button marked EVAC.

"Everybody get ready," he called out.

The droid came in over the trees, drives whining steadily. Several green bolts lanced into the air from the woods around them, slamming into the robotic hauler's underside. The hand weapons didn't seem to hurt it much, but Mike had no illusions what one of the Grugell's flying spider-ships could do to the ponderous droid. He was certain they had little time to spare.

The droid hit its landing lights suddenly, blinding everyone on the ground. The robotic voice boomed out, "EMERGENCY BEACON DETECTED. STAY CLEAR OF LANDING AREA." With a crash of tree branches, the droid crunched down through the forest, settling to a landing a few meters away from the beacon – and the scouts.

They scrambled for the droid's slowly opening cargo door, pursued by blasts from the Grugell's energy weapons.

Yuri Pyak took a glancing hit and spun to the forest floor in front of Mike. Mike grabbed for the little Nenets, missing as Yuri rolled once and came up running, dropping his pack but retaining the giant Krupp cannon. Thomas Quiet Water appeared out of nowhere, bearing his rifle in one hand, holding the unconscious Albert Greene over one shoulder with the other. He tossed the Englishman in the cargo door and turned to face the others.

"We must go now!" he shouted.

"*Pas de merde!*" Rousseau barked back. He was retreating slowly backwards towards the droid, firing his Parks double at the sources of each green bolt. Mike did the same, firing, breaking the action open, dunking in fresh rounds, and firing again. On his third shot, he was rewarded with a thin screech of pain from the unseen assailant behind the burst of green light.

Yuri Pyak appeared on the top of the droid, having scrambled up the side of the cargo bay. He crawled to the flat driver housing at the rear, dragging his Krupp cannon to a good firing position from which to punch high-explosive rounds into the trees. A Grugell flying platform appeared from the direction of the river, spitting green fire at the droid. Pyak fired at the platform, hitting it at the base of the T-handle and exploding vehicle and driver both in a white-hot flash. He shouted something in Nenets that sounded triumphant.

Mike and Rousseau arrived at the droid together, firing their last 15mm rounds at the tree line before tumbling backwards in the door. "'Ow we make dis t'ing go now?" Rousseau shouted.

Mike's heart leaped. "The beacon!" The others stared. "It's still out there!"

The droid lurched suddenly and began to climb out of the trees. "How?" Mike and Rousseau exclaimed together. They looked at each other, looked up to the trees rapidly falling away beneath the high steel walls of the cargo bay, and then towards the sounds of mad laughter from the top of the driver housing, where sat the grinning Yuri Pyak at the open panel containing the emergency manual controls.

"Yuri, Yuri fly, *da*?" he called down to the others.

"*Je serai damné*," breathed Rousseau. Mike nodded in agreement.

The scouts collapsed against the walls of the cargo bay as the droid fled into the night sky. The whining of drivers and the laughter of the little Nenets echoed in the night as the robot hauler turned south for Settlement.

## The Grugell base camp

"Sir," the communications technician turned from the panel to face Group Commander Dispotratik. "We have reports that our patrols on the river have made contact with an armed party of aliens. They've taken casualties, sir, but report that the perimeter is now secure. They repelled the aliens, and report at least five of the enemy killed."

"Very well," the newly anointed Group Commander replied. He glanced at his new rank insignia, which he'd placed on his uniform jacket immediately on receiving the message from the Imperium assigning him the task of completing the Occupation. "They know we're here now. Send orders to the subunit commanders. All available troops are to begin movement to the river. Only minimal security and administration staff are to stay here at the base camp. We'll attack as soon as possible." He stood up, straightening his tunic. "I'm going to my quarters to prepare my gear. I'll lead the attack myself."

Dizzying visions of glory swam in Dispotratik's head. Whatever these aliens were, they would doubtless be no match for Grugell military prowess.

# Twenty-Four

**Settlement, the following evening**

"You ready to go back out again?"

Mike opened his eyes to see Major Wells standing over him. "Oh, crap, Major, how's next month grab you?" Jenny tapped his head with two fingers. The young couple had been dozing in the light of the setting sun. Jenny was sitting in a clump of ferns against the wall of their borrowed shack, Mike was reclined with his bandaged head in her lap.

"Come on," Major Wells chuckled, "There's someone I want you to meet. Miss, I promise I'll have Lieutenant Crider back to you in an hour."

"I'll hold you to that, Major." Jenny smiled.

Mike got to his feet slowly, grumbling. "How's the head?" the Major asked.

"It'll do," Mike informed him. "It still hurts, but not so bad. The doc tells me it'll heal up fine, but I'm lucky to be here. Another centimeter to the side, and I wouldn't have a head." Jenny grimaced at that but didn't offer any comment.

"Let's go over to the briefing room. Your men should already be there. I've got two replacements for you, and we've got another mission in mind. Something that might stop these things once and for all."

"Really? How?"

"I'll let Doc Richfield explain that."

The briefing room in the Security HQ was only five minutes' walk away, and when they arrived, Mike's scouts were already there and seated. Yuri Pyak had taken an energy bolt burn across his ribs on the left, Rousseau a glancing hit on one shoulder, but both had been examined and pronounced fit for duty.

The two replacements were seated at the front of the room. At a wave from Major Wells, they came forward to shake hands with Mike.

"Mike, this is Mick Menmunny. He's been living on the edge of the forest south almost to the ocean, and just now brought his family in to Settlement." Menmunny was brown-skinned, with a shock of light-brown, frizzy hair.

"G'day, Mike. I've 'eard a lot about you, mate." He stuck out a calloused hand to shake Mike's.

"You're from Australia?" Mike asked.

"That's right. A little place in Queensland called Yarrabah. My people have been thereabouts a long time."

Mick wore only tattered green cotton shirts, leather sandals, and a tooled leather bag on a strap over one shoulder. His weapon was a surprise, a beautifully maintained Berne & Kobel 14.5mm Recoilless. The weapon's sling doubled as an ammo bandolier, lined with a dozen or so of the 14.5mm rockets for the single-shot arm.

Major Wells turned to the other man, a tall, powerfully built black man wearing khaki shorts and a black cotton shirt. "And this is Nathaniel Tzukuli, Mike. He's our resident zoologist, but he's volunteered to scout with your group."

Tzukuli's huge hand engulfed Mike's in a powerful grip. "Pleasure to meet you, Mr. Crider." His voice was deep, sepulchral, his accent upper class British. Tzukuli threw back his head and laughed at Mike's surprised expression.

"Yes, the accent. My father was in the KwaZulu regional government, Mr. Crider. I was educated in England."

"Don't be so modest, Nathaniel," Major Wells broke in. "Mike, Nathaniel here went to Oxford on a Rhodes Scholarship at age fourteen. He's got PhD's in Animal Behavior and Xenozoology. He's probably the smartest man on the planet, so we all listen to him, don't we, Doctor Tzukuli?"

"Well, the brighter among you do, yes," Tzukuli replied seriously.

"What's a xenozoologist?" Mike wanted to know.

"I study extraterrestrial life forms," Tzukuli said. "You know what a zoologist is, yes?" Mike nodded. "'Xeno' means 'outside' or 'external.' In this case, it means outside Earth's biosphere. I specialize in the study of large predators, which is why I'm here on Forest."

"The rocs," Mike said. "I've got to ask, why are you signing up with us? I mean, if you're a scientist, wouldn't you be better off working with the Company people here to figure these things out?"

"Two reasons, Mr. Crider. One, I was a Zulu before I was a scientist. Forest is my home now, and now I find an enemy threatens my home. The *impis*, the war regiments, are forming, and I've come to join them.

"Two, the physics and technical people don't need a field zoologist getting in their way. My field is specialized and of little value to the problem at hand. However, I am an experienced field zoologist and here on Forest that means I am also an accomplished hunter. I've fed myself in the wild for months at a time, and I've observed rocs extensively at close quarters without being detected. I think my skills will prove useful to your party. Besides," he added, grinning, "I understand you've quite a challenge facing you. I think you'll need all the hands you can get."

"Ah, I don' know if I like de sound of dat." Beauregard Rousseau came forward, placing one huge, calloused hand on Mike's shoulder. "But I tell you somet'ing. Dis boy 'ere, there be more to 'im than you see. We 'ad our tits in a wringer night before las', and 'e keeps 'is 'ead. Brings us out in good shape. Before dat, I was t'inking, 'Dis one, 'e is only a wort'less boy. I was wrong. We go after dem t'ings again, I jes' as soon go with dis boy in front."

Mike's face reddened with embarrassment at this unexpected benediction.

Yuri Pyak piped up, "*Da!*"

Thomas Quiet Water nodded once.

"We're in with a good crew, Doc," Mick Menmunny observed.

The briefing began a few moments later, with Major Wells once again at his place in front of the room. Gerald Richfield hurried in just as the Major began speaking.

"OK, our technical team, led by Doctor Richfield here, have found out something very interesting about the enemy we're facing. Doc?"

Gerald Richfield stood up, adjusting his glasses. He glanced once at a thick sheaf of papers in his right hand, and then set them down.

"We've been examining the flying skimmer that Lieutenant Crider brought in. We were pretty baffled at first, because it doesn't seem to have any power source, but the vehicle still functions. In fact, our research team's been riding it all over Settlement." The scouts chuckled at that remark.

"So, anyway, we were a little confused until we noticed what looked some kind of receiver wired to the presser field generator. They use a generator that's really pretty similar to the ones on our skimmers, but they don't operate on a fuel cell. When we noticed that, we cobbled together a wideband signal detector, and we found a broadcast signal that's almost off the scale."

"Broadcast power?" Nathaniel Tzukuli said in a wondering voice. "Isn't that supposed to be impossible?"

"Evidently not," Richfield replied. "These Grugell have figured it out. Let me tell you what that means."

He pointed up at the ceiling. "Somewhere up there, the Grugell must have some kind of satellite with a massive solar power array. Well, we can't get at that. It would take at least sixteen months to get any help from Earth, by the time a signal gets to Earth and any help can get here. We don't have any ships on the ground here at the moment, and none are expected for another three months, so we can't even ram the thing. So, we can't do anything about the satellite."

"I see where you're going," Mike said. "If we can kill the broadcast power, we kill all their vehicles, maybe all their equipment. But since we can't get to the satellite, how do we take out their power?"

"That's what we were worried about, until we analyzed the signal. It's strong, but not as strong as we expected. They're not broadcasting from the satellite. Forest is a magnetic planet like Earth, and our best guess is that the magnetic field interferes somehow with a direct broadcast. What we got to thinking is that they're beaming the energy from the satellite to a receiver here on Forest, and broadcasting it from there. So, we analyzed the source of the broadcast signal, triangulating from ten klicks east and west of Settlement. Here's where the signal is originating." He walked to a large map on the back wall, indicating a spot with a pen taken from his shirt pocket. "Right here, in the New Pyrenees."

"That's where our cabin is! Was, anyway!" Mike burst out.

"That's where they've set up their base camp," Major Wells interjected. "And that's where we're sending you men. To find whatever receiver they've got up there receiving the broadcast power from orbit, and destroy it."

"What will it look like?"

Major Wells and Doctor Richfield traded a sheepish look.

"We don't know," Richfield admitted.

"So, 'ow we supposed to blow de damn t'ing up?" Rousseau demanded.

"That's where Doc Richfield comes in," Major Wells announced, taking the stage again. "He's going with you."

"If I can get a look at their camp, I should be able to spot the receiver. I'm not sure what it will look like, but I should know it when I see it."

"You should know it when you see it?" Mike asked, doubtful.

"That's the best guess I can give you, Lieutenant."

"Oh, boy, dis is somet'ing. We gon' drag all de way up in dese mountains, and den hope we can figure out what dis t'ing is, *oui*? Hoo boy."

"Yeah, Beau, but if we can kill it, that kills their power to everything. We'll be able to mop them right up," Mike chided the older man. "I don't think it's a bad idea at all. Doctor Richfield, can you be ready to leave at first light?"

"My stuff's already packed," the scientist replied. "I'm not much of an outdoorsman, but I'm in pretty good shape, and the Mercantile has set me up with gear. I'll try not to slow you down too much."

"Mick, Nathaniel, are you ready?" Both men agreed.

"That's it, then. Major Wells, can you arrange a skimmer to get us to Outskirts? We'll jump off from there."

"You've got it, Lieutenant Crider. Get some rest, men, you've got a long walk tomorrow."

*I'm going to have fun explaining this to Jenny*, Mike told himself as he walked back to the shack.

"You're going to do *what?!*"

"Baby, this is important! If we can knock this thing out, we kill all their equipment. We'll have them beaten!" Mike hugged Jenny against his chest, kissing the top of her head. "We've got to do it. It might be our only hope of beating these things."

"Why you?" Jenny sobbed. "Why can't they send someone else? Haven't you done enough?"

"There's nobody else that *can* do it. I know that country, I know how their camp is set up, and I know how to get in and out of there without being picked up."

"I wish I was going with you," Jenny relented. "They say they need every gun they can get here, in case they come looking for us."

"No way I'd let you come anyway, baby. Too dangerous."

"You and your tough cowboy attitude. Well, don't you 'little woman' me, Michael No-Middle-Name Crider. I'm going to be on the palisade with my rifle if they come down here looking for trouble."

"I know, honey. We are in a hell of a spot, aren't we? I bet you wished you'd stayed on the Moon."

"Not even close. If this is as far as we go, Mike, then this is as far as we go. But loving you for the last year is worth more than living another fifty without you."

"Me too, baby. Me too."

"Now, let's go in this horrible little shack, and go to bed. I've got an idea it will be a while before we get another chance to, well, you know." She thrust her flat little stomach against Mike's belt buckle, quickly, before taking his hand and leading him inside.

# Twenty-Five

**Outskirts, the next morning**

"Not much of a town, this," Nathaniel Tzukuli noted as the scouts climbed out of the same skimmer bus Mike had ridden to the little village on his first day on Forest.

Mick Menmunny reached down to shake the shoulder of a thin-faced boy who dozed in a seat. "Wake up, Tak."

Menmunny had created quite a stir when he'd reported half an hour before sunrise with his oldest son in tow.

"What do you mean, he's coming with us?"

"He's fifteen, mate. Old enough, he's a man now. Besides, he's a slick little bastard, really sneaky, and a good shot. You said we needed every hand we could get, right?"

"He's just a kid!" Major Wells objected.

The argument had gone on for a few minutes – until Major Wells reached out to take hold of Tak's shoulder and found himself on his back in the red dust in front of the Mercantile. He looked up to see skinny Tak Menmunny standing over him with a large, razor-edged knife.

"If you were one of those things, you'd be dead, mate!" the boy chided him.

The scouts had burst out in laughter to a man. Tak Menmunny was accepted into their fold without further question, despite Major Well's objections.

"We do need every man we can get," Mike pointed out. "He'll do."

Now, an hour and a half later, they scrambled off the bus in Outskirts, yawning and stretching. Beauregard Rousseau and Yuri Pyak were particularly bleary-eyed, both men were vague about their whereabouts the previous evening.

"You know 'ow it is, boy, when a man is goin' off to th' wars, eh?" Rousseau had confided in Mike with an exaggerated wink. Mike suddenly remembered walking past the "Blue House," Settlement's legal, if not too discreet, brothel. Yuri was grinning, but not as broadly as usual, and he blinked painfully at the bright morning sunlight.

"Well, anyway," Mike stammered, somewhat embarrassed. "Let's get going. Thomas, why don't you lead off? I think we'll leave Beauregard and Yuri back in the column for now. Will you two please look after Doctor Richfield?" The scientist was struggling with his pack straps. *The guy may be a rocket scientist*, Mike thought, *but he sure isn't an outdoorsman. I hope he doesn't get hurt or killed out here.*

The column snaked off into the morning woods, following the same course Mike had taken out of Outskirts that first afternoon.

They covered only a few kilometers that first day. "We'll stop a little while after noon, lay up until dark, and then move on after dark," Mike informed the group. "Once we get to the river, we'll only move at night. I figure that's about where we cross into enemy territory now."

Evening found the scouts in a dry camp a kilometer or two short of the bend in the Settlement River. Mike planned to cross the river in the dark, dodging any Grugell patrols on the crossing – or dealing with them as quietly as possible if necessary. "We can't let them know we're out here," he pointed out.

Nathaniel Tzukuli spoke up then. "I think I can handle one or two of them fairly quietly, if it should come to that, and I'm told our young Cheyenne friend here is quite good in that respect."

Tzukuli had been carrying a two-meter-long wooden staff, using it as a walking stick. Mike had assumed that's all it was, but now the tall Zulu delved into his big frame pack and retrieved a half-meter long polished steel spearhead. A few moments fiddling, and Tzukuli had a silent, formidable and deadly weapon to go along with his 15mm Transvaal Express double rifle.

"My ancestors used to hunt lions with these," he pointed out. "I've killed bosers with this one. I'm sure it will work for one of our alien friends, should the need arise. Wouldn't you agree?" he asked, holding the spear up with the point in the dim light of the scout's tiny fire.

"*Mon Dieu*," Rousseau muttered. Thomas Quiet Water nodded appreciatively but said nothing.

They moved out again when the woods fell fully dark, ghosting silently through the darkened woods. To everyone's surprise, Gerald Richfield quickly picked up the knack of moving quietly in the night. Tak Menmunny was another pleasant surprise, with movement skills that rivaled Thomas Quiet Water's. The scouts moved in a loose formation, each at least twenty meters from the others, with either Thomas Quiet Water or Mick and Tak Menmunny ranging five hundred meters or so ahead to check the route.

The river crossing was accomplished without incident and the group covered another six kilometers towards the mountains before they stopped to spend the day in the shelter of a rock overhang. They set off again at dusk. "We've got another good hundred klicks up there, and we'll want to be there as fast as we can," Mike informed them. They filed silently into the trees, resigned to another four or five night's marching. Open country leading up to the foothills was coming up ahead and in those mountains. Mike knew the Grugell camp was laid around the ruins of a tiny cabin. He grinned savagely into the night muttering under his breath to invoke one of the oldest of all human philosophies:

"Payback's a bitch."

## Settlement, five days later

"OK, swing the top a little to the right – there you go – now forward!" Another mammoth tree trunk fell into place, and four men swung in to hammer crossbeams in place.

Someone had been designated as foreman of the work gangs building the palisade around the main Company buildings in the town, and the work was proceeding quickly now. The work crews expected to have the palisade finished later in the afternoon. Most of the homes and some of the smaller businesses would lie outside the wall, but the main Company buildings and the Mercantile were inside, and there was enough room to get most of the non-combatants inside and under cover.

Jennifer Aggruder/Crider didn't belong to that group.

She stood on the firing step built below the edge of a completed portion of the palisade wall, staring out into the endless forest. Just to her right, the red-dirt road to Outskirts led north. Outskirts, she knew, stood empty now except for five OWME Security officers with light weapons and a comm-link for raid warning, plus one other nasty surprise for the invaders. Two other small villages to the east and south, Fairport and Glen, were likewise empty now, their tiny populations brought into Settlement for safekeeping. Every able-bodied adult that owned a weapon had been pressed into service in the colony's defense, but the line was thin – a little over a thousand men and women all told. Forest's total population was almost four thousand, but almost half were Company specialists that had no arms to bring to the fight. The Company supplied weapons only for the two hundred or so trained Security troops. The armed colonists themselves, bearing their own weapons they'd brought from Earth for hunting, would fight the battle for Settlement. It was to be a battle fought by a civil militia, in the oldest and truest sense of the term.

*Where are you, Mike?*

Her old Remington leaned against the wall next to her. An old pair of optical binoculars from Mike's hunting gear hung around her neck. For the thousandth time that day, she lifted them to her eyes to scan the sky and the trees. Somewhere out there a horde of armed aliens was biding their time, no one knew where or when they'd attack.

But attack they would.

A married couple, Sam and Karen Dix, farmers from Out-skirts, held a position a few meters to her left. The hard, fortyish red-haired doxie from The Blue House standing watch to the right was holding a vicious 5.6mm Steyr Magnetic assault rifle, a state-of-the-art piece of military hardware. The doxie, Carrie Manns, was rather evasive about how she'd obtained the weapon and why she had it, but nobody was too concerned. She was better armed than OWME's Security troops, and Jenny imagined she could fight like a logger having a bad day.

Whenever the Grugell came down from the mountains, they'd be in for one hell of a scrap.

**North of the river, a temporary assembly point**

Dispotratik surveyed his gathered forces. At least a hundred scooter troops, six scout ships, two-hundred-foot soldiers on cargo scooters, and they all awaited his orders.

Activating a throat mike attached to his uniform collar, Dispotratik barked orders.

"Scout ships Two and Four, proceed to the northern village and destroy it. Report back here when that's completed." He turned to his new Assistant Commander, Lepotraskit VI., "We'll smash that northern village first, then mass all our forces and strike the main colony all together. The smaller villages to the south we can clean up later."

"It will be a great victory, sir," Lepotraskit fawned. Overhead, two of the hovering silver scout ships peeled off, floating across the river towards the south.

**Outskirts**

"Roger that, we'll keep an eye out up here."

"What's up, Sarge?"

"Two spiders just crossed the river, heading south. They may be headed our way. Get the others up, everybody stand-to."

The attack came without further warning, a spidery silver Grugell ship descending suddenly from the sky, firing bolts of jade-green energy into the empty houses. Another ship followed within seconds.

"Base, this is Eyes One," the Sergeant in charge of the detail at Outskirts whispered into the comm-link microphone. His squad was dug in hard into a concealed position on the southern edge of the village. "We've got two, say again two spiders firing into the houses – whoa, and there goes the Mercantile. One spider's landing and unloading troops."

"Eyes One, engage at will," Base responded. "Weapons are free, say again weapons are free. Remember, ships are likely to be shielded. Be careful, disengage and get your men out as soon as your position is compromised."

"Roger that, Base. We'll get back to you. Eyes One out."

Roughly a fourth of OWME's supplies of explosives had been sunk into the ground in the open center of the rough square of buildings that made up Outskirts. Somewhat predictably, the slightly confused Grugell troops began to congregate there when they found no sign of the village's inhabitants.

"Wait, not yet," the Sergeant advised the troop holding a radio detonator. "Let them gather around a little more. Looks like that one's in charge, he's yelling orders."

One tall, stick-thin figure was shouting in a thin, reedy voice. At his apparent command, the rest of the alien troops came trotting in to gather around. "Looks like an orders group," one of the OWME men whispered.

"No, I think they're getting ready to pull out," the Sergeant replied. "See, here comes one of the spiders in to pick them up again." He pointed at the silver ship that was floating gently to the ground.

"Yeah, they're going to pull out. Time to give them something to think about. OK, when I fire, hit the charge," the Sergeant ordered. He raised his OWME-issued Marquardt magnetic rifle, flipped the selector switch to Single, and aimed carefully. The rifle discharged with a loud crack, the electrets driving a steel dart at two thousand meters a second. The Grugell leader's head disappeared in a puff of black, a second before the massive HE charge exploded.

The entire enemy squad and their transport disappeared in a thundering flash. In their covered hiding place, the OWME troops rode out a sickening shock wave, coughing as dust and dirt filled the air. The Sergeant clung to the firing port, watching as one disconnected driver pod from the spider cartwheeled into the sky above a rising column of smoke. "Damn!" he exclaimed. "I guess their shields aren't completely impossible to beat, huh!"

The second ship had been almost flipped over by the blast where it hovered a hundred meters away. Recovering, it swooped down on the blast site, the white guide beam of its primary weapon scanning the ground. "Let 'em know we're here," the Sergeant ordered, and the five opened fire, five magnetic rifles cracking away, sending high-velocity steel darts glancing off the ship's energy shields.

The spider swung towards the source of the troop's firing position, the white guide beam flickering towards them. "Now!" the Sergeant called. One by one the troops ducked down a tunnel to the rear of their hide, the Sergeant last. They had to crouch-walk down the hastily dug passage, moving as quickly as the hunched gait would allow. Behind them, their hiding place erupted in a blast of green energy fired from the Grugell spider, the edges of the blast singeing the Sergeant's clothing slightly. They emerged in the woods a hundred meters beyond the tree line.

"I guess that gave them something to think about," one of the troops muttered.

"That was nothing," the Sergeant replied. "They'll be on their way to Settlement next. Let's get out of here."

## Settlement

The word percolated out from the Company Security offices. Colonel Davies himself had made the announcement to a small group gathered in the courtyard of the Security building, and the news traveled out quickly to the people standing watch on the wall.

"Everyone's supposed to look sharp," Carri Manns informed Jenny. "The bad guys have hit Outskirts. They'll be headed here next."

Jenny nodded and walked over to tell the Dix's the news. The day dragged on, stress levels slowly building in all of Settlement's defenders. Dark clouds were gathering in the north, and thunder muttered in the distance.

A storm was brewing.

# Twenty-Six

**That night, the New Pyrenees Mountains**

"There, see over in that tree line?" Mike whispered. "Two guards, right where they were last time." Thomas Quiet Water nodded. "The meadow is less than a click away, right up that hill." They could hear the activity coming from up the slope. A low chatter of voices, the humming of equipment, and an occasional slamming door all echoed faintly down to where Mike and Thomas hid under the overhanging branches of a large pine. "We'll have to get around them quietly. Come on, let's get back to the others."

The two scouts slipped silently away to where the rest of the group waited in a cluster of tall ferns at the edge of a ravine. Thunder rumbled overhead as a faint strobe of lightning lit the woods briefly. "Storm might work for us," Thomas pointed out.

"There's two guards watching the valley leading uphill," Mike announced. "I can get at least one of them with my bow. Nathaniel, can you take out the other one?"

The tall Zulu nodded.

"OK," Mike continued. He struck a small light-stick and dropped it on a bare patch of ground, squatting to draw with a stick in the dust. "Here's the valley, it sort of curves up this way and hooks into the meadow at the bottom edge. The two guards are right here," he made two small X's in the dirt, "Nathaniel and I can come in from these big trees on this edge to within about ten meters. Close enough for you, Nathaniel?"

"Yes, I should think so. As long as there isn't any brush or fern in the way, I should be able to hit a target at that distance." He hefted the intimidating Zulu spear.

"Good. I'll take out the far one with my bow while you take out the near one. Beauregard, you and Mick can slip up the other side of the valley, there's a really huge old pine right about here," he pointed, "and cover us with your rifles, in case something gets messed up. The rest of you wait right here. Everyone know what a coyote sounds like?" There were several blank looks, so Mike demonstrated. "If you hear that, come on up the valley, and Nathaniel or I will meet up with you to go up the rest of the way to the meadow. If there's any shooting, everyone get away as fast as you can, break up and scatter. We'll meet up back at the place we stayed over the day yesterday. Everyone got that? Anyone got any questions?"

"Yeah, mate, what do we do once we get up there?" Mick Menmunny asked.

"Then it's up to me, I guess," Gerald Richfield interjected. "I'll see if I can spot the receiving station for their broadcast power and then we'll have to figure out how to wreck it."

"Anyone else? OK, that's it then. Beauregard and Mick, we'll give you ten minutes' head start to get set up to cover us. This is it, guys. Good luck, everyone." The Cajun and the Aborigine faded silently into the night.

"You know, Michael," Tzukuli observed, "You've the makings of quite the revolutionary leader, old chap. You've got a head for tactics."

"Yeah, well, the heck with tactics. I'll take a nice quiet life in the mountains anytime, with a nice cabin, my girl, and some good hunting."

"Wouldn't we all?" A deep chuckle rolled from Tzukuli's barrel chest.

"Time for us to get moving," Mike said a few minutes later, glancing at the treetops that were beginning to bend and whip in the freshening wind. "The breeze is blowing across, that ought to help." They set off into the darkness.

Ten minutes later, they were watching the two bored, tired Grugell sentinels from the shelter of a massive pine trunk.

"Are you ready?" Mike whispered as he nocked an arrow.

The tall Zulu merely nodded and raised the great spear in his right hand, point aimed at the nearest Grugell soldier. Tzukuli's target turned away from the two hidden scouts briefly, calling in a low voice to his comrade.

"Now," Mike hissed, and the two let loose their weapons.

Both struck true. Mike's arrow struck home in his target's eye, slamming though his brain and dropping him to the forest floor. Before his colleague could react, Tzukuli's spear struck him in the back, the long steel head penetrating all the way through his chest. The stick-thin figure looked down once, shook his head, and fell silently to the side.

The two scouts retrieved their weapons and rolled the bodies into a clump of ferns. Mike let out the characteristic yipping howl of the small predator of his native Idaho then the two found a sheltered spot to hide and wait.

In the space of a few moments, the Cajun and the Australian native crept down the hill, almost tripping over Tzukuli before the Zulu whispered, "Careful, lads."

Five minutes later, the rest of their party arrived.

"OK, this is it. Two by two, keep the pair in front of you in sight, but don't shoot unless you're shot at. Nathaniel, let's you and I go first. Doc Richfield, you and Yuri follow Nathaniel and I up.

I know a spot where we can see most of the meadow from a big tree."

# Twenty-Seven

**Settlement**

Darkness had fallen over the besieged town of Settlement, and still the sentinels on the palisade kept their vigils, weapons in hand.

A shout rose up from Security Headquarters. "Heads up! Our sensors on the river just went down. We're gonna have company!"

Jenny traded a look with Carrie Manns. "It's really going to happen," the doxie noted.

"Any minute now," Jenny agreed. She crouched down, peering over the edge of the palisade wall into the darkness beyond. Behind them, the Company troops ran to their firing positions. The colony's two precious twin-barrel 30mm cannons were set up on their heavy tripods, one on the southwest corner, the other on the northeast, and Security troops frantically fitted heavy, metal-linked ammo belts to the massive weapons.

A faint whine in the distance grew slowly louder. It seemed to come from all directions, underscored by a faint buzzing sound.

"They're all around us!" someone shouted from the far wall.

"Y'all keep your heads! Make every shot count!" Colonel Davies' voice bellowed out from somewhere in the darkened compound.

The whining and buzzing sounds grew louder.

"Mike, please, be alive out there," Jenny whispered. "No matter what happens here, please be alive." She shouldered her antique Remington and squinted over the sights into the night.

A spider-ship shot out of the darkness, angling for the northwest corner of the palisade. The ship roared overhead, spun on one of its four drivers, and aimed downwards, stabbing its white guide beam onto the roof of the Mercantile. But before it could fire its main weapon, both 30mm cannons opened up with chattering roars, lancing depleted uranium rounds through the spider's shields. The ship exploded with a roar, the wreckage falling within the compound and ripping the south wall off the Mercantile building. Screams from the darkness echoed from people hiding in the buildings.

Two more spiders shot overhead, raking the buildings with green bolts. The cannon crews returned fire, damaging one ship that limped away trailing an incandescent cloud of sparks.

**In the forest near Settlement**

Dismayed by the loss of one of his four remaining scout ships and the severe damage of the other, Dispotratik barked orders through his throat mike. "Send in all the scooters – all of them! Use one of the scout ships to knock out those big weapons from a distance, then punch holes in the walls."

A chorus of replies acknowledged his orders, the Grugell forces hurried to do their Group Commander's bidding.

## Settlement, on the wall

A faint form in the starlight moved against the trees. Then another, and another came into view. Jenny raised her voice in a shout that rose to a shriek: "They're coming in on the ground! Watch the trees!" She snapped off a shot at one of the racing forms, tumbling the platform's driver backwards.

A green energy bolt slammed into the cannon on the northeast corner of the palisade, destroying it and killing the gun's three-man crew. The surviving crew sent a hail of depleted uranium slugs over the compound into the darkness, striking sparks off the unseen spider that had just killed their comrades. A green bolt from the opposite direction blasted a hole in the south palisade wall, then another. Before the cannon crew could traverse their heavy gun around, another bolt shot into the east wall, blasting a large hole and sending the defenders flying. Cracking rifle fire sounded from all about the walls as the Grugell charged for the gaps in the palisade on their flying platforms. Bolts of green energy lanced through the air from Grugell platform projectors and hand weapons, to be answered by rifle and cannon fire from the defenders.

"They're inside the walls!"

## The Grugell base camp

"Doc Richfield, come have a look at this thing." Mike motioned the physicist forward to the base of a giant spruce.

A small town had sprung up in the meadow since Mike had seen it last, at least twenty of the thin-walled metal buildings had sprung up among the ferns. The structures were arranged in a rough square, but in the middle was a tall, featureless black obelisk, rising from a rectangular base, tapering away as it rose thirty meters above the surrounding buildings. A thin, cold drizzle fell now, and an ominous muttering came from the clouds overhead.

"It wasn't there before, but that was only a day or so after they landed. Could that be what we're after?"

Richfield squinted at the structure, shivering in the cold rain. "It doesn't really look like it. It looks almost religious." He pulled a small gizmo with a pistol grip from his jacket pocket, fiddled with a pair of dials, and pointed it at the black idol.

"Wow!" he exclaimed. "I guess that's it after all – the thing's throwing off energy readings that are off the scale. Don't get too close to it – your kids might have three heads."

"So," Nathaniel Tzukuli wanted to know, "How do we go about disabling this thing, then?"

"It looks like it's a pretty hard target," Mike noted. "Looks like armor plate around the thing. I suppose they thought that someone like us might happen along to try to blow the thing up?"

Doctor Richfield was staring into his gadget's tiny screen. "You know," he said, "if you could get me up to that thing, and if we could find a way to get a look inside…"

"The thing ought to have an access panel, right?"

"I hope so. They're taller than we are, it may not be easy to reach."

"Only one way to find out, right?" Mike raised his head, looking out over the Grugell occupation camp. "Doesn't seem like there's too many of them around, does it? I wonder where the rest of them are?"

"I think the answer to that is rather obvious, old chap," Tzukuli noted.

## Settlement

The Battle for Settlement had degenerated into a free-for-all inside the palisade walls, the darkness punctuated by muzzle flashes of human firearms as well as blasts of emerald lightning from the surviving spider, flying platforms and Grugell hand weapons. The second cannon and crew disintegrated in crossfire between the undamaged spider and several flying platforms, depriving Settlement of its last heavy weapon.

Jenny crouched on the wall, alternating glances inside the wall and out. One more Grugell tried to make a run at the wall near her, only to be transfixed by a near-solid stream of steel darts from Carrie Mann's assault rifle. Jenny snapped one shot at a buzzing platform but missed, as a green bolt slammed into the wall beneath her feet. Jenny and Carrie Mann landed hard, stunned, a few feet apart on the ground inside the palisade wall, chips and splinters of wood pattering into the red dust all around.

A stick-thin figure appeared in a gap in the wall, silhouetted against the faint moonlight, aiming a hand weapon at Carrie Mann. Jenny shook her head, frantically trying to rid herself of the sparkling lights in her vision. Rolling to her side, she brought the Remington to bear, firing once as the alien released a green bolt at the stunned doxie. The bullet took the alien in his leg, and he staggered sideways, screeching his agony even as Carrie howled in pain with a badly burned shoulder. Jenny stood up, somewhat unsteadily, and aimed remorselessly at the hobbling alien. A second shot finished him.

"There's more, coming for the gap," Carrie ground out through gritted teeth. A white light suddenly bathed the two women and everything around. A parachute flare, fired by a panicked farmer somewhere inside the compound, revealed at least ten dismounted Grugell troops racing for the gap in the palisade.

Carrie Mann's Steyr Magnetic swept three of the racing figures down to the ground before her magazine of darts ran dry. Jenny's Remington roared once, twice, dropping two more. The others darted to either side of the breach in the wall. A moment passed, and a black, oval object rolled in through the gap.

Jenny was stuffing fresh rounds in her Remington when the grenade exploded.

**The Grugell base camp**

"OK, let's go!"

Mike and Thomas Quiet Water wriggled frantically through the soaking wet ferns towards the Grugell broadcast device, with Gerald Richfield crawling between them. Nathaniel Tzukuli crawled along behind them. Beauregard Rousseau and Yuri Pyak kept an over watch from the tree line, as the Menmunnys crept towards a large building that they reckoned to be some kind of dormitory. "A diversion," the older Australian had announced while Mike was describing his plan. "Relax, mate – it'll keep them from noticing you blokes going for the energy thing. Trust us!"

It didn't take long for the 'diversion' to become apparent, as a rocket from Mick's 14.5mm launcher screamed through the falling rain and exploded against the far side of the dormitory, punching a large hole in the wall and starting a fire. Shouts rose from within even as the blast echoed off the hills, and within moments lances of green fire were slamming into the tree line. A squad of Grugell troops bolted from the structure, quickly forming a rough skirmish line and running for the trees, heading for the spot where the rocket was fired.

"They won't find anything," Thomas Quiet Water whispered. "Mick and Tak, they're of the old people. They know how to disappear."

"I hope so – come on, let's keep moving."

A moment later they arrived at the base of the tower. As Richfield searched for an access panel, the others took up prone firing positions to defend him as he did his work.

"I think I've found it," the scientist hissed. "Someone pass me a knife." Thunder rolled overhead as the physicist pried at a ground-level access panel in the driving rain.

## Settlement

Jenny came to slowly. A haze of red obscured her vision and when she raised a hand to wipe her face, it came away bloody. A fragment from the Grugell grenade had lacerated her scalp and other fragments had sunk into her right side. When she tried to move, white-hot needles of pain shot through her from armpit to hip.

She managed to clear her vision and sit up, bracing herself against a fallen portion of the palisade. From farther inside the compound, she could hear shots, shouting, and the snap of Grugell blasters.

"You OK?" A weak voice from nearby, Carrie Mann, lying on her side in a pool of blood. "I guess they thought we were dead."

"Where are you hurt?" Jenny gasped. "You're bleeding like a stuck pig."

"My leg – I took a big chunk of something. I've got it tied off now, but I sure don't feel too good." A weak grin. "Good thing I work on my back, eh?" The veteran doxie let out a coughing laugh.

"They're still fighting inside." Jenny caught sight of her Remington a few meters away and managed to crawl over to it. She checked the action quickly – two rounds in the magazine, one in the chamber. Another .338 cartridge lay in the dust nearby. She picked it up, cleaned the red dust from it with her tattered shirt, and stuffed it into the magazine.

"I'm going to see what's going on," she told the doxie. Using the rifle as a prop, she managed to get to her feet, only to be hammered to her knees by a wave of dizziness.

"Girl, you're about to fall over," Carrie chided her, but weakly.

"No, I'm not." Shaking her head, Jenny managed to get to her feet once again. "Can you get up?"

"I don't imagine I can walk on this leg."

"Where's your rifle?"

"Right here," Carrie pulled the Steyr up from behind her. "I'm reloaded. Go on, I'll be fine – I'll play dead if too many come towards me. Worked once."

On an impulse, Jenny went to the doxie and hugged her, and then she turned towards the interior of the compound. The shooting seemed to be slacking off somewhat now. In the fading light of another parachute flare, Jenny staggered towards the Mercantile building.


## The Base Camp

The rain was falling harder now, thunder rolled overhead as bolts of lightning lit the landscape at irregular intervals. A full-blown thunderstorm had settled in on the mountain meadow.

The power transmitter's access panel was open at last, pried open with Nathaniel Tzukuli's spear point after the point of Mike's skinning knife had broken off in the first attempt.

"Say, now this is interesting," Richfield commented. He was using a penlight to peer inside the apparatus. "I think I see how this thing works."

"Well, wreck it and let's get out of here," Mike hissed.

"I think I can do better than wreck it," Richfield answered. "I think I can reverse the field polarity from here. If I do that, and they don't know to adjust for it at the other end, that might turn this thing from a receiver to a reflector."

"And that would do what, exactly?" Tzukuli asked.

"Well, it would bounce all that power being beamed here from that satellite straight back up to orbit," Richfield said. "It ought to be, well, pretty spectacular. If it works."

"And if it doesn't?"

"Then this thing will overload and explode, and we'll be incinerated."

"Win-win situation," Mike announced. "Go ahead – it's worth a shot."

A flash of lightning strobed across the sky, lighting up the fern meadow. A moment later, another rocket shrieked into the Grugell camp, this time from a different direction, exploding a parked flying platform.

"Those Aussies, they take their diversions seriously," Tzukuli noted with a dark chuckle. A Grugell voice shrieked in pain somewhere out in the darkness, then was silenced.

A shout came from the trees where Pyak and Rousseau waited. "*Ils vous voient*! Look out – dey's a-comin' your way!"

A bolt of green flared, missing Richfield's head by millimeters. Mike returned fire at the two Grugell soldiers who had spotted them, dropping one with a 15mm solid. The other alien threw himself flat in the ferns, shouting. A round from Yuri Pyak's monstrous Krupp cannon slammed into the ground beneath the alien and exploded, hurling him bloody and broken into the air, but too late. The alarm had already been sounded.

## Settlement

A pair of bodies lay, broken and burnt, at the corner of the small house half a block from the Mercantile. Jenny crouched, checking for pulses, but the middle-aged man and woman were both dead. From her position, she could see the open area in front of the Mercantile.

Several bodies, both human and Grugell, littered the area. Sporadic shots were still being fired from within the Mercantile, while the Grugell returned fire with blasts of green from various positions outside.

The aliens were advancing, mercilessly, on the last holdouts in the giant store. Beneath the building, in the cavernous storage spaces, Jenny knew the bulk of Forest's colonists were hiding – including all of the colony's children. Overhead, the whine of the undamaged spider grew louder. The white guide beam flickered down towards the building, followed by two blasts that silenced the rifle fire from within. A squad of ten Grugell troops appeared, trotting towards the building, firing as they went. The spider dropped in closer, hovering, the white guide beam playing ahead onto the Mercantile to cover the troop's advance.

## The Grugell Base Camp

"To your left!" Mike rolled and fired twice with his Colt, another Grugell fell into the ferns. An emerald bolt glanced off the tower just over his head.

"Keep them off for just a couple minutes more," Richfield snapped. He shook his head, sending drops of rainwater flying from his close-cropped hair.

"Doing our best, Doc, but we're on the clock, here."

"One to your right," Thomas Quiet Water warned.

"On him," Tzukuli replied, snapping off a shot from his Transvaal double. The Grugell soldier dodged the shot, retreating over the lip of a small rise. The scouts could hear him screeching for reinforcements.

"This isn't looking good, lads," Tzukuli noted.

Running footsteps approached quickly from the western tree line. Mike rolled and swung around to face the sound, rifle pointed, only to see Tak Menmunny racing towards them through the pounding rain.

"You almost got yourself killed, boy," Tzukuli snarled.

"Never mind that, mate – you've got about twenty of those things hiding on the other side of that little ridge, fixing to come settle your hash. Me Pop's going to fire a hi-ex rocket right into the thick of 'em just as they get up to rush you – I already been over to the others, they're in a good spot to fire from."

"Doc, keep at it," Mike ordered as Richfield looked up. "We'll keep them off you."

Thomas Quiet Water crept around the side of the tower, dripping wet, his large dressing knife in one hand. "He's right," the Cheyenne confirmed. "Twenty, right over there."

"You mean to tackle them with a knife, mate?" Tak asked.

"No ammo."

The crack of a 14.5mm rocket exploding marked the Grugell charge. Sixteen of the stick-thin soldiers rushed over the little rise, silhouetted by the glow of the burning dormitory building behind them. Bolts of green fire lanced ahead of them.

The scouts returned fire, aided by shots from Rousseau and Yuri Pyak, but before they repelled the charge, several green bolts raked the ground at the base of the broadcast tower. The Grugell retreated over the rise, four of them, dragging one wounded comrade.

A groan led Mike to look over at where Gerald Richfield lay on his side at the open panel. A flash of lightning revealed the scene with unreal clarity. A Grugell energy bolt had lanced through Richfield's chest a few centimeters to the right of center. The physicist coughed hard, spraying blood into the wet ferns.

"Oh, shit," Mike breathed. "Doc, can you hear me? Doc?"

Richfield's eyes rolled up at Mike. "Yeah, I can hear," he gasped, "Just can't breathe too good…" His voice trailed off into another fit of coughs. A bolt of lightning slammed into a tree to their rear, the clap of accompanying thunder rolled over the scouts.

Mike looked up at Nathaniel Tzukuli, who had rolled to crouch on the other side of the scientist. The Zulu looked up at Mike and shook his head once, his liquid brown eyes huge in the dim light of the distant fire.

"Doc, can you tell us what to do? We've got to kill this thing, Doc!"

"Help me roll over," Richfield gasped.

**Settlement, in front of the Mercantile**

"All forces, hold your fire! Hold your fire!" Dispotratik shouted. He strode forward, gesturing at the gathering foot soldiers around the large wooden building. "They're about finished. We'll advance on line, get troops into that structure and wipe them out." A loud bang sounded to the rear. Dispotratik barked into his throat mike, "Lepotraskit! There's one of them around to the rear by the wall someplace. Get a squad out there to find it!"

**Near the palisade**

"We're losing, aren't we?"

Jenny almost jumped out of her moccasins at the voice. She turned to see the farm couple that had been next to her on the palisade.

"No, we're not going to lose. Have you two still got ammo?" The husband and wife nodded. "Follow me, then," Jenny ordered.

They crept from cover to cover, from building to building, until they reached the corner of a small shop with a good view of the Mercantile. The Grugell were at the main doors now, the firing from inside had stopped.

"We've got to draw them off," Jenny said. "You two stay here. When you hear my shot, both of you shoot one of them and then run back to the wall. Circle around behind the buildings, and try to get back from the other side. Shoot once, then move. We've got to give those people inside a chance."

"This is pointless, we should get out of there," the farm wife pleaded. "There's too many of them."

Jenny grabbed the woman by her shoulder. "Listen, my Mike is up there in the mountains with his scouts. They should be at those things' base camp by now. We've got to buy time – they can shut the alien's power off from there!"

"Power?" the husband asked. "How?"

"I don't know exactly, but you've got to trust me. Now do as I tell you!"

Cowed, the farm couple nodded.

Jenny left them there and scuttled to the corner of Settlement's lone café. At the rear of the Grugell forces, one tall, caped figure stood alone in the light from several fires around the compound, with two armed soldiers a pace or two behind him. He appeared to be barking orders at the others.

*That's the boss*, Jenny told herself. *Taking him out will screw their night up. Fifty meters – piece of cake.*

She aimed carefully. A trickle of blood ran into her eyes, she had to stop to wipe it away. Trying to calm her ragged breathing, she aimed again. The sights settled on the alien's chest. Her father's voice came back to her, explaining, *take a deep breath – let half of it out – and squeeze!*

The ancient Remington roared into the night. The Grugell commander let out a weak screech and collapsed into a tangle of sticklike arms and legs.

Two shots roared from somewhere to Jenny's left, and two more Grugell troops hit the dirt. She ducked and ran to the rear, working the Remington's bolt as she ran. Green energy bolts and shouting followed her flight.

She ducked around a shack, through a badly damaged storage shed, and crawled under a tool shed next to the Blue House. From there, she could see three Grugell troops carefully edging up to the corner of the building she'd last shot from. Aiming carefully, she dropped one of them twitching into the dust. The other two hit the ground and fired wildly, sending emerald bolts flying in her general direction, but Jenny had already crawled out from under the shed and was racing to a new spot. Somewhere behind her, more rifle shots barked.

## The Grugell Base Camp

"I think I've got it," Richfield gasped. His breath was coming hard now, a pool of blood gathered under him where he lay on his stomach. Sporadic fire still came their way from several directions as occasional rifle shots barked from the trees around. At one point another 14.5mm rocket raced right-to-left from Mike's perspective, slamming into a small building. A Grugell voice screeched once, thinly, before fading out.

"Doc," Mike asked. "You still with us?" A nod. The scientists' hands were still inside the open panel, still moving.

Richfield was holding the darkness back by sheer willpower alone. He was wet and cold, the rain driving into his eyes made it hard to see. Breathing was almost impossible now, his mouth kept filling with blood, his arms were growing weaker by the moment. *This lead*, he thought, *disconnect that, attach it to this here, turn this contact off – that's got to be a hyper wave modulator, unplug that, turn it around, hook that lead back up, and then when I put the modulator back in, that should do it…* His hands were heavy as lead now, his vision narrowing, fading.

*That should get it – plug that back in now – oh, God, I'm dying…*

## High orbit, over Forest

Roptamaktik IX was the technician in charge of the power satellite's crew of three. A boring tour of duty was about to turn suddenly – and briefly – exciting.

"Sir," a shout came from the watch technician, waking Roptamaktik where he dozed in his chair, "There is feedback from the receiving station, sir, rapidly rising…"

The satellite exploded a millisecond later, vanishing into a cloud of expanding gas and rubble.

## Settlement

Jenny's luck had run out. A wave of dizziness overcame her as she tried a dash between buildings, hammering her to her knees. She struggled to get up, dimly hearing the thin shouts of Grugell soldiers. She looked up, wiping blood out of her eyes, to see a stick-figure alien standing over her.

The aliens' hand extended, bearing an energy weapon. His face lit up in a sharp-toothed grin as he pushed the firing stud.

And nothing happened.

Behind him, the spider ship's driver orbs went dark, and the spider dropped from the sky like a stone, crashing into the group of Grugell troops facing the Mercantile. All around the compound, flying platforms crashed into the ground, slamming their drivers against the control T-handles or spilling them onto the ground.

*They did it!* The thought exploded in Jenny's head. A burst of adrenaline brought her to her feet, screaming a victory cry. The Grugell in front of her stepped back, alarmed. He tried to fire his weapon again, with no result. Panicking now, he turned and ran.

Jenny ran for the Mercantile, firing her Remington from the hip at stunned, helpless Grugell soldiers, shouting as loud as she could, "Come on out! Their power's gone!"

A dozen OWME Security troops burst from the big main doors, firing as they ran. Colonel Davies was right behind them, shouting orders. The panicking, weaponless Grugell fled into the night.

"Ah'll be damned," the Colonel exclaimed, "Ah've never seen tables turn as fast as that before. Major Wells!"

The Major appeared from the open doors, grinning. "Yes sir!"

"Y'all get a squad out there, get some lights back on around the area. Get some folks organized to look for wounded and get a detail to look after any prisoners."

"Yes, sir – I think you've got your first wounded right there, sir." Major Wells pointed.

Jenny staggered towards the Colonel, battered, filthy and bleeding, and collapsed in his arms.

"They did it, didn't they Colonel?" she asked. "They really did it."

"You bet they did, Miss. You bet they did," he assured her as she slipped into a faint.


**The Grugell base camp**


"You did it, Doc! Lights are all off, all around – you did it!"

A cloud of smoke burst from the open panel. Sparks shot out, bouncing off Richfield's unresponsive face.

Mike grabbed at Richfield's shoulder, shaking him once. There was no reply.

"Doc?"

Nathaniel Tzukuli leaned over, feeling for a pulse. "He's dead, lad."

Thomas Quiet Water muttered something in his native language. He rolled back, sat up with his back against the defunct broadcast tower, and began a singsong chant. Silence closed in around them as the lights from the fires slowly died out, Thomas continued his chant as the scouts gathered around the body of their savior. Mike explained to the others what had happened.

"*Cet homme, il est un lion!*" Rousseau exclaimed softly.

"We'll take him home with us," Mike announced. Murmurs of agreement came from the group. "Let's get him back down the valley a way. We'll get some sleep and start out tomorrow. I don't think the Grugell will be bothering us any."

The rain continued to fall all around the scouts as they gathered around their fallen comrade. Of the Grugell there was no sign. A bolt of lightning lit up the scene briefly, revealing Gerald Richfield's open, unseeing eyes still staring at the open panel. Mike reached down and gently closed the scientists' eyes.

# Twenty-Eight

**Settlement**

Jenny woke once, just as dawn was breaking. She found herself on a rough pallet in the middle of the Mercantile, an IV line running into her arm. She turned her head towards a familiar voice.

"Hey, girl," Carrie Manns greeted her from the next pallet.

"Hey," Jenny replied. Carrie reached out and took Jenny's hand, giving it a squeeze.

"Whole town's talking about you, girl."

"Really?"

"Really, really," Carrie smiled. "Jenny Crider, hell-cat of the Battle of Settlement." The doxie laughed, wincing at the pain of her injuries. "Some farm couple is telling everyone who'll listen how you shot up half the Grugell troops single-handed."

"Half the Grugell troops?" Jenny laughed once, wincing at the pain of her injured side. "I think I only got two or three of them. Is there any word from Mike or the other scouts?"

"Not that I've heard, honey."

**Two days later**

"Jenny! Jenny! Wake up!"

Jenny grumbled awake. Her head still ached, but she felt a great deal better, and had moved back into the borrowed shack that had been assigned to her and Mike. She opened her eyes to see Carrie Manns standing over her, her crutches tucked under one arm.

"A provisioning droid just lifted off out of the Mercantile's lot. They picked up a beacon signal from just north of the river! Jenny, it's got to be the scouts coming home!"

Jenny jumped from her chair and ran for the door, followed by the chuckling Carrie Manns. "Girl!" she shouted after the slim form sprinting for the landing field behind the Mercantile. "It'll be an hour or more before the droid comes back!"

Carrie stumped around the corner of the Mercantile building, sweating in the hot sunlight, to find Jenny standing expectantly on the edge of the landing pad the provisioning droids used. Two of the flying dump trucks sat idle nearby.

"Honey," she asked Jenny, "Why don't you go on back to your house and wait a while?"

"Because Mike's going to be on that droid!" The light in her eyes was all the veteran doxie needed. As rarely as she saw such emotion in her own line of work, she recognized love when she saw it.

"All right, then, let's sit down, at least. This leg is killing me."

They sat in the dust, leaning against the clapboard wall of the Mercantile, and waited. It was an hour and ten minutes before the clumsy droid floated in over the trees, settling to the red dirt of the field with agonizing – for Jenny – slowness.

She ran to the craft as the great cargo door opened. Mike was the first one out. She grabbed him, squealing her joy, kissing him hard before noticing the look in his eyes.

"Mike, what is it?"

Mike smiled sadly, and stepped aside just as Beauregard Rousseau, Yuri Pyak, Nathaniel Tzukuli, and Thomas Quiet Water appeared carrying the cloth-wrapped body of Gerald Richfield.

"He saved us all, baby." The scouts laid the body gently down in the red dust of Forest while Mike explained. Carrie Manns crutched up to listen, smiling at Rousseau as she approached.

"We lost a lot of people here, too, Mike. Forest isn't short on heroes today."

"And that includes all of you boys, Lieutenant," Colonel Davies' voice boomed out as the heavy-set Security Chief walked up to the group. "Damn, though," he grimaced, looking at the cloth-wrapped form. "That was a hell of a thing the Doc did, but y'all best remember that it was you, boy, that made the whole thing possible."

"And, it was your girl here that fought off half the Grugell army down here," Carrie Manns added. She looked sideways at Rousseau, winking at the old hunter.

"*Comment allez-vous, des ma petite douce?*" the Cajun grinned at her.

"I'm just fine, you old devil," Carrie answered. "I see you came through safe and sound!"

"*Oui*, and I reckon a' some point I'll tell you about th' hero Rousseau!"

Mike and Jenny looked at each other and smiled. "Life goes on," Mike observed dryly.


**A Grugell freighter, ten light years away**

"Message from the Imperium, sir."

Ottrattatisk VII sat up I the bridge chair suddenly. He'd been expecting this ever since a landing craft had brought the battered, broken remnants of the Occupation Group back to the Fleet transport in orbit.

"Very well. Play the message."

"Commander Ottrattatisk, commanding Tactical Logistics Group XIX in support of Occupation Group XIX. You are ordered to return all surviving Occupation Group personnel to the Imperial Navy Base on Grugell for court-martial."

Ottrattatisk winced. Grugell court-martials were short, and Grugell punishment was swift and brutal. The Emperor did not suffer failure lightly.

This Occupation Group had failed spectacularly, first suffering the loss of the Group Commander and his Assistant, and then stupidly allowing their broadcast power station to be sabotaged.

"Acknowledge the message, Technician. Helm, adjust our course to take us directly to Grugell."

For the first time in Grugell's history, an Occupation had failed, and the Occupation Group had taken serious losses. This planet was going to have to be abandoned to the occupying aliens, and the Grugell Empire was facing, also for the first time, a major adjustment in their expansion policy. There was now known to be another race of spacefaring, intelligent life forms in the Galaxy, and they were warriors to match the Grugell.

There was going to be hell to pay.

## Settlement

The days that followed were filled with goodbyes, with surprises, and with news from the north. The remnants of the Grugell occupation force fled north on foot, watched but not attacked by OWME Security troops in Forest's one available flyer. While OWME Security hadn't bothered the retreating Grugell, Forest's native predators showed no such compunctions. When the rocs started to close in, the OWME Security troops weren't of a mind to be forgiving, and so they didn't interfere as one of the great predators after another homed in on the column of weaponless aliens. Only ten or so made it back to the largely wrecked base camp, where a small shuttle was waiting to take the survivors off the planet.

A week after the scout's return, a funeral service was held for Gerald Richfield, which Jenny, Mike and the rest of the scouts attended. An hour afterwards, Yuri Pyak came to shake Mike's hand. His pack was loaded, and the monstrous Krupp cannon slung on his back.

"So, you're off to the woods again, eh Yuri?" Mike asked him. "Back out to hunt loggers?"

"*Da!*" the little Nenets replied, laughing. "Logger! *BOOM!*" His ever-present grin widened as he embraced Mike, kissing him on both cheeks. "*Do svidanyia, tovarisch,*" he said, and then he turned and walked away, bearing north by northeast, his short, bandy-legged form vanishing at last into the timber.

"You know," Mike told Jenny, "I never did understand much of anything the little guy ever said."

"An' neither did I," Beauregard Rousseau's voice boomed out from behind them, "But 'e was a 'ell of a shot, I tell you dat!" The Cajun laughed, slapping Mike on the shoulder. "Well, boy, we gon' be off to th' woods agin, too."

"We?" Mike and Jenny turned to see Rousseau and Carrie Manns, both with loaded packs. Rousseau cradled his Parks double, while Carrie Manns had her Steyr Magnetic slung on her shoulder.

"Well, I'll be!" Mike grinned widely. Jenny went to Carrie and hugged her.

"Someone has to keep this old gumbo-eating bastard out of trouble," Carrie explained seriously. Her eyes sparkled as Rousseau sputtered in feigned outrage.

Thomas Quiet Water took his leave that evening, coming by the borrowed shack to squat in the dust next to where Mike and Jenny sat on the step, watching the sun set.

He placed his hand on Mike's shoulder and spoke once.

"You will always be my friend. Walk in peace for the rest of your days, Michael." Then the tall Cheyenne turned and walked off into the forest.

"I think that's the most I ever heard him say at one time," Mike noted.

"When can we go back home, Mike?" Jenny asked, watching the tall, lean figure disappear into the trees.

"Soon. I've got a few things I want to work out down here first."

"Like getting a bunch of wrecked Grugell equipment out of our clearing?"

"Something like that, yeah. I've got a feeling that Colonel Davies may be able to help us."

"I'd say the Company owes us a favor or two," Jenny agreed, fingering the bandage on her head.

# Epilogue



**Settlement, OWME Security Headquarters, a week later**

"Kids, Ah don't rightly know how we can properly thank y'all," Behind an expansive desk of native Forest wood, the Colonel rocked back and forth in an old-fashioned swivel chair. In fact, he did have a pretty good idea. A team of construction engineers was already assembling for just that purpose.

Mike and Jenny were seated across the desk from Forest's number one Security Officer. Mike reached over and took Jenny's hand.

"Colonel," he asked, "if OWME wants to express its appreciation, I may just have an idea how they could do it."

"And how would that be, son?" the Colonel asked. He had an enigmatic grin on his face.

"How long would it take for a team of engineers to clear all the junk out of that meadow and help Jenny and me rebuild our cabin?"

Colonel Davies leaned back in his swivel chair, an expansive expression on his broad face. "Well, son, seein' as what you and the Missus have been through, and how y'all warned us about these here Gru-Gell landing on our planet, well, mind you Ah can't speak for the Company, but with mah favorable recommendation, Ah imagine the Company will most likely approve y'all's request. In return, son, for mah favorable recommendation, can Ah prevail upon you to perhaps give trespass permission and guide an old boy on a huntin' trip up in those mountains of yours sometime?" He motioned to the five-by-five elk head on the wall over his desk. "Ah've got some mighty fond memories of the last time y'all guided me on a hunt, son, and Ah'd be delighted to repeat the experience. Ah'm right pleased y'all found your way here to Forest, boy!"

"I'll take you on a hunt anytime you like, Colonel, but they aren't our mountains," Mike replied. "I'd be happy to guide you, but you don't need my permission."

"Ah, boy, that's where you're wrong," Colonel Davies grinned. He produced a framed piece of paper from his desk drawer. "Kids, the OWME Forest Project Board O' Directors met this very morning, at which meetin' Ah was privileged to be a guest."

"It didn't take the Company bigwigs long to resurface once the shooting stopped, did it?" Mike chuckled.

Smiling, Colonel Davies got up now walked over to a large map of the area on his office wall. "You should know, boy, that executives never do any of the dirty work. Not in a big company like OWME! Anyway, now, at this here meeting, the Board voted unanimously to give you and Mrs. Crider clear title to the land from the big river here," he pointed, "To the divide of these mountains on the north, over to the coast on the west, and down to an east-west line here," he concluded, drawing a line with one finger what had to be fifty kilometers south of the cabin site. He'd just outlined a stretch of land approximately the size of the American state of Ohio. "Now, since the Company has rights to land apportionment under the Settlement Act of 2169, Ah'm pleased to say this document yields y'all full legal title and all rights to the land described, without lean or qualification.

"Congratulations, kids. Y'all are unquestionably the biggest landowners this old boy's ever met." He strode over to shake

Mike's hand. He extended his hand to Jenny as well, but she ignored it, choosing instead to kiss the Colonel on the cheek. He blushed.

"Colonel," Jenny said warmly, "I don't know what to say."

"You kids are the heroes of Forest," the Colonel replied, still a bit embarrassed. "Hadn't been for you, the Gru-Gell could have landed a whole army before we'd a known what was what. You told us what they were up to, and where they were, and you risked your lives to get here to tell us. Hell, you even brought in the first P.O.W.!"

Clomonastik, having been summarily abandoned by the Gru-gell Occupation force, was still being held in a security cell in the Security Headquarters two stories down. He was rapidly learning English and, as the old Earth saying went, 'singing like a bird.'

"In that case, Colonel, if you'll excuse us, we've got one more errand to run before we catch a ride back home," Mike said, and shaking the Colonel's hand, he ushered Jenny out of the Security Headquarters and towards a large, white-painted structure across the dusty red-dirt street.

An hour later, Mike and Jenny stood, facing each other, in front of a gray-haired, black-robed Magistrate, who smiled broadly as he concluded, "You can kiss the bride, son." Mike did so, for all he was worth.

**Two years later, in the mountain meadow**

The battles fought for Forest seemed far away as Mike stepped out of the cabin on a bright, warm morning for another session of archery practice. As he walked towards his practice field at the far edge of the meadow, his thoughts were drawn back to the two years gone by since that great turning point in his life.

Colonel Davies was now a regular and welcome visitor to the mountain home of the Criders. Mike and Jenny had been thoroughly surprised one morning only two weeks earlier when the Colonel had showed up with two Security troops and a subdued Clomonastik in tow.

The former Grugell Occupation Commander was speaking excellent English now. "He's smarter than Ah care to admit," Colonel Davies informed Mike. "Ah hope, for our sake, that the rest of the Gru-Gell are a little dumber than this one."

Clomonastik approached Mike that afternoon, after the Colonel and the Security troops had taken him on a tour of the area and explained the circumstances of his Occupation's defeat.

"Ah, Mikecrider," Clomonastik had grinned down at Mike from his nearly three-meter height. He leaned over to lay one white, long-clawed hand on Mike's shoulder. Mike flinched, but there was no malice in the motion.

"You, my friend, were a worthy adversary indeed. I've recently been made aware of some of your human scribes and philosophers. One of them, whose name I don't recall – such odd names you humans bear – said, 'the true measure of a warrior lie not in the loyalty of his friends, but in the caliber of his enemies.' You, Mikecrider, are a worthy enemy. Since my own personal lot would now seem to be cast with your people, it is my wish that you will one day accept my own friendship, and find that the Grugell can be as faithful in friendship as we are in war." Given that Clomonastik's fate should he return to the Grugell would be disintegration for failure, he had quickly seen the wisdom in self-preservation.

"I guess that remains to be seen," Mike equivocated. "Are they going to keep you here on Forest?"

"No, Mikecrider," Clomonastik made a weird sound – if bats could laugh, Mike imagined it would sound much the same. "It seems I'm too valuable to be left out here on the edges of space.

No, in ten days' time I will be placed on a ship returning to your home world, 'Earth.' What wonders will I see there, could you begin to describe them? No? Perhaps another time, then." He removed his feather-light palm from Mike's shoulder. The Grugell straightened up, looking around at the meadow that was to have been his Occupation headquarters.

"I'm reminded of the words of another of your great philosophers, my respected adversary," Clomonastik said at last. "This one said, 'I have not come to bring peace, but a sword.' The Grugell will face your people again, Mikecrider. Be on your guard, always. My people are great warriors. I think that a great conflict will be our portion one day."

Clomonastik turned, smiling and waving one thin hand to a scowling Jenny as she watched from the cabin doorway.

"You should have more than one wife to care for you, my friend," the tall, thin alien chided him gently. "With this large home, you should have, oh, six or seven. A warrior of your caliber should have many females and children."

Mike offered no comment.

Possible wars were far from Mike's concern this morning, however. The morning sun was warm on his back as he sent a fifth arrow slamming into his leather target. Smiling, he tipped back his battered old Stetson and rested the lower limb of his longbow on the toe of his moccasin. His new batch of arrows was just fine. Twisting one handlebar of what was now a truly enormous Zapata mustache, complimented now by a dark-blonde goatee, Mike turned at the sound of the cabin door slamming.

The new cabin stood on the site of the old one, but was built of mill-hewn lumber rather than logs, and had four rooms instead of one. Water from a drilled well, put in place by the engineers sent by a grateful Company, replaced the two buckets Mike had previously used to haul water from the sparkling clear stream. A geothermal power source even provided them with electricity and hot water for a tiny shower stall in the bathroom.

His Jenny was walking towards him, dressed as usual in a knee-length leather dress. The leather tented over the swell of her six-month pregnancy, and behind her padding bare feet toddled their year-old son, Little Mike. Jenny had one hand behind her back and was smiling warmly at her husband. She kissed him warmly, whispering, "Close your eyes and hold out your hand."

He complied, hearing her giggle as a hard, paper-wrapped object dropped into his hand. He opened his eyes.

"A Nutty Crunch Bar!"

Mike picked up Little Mike, seating him on one shoulder for the walk back towards the cabin. A heavy cargo flyer sailed overhead at high altitude, bearing for the new town of Edgewater, a growing community on the shore of the Northern Ocean. Docks were going up there, and a shipyard, to complete the exploration of Forest by sea.

Mike and Jenny's new home planet of Forest remained, mostly, a primeval wilderness. The fearsome, dinosaur-sized rocs still stalked the lowland fern prairies, and travelers still had to exercise caution when moving through the haunts of the huge predators as well as the areas frequented by the giant, ill-tempered loggers. More people were moving onto the planet every month, roads were pushing farther into the wilds, and farms had sprung up as close as the base of the New Pyrenees. But in the mountain meadow, high above the hunting grounds of the rocs, the Crider family enjoyed their hard-earned peace and solitude.

"Life," Mike observed to Jenny that bright morning as they walked hand in hand towards the cabin, "just couldn't get any better than this."

Forest's best-known family went inside their cabin as the flying freighter disappeared overhead, bearing north.

Book Two

# Confederacy!

# Tarbos

*The year 2234CE was to be a momentous one in human history. Early in that year, Robert Pritchard, the Project Director for Off-World Mining & Exploration's operations on the planet Tarbos, called a meeting of delegates from the thirteen worlds to discuss solutions to the loss of OWME freighters. While the causes of the losses were not known at first, the hostile Grugell were suspected, and this was later confirmed.*

*However, Director Pritchard's meeting was to have far more lasting results than initially planned. Even before the delegates began to arrive on Tarbos, the meeting evolved into what would become a Constitutional Convention founding the Confederated Free Planets.*

*The Grugell swiftly discovered the intent of the various planetary officials gathering on Tarbos, and moved to prevent the formation of an interplanetary human government. Efforts were undertaken by at least one Grugell warship commander on several different fronts, all ultimately unsuccessful.*

*The new Confederate Constitution was swiftly ratified by the thirteen settled worlds. Tarbos Project Director Robert Pritchard was elected the first Confederate President; a key point in his campaign was the founding of the Confederate*

*Navy. The human expansion continued, at a faster pace now, borne by ships carrying the blue banner of the Confederacy.*

*—Morris/Handel, "A History of the First Galactic Confederacy," University Publications, 2804CE*

# One

**Grugell**

The small desert world of Grugell orbited a large blue-white star, at about 1.3 Sol-system Astronomical Units – about 1.3 times the distance of Earth from Sol. Slightly smaller than Mars, Grugell was a light world. The planet was light in gravity, light in atmosphere, light in biosphere, and especially light in water. Even at 1.3 AU, the blue-white type A star blasted Grugell with a burning heat, resulting in a planet that was desiccated, shriveled, and hot. Only a fierce, competitive species could survive here, and the Grugell were nothing if not ferociously competitive.

Dominated by the endless desert, the small planet boasted only one small, salty ocean, taking up less than a fifth of the planet's surface. Over most of the planet, a variety of small forbs and tough, grass like plants clung precariously to life in sheltered areas of the dunes, and tiny crawlers eked out a living by feeding on the plants and on each other.

On the shores of the ocean there were small, stubby trees and a richer variety of lower plants. Several species of herbivore fed on the plants, and precisely four species of predator hunted the herbivores. One of those species was closely related to the Grugell themselves and indeed was considered by some Grugell scholars to be much like the ancestral Grugell; the Gouge were semi-bipedal, savage, fanged creatures that hid among the stunted trees to leap screaming in ambush upon the unwary passerby, be they Grugell or beast. Young Grugell on their adulthood adventures often hunted the Gouge as a ritual challenge, and it was not infrequent that such ambitious young warriors did not return from these quests.

The city Gormapa, the capital of the Empire, had sprung up from the ancestral village of the first Emperor, Krickstask I. Gormapa lay forty kilometers north of the seashore, and in this modern era had sprawled out across the sands to house fifteen million Grugell. The base of the Imperium, the Emperor's military command structure that ruled every aspect of Grugell society, was here; so also was the Emperor Himself.

Rising like a fang above the desert, the gleaming silver spire of the Imperial Palace stretched a good five kilometers from the dry, sandy surface of Grugell, from the very heart of Gormapa. This fortieth day of the Grugell month of K'kitik, at the height of the Grugell summer, the blue-white rays of the sun were seething on the polished silver exterior of the palace's soaring spire and sizzling the walkways and gardens far below.

In the Imperial quarters, though, all was cool and dim, and the faint sound of water trickling through ornamental fountains and pools echoed through the high, arching stone and metal chambers. The ostentatious display of water was a sign of the Emperor's wealth; on a planet critically short of water, only the Imperial palace had water to spare for such ornamental frippery.

And Emperor Ignostak XI wanted it known. Especially to lowly types like the two Imperial Navy officers that stood nervously before him now in the vast, cool, humid expanse of his audience chamber, escorted by his chief advisor Kaxatrisk II.

Yawning, the Emperor reached into a small silver canister next to his desk chair and extracted a small, wriggling animal. The legless crawler was native to the desert sands south of Grugell's ocean, and was imported as one of the Emperor's favorite delicacies. Inspecting the struggling creature dispassionately for a moment, Ignostak XI brought it to his mouth and bit its head off, chewed briefly and swallowed before speaking.

"Well?" he demanded. "What have you learned?"

"Your Majesty," Kaxatrisk began, "Admiral Pokatak IX and Admiral Gilgakat XII have gathered all intelligence regarding the human activity in the few worlds they have settled. They have established patterns of shipping activity, and their armed ships have attacked and destroyed four human ships."

"Only four?"

"Four, Your Majesty. We have concentrated our efforts on learning about their organization and social structure rather than engaging in direct warfare."

The Emperor took another bite of the crawler, chewed, and wiped his mouth with a forearm. "Wise, that, after the debacle on Forest."

"Indeed, Your Majesty. What we have discovered is intriguing."

Ignostak XI merely raised his eyebrows.

Admiral Pokatak IX, Fleet Commander of the Grugell Imperial Armed Navy, stepped forward now. "Your Majesty, if I may speak?" The Emperor nodded. "We have analyzed the wreckage of four human ships. The four ships we have engaged were all unarmed, Your Majesty. They carried cargo and passengers but no weaponry. Further, and better still, they seem unable to cloak even their smaller ships, which only operate near planets. They have evidently not discovered the wave-bending technology."

"Good."

"We are not yet certain which of the human planets is their home world, but we expect to discover that within a year by analyzing travel patterns of their cargo ships. At present we have only eight armed ships, as you well know, Majesty, and only six of them are equipped with the wave-bending devices that allow them to pass undetected."

"So?" the Emperor looked mildly puzzled.

"Your Majesty," Kaxatrisk interceded, "The Admirals feel that the proper strategy would be a strike directly at the human's home world, before they can devise armed ships of their own or, if they should already have them, before they can discover the where-abouts of the bulk of our own population."

"And I must point out, Majesty, that we will need at least two heavily armed Occupation forces and several more armed ships to carry out the task," Pokatak added.

"The Occupation ships will be available within that time, Majesty," Gilgakat said; as Commander of Occupation Forces, his life depended on accurate dispositions of the five Grugell Occupation ships. "We will, of course, need combat troops and crews."

"These will, presumably, be made available?"

"Yes, Majesty. We have already begun conscription of the youngest crèche troop classes."

"You favor this pre-emptive strike, Kaxatrisk?"

"I do, Majesty."

"You two, you Admirals of my fleets, do you as well?"

Both Admirals nodded.

"Very well. Proceed as you have described. You have my authorization to begin ship construction as necessary. You are dismissed."

"By your command, Majesty." The three made to back slowly from the room, heads bowed as protocol demanded. "Kaxatrisk, you will remain," the Emperor barked.

Kaxatrisk waited until he heard the Admirals leave before raising his head. The Emperor motioned him forward. "Come, my trusted advisor, sit here beside me. Have a crawler."

"Thank you, Majesty." Kaxatrisk seated himself carefully at his Emperor's feet and selected a small crawler from the canister.

"There is more to this other space-going race you are not telling me, my old friend," Ignostak IX observed.

"Nothing of consequence, Majesty." More at ease with the Admirals gone, and comfortable with his role as the Emperor's most valued personal advisor, Kaxatrisk relaxed visibly. "It is only that…"

"Yes?"

"Majesty, they differ from us in significant ways. The interrogations of the survivors of the failed Occupation troops revealed much."

"Continue."

"They do not seem to be organized, Majesty. They move freight, but with little central direction. They are armed, but lightly so, and there is no regularity to their uniforms, their armaments, or their tactics. And, Majesty, strange as it seems…"

"Strange as what seems?"

"On Forest, their females fought alongside the males." Such a thing was unthinkable to the highly dimorphic and fiercely patriarchal Grugell. "And ferociously, it seems. It was a human female that was suspected of killing the acting Commander during the final battle in the human village. And as individuals, they are physically very formidable – I'm told that it is probable they originated on a planet with considerably heavier gravity than Grugell."

"Then we must take them in space, where our armed ships give us the advantage."

"As ever, Majesty, you see to the heart of the matter."

## Washington D.C., Earth

"Ladies and Gentlemen, the President of the United States!"

A round of applause followed the announcement heralding the entry of President Anthony Ignacio Gomez. He strode to the podium to address the crowd gathered for the Inaugural, Vice President Hector Gutierrez at his side.

President Gomez was an impressive figure, less than two meters tall but a commanding presence in a gray suit, steel-blue tie, and his iron-gray hair combed carefully back. He looked over the throng with coal-black eyes, past a nose that was slightly hooked, giving him an almost raptorial appearance. The Secret Service had already given him the code-name EAGLE, which he jokingly corrected them to pronounce *ÁQUILA*. Unfortunately, the Secret Service agents assigned to protect the President were a somewhat humorless lot.

The President placed his work-hardened hands on the podium – he'd started his adult life as a contractor. He rocked back on his polished Italian shoes for a moment, looking out at the crowd, lost for a few seconds in the memories of all that had brought him to this moment. He had spent twenty years of building a nationally known chain of construction companies, including major contracts with Off-World Mining for the Peru Skyhook and the orbital graving dock. Following an offer for sale of the chain, he'd retired at 40 and, seeking an outlet for his restless, aggressive energy, he'd entered politics as a campaigner in the Libertarian Party, quickly rising to be Governor of Colorado at 48. With his childhood friend Hector Gutierrez as Lieutenant Governor, they'd served two terms, re-elected for the second in a landslide, then sought and won the nomination for the Presidency on the Libertarian ballot, winning that race by a wide margin. "A Common Man with Common Sense" was the wildly successful slogan, printed on posters showing Gomez as a twenty-five-year-old carpenter in overalls and tool belt next to the present-day Gomez, likewise in overalls.

Now, at 57, he'd achieved a goal he'd never contemplated until the year before.

"Ladies and Gentlemen. Good afternoon," he began. He still spoke directly, in short, barked sentences, as though he was issuing orders to a gang of workmen.

"In our campaign, Vice President Gutierrez and I promised you all several things. A reduction in the Federal bureaucracy. A half percent decrease in the Federal sales tax rate. And, most important of all, a planetary defense against the hostile Grugell Empire."

A few catcalls followed the last remark. The hostility of the Grugell had been a contentious issue during the campaign. Gomez' Republican opponent had made some political mileage with his stated intent to "seek common ground" with the Grugell.

Gomez fixed the crowd with his raptorial glare. "I know what some of you are thinking. Why does America have to protect the globe? Why does America have to baby-sit the rest of the planet?" There were a few shouts of agreement.

"I ask you," he continued. "If not America, then who?"

He surprised the Secret Service by walking around to the side of the podium, abandoning the armored poly-steel box and the all-but-invisible force field that shielded his upper body. He strode to the edge of the platform, looking down now into the crowd. "Who?" he demanded. His presence was more commanding than ever, standing over the front rows. The Secret Service fanned out nervously, scanning the crowd for any signs of trouble, but the people had gone quiet, still, their attention captured.

"I'll tell you who. Nobody. Nobody else can." Trailing a pair of Service agents, he walked across the front of the stage, gesturing with one hand as he spoke. "Who else will do this? The European Union, still struggling out of depression? The nations of Africa, decimated by plague and war? China, still recovering from their own Civil War? Brazil? Argentina? Peru? Who, if not America?" He invoked a phrase out of history, borrowed from another President who had presided over another crisis, over a century before: "If not us, who? If not now, when?" He paused for a moment, apparently thinking about what to say next.

"I don't know that much about politics, really. I don't know much about diplomacy. I know about running a business. I know about meeting deadlines. I know about cutting the fat from an operation. But you know what's more important than that? I know about the importance of helping a brother or sister who needs a hand up. Not a hand out, a hand up." He pointed at the sky. "Twenty years ago, up there somewhere on a planet called Forest, humanity met the Grugell Empire for the first time. We met them, because we were on that planet, and the Grugell intended to take it from us. Not to share in its resources, not to establish their own colonies and live with us as neighbors. They intended to kill all of the people on that planet and take it for themselves. Well, you know what? We didn't let them. The colonists of Forest fought off a heavily armed alien invasion with hunting rifles, and with farming and mining equipment."

He walked to the center of the platform now, eyes constantly roving over the crowd. "But I'll tell you something. Since that time, we've seen and heard more of the Grugell. We know their ships are operating in our space, the space we've already colonized. There has been very limited contact, but that will change, I assure you."

"Eventually we'll have to have some kind of relations with them, but for now there are no embassies, no diplomatic relations. We must make no mistake – the Grugell are *hostile*. They are an armed, totalitarian, militaristic society, and they know where humanity's home planet is. They probably know where eighty-five percent of humanity still lives. And, unlike humanity, they have armed ships to enforce their policy of expansion."

"We can't protect the colonies. But we can protect Earth."

The speech drew cheers, but the crowd seemed subdued. The new President had just offered support for what the national media was calling a massive, expensive planetary defense of dubious effectiveness.

The Vice President was the first on the platform to stand as the President concluded, and as he stepped forward to shake the President's hand, Gutierrez leaned in to whisper *sotto voce*: "You had 'em, *ése*, but you lost 'em. Should have waited for that one."

"Better that they know up front," Gomez said. "You got the same briefing I did."

"Yeah, but shit, Tony, you laid it right out…"

"I'm not a politician, *mijo*, and I'm not going to start acting like one now. First step of a job is letting the people know what they're supposed to be working on."

"You say so. Come on, time to meet the media."

Gomez let out a groan. "Tell me again how I let myself get talked into this."

"I seem to remember you saying something about, 'if you want the job done right,' bro."

President Gomez threw back his head and laughed, drawing a stare from the Secret Service agents.

# Two

**Tarbos**

Tarbos Project Director Bob Pritchard looked out of his twelfth story, corner office window at one of the most spectacular views in and of the settled worlds. Off-World Mining and Exploration's offices on Tarbos were located in a remarkable setting.

The city of Mountain View had grown up just downhill from the first landing site. While the city overlooked a bay and natural harbor on the northern edge of Tarbos' one ocean, a mountain range reared its head just to the north of the city, and on a peak forty kilometers north of city center the planet's Skyhook soared to the heavens. Hardwood forests and long-grass prairies covered most of the one continent, dotted by the small, efficient mining operations extracting a wild panoply of mineral riches from the crust. Tarbos was a slightly "heavy" planet, with gravity about ten percent greater than Earth's, but this was compensated by an atmosphere slightly higher in oxygen.

In his office on the twelfth floor of OWME's triangular, gleaming black headquarters tower, Pritchard stood looking out his window at the surf lapping gently against the beach just five hundred meters away. Already, at two in the afternoon local time, (Tarbos ran on a twenty-one-hour clock) the first after-work sunbathers were showing up on the wide expanse of snow-white sand. Below his aerie perch, the beachgoers lay on blankets, splashed in the surf, batted around beach balls, threw flying plastic discs. Pritchard couldn't share their joy.

A thin binder lay on Pritchard's expansive black polymer desk. The cover bore a legend – OWME Freight Losses, 2130-2132.

Page 38 contained the entry that had Pritchard concerned.

> 16 April 2131: OWME Freighter *Narwhal* lost en route Earth to Tarbos. Ship black box log indicates three strikes by unidentified energy weapon, one to the drive tunnel, one to the Navigation suite and one to the Bridge. Drive tunnel hit resulted in failure of an anti-matter conduit, causing a matter-antimatter explosion resulting in the complete destruction of the ship and cargo. All hands lost in the attack: Seven officers and sixty-three crew. Estimated cost of ship and cargo total $1.26 billion. Additional insurance/compensation/compound interest losses total $43.68 million.

> No other ship traffic was detected in the area in the eight-hour period prior to the attack. The identity of the attacking craft has not been determined.

> The hostile Grugell Empire was known to have a device that rendered their ships impossible to detect.

*Unidentified energy weapon, my ass*, Pritchard thought bitterly. *It was a Goddam Grugell warship.*

What Tarbos, or any other settled planet run by Off-World Mining and Exploration was to *do* about the Grugell, was another question entirely.

## Forest

The cabin in the mountain meadow had grown into a three-bedroom house now, but other than that the clearing in the giant conifers looked much as it had when Mike and Jenny Crider had returned there as newlyweds twenty-two years before. This morning, the sun was rising bright and hot in the west after a night of scattered thunderstorms, leaving the great trees and fern meadows steaming.

Heat and humidity or not, it was a perfect late-summer day. The cabin door swung open with a bang, and Mike stepped out to greet the morning.

His frame was as tall and thin as ever, his face marked with a few more wrinkles above his dark-blonde goatee. Crows-feet crinkled the corners of his ice-blue eyes now as before. A few streaks of gray showed in his shoulder-length hair.

His ancient gray Stetson had been replaced, and replaced again in the last twenty years, but only by another, identical model. Finding duplicates was no difficulty; following the long-ago Battle of Settlement, gray Stetsons had rapidly become a wildly popular fashion on Forest, and remained so to this day. He still wore his favored blue cotton shirts, and while blue jeans had replaced his boser-skin leggings of long ago, he still preferred his wife Jenny's hand-made knee-high moccasins. This morning he carried his longbow and a quiver of arrows.

"Ready to go, Junior?" he called over his shoulder.

From the cabin emerged a near duplicate of the Mike of twenty years before. Mike Junior was twenty-one, tall and lean as his father, with his sire's long blonde hair. Mike Junior kept his face shaven, though, and eschewed the Stetson for a floppy leather hat.

"I'm ready, Dad. We heading up the mountain today? I saw a group of bosettes up there yesterday, right at the top of the Turkey-foot." Mike Junior shouldered a longbow and quiver similar to his father's.

"I figured as much. Maybe it'll be cooler up on the high benches."

"Wouldn't bet on it, Dad. It's going to be a steam bath no matter where we go. Sure you don't want to run down to Outskirts for anything today?" Mike Junior grinned at his father.

"You spend too much time messing around in town as it is," Mike grumped.

"No girls up there on the high benches, Dad."

"All right. Let's get going. We're burning daylight."

The two set out with mountaineer's strides, into the trees, bound upwards for the high benches above the cabin.

"You saw on the news this morning, the US has a new President, didn't you Dad?"

"Yeah. I sent in my absentee ballot. I think he'll do OK – 'bout time we had someone in there who's worked for a living."

"Yeah, I guess." Mike Junior was of an age where girls were far more interesting than politics, but the particulars of his father's comment weren't lost on him. "Uh, 'we,' Dad? Are we Americans, or are we Forestians? I hear tell some of the people on Earth are wondering whether we're citizens or not."

"I am. You, son, well, that remains to be seen, I guess. Forest isn't an independent world, you know. It's a Company planet, and OWME's an American corporation. I'm still an American citizen, so's your mother – she was born on Earth, in Baltimore - and I'd guess that makes you and your sister citizens too." He looked up through the trees. On the slope ahead of the pair, the lush ferns under the trees hung limp in a haze of humidity. "Getting hot, isn't it?"

Mike Junior wasn't ready to let the conversation go, but a youth spent in a remote cabin with only his parents and sister for company had gifted him with insight. He dropped the subject.

"Right up there, Dad," he pointed, "up on the second bench up from the left-hand side of the Turkey-foot, that's where I saw the bosettes. Company is paying premiums for meat still, right? What with this latest ship of settlers coming in?"

"Yep." The old *Mayflower* was on a dedicated Earth/Forest run now.

"Well, let's go get 'em!"

Under the trees, the air was a little cooler, but not much. Before they'd gone a kilometer, both men were sweating. Mike Senior stopped to wipe sweat from his forehead.

"We get anything today, we'll just dress it and beacon it for the retrieval droids. We don't need meat at the house, and I'm not carrying anything down the mountain in this heat."

"OK with me."

## The White House, Washington D.C., Earth

While President Gomez had seen pictures and video of the Grugell race, not much could have prepared him for the sight of a living, breathing alien. But it was just such a being that sat before him now, in the ancient, historic Oval Office, flanked by his Secretary of State and Secretary of Defense. Two Secret Service agents watched, hawk-like, from the far wall.

The weird, sticklike creature leaned forward slightly, adjusting his three-meter frame uncomfortably in a chair designed for humans. "You must pardon me for fidgeting, Mr. President," he said, "I have adjusted somewhat to the gravity on your world over the years, but I find your furniture rather uncomfortable." His English was impeccable, almost without any trace of an accent.

"I can imagine, Mr. Clomonastik. I apologize for not having more comfortable accommodation for you here, but you're the first Grugell to visit the Oval Office."

"Indeed, Mr. President, since I am the only Grugell on your home planet." The alien grinned, revealing serrated, predatory teeth. "Which brings us to the reason you have brought me here today, yes? Away from my poor Silver Spring restaurant?"

"I've dined in your restaurant, sir," Gomez replied. "I wouldn't describe it as 'poor.'"

"I trust you enjoyed your visit, Mr. President, but I suspect you didn't 'invite' me here to discuss Grugell cuisine, am I correct?"

"Yes, that's true. Before your capture on Forest, Mr. Clomonastik, you were a fairly high-ranking officer in the Grugell military, is that right?"

"You could say so, yes. I held the rank of Group Commander, which is roughly equivalent to a Rear Admiral in your seagoing Navy here on Earth. I was tasked as Occupation Commander on Forest, a mission which, as you know, failed."

"Yes, and you chose freely to come to Earth."

"It was either that or face disintegration for failure on my return to Grugell," Clomonastik pointed out. "In my case, sadly, self-preservation won the day over patriotism." He looked anything but sad; his Grugell restaurant in nearby Silver Spring, Maryland, was a wild success. Clomonastik was somewhat limited by only having Earth materials available, but the novelty of Earth's first extra-terrestrial restaurant – cynically named "End of the Universe," after some obscure twentieth-century science-fiction novel that the former Grugell officer had found amusing – had made Clomonastik a very wealthy Grugell, and the United States' first *truly* alien "permanent resident."

That last item had caused the government's Immigration service no small amount of consternation. The bureaucracy had, not surprisingly, been caught off guard, and, being a bureaucracy, had reacted in the only way possible – by mindlessly following procedure to the letter. Clomonastik now was the proud owner of a "green card," which he regarded with distinct amusement.

"You wish to question me about the composition and structure of the Grugell military," Clomonastik observed.

"Well, yes."

"Then, Mr. President, I must begin by clearing up the misconception you may have about Grugell society. First of all, the Grugell Empire has no 'military' as you know the term. The Grugell Empire *is* a military organization. Every adult male is in our military, he holds a rank, and his level of achievement in life is measured by the attainment of rank and military honors. We simply have no 'civilians' in the Empire."

"Except the women, of course," the Secretary of State, Claudia Stetson, pointed out.

"I appreciate your sensitivity to that, Madame Secretary," Clomonastik replied, inclining his head graciously. "Our females, it is true, have limited rights and status compared to our males – they are expected to obey their Estate-Master, bear and raise children, and maintain the estate."

"Estate-Master?" Stetson frowned.

"You understand that the phrase loses something in translation, but that is roughly your equivalent of the Grugell term."

"We're not here to discuss equal rights for Grugell women, Claudia. We can take that up another day, all right? We've got bigger fish to fry." Gomez wasn't pleased with the sidetrack the conversation was taking, and his scowl made that plain.

"Yes, Mr. President." The Secretary of State backed off but remained uncowed.

"Mr. Clomonastik, you were describing your military culture?" Gomez prompted.

"Yes – where was I? Oh, yes. The Emperor is a hereditary monarch, as you've had here on Earth in the past. The Emperor is the absolute ruler of the Grugell; his every whim is law. There is no legislative body, no civil court, and no police force. Crimes against the Empire and petty crimes against a fellow Grugell are punished by what you would describe as a military court-martial."

"How do you handle consumer goods, food production, all that sort of thing?"

"All done as a function of our military structure," Clomonastik replied. "As in your military services, our Imperial Navy has a range of military specialties, which include manufacturing and raising of food animals." The Grugell, being essentially a predatory species, had no vegetable agriculture as such; this was reflected in the offerings of Clomonastik's restaurant. Vegetables and salads were all but unknown there. Almost all the menu items were purely meat dishes.

Clomonastik continued. "Now, until we encountered your race on the planet Forest – we called it something different, of course – we had no armed spacecraft. There was no need for any. Our Occupation forces were armed when making planetfall on new worlds, but all we have encountered so far are less developed, unintelligent species.

"Of course, that has changed. We were fortunate enough to detect signs of your spacecraft operating in the vicinity of Forest without being detected in return, and the Emperor's decision was swift. Shipyards on Grugell and another developed Grugell world, Gorbinia, immediately began building armed spacecraft."

The Secretary of Defense, Titus McAlester, spoke up now. "And how are those craft armed?"

"Bear in mind, Secretary McAlester, that my knowledge is over twenty Earth years out of date. But at that time, standard armament for an Imperial Navy armed frigate consisted of two anti-proton projectors and two anti-ship torpedo bays, carrying five torpedoes each. And, as you are no doubt aware, Grugell engineers have discovered a means to render these frigates undetectable with a cloaking field. The nature of that field is a closely guarded secret; I've never been on a ship that possessed such a device. The device only works, it seems, on small ships, frigate class or smaller. The Occupation ships are too large to conceal."

"Have you any knowledge of how many of these armed frigates your Navy has built?"

"Indeed, Mr. President, I do not. As of my last first-hand knowledge, there were but two. In twenty years, it is safe to assume that there have been a significant number built. The Emperor is not, shall we say, encumbered by dealing with a recalcitrant Congress in organizing such projects. He simply commands, and his commands are carried out. And, Mr. President, I'd like to correct your use of the possessive; the Grugell military is "mine" no longer. I have cast my lot with your people, your society. My loyalty is now to America."

"I appreciate that, and I appreciate your loyalty. Most of all I appreciate your being so forthcoming with information that would certainly be considered *dis*loyal by your fellow Grugell."

"In Grugell society, Mr. President, I am already considered guilty of the most severe of crimes; I failed in a mission to which I was assigned by the Emperor Himself. Nothing I may tell you could further compound that offense, sir. And as I've said, America has earned my loyalty. Besides," he chuckled, a strange, thin sound, "a race that produces such a tenacious and canny adversary as your fellow American Michael Crider will prove to have a great destiny, I think. I would one day enjoy seeing my respected friend Michael again."

"We'll have to see if we can arrange that. Mr. Clomonastik, I'd like you to spend a few days interviewing with Secretary McAlester's senior staff."

"I'd be delighted to help, Mr. President. Fortunately, I've got a very capable assistant that can oversee operations at the End of the Universe."

"Good – it's all settled, then. Jorge," the President called to one of the Secret Service men, "Will you see to it that Mr. Clomonastik has a suite at the D.C. Marriott, and anything else he needs? Thank you. That's all for now, everybody. Mr. Clomonastik," Gomez extended his hand, managing not to flinch as the Grugell immigrant shook it with his bony, clawed one. "Thank you for coming in to see us, sir. I'll speak with you again before you return to Silver Spring, if that's all right with you."

Clomonastik nodded and left, the Secret Service agent on his heels.

**Caliban, the Capital Archipelago**

Caliban was a "wet" planet, being, as it was, over 80% oceanic. The first landing site on Caliban, on a large island in a chain that stretched halfway across the southern hemisphere, had now grown into an impressive city called Capital.

Stefan Ebensburg always thought the name unimaginative, which was a common problem on the worlds settled by OWME. But his powers as the fourth Caliban Project Director didn't allow him to change the name of what was fondly called the most beautiful first-landing city in the Galaxy, so he accepted it graciously.

At least he had miles of beach to walk along, and the climate here in Capital – on Capital Island, in the Capital Archipelago – was sunny and warm, a far cry from Ebensburg's native Berlin. He enjoyed many an afternoon walk a few kilometers down the beach from the office/dormitory complex, as he was doing even now – but his walk today was overshadowed by a crisis he wasn't prepared to face.

His native Berlin was as far from Ebensburg's mind as it was in reality, today. Berlin was roughly two hundred and sixty light years from Caliban, but the problem facing Ebensburg was quite a bit closer – in orbit around the planet, in fact.

Two Grugell Occupation ships had been sighted by an orbiting freighter.

The ships were up there even now, no doubt loaded to capacity with a heavily armed Grugell Occupation force. An orbiting OWME freighter was keeping them under surveillance at a safe distance, but the great disk-shaped cargo hull could do nothing to stop the Grugell ships from launching landing craft. Unless, that is, they wanted to ram. The freighter, the old, space-worn *Rorqual*, was overdue to depart for Earth. The Company would want their ship back soon.

If the Grugell decided to start landing, Ebensburg wouldn't be able to stop them. He had only a thousand or so lightly armed Security troops to hand; Caliban had no dangerous indigenous life forms. All the colony had needed was a modest police force.

Until now.

A frantic message was on its way to Earth, using a tight-beam subspace transmitter called a "hyperphone" – a new toy invented by OWME's technical geniuses on Earth, and only arrived on Caliban the month before. But even a subspace hyperphone message would take weeks to reach Earth, and more weeks would pass before the Company could reply.

A polite cough distracted Ebensburg from his worry. He turned to see his Executive Secretary, Ingrid Holtz, smiling at him.

"Good news, Herr *Direktor*," she told him. "A message from the *Rorqual*."

"Must I stand here and wait for it?" Stress had made the normally affable Ebensburg short-tempered.

"The Grugell ships were seen leaving orbit, *Herr Direktor*. They went into hyper drive just north of the ecliptic and appear to have left the system."

Ebensburg's shoulders sagged in relief. "Very good," he replied. "Very good, for now."

"But what shall we do if they come back?"

*Fraulein Holtz* could only shake her head.

**Tarbos**

"Mr. Pritchard? Hyperphone message coming in." Bob Pritchard started awake at the sudden buzz from his desk comm panel.

"All right, forward it to my terminal, please." His secretary, Ophelia Mae, quickly tapped the message forward from her outer office desk terminal to his.

"Hmph," Pritchard grunted. "From old Steve Ebensburg, eh? Wonder what's up on Caliban." He tapped a key to open the message, reading quickly through the sparse text allowed by the horrendously expensive hyperphone signal.

BOB

FOND HOPES THIS MESSAGE FINDS YOU WELL.

TWO GRUGELL OCCUPATION SHIPS WERE
SIGHTED IN CALIBAN SYSTEM. BOTH SHIPS LEFT
SYSTEM 1812 LOCAL CAPITAL TIME YESTERDAY.

THE GRUGELL ARE BECOMING A PROBLEM OLD
FRIEND. I DO NOT KNOW WHAT WE COLONIES
ARE TO DO IF THEY ATTEMPT ANOTHER
INVASION.

WE ARE ON THE FRINGES OF EXISTENCE WHILE
EARTH DEBATES DEFENDING ONE PLANET. THE
GRUGELL COULD STRIKE AT EARTH HERSELF
TOMORROW ALMOST UNOPPOSED. OUT
HERE WE ARE UTTERLY HELPLESS AGAINST A
REMORSELESS FOE.

WE NEED A NAVY, OLD FRIEND. YOU ARE
THE SENIOR ACTING PROJECT DIRECTOR.
YOUR INFLUENCE IN THIS MATTER WOULD
BE INVALUABLE. I ASK YOUR ASSISTANCE IN
APPROACHING THE BOARD OF DIRECTORS ON
EARTH TO DISCUSS THE MATTER OF ARMED
SHIPS FOR LOCAL DEFENSE.
YOUR TRUSTED FRIEND,
STEFAN EBENSBURG
CALIBAN

"You always had a gift for understatement, Steve old man,"
Pritchard muttered. He hit the "reply" key and typed his response.

STEFAN
I AM WELL. HOPE YOU ARE SAFE AND WELL ALSO.
I HAVE HYPERPHONED BOARD OF DIRECTORS
EARTH ON SUBJECT OF LOST FREIGHTERS. EVEN
THOUGH COST OF LOST FREIGHT SHIP AND
CREW IS GREAT EARTH BOARD CAN DO LITTLE.

COST OF WARSHIPS AND CREW IS ABOVE THE
POSSIBLE MEANS OF OWME.
I HAVE HYPERPHONED UNITED STATES
GOVERNMENT AS WELL. US GOVERNMENT IS
EMBROILED IN DEBATE OVER LOCAL DEFENSE.
PRESIDENT GOMEZ RECOMMENDS COLONIES
CONSCRIPT AND TRAIN MILITIA TO GUARD
AGAINST LANDINGS.
WE ARE ON OUR OWN OLD FRIEND.

An incredible thought slammed into Pritchard's head as he
re-read the last sentence. "We are on our own," he whispered.
"*We* are on our own."

Pritchard leaned back in his chair, staring back at the ceiling.
"The hell we are," he grinned, speaking out loud to the empty
office. "What's Earth got besides a lot of squabbling politicians?
Leave it to businessmen to know how to get things done." He sat
forward and resumed typing.

I BELIEVE IT IS IN OUR BEST INTERESTS TO
FORM AN ALLIANCE OF THE SETTLED WORLDS.
BETWEEN US WE POSSESS RESOURCES THAT
DWARF EARTH'S. AN ALLIANCE COULD FORM AN
ARMED FLEET TO RESIST THE GRUGELL, AND
WITH OUR COMBINED RESOURCES ALL PLANETS
COULD BE PROTECTED ALIKE.
I WILL PROPOSE A MEETING OF
REPRESENTATIVES FROM EACH OF THE COLONIES
HERE ON TARBOS. THE LOCATION IS REASONABLY
CENTRAL AND WE HAVE MORE THAN ADEQUATE
FACILITIES.
OUR FATE IS IN OUR OWN HANDS STEFAN. PRAY
THE CHALLENGE BEFORE US WILL NOT FIND US
WANTING.

REGARDS

ROBERT PRITCHARD

TARBOS

Pritchard hit the key that would send the message to Tarbos' hyperphone transmitter at the top of the Skyhook a few kilometers away, and called up a "New Message" screen to write out the proposal he'd referred to. It would take weeks, months, for all the messages to be received and answers returned, but Pritchard felt certain it would prove to be worth the wait.

He knew he was starting something. But he didn't know yet just how far his proposal was destined to go.

# Three

**Grugell, Imperium Fleet Command Complex**

Kadastrattik XII had been expecting the summons for some time. He strode into the Fleet Commander Pokatik's office with as much confidence as he could muster. His think black hair was oiled down, his black uniform cleanly pressed, his black cloak well brushed; in short, he was as well turned out as the attentions of his three wives could make him.

"You summoned me, Fleet Commander."

"Yes, Commander Kadastrattik. Sit down." The Fleet Commander had his back to the entryway, and didn't bother to turn as Kadastrattik walked in and took a seat on the room's single high stool.

"Are you aware of the ongoing project to determine the shipping lanes used by the humans in their travels between their settled worlds?"

"Yes, Fleet Commander."

"You are aware, then, that the Emperor has taken a personal interest in this project?"

"Yes, Fleet Commander."

Pokatak turned his chair around now, finally, to face his subordinate. "Then you'll appreciate the importance of the orders you are being given, Commander. You have recently completed a tour of duty as Subcommander of a frigate, so you're prepared for this mission." The Fleet Commander reached into his desk, tossed Kadastrattik an information storage crystal. "Examine that carefully. You are being assigned Commander of the newest of our frigates, the K-101. Your first mission will utilize the initial findings of our traffic analysis project."

"A strike mission, Fleet Commander? Surely the time is not yet ripe?"

"You are astute, Commander, and cautious, although not overly so. No, your initial orders are to proceed to the planet indicated on that crystal – the humans call it Tarbos – and monitor ship traffic and transmissions. Your ship's main computer has the latest data on human language that we've been able to decipher."

"Do we suspect this is the human's home world, Fleet Commander?"

"No. The population density is lower than the demographers say it should be, and the settled areas are too recently built. But it seems to be a communications and traffic nexus. It sees far more traffic than any of the other worlds we've located. The home planet would seem to be in a sector we haven't explored yet, and we're hoping that a listening post at Tarbos will lead us to it."

"And when that happens?"

"As the Commander of the successful listening post mission, you'll be ripe for promotion, Kadastrattik. If you earn it, I may place you in command of the Occupation force to invest the human's home world." Pokatak leaned forward, his jet-black eyes narrowing. "And I remind you, the Emperor has taken a personal interest in this matter. In fact, I have had a personal audience with His Majesty myself, and I know the degree of his interest. If you fail in this, Kadastrattik, then the consequences will be dire. Do you understand?"

An image flashed through Kadastrattik's mind; an image of the Imperium's disintegration chambers in the Penal facility. "I understand perfectly, Fleet Commander."

## Forest

"Hey Dad, aircar coming in!" Mike Junior's call from the archery practice area at the lower edge of the meadow broke through Mike's customary late-afternoon doze in the porch swing he'd built some years earlier. He opened his eyes, stretched his arms and yawned. "Who'd be coming in this late in the day?"

Jenny, seated next to Mike in the swing, looked up from her book. "I don't know, honey," she said. "I suppose we'll find out in a minute – here it comes over the trees now."

"Well, there goes my quiet afternoon." Mike stood up and stretched again. The aircar was just settling to the mowed area fifty meters from the front door Mike maintained as a landing area. Mike and Jenny's daughter Andrea, two years younger than Mike Junior, came outside just as the car touched down. "What's going on?" she asked.

Mike didn't expect the first figure out of the air-car, nor the two that followed.

"Beau! Beauregard Rousseau!" Mike burst out. "Look Jenny, it's Beauregard Rousseau!" Mike waved at the gray-haired figure that emerged from the air-car. "And Yuri Pyak? And who's that – Tom Quiet Water?" Mike strode quickly out to greet his former comrades-in-arms.

Beauregard Rousseau was thinner, his hair shot through with gray, but his eyes still glittered with the old mixture of humor and irascibility. "*Comment ça va, garçon?*" he asked, extending a gnarled hand with the little finger missing. "How you been keeping, boy?"

"Great, Beau, just great. You look good!"

"Eh. The knees, they be going, but the heart is still strong," the old Cajun answered, *thump*ing his chest.

"And you, Yuri? Still hunting loggers?"

"*Da*," the little Nenets grinned, as madly cheerful as ever, but much more fluent in English – thanks to the Company's newly developed hypnopedia sleep-teaching programs. "The hunting, it goes well, Mikhail Nelsonovitch. One day you must come on a hunt with me."

"I don't know," Mike laughed. "I don't know if I could handle a cannon like that old Krupp you used to carry. Tom, how are you?"

"Well, my friend." The tall Cheyenne's hair was iron gray at the temples now, but other than that he had changed not a bit. Even his former taciturn nature was still obvious.

"So, what's going on? Why the sudden reunion?"

The air-car's pilot finally emerged, removing a helmet to reveal a cascade of bright-red hair.

"Mr. Crider?" the woman asked. "That'd be me," Mike answered, gaping a little.

The woman wore the uniform of a Colonel in OWME Security, although she looked to be no older than thirty. She was short, like most OWME air-car pilots, and slight – she probably weighed no more than 45 kilograms soaking wet. Her eyes shone a bright, steady green from a narrow, ivory face stippled with freckles.

"I'm Colonel Celia MacFarlane," she said, extending a narrow hand to shake Mike's. "I'm the new Head of Security for Forest, since Colonel Wells retired. It's an honor to meet you, sir."

Mike waved a hand in a dismissive gesture. "Don't believe everything you hear, Colonel."

Colonel McFarlane regarded Mike closely for a moment. "Sir, there's a matter of some importance I've been asked to discuss with you. Could we talk inside?"

"Yes – yes, of course."

They crowded into the Crider household's tiny living room, finding only a small fireplace, a tiny vidscreen/terminal, a small couch and two old, upholstered chairs.

"I'm afraid there's not too much room," Jenny apologized, bringing in two extra chairs from the bedroom. "We don't get many visitors up here."

"This be fine," Rousseau half-bowed gallantly. "You be as pretty as ever, *belle*." Jenny dimpled at the old Cajun. Mike motioned the others to seats and took his own accustomed place in the chair nearest the fireplace. His old Parks double, still clean, oiled and well maintained, hung over the mantle.

"So, Colonel," he began, "You said you had something important to talk about."

"Yes, Mr. Crider, I do. Bert Grolier, the Forest Project Director, sent me to speak to you." Mike raised his eyebrows questioningly.

"To put it rather bluntly, Mr. Crider, we'd like to ask you to represent Forest at a meeting on Tarbos."

"Me? Why me? What kind of meeting?"

"A meeting of representatives from all the colonized planets, sir, and from Earth, too. They're going to discuss forming an association of the colonies to form a Navy."

"The Grugell, right?"

"Yes. The Grugell. They've been picking off freighters, four this year alone, and several of their Occupation ships have been sighted orbiting worlds we've already colonized. So far there haven't been any landings, but…"

"It's only a matter of time," Tom Quiet Water added softly.

"You didn't answer my first question. Why me?"

"The Director will never leave Forest again, Mr. Crider," Colonel McFarlane said. "His heart condition won't allow it. The

Assistant Director is too young and inexperienced; the Director doesn't have any confidence in her."

"While you, *tovarisch*, are the Hero of Forest. Your voice carries much weight, Mikhail." Yuri Pyak was actually solemn, adding greatly to the gravity of the moment.

"And they're going to be needing sensible voices in this thing," Rousseau grunted. "Old Rousseau, I'd go myself, but these old bones, they ain't going to take no rocket launches. An' Carrie, her leg gets worse these last few years. She don't need to be alone for nine-ten months."

"You're talking about a Constitutional Convention," Mike observed. "I did study history in school, you know. You're talking about setting up a Galactic government. That's what it will take to form a Navy. You'll have to combine resources of all the colonies, and Earth, too."

"*Da*," Yuri agreed. "It's a Navy we need."

Mike stood up and turned towards the fireplace, more deeply troubled than he cared to admit. He turned to look at Jenny, who was looking into the cold fireplace with a contemplative expression. Mike Junior stood in the doorway next to Andrea; both of them looked thunderstruck.

"Kids, you may as well come in and sit down. This affects all of us," Mike told them. Mike Junior and Andrea seated themselves on the stone hearth, looking up at their father, alarm registering on the young faces.

"I still don't see why you want me to go," Mike said at last. "I'm not qualified for anything like this. I don't have any education in government or politics. Hell, I never went to college, I only just graduated high school." He turned to face the others, his hands held out almost pleadingly. "I'm just a Company hunter and pioneer. What business do I have at a Constitutional Convention?"

"You're an American, are ye not?" Colonel MacFarlane asked, her brogue deepening somewhat.

"Yes, born and raised in Idaho. I don't see the connection."

"Who founded your country, Mr. Crider? Who fought and died for it?"

"Farmers. Plantation owners. Shopkeepers. Woodsmen." Mike answered.

"People like you, sir. You're the Hero of the Grugell Invasion, Mr. Crider."

"You the man, Mike." Rousseau agreed.

"There's no one on the planet better suited to represent Forest's interests at the meeting."

"I don't know," Mike equivocated.

"Michael." Mike turned to see Thomas Quiet Water standing up, his arms folded across his chest.

"This thing that we ask you to do is a tremendous thing. You will be spoken of in history classes for hundreds of years. So will all that attend this convention."

"But think well on your answer, Michael. You wish to stay here in the home you have built, with the family that you have raised here. These are the normal wishes of any normal man. But you are not a normal man, Michael. Events in the past, when the four of us fought alongside the other heroes who are not here tonight, Nathaniel, Mick and Tak, they have proven you to be more than the ordinary man.

The tall Cheyenne took two steps to face Mike, placing one hand on his shoulder.

"This meeting, this convention, it will have many men of education, many of sophistication, many of political learning and experience. But such men are not frequently men of courage, Michael. They are thinkers, not actors. Forest is not like the other worlds, my old friend. Forest is not a world of industry and trade.

Forest is a world of hunters, farmers, and pioneers. We do not need a politician or a businessman to represent us. We need a man of courage and vision. You are that man, Michael."

Mike turned to his wife. "Jenny?" he asked.

Jenny looked into the cold ashes of the fireplace for a few more moments before answering.

"I hate the idea, Mike. I hate the idea of you being gone for what, nine, ten months? But Mike, I have to admit, I agree with Tom and the others. You're the logical person to go."

"Can I take my family with me?" Mike asked, still looking into Jenny's eyes.

"The Company will cover transport for you and your family," Colonel MacFarlane answered.

"For you," Jenny corrected. "Andrea still has a year of hypnopedia and cyber-school. We're staying here."

"Mom!" Andrea protested but subsided quickly at a gesture from her mother.

"What about me?" Mike Junior asked. "I graduated cyber-school a year ago."

"I'd like to have Junior come with me," Mike admitted. "Jenny?"

"It is time he got out, broadened his horizons some. I think it'd be good for him," Jenny agreed. She was smiling, but a tear glistened in the corner of her eye.

"When would we have to be ready to leave?"

"There's a passenger liner inbound from Earth in nine weeks. It stops here for four days, then ships for Tarbos."

Mike threw up his hands. "All right. All right."

"I knew when I met you, Mike, that you were something more than just an ordinary man," Jenny noted. "And you've always shown that to be true. Thomas is right, Mike. They'll need someone like you to speak for the little people in this new interstellar government."

"Oh, man," Mike Junior exulted. "Tarbos! I've heard stories about Tarbos!"

Mike looked at his grown son with some dismay. He turned to Colonel MacFarlane.

"All right. Nine weeks from today, we'll be in Settlement with our bags packed."

"Thank you, Mr. Crider. Mr. Grolier will be delighted at the news."

"I just wish I could say I was delighted," Mike frowned. He shook his head. "Well, that's decided. Colonel, please sit down. Tom, Beau, Yuri, let me get us all a drink. We've all got a lot of catching up to do."

# Four

**High Earth Orbit**

An enormous disk of a ship coasted slowly towards high Earth orbit. A slight glow of a Gellar drive under one-quarter power slowly edged the enormous disk into the parking orbit recently vacated by the passenger liner *Star of Carolina*, just departed on the Forest – Tarbos - Harvey run. Once the huge cargo hull made a good orbit, the immense disk would detach and descend through the atmosphere to Off-World Mining & Exploration's Fairplay, Colorado warehousing complex to be unloaded and reloaded. The command module would remain in orbit.

As the huge hull turned slowly in the bright light of the Sun coming over Earth's north pole, the name of the ship became visible on the edge of the gray-painted disk:

CACHALOT

**The White House**

President Gomez stared at the message form before him, reading the last paragraph again for the thousandth time that day.

THEREFORE, IT BECOMES APPARENT THAT WE
MUST FORM AN ASSOCIATION OF SETTLED

PLANETS TO PROVIDE FOR THE COMMON
DEFENSE. I PROPOSE A MEETING OF THE
PROJECT DIRECTORS AND SENIOR STAFF OF THE
COLONY PLANETS AND MAJOR GOVERNMENT
LEADERS FROM EARTH HERE ON TARBOS IN JUST
OVER EIGHTEEN MONTHS, JUNE 1 2233. LIST OF
PROPOSED ATTENDEES FOLLOWS.

Halfway down, *following* the list of OWME's Project Directors, came four heads of state from Earth:

UNITED STATES OF AMERICA PRESIDENT
ANTHONY GOMEZ
UNITED KINGDOM PRIME MINISTER JUSTIN
MACDOWELL
RUSSIAN FEDERATION PRESIDENT KONSTANTIN
GOGOL
REPUBLIC OF CHINA PRESIDENT KEE CHOW AN

*The Japanese aren't going to appreciate being left off this list,*
Gomez thought with a dark chuckle. *They pretty much own the
low-Earth orbit commercial satellite business.*

"There's a word for what they want to form, Tony," Hector
Gutierrez told him from his seat on the other side of the massive
desk. "It's not a nice word here in the States, thanks to a dark bit
of our history, but it's accurate. They want to form a Confederation. A limited association of sovereign states formed to regulate
trade and provide for a common defense."

"You're right, *ése* – and when you're right, you're right." In
private, the two tended to talk like the old childhood friends they
were. "And it's not a bad idea, either. That's what America was
founded to be." He dropped the message form on the polished
desktop. "Remember the Liberal/Progressive movements of the
late 20th century? The old Democratic Party? That almost sunk

that notion altogether, until the Third World War and the Liber-tarian Party's becoming a force in national politics." Gomez stood up and turned to look out the window, hands clasped behind him, unconsciously adopting the posture made famous by another President, many decades earlier. "Can you believe the Republican Party was on the *right* of national politics those days, and it was the old Democratic Party that was considered the 'left?' It's only been the last fifty years that we managed to undo a lot of what they did back then – at least now Congress and the Supreme Court remembers that there's a Constitution. I hear tell that some of them have actually read it."

Vice President Gutierrez was looking thoughtfully at the ceiling, his mind turning over very rapidly. "And what's more, if they manage to put something together, they'll have to have a plebiscite of the various planets to put it in place – at least, if they want to have a free population. How's that going to work on Earth, with all these different nations? Most all the planet has elected governments now, but there hasn't been a serious international forum since the old UN collapsed in the mid two-thousands."

"I'm not too worried about that. There's the European Common Market, the African Confederation that's still trying to form up, the Asian/Pacific Co-Prosperity Alliance, and the North American Free Trade Organization – and for that matter, there's still technically a UN office in Belgium, you know. We'll work something out, if there ends up being a good reason to do it."

"So, are you going to this meeting? We can sure get passage on an OWME passenger liner, but you're looking at being off-Earth and out of touch for at least a year, *amigo*. The 'esteemed opposition' is gonna take it out of your hide in the next election, bro, if you leave planet for a year."

Gomez smiled lazily, like a cat contemplating a canary with a broken wing. "I know. That's why I'm sending you."

"*Me?*"

"You, Heck," Gomez grinned at the Vice President as he invoked an ancient childhood nickname. "You're the man this time. You'll have to speak for the United States. I can't go – you just explained one reason, and there are plenty of others. We still have a domestic agenda, remember?"

"You still want to push ahead with a planetary defense?"

"Damn right. Let's be real, Heck – there isn't likely to be too much come out of this meeting. You expect a bunch of business-men to form a Galactic government?"

"From where I sit, *mijo*, it doesn't seem all that unlikely. You and I have only been pols for what, nine years? What were we doing before that?"

Gomez shrugged, conceding the point. "Well, that's all the more reason for you to go – I can't send a second-level functionary to something like this, and besides, I can trust you. These others," Gomez waved a hand vaguely at the Oval Office doors, "they're all Washington regulars. You and me, we went to school together, built a business together, we were in the trenches together. I need *you* to go to Tarbos, Heck."

"I guess I can't argue with that. So, when should I figure on leaving?"

"There's an OWME liner leaving for Forest in three weeks, and then it goes from there to Tarbos. I've already got berths for you, Sandy, Maria and Manuel."

"Well, at least my family gets a year-long space vacation. Say, will there be any landfall on Forest? Manuel always wanted to see it, ever since he read about the Grugell Invasion in middle school."

"I'm sure you can arrange something," Gomez said.

## Tarbos

A scattering of hyperphone replies lay on Bob Pritchard's desk. Aside from his old friend Stefan Ebensburg on Caliban, he'd received replies in the affirmative from all of the thirteen inhabited worlds. He read the names with a great deal of satisfaction:

FROM EARTH:

UNITED STATES, VICE PRESIDENT HECTOR GUTIERREZ

UNITED KINGDOM, PRINCE HARRY IV, PRINCE OF WALES

RUSSIA, VICE PRESIDENT VLADIMIR TARAKANOV

CHINA, PRIME MINISTER KEE CHOW AN

*Only China's Head of State is coming in person*, Pritchard noted. *Well, that's to be expected – a major nation's President can't really be off world for a year. I wonder how Kee Chow An is getting away with it? His Parliament must be going nuts…* He continued reading.

Caliban, Halifax, Forest, Selin, Chernov, New Albion, Zed, Harvey, Coronado, Arabia; all the names of attendees were of Assistant Directors or other high-level executives, but only Caliban's Stefan Ebensburg was coming in person; and as yet, there was no answer from Corinthia. The name of the attendee from Forest was familiar, but didn't belong to any OWME executive that Pritchard could remember. *Crider*, he asked himself, *Crider, where have I heard that name before?*

*Of course! The Grugell invasion on Forest, he's the big hero that led the scouts. The Battle of Crider Meadow, when they shut off the orbital broadcast power. Well, that's interesting – he'll be the only ordinary citizen here, not a politician or an executive. I wonder why they picked him? Old Bert Grolier's heart probably won't stand a shuttle launch from Forest, but he's got assistants. Why this Crider fellow?*

But the meeting was on, and it was only now that the thought occurred to Pritchard that had occurred to several other people in the process already: *We're forming an interstellar government, here.*

*I wonder what we should call it?*

He stood up, gathering the stack of replies and dropping them in a drawer. A stab at a silver button on his desktop opened an audio channel to his primary assistant. "Marie? I'll be over at the Central Library for a while."

"All right."

Pritchard strode from his office, thinking hard: *I've got a lot of preparation to do in the next few weeks.*

# Five



**A shuttle approaching the OWME Passenger Liner *Star of Carolina*, orbiting Forest**

"Geez, Dad, that thing is huge."

"It's not as big as the old *Mayflower*, but it'll do," Mike Crider agreed with his son, staring at the huge, slate-blue mass of the passenger liner from his window seat in the orbital shuttle. "It's going to take us a while to get to Tarbos, wherever that is, so we may as well be comfortable." He dropped back into the bucket seat with a sigh. "At least the Company is picking up the tab for this trip. I don't want to think about what a trip on a liner like that would cost. It cost me everything I had to get me to Forest twenty years ago," he exaggerated.

Mike Junior craned his neck to keep the liner in sight as the shuttle adjusted course. "Why'd you pick Forest anyway, Dad? Don't they use hunter-pioneers on other planets?"

"Yeah, I'm sure they do. It's a long story, Junior, but basically, I saw a recruiting poster in the market one day, and an old friend sort of talked me into it. Next thing I knew, I was on the way." He tilted his big gray Stetson back on his head. "Not that I'd change anything, if I was to do it all over again. If I hadn't come to Forest, I wouldn't ever have met your mother, for one thing."

"And Mom would have been killed by a roc, along with our grandparents."

"That's right. Anyway, from what I hear, Earth's more crowded than ever. Idaho is a great place, son, and I hope one day you'll get to see it, but there's sure a lot of people. Forest is nice and quiet."

"Too quiet, sometimes." The younger man lapsed into a pensive silence for a few minutes before speaking up again. "Dad, by the way, do you think you could not call me 'Junior,' while we're on the ship and on Tarbos?"

Mike turned to stare at his son. "What? We've called you Junior since you were born."

"Come on, Dad, I'm a grown man now. 'Junior' just doesn't get it, you know? Can't you just call me Mike?"

"Not 'Little Mike?' We used to call you that, you know. How about 'Mikey?'" his father teased.

"Dad!"

"I think I'm following you, son," Mike Senior teased. "There sure aren't very many girls on Forest, but there's bound to be a bunch of them on that liner," he pointed out the viewport, "And more on Tarbos. Especially with this big convention going on."

"I don't know what you're talking about, Dad," Mike Junior chuckled.

"Uh huh." It would be another hour before the cranky old shuttle made it to the *Star of Carolina*'s docking bay. Mike smiled and, tipping his big hat down over his eyes, leaned back for a short nap.

## The *Star of Carolina*'s docking bay

Eighteen-year-old Maria Gutierrez found the trip from Earth of differing levels of interest, in stages.

The trip up the Quito Skyhook and the shuttle ride to the ship was exciting. Settling into one of the giant liner's VIP suites was exciting. Watching on the terminal viewer as the ship accelerated and leaped into subspace was exciting.

The weeks-long stretch after that was boring.

Now things were getting exciting again, as Maria stood with her father at a port, watching the shuttle approach. She didn't find the vast green and blue expanse of the wilderness below interesting; there were no cities, no air traffic was visible, and the liner's planetary information system told her that there wasn't much there for a big-city girl (as Maria invariably thought of herself, having grown up in Denver) to find interesting. There wasn't even a Skyhook; the boarding passengers had to batter their way up the gravity well in an old orbital shuttle.

But the rather banged-up old shuttle that was approaching the ship now carried a living, breathing historical figure about whom Maria had read in her recent history classes. The Hero of Forest, Mike Crider, was on that ship, and she was going to get to meet him!

"Maria, honey, back away from the port, let your brother have a look." Sandra and Hector Gutierrez stood behind their children, awaiting the arrival of the representative from Forest. Maria stepped back to let her fifteen-year-old brother Manuel peer through the heavy polymer port.

"Hey, that's some busted-up old junk," he commented.

"Forest isn't a real profitable venture for OWME," his father informed him. "There's no mineral wealth, not much for petrochemicals, no precious metals. Mostly farming. It's going to be the breadbasket of the Galaxy one day, but right now, it's still mostly wilderness."

"That's still some busted-up old junk," Manuel repeated.

The shuttle coasted into the cavernous docking bay of the *Star of Carolina*, stopping with a puff of maneuvering thrusters. A docking tube extended outwards, connecting finally to the hatch on the side of the craft.

"Let's head over to the gate. I want to meet Mr. Crider as soon as he debarks."

"Yes, I suppose we should. Kids, come on." Sandra Gutierrez tapped both teenagers on the shoulder. "Let's go."

Only a handful of people debarked from the shuttle. Hector Gutierrez lined his family up at the port and waited patiently as the passengers filed off.

"There he is," he said suddenly. The figure that emerged from the port was easily recognizable from old pictures Gutierrez had seen; all of the settled worlds had seen photos of the Hero of Forest, and anyone would recognize the tall, lean, taciturn frontiersman with the trademark blue cotton work shirt, blue jeans, laced boots and big gray Stetson hat. Behind him stepped a second man, younger, but otherwise a near duplicate of the veteran of the Grugell Occupation.

The Vice President stepped forward, hand extended. "Mr. Crider?"

Mike smiled, a little intimidated at being so far out of his element. "Yeah, that's me. This is my son, Mike Junior."

Gutierrez shook Mike's hand in a rock-hard grip. "Hector Gutierrez, Mike. I've looked forward to meeting you." He turned to introduce his family. "This is my wife Sandra, my daughter Maria, and my son Manuel."

Mike Junior felt his heart take a sudden lurch. Maria Gutierrez looked at him with a dazzling smile. Her dark eyes sparkled, her raven-black hair shone, her teeth were even and white, her skin smooth and silken. She extended her hand towards him, smiling sweetly.

"Hi. This is all pretty exciting, isn't it?"

"Uh, yeah," Mike Junior stuttered, shaking her hand lightly, suddenly conscious of her soft, warm fingers clasped in his own thick, callused hand. "Yeah, I suppose it is."

"Have you ever been off Forest before?"

"No, this is my first time," he replied, finding his voice again. "Heck, I've only been as far as Settlement a few times. Dad doesn't have much use for towns."

"Oh, well, I guess we'll be seeing quite a city on Tarbos."

Mike Junior suddenly realized he was still holding her hand. He let go as though her slim fingers had suddenly turned red-hot. *Wow*, he thought.

Mike Senior and Hector Gutierrez hadn't missed the exchange. They looked at each other with raised eyebrows.

"I think this is going to be an interesting trip," Gutierrez observed.

"I think you're right, Mr. Vice President," Mike grinned.

"Call me Hector, Mr. Crider, please. Oh, hell, call me Heck. That's what all my friends call me."

"Only if you drop the 'Mr. Crider' business and call me Mike," the Hero of Forest answered.

"Agreed. I only hope the rest of the issues at this conference can be settled that easily!"

Mike frowned, remembering the stack of notes he had in his luggage, products of a week's reading in the Settlement Library. "I'm not betting a penny on that."

**Earth, high orbit**

OWME's high orbit spacedock contained, among other things, the best zero-gee physics lab that had yet been devised. Hans Richter, as one of Earth's foremost working physicists, was

OWME's first choice to head up the staff at that lab. Hired away from The Planck Institute three years earlier, he had immediately gone to work cataloging interstellar dark matter ratios, hopefully to improve the efficiency of the Gellar Star Drives mounted by OWME ships. To that end, he had sent scanners out on OWME ships traveling all the standard trade routes, and kept his staff working late into the nights analyzing the data each time a ship returned.

What his scanners had found, on three occasions, were strange clear areas in his spatial matter density scans – "blank spaces" in space, baffling to Doctor Richter, intriguing to the American government's Air Force Chief of Staff who had visited the labs. Three weeks after Air Force General Janine LeBlanc had visited the lab, she'd returned with a question.

"A cloaked ship? You mean a Grugell ship?" Doctor Richter hadn't even considered that possibility.

General LeBlanc answered tersely. "Yes, exactly that. We want to know if a cloaked Grugell ship could be responsible for those blank spaces."

"It's possible. We don't have any idea, really, how the Grugell cloak works. We assume it either renders the ship transparent to the electromagnetic spectrum, or that it somehow bends light waves around the ship's mass. A strong gravimetric field could conceivably do that, but we've no idea how they would generate or control such a field, and the stresses on the ship's structure would be far, far beyond the capabilities of any material we know of."

"So, it's more likely the former, then."

"Jah. And while the ship is shielded from observation, it still 'sweeps' an area of space in passage, either displacing or removing the normal traces of interstellar matter. They may well use them as we do, to power their drive systems."

"Could you adapt your scanner to track the passage of a cloaked ship?"

"Easily, given some added computer support."

General LeBlanc stood up. "I'll have a funding voucher faxed to you from the Pentagon within the hour. I've already cleared it with your bosses at the Company HQ in Denver. This will be your top priority now – get your plans together, build a prototype if you have to, and get us documents on how to build a tracker."

"Yes, I'll start right away," Richter answered softly, his scientist's mind already turning over with procedures and plans.

That had been five months ago. Today, Doctor Richter had learned that the plans for his adapted scanner had been hyper-phoned to Tarbos. For what reason, General LeBlanc had declined to say.

## Half a light-year outside the Tarbos system

Not even a shimmering in the star field betrayed the passage of the cloaked ship; the Grugell frigate slid through space like a wraith, invisible, undetectable. Alone and unsupported, the diminutive warship coasted towards the Tarbos system, decelerating slowly at a rate that would bring it out of subspace a little over a hundred thousand kilometers (the Grugell, of course, used their own units of measure) outside the orbit of the sole inhabited planet.

The *K-101* was built on the standard frigate pattern, a sleek, shining silver fuselage between two arms supporting the drive pods. The main cabin was somewhat cramped for the crew of six officers and twenty crew, but Grugell society was Spartan in nature, and none of the crewmembers thought that things might ever be any different. There was one recent innovation that made life easier aboard ship; this newest frigate had special deck plates that produced a gravity field, approximating the sea-level gravity of Grugell itself.

And deep in the bowels of the ship, shielded by three different energy fields and wired to a self-destruct charge, was the unfathomable black sphere of the cloaking unit. It hummed now in its darkened compartment, exerting its unknowable influence to warp all forms of electromagnetic energy around the body of the *K-101*.

Two decks above the crew quarters and tiny dining area and one deck above the officer's staterooms, the bridge was small and claustrophobic as was the rest of the ship. The Commander had the only really comfortable seat on the ship, a large chair in the center of the Bridge that swiveled to face the various stations on the circular compartment: Navigation, Helm, Weapons, Signals, Scanning. A large viewscreen dominated one wall, at present displaying only the weird, shifting patterns of subspace.

"All stations, report status," Commander Kadastrattik XII barked from his bridge chair.

"Helm, Commander. We are on course, scheduled to leave subspace as planned, we will assume station one hundred thousand kilos from the planet as you have commanded."

"Navigation, Commander. Confirm we are on course."

"Scanning, Commander. All scanners are nominal. No other detectable ships are in the area." He didn't bother to explain that detecting another ship in subspace was all but impossible without actually running into it. "We are prepared to begin detailed scans of the planet and surrounding space upon reaching station."

"Weapons, Commander. Torpedoes are stowed, all units tested and operational. Anti-proton projectors are fully charged and functional. Cloaking device is functioning normally."

"Signals, Commander. No incoming messages."

"Excellent." Kadastrattik was a careful Commander, a cautious and prudent Grugell, and a veteran of the debacle of the failed Occupation under Clomonastik III. His orders were simple, if somewhat cryptic, and the manner in which he was to accomplish his final goal had been left to his discretion.

Communications intercepts indicated a meeting of some sort was to take place on this planet. The humans were, Fleet Intelligence predicted, attempting to form an interplanetary alliance. His orders were to prevent that from happening.

All he needed was a brief window of opportunity.

And, to his good fortune, he had an idea of how to achieve that as well.

He leaned back in his chair now, smiling slightly, visions of Group Commander rank floating deliciously through his head.

# Six

**The *Star of Carolina*, in transit**

"Did you ever imagine anything like it?"

One of the *Star of Carolina*'s outstanding features was its observation bubble, a large poly-steel blister on the outer hull that offered a slowly rotating view of space – or, in this case, the weird, continually shifting, unfathomable patterns of subspace. The only down side was that, to accommodate the passenger compartment's rotation to provide gravity, you had to strap into seats that rotated into the bubble at the touch of a switch – and the ship's rotation made you feel as though you were hanging upside-down.

"Not me. I've seen stars before, from Forest, but nothing like this."

Mike Crider (Junior) and Maria Gutierrez sat in the observation bubble, ostensibly watching the streams of subspace whipping past but really just enjoying each other's company. Maria's raven-black hair cascaded down, framing her face. Mike's attention was constantly torn from the spectacle of subspace by the nearer, more fathomable, and yet more beautiful sight seated next to him.

"Daddy says you don't see stars in subspace. He's not even sure that there are stars in subspace. Oh, look there!" Maria pointed at a vermilion whorl that spun, danced at the edge of vision and was gone, somewhere far aft of the hurtling ship. "I wonder what that was."

"Beats me. Most impressive thing I've seen before was a logger out on the eastern savannah, and that wasn't a patch on this."

"What's a logger?"

"Big things, herbivores, live out on the fern prairies and savannahs east of our mountains. They're about six to ten meters long, armor-plated, with big horn blades sticking out to the sides." He held his hands a meter apart to show the size of a logger's side spikes. "A beak like a turtle – they can bite right through a tree trunk. They've got big plates of horn on their backs and necks, and they walk on their hind feet and the knuckles of their hands. First one I ever saw was a big bull, leaning back on his tail to strip a tree along a branch of the East Fork River. He was leaning back on his tail, using the big, hooked claws on his front feet to hook down branches to eat. Thing was like two stories tall.

"Dad knows a guy who hunts them, but I'm not about to try it. Rocs are plenty exciting enough. Plus, you have to use a rocket launcher or a cannon to kill one."

"I've never seen anything much bigger than a deer, but I've always been a city girl," Maria confessed.

"Well, you've got me beat there. I've hardly ever seen a town. Just Settlement, and it isn't much. Heck, Forest doesn't even have a Skyhook yet."

"Daddy says it's mostly farmers."

Mike Junior smiled as he watched a pattern of violet sparkles cascade past, fading to a dull green as they went. "Yeah, I suppose it is, ships always re-provision at Forest – this one did, we watched two cargo hulls of food shot up before our shuttle took off from Settlement. But we're not farmers, we're pioneers. We hunt for meat, hide and feathers for the colony."

"You hunt wild animals?" Maria asked, frowning a little. "Doesn't it bother you, killing animals?"

"What'd you have for breakfast this morning, Maria?"

"Oatmeal, eggs, sausage – a little chorizo," Maria answered.

"Sausage, eh? Think the pig gave it up voluntarily?"

"OK," she smiled. "I see your point. But it's got to be lonely, living way up there in the mountains." Maria leaned a tiny bit closer; the herbal scent of her glossy black hair filled Mike Junior's senses. "Don't you ever miss being around people?"

"Sometimes. Can't really miss what you never had."

"I guess."

A trail of salmon-pink ripples cascaded past the viewport, turning rapidly through white to end up bright blue.

"What do you think Tarbos will be like?"

"Beats me," Mike answered. "I guess there's a big city, just down from the hills where they Skyhook comes down – Dad says it's called Mountain View. It's supposed to be one of the prettiest cities in the Galaxy. Well, that we know of, anyway."

"I've never been off Earth," Maria said softly.

"Yeah, I've never been off Forest."

"It's a little scary, isn't it?"

Mike Junior thought about that for a moment. "Well, maybe a little, but not like a guts-turning-to-water kind of scary, like when you make a bad shot on a roc and he turns and comes after you, twenty feet tall and screeching bloody murder. It's more like a final-exam-in-cyber school kind of scary, when you know you've been goofing off out in the woods and not studying."

Maria laughed, tossing her raven hair in a way that made Mike's heart hammer in his chest. "I hadn't thought of it quite like that. Has that really happened to you? I read about rocs in science class when I was in high school – you really had one come after you? A wounded one?"

"Yeah," Mike answered, remembering. "I was only sixteen, and my shot went a little low. I had the other barrel loaded with a shotshell, too – stupid. Dad gave me some hell about it later."

Maria sat quietly for a moment, waiting, and then impulsively punched Mike on the upper arm. "So, tell me what happened!"

"Oh, yeah. Well, Dad got him with a high-ex round. Dropped him in a full charge – he slid up to about ten feet from my boot toes. I couldn't move for about five minutes." He omitted mentioning another, more embarrassing consequence of that close call – one that had required a change of undergarments.

"I imagine so!" Maria casually reached for Mike's hand, intertwining her fingers with his. "I hope that sort of thing doesn't happen very often. I'd just as soon you stayed safe, you know."

"Uh, no. Not very often." Mike's powers of articulation had suddenly diminished, but he managed to give Maria's hand a squeeze.

Outside the bubble, a swirl of light blue faded through purple to a light pink, culminating in a starburst of brilliant white.

Maria and Mike Junior sat quietly watching the weird, unpredictable lightshow of subspace as the *Star of Carolina* plunged on through the unfathomable continuum of subspace towards Tarbos.

## Corinthia

Of all the settled worlds, there was only one that was not a project of Off-World Mining & Exploration.

Twenty-six years earlier, the younger brother to the United Kingdom's King Charles III led an expedition to an undeveloped planet. Prince Harold intended to re-establish a true monarchy, and with the wealth of the Royal Family behind him, he contracted an OWME liner to transport himself, his family, and six thousand, two hundred and forty-three followers to Corinthia, where he was crowned King Harold I.

Corinthia was then discovered to have an amazing, no, a stunning wealth of mineral riches. Corinthia's crust contained incredible amounts of titanium, germanium, rhodium, all the valuable construction and power metals, silver and gold as well. In the space of five years, mining operations made the privately held planet very, very wealthy indeed, and King Harold I became the wealthiest man in the Galaxy by a considerable margin, surpassing even the recently deceased Hiram Gellar.

But the message from Tarbos had come as a shock. Harold I had what he liked to refer to as "a very nice little arrangement" on Corinthia, and he wasn't enamored of the idea of a Galactic government suddenly wanting to impose rules and regulations on his privately held planet.

And so, it was a very disturbed King Harold I of Corinthia that called a meeting of his chief advisers to discuss the proposed meeting on Tarbos.

"Would someone please tell me what precisely is to Corinthia's benefit in all this?" The King glared at his Ministers, seated before him around an enormous conference table of local wood.

"Sire, we need to examine the logic carefully." Lord Alfred Roth was the King's Minister of Planetary Affairs, his best and most trusted friend. "This Pritchard, he makes a compelling argument. I would point out, Your Majesty, that Corinthia is unfortunately located on the far edge of settled space. There are no colonies farther from Earth than we in this direction; there are no other settled worlds to serve as buffers between the Grugell and us, or for that matter any other hostile races who may exist. The common defense alone is worthy of serious consideration."

"We will have our own shipyards operating in three years," the King pointed out. "Can we not build our own ships, our own defenses?"

"We could, sire; but the cost would run into the billions."
This came from Lord Nigel Sands, his Minister of Finance. "I've
researched the issue. A modest fleet of ten armed ships for local
defense would cost a great deal indeed." He handed the King a
pad. "I've taken the liberty of summarizing the costs involved. It's
important to note that we would also be required to seek technical
experts in the area of weaponry. We have successfully recruited
drive engineers and spaceship architects from Earth, but we have
no weapons experts."

The King took his time perusing the pad's screen while his
Ministers waited patiently.

"I'm not entirely convinced, you know," he said at last.

"It would be imprudent of you to make a decision so quickly,
Your Majesty," Lord Roth answered.

"Yes, but it would also be imprudent for us to fail to attend
this conference, would it not? And so we shall. In fact, I'll go
myself. Lord Roth, you will accompany me to Tarbos. This conference is scheduled to begin in," he shuffled through a pile of papers
on the table, "six weeks. The Royal yacht will take less than four to
make the journey to Tarbos; this gives you two weeks to prepare."

"As you wish, sire."

"Prepare a message for this chap Pritchard. Tell him Corinthia
will be represented."

**Tarbos, five weeks later**

Mountain View had never been this busy. For that matter, Bob
Pritchard had never been this busy before, either.

A month's worth of research went into the conference's
program. A month spent in the Tarbos Main Library, researching
Earth history, government, economics, trade issues, a dozen

or more smaller topics. The result was a pad bearing roughly a terabyte of data, to be handed to each delegation on their arrival.

Pritchard had arranged quarters for the delegates at the Tarbos-Mountain View Marriott, which wasn't nearly as impressive as it sounded. Tarbos had little need for hotel facilities, and the hotel was crammed to capacity with the seventeen delegates, their families and aides. In fact, the big new Tide Pool hotel/casino up the coastline from Mountain View would have been far more suitable, but the commute – even by air-car – was considerable.

And the delegates were beginning to arrive. Three this morning, and the rest expected within a week.

### The *K-101*, outside Tarbos' orbit

A hundred and twenty thousand kilometers outside Tarbos' orbit, the undetected and undetectable still held station. Boredom had set in long since; a warrior race with a violent history, the Grugell society did not cultivate patience.

"Incoming message from the Imperium, Commander." Kadas-trattik turned in his bridge chair to take the message form.

> MONITOR COMM-CHANNEL 175 STANDARD.
> IMPERIUM INTELLIGENCE SERVICE HAS MADE
> CONTACT WITH AN INFORMATION SOURCE ON
> THE PLANET.

A series of codes and alternative action plans followed the terse opening. In due time they'd receive a message. The message would tell them how to proceed.

## The *Star of Carolina*

The *Star of Carolina* had dropped out of subspace the day before, and was now proceeding towards Tarbos on one-third drive.

"That's Tarbos now." Hector Gutierrez pointed out a blue and white sphere to his family as they stood alongside the Criders in the Star's Stellar Cartography suite, looking at a playback of the main navigation scanner. "It's a heavy planet, I understand – you'll feel about ten percent heavier than in the one-gee they keep on most of the liner's passenger compartments. Lots of minerals. Rich planet. They say Mountain View is the most beautiful city on any of the settled worlds. It's even got nice beaches."

"Not like Forest," Mike Senior observed. "I'm afraid Forest's always going to be a poor planet."

"How do you figure?"

"Well, we're mostly farmers on Forest, you know. There are no mineral deposits that anyone has ever found, nothing to mine or manufacture with. We have to import almost all of our manufactured goods. The soil is fantastic, Earth crops grow really well and there are a couple of native plants that the science guys say they'll be able to alter for crop growing. But farmers are always on the bottom of the economic heap. In good times there's plenty to go around and crop prices are low, so the farmers don't make much money. And in bad times… well, you remember reading about 1930's America? The Dust Bowl?"

"That was mostly due to bad farming practices, but I see your point."

"Yeah. Well, this is going to be a whole different deal. Maybe things will change. They say Forest is going to be the breadbox of the Galaxy one day," Mike Senior added hopefully.

Beside him, Mike Junior's hand sought out Maria Gutierrez's. She returned the pressure of his thick, work-roughened hands with a squeeze of her own slim fingers, and smiled a small, secret smile.

"Is there a moon, Daddy?" Maria asked.

"One little one," Hector Gutierrez answered his daughter. "About the size of Phobos."

"That's sad," Maria whispered in Mike Junior's ear. "Nights aren't very romantic with no moon."

"They will be," the younger Crider promised her. "Trust me."

# Seven

**Tarbos, the Main Conference Hall**

The Main Hall was full, full of delegates and their aides in the front, families, friends and curious Tarbosians in the rear. Bob Pritchard strode into the room, walking purposefully up the main aisle to the front of the room.

The Main Hall was, at least, a suitable forum for the Convention. A hundred meters long by fifty wide, made completely of petroleum-based polymers, the Hall had transparent side walls, which curved gently up to a gleaming black roof. Polished black struts supported the Hall's roof and held the power cabling for the wall's rather unique polarization system, an innovation cooked up right here on Tarbos.

"Ladies and gentlemen, please come to order," he called out. Fifteen assorted delegates and perhaps forty more aides, assistants, and hangers-on fell slowly silent.

Pritchard stood behind a black polymer podium at the front of the Hall.

The morning sun glared in from over Mountain View Bay, striking through the walls; Pritchard, noting the squints of delegates seated near the windows, turned a dial on the podium's smooth black top. The windows polarized, dimming the glare of the sun considerably. He nodded to acknowledge the murmured thanks of the group.

Resisting the urge to say, 'I suppose you're all wondering why I asked you here today,' Pritchard instead began with a simple preamble.

"I've been doing a lot of reading since I first messaged you all to invite you here." He walked away from the podium, gazing idly over the delegate's heads. "I've been doing a lot of reading, and a lot of thinking.

"When Stefan Ebensburg and I first conceived the idea of an interstellar alliance," he began, graciously extending half the credit to his old friend, "We were thinking of a business arrangement, some kind of deal worked within the framework of the Company, perhaps. Well, it's become apparent that a business alliance isn't what we need." Walking back to the podium, he flipped a switch; in mid-air above the delegates, a three-dimensional, holographic image shimmered into view.

"This image and the plans that accompany it were hyper-phoned to me from the Company's Chandler Aerotech Spaceship Architect division on Earth. It's hard to get any sense of scale, of course, from a hologram, but this ship is only about a hundred and fifty meters long, and carries a crew of one hundred and forty-one. Now look closely, ladies and gentlemen."

Pulling out a laser pointer, Pritchard indicated the oversize Gellar tunnel which seemed to make up three-fourths of the ship's mass – which it did – the stub wings, the bumps on the upper and lower fuselage. "These stub wings contain hard points designed to carry the new Shrike ship-to-ship missiles that Lockheed-Boeing Aerospace is developing. These bumps on the fuselage are high-energy particle beam emitters, turreted to allow a wide range of fire in an arc to the ship's front, rear, and sides, above and below. There is also a passive defense, in the form of force-field emitters that can surround the ship with an energy shield that should repel most current weaponry."

"This, ladies and gentlemen, is the design of an armed frigate, at the moment known to the engineers as the 901 Project, although the first ship – if it's built – will be named the *Farragut*."

A hand went up in the room. Pritchard pointed at the King of Corinthia.

"So, my good man, what you're saying we need is a fleet of these things, is that right?"

"These, and larger, more heavily armed ships as well." Pritchard left the hologram floating overhead and walked to the front of the small, raised stage. "Plans are being developed for cruisers, battleships, and carriers that will carry wings of fast, agile sub-light fighters and strike craft.

"What we need is a Navy. In order to have a Navy, we have to pool our resources; the *Farragut* will cost on the order of sixteen billion dollars, and we'll need more than one ship.

"And planets like Forest can't build even one, if we're on our own," Mike Crider pointed out."

"Yes, exactly," Pritchard continued. "We need a Navy, and to build a Navy, we need a government. An interstellar government."

The reaction wasn't the pandemonium Pritchard expected, but rather a thoughtful murmur.

"As you all know, our program allows ten minutes for a statement by each representative to open the convention. A computer randomly selected the order of speakers; we'll begin with the Vice President of the United States of America, Earth, Mr. Hector Gutierrez. Mr. Vice President?" There was a smattering of applause.

Hector Gutierrez took the stage, straightening his tie as he went. *Some days I wonder if I shouldn't have stayed in the contracting business*, he told himself wryly. Striding to the podium, he took the tiny mike he found there and clipped it to the lapel of his dark blue jacket and took a deep, careful breath.

"Ladies and gentlemen," he began, and then paused a moment, frowning in deep thought. "I'm kind of used to saying, 'My Fellow Americans,' but that's not really appropriate here, is it?" A smattering of laughter, but mostly just patient expressions followed his opening remark. *This isn't a political crowd*, he reminded himself. *These are chiefs of State, and top planetary executives — really chiefs of State themselves. It's a savvy crowd, and a sophisticated one. Don't talk down to them, Heck.*

"We live in interesting times, my friends. Eighty-five percent of humanity is still on one planet, but most of you here are pioneers on new worlds. I'm a politician now, but I was a businessman for most of my adult life, just as most of you are businessmen and —women now. And as executives, most of you are responsible for administering a whole planet, all of you know how to get things done – quickly, efficiently.

"I know that almost all of you here were born on Earth. Our first off-world generations are only now reaching adulthood. You are all familiar, I'm sure, with Earth's history over the last two hundred years, but I'll recap a few items.

"Earth was once a much less inviting place to live. Only a little over two hundred years ago, half of Earth's population lived under the iron fist of dictatorships. It took three World Wars and eighty-six million people dead to change that, and since the Third World War, representative governments have ruled the nations of Earth. The rule of law and the concept of one citizen, one vote, are now accepted facts all over the globe." Gutierrez paused to sip some water from a tumbler on the podium.

"The colonized planets are run by a private company, and Off-World Mining and Exploration has done a first-rate job at administering these projects. Indeed, OWME has acted as a de facto government for these worlds until this point. But we are met here today on Tarbos, the most centrally located of the settled planets, to discuss a new form of government, an interstellar government, a government that can build a fleet of armed starships to protect us from the threat of another dictatorship, a heavily armed and militarized dictatorship, this so-called 'Grugell Empire.' After millennia of fighting, after millennia of sacrifice, the people of Earth now know freedom, but the cost of freedom is eternal vigilance – and this is proven by the threat we face now, where once more the mailed fist of tyranny reaches across the light-years to threaten humanity."

"If there are any lessons to be learned from Earth's history, especially from the World Wars of the twentieth and twenty-first centuries, it is that a free people must always be vigilant to protect their freedom; that dictators and despots will always seek to usurp free societies, to attain through force the wealth that only a free people can achieve, though their own efforts in a society that rewards individual effort and hard work.

"In all three World Wars, the United States fought on the side of freedom. We fought our own internal battles as well, and in both cases freedom and individual liberty emerged triumphant. I urge you all here to bear that in mind as we continue; if we are to form a government, let us form a libertarian government, a limited association of the sovereign worlds, a Confederation of equals that prizes the liberty of the individual and the rights of the planets to govern themselves. Let us establish our armed force, but let us balance that with a Bill of Rights that assures the sovereignty of the individual above all else. Let us do those things, and as the representative of the United States of America, I guarantee that America will fully support this Galactic Confederacy."

**The *K-101*, high Tarbos orbit**

"Commander, our first coded signal has arrived. The humans' conference has begun as scheduled."

"Good. Good. Our agent is in place, then."

"Yes, Commander."

"Good. Good. Send a message to the Fleet Commander personally; inform him of events to this point. Move the ship into a high orbit, geosynchronous over the human's main city."

"By your command."

# Eight

**Tarbos, the Main Conference Hall**

Mike sat in the audience, watching the President of the Republic of China drone on about China's role in Earth history. He glanced down at his sparse notes; he was next up to speak, preceding Harvey's Assistant Project Director, Nancy Kawasaki.

*Boy, am I out of my league here.*

In the seat next to him, Mike Junior was fighting to keep his eyes open as Kee Chow An went on about the rise and fall of Communism in China, and how an ancestor of his fought in the Rebellion against the Communist People's Liberation Army to liberate China from Communist rule.

*I wonder what's for lunch. Tarbos is supposed to have some sort of local delicacy, some kind of big hairy turtle-thing.*

Seated on the other side of Mike from his son was some sort of aide to the King of Corinthia; the man reeked of perfume and was dressed like a peacock. Mike glanced down at his trademark blue cotton shirt; he'd put on black pants, a new pair of tooled boots, a light gray suit jacket and an old-fashioned string tie as a concession to the formality of the occasion. His gray Stetson hat lay in his lap.

*Oh, boy. Sounds like the old boy's winding down. Get your shit together, Mike old boy.*

Next to him, Mike Junior started up suddenly out of a doze. He rubbed his eyes and looked around the room for the hundredth time, his gaze finally settling on Maria Gutierrez, seated with her family a few meters away. Maria looked back over her shoulder at Mike Junior; she winked once and smiled.

*This is going to be serious*, Mike reminded himself; he knew all the signs of young love, having been through it once himself. *Hell, Jenny still looks at me that way. I probably look at her just like Junior looks at Maria Gutierrez. Oh, boy.*

And then it was his turn. Kee Chow An stepped off the stage, and Bob Pritchard was introducing 'The Hero of Forest, Michael Crider.' Mike got up, seated his hat on his head, and made his way to the podium like a man on the way to a hanging.

"Good morning." He shuffled his notepaper, squinting at his own scratchy handwriting. "Excuse me," he apologized, reaching in his jacket to extract the reading glasses he'd begun to need a few years earlier. A smattering of friendly laughter flickered through the room as Mike gave the glasses a quick polish with his jacket sleeve before threading the earpieces behind his ears. "That's better," he said with a note of satisfaction.

"I've spent the last few days wondering why, exactly, I'm here. I'm not like the rest of you. I'm not a political or a business leader. I'm just a hunter and pioneer. The rest of you are used to managing the affairs of nations and planets. Me, I'm just used to hunting the occasional boser or roc to send down to the colony for meat; that's how I earn my humble living. And it's a pretty darn humble living, too." Mike paused, smiling at the laughter his dry wit engendered.

"You all know the reason I'm here. I'm the only one here who has faced the Grugell firsthand. I fought the Grugell Occupation on Forest, my wife fought in the Battle of Settlement, and I led a party of scouts to destroy the broadcast power station in the very meadow I still live in today. You've all read the accounts of those battles, and so it's obvious – at least to me – that any of my fellow scouts would be as well suited to this as I. Maybe more so – Nathaniel Tzukuli was one of those scouts, and Doctor Tzukuli is probably one of the smartest men in the Galaxy.

"But they're not here. I am. So, I suppose I should tell you what I'd like to see in this Galactic government we're here to form.

"Vice President Gutierrez spoke about freedom. That's the first thing I'd like to see. The freedom to earn my own living as I please. The freedom to be left alone to live my life as I please. The freedom to raise and protect my own family.

"The Vice President also spoke about the dangers of dictatorships. That's the second thing I'd like to see. I'd like to see a provision for a military force, one strong enough to ensure that the Battle of Settlement won't be repeated. On Forest, we beat the Grugell because they didn't understand us; they didn't understand the power of an armed citizenry, the power of free people fighting to protect their freedom. They know better now, and if they try to strike at one of our planets again, they'll come in force, and we'll need more than farmers and pioneers with hunting rifles to stop them.

"Finally, the Vice President spoke about history. That's what we're here to do; we're going to make history. Well, I was born and raised an American, and there's one thing America had right from the start, and that was ensuring the rights of its citizens. That's the third thing I'd like to see. A Bill of Rights, to grant those rights – no, that's not right. I don't believe a government can grant rights. We, as human beings, have certain rights that are inherent in being human. Natural rights. We must have a Bill of Rights to guarantee the natural rights that every person is born with, by virtue of their humanity.

"Like I said, I'm a simple man. Just a hunter and a pioneer. But there are billions like me on Earth, and in the colonies. We're the people, the ordinary people, who are going to live under this Confederation. And just like America was the beacon of freedom that finally removed the scourge of dictatorship from Earth, so should this Confederation be the beacon of freedom for the Galaxy."

Mike paused, tipping back his hat. The delegates were dead silent; Mike lacked the experience to gauge their reaction.

"I find it interesting that America was founded with thirteen colonies. We have representatives from thirteen planets here today. Let's take that as an omen. Let's proceed with the same commitment to liberty and freedom that those Founders did back then.

"That's all I have to say." He folded his notes and placed them in his jacket pocket, removed his glasses and tucked them away as well. The room was still silent.

And then Vice President Hector Gutierrez stood up, clapping. His family followed suit, followed by Bob Pritchard, by the Russian Vice President whose name Mike had forgotten, and then by the room en masse. The applause washed over Mike like a wave, leaving him a trifle bewildered. As video and still cameras recorded the scene for history, capturing a pose that would be immortalized in textbooks for a millennium, Mike Crider smiled slightly, touched one finger to his gray Stetson in a half-salute, and left the stage.

# Nine



**Washington D.C., Earth**

President Anthony Gomez was finding the White House a little too quiet these days, with his best friend and most trusted advisor gone over a thousand light-years away. Gomez presided over a United States enjoying an unprecedented economic boom, an America that sat at the heart of an Earth that was now a rather quiet and idyllic place.

But President Gomez had other advisors as well, and one of them sat in front of the historic Oval Office desk now.

Army General Horace Julesberg was the Chairman of the Joint Chiefs of Staff, the top military officer in the country, serving in a position that the global political climate had made almost irrelevant – until the word came of the attempted Grugell occupation of Forest.

"At any rate, sir," the General was concluding, "we'll be ready to launch the first auto-defense satellite later this year, by October 1st at the latest. Each satellite will have a high-resolution-video and a millimeter band radar targeting system, twin particle beam projectors, a laser designator and two Shrike missiles. The computer targeting system can engage three targets simultaneously, and can shift fire to deal with as many as sixty targets a minute with particle beam fire."

"And there will be twelve of these in geosynchronous orbit by May?"

"By the end of May, yes, sir. Earth will be surrounded at the Equator by a belt of these defense satellites."

"The Skyhooks are still our weak points. We've got almost no orbital lift capacity that doesn't depend on these three Skyhooks."

"Yes sir, that's a major bottleneck in the overall strategic situation. At least Off-World Mining is volunteering the use of their orbital shuttles to launch our satellites from the Quito Skyhook, for the cost of crew and fuel. Saving the taxpayers a bundle there, sir."

"That's what it's all about, isn't it?" President Gomez smiled. "Tell me, do you think we did the right thing sending another representative to Tarbos?"

"Yes sir, I do. Vice President Gutierrez could use the input from a unique viewpoint."

"Yes, I suppose he could."

"I just wish I'd thought of it a few weeks earlier."

**OWME cargo ship *Cachalot*, en route Earth to Tarbos**

The cargo hull was ungainly, awkward, built along wholly different lines than most OWME exploration ships and liners. A giant disk formed the cargo carrier, docked beneath a smaller drive unit housing a Gellar tunnel that was rather small for the mass of the ship. The result was a carrier of massive capacity that handled, according to its pilots, like a hog.

But it was efficient.

On reaching a planet's orbit, the disk portion would detach from the star drive unit and descend through a planet's gravity well using chemical rockets and pressor beams to balance the load;

when their planetside chores were done, the disk would rise on four columns of ionic flame, back to orbit, there to dock with the star drive unit.

It was ugly, but it had the virtue of effectiveness. Twelve such cargo hulls, all named for Earthly whale species, roamed the trade lanes now.

Command of a cargo hull was considered a punishment posting for an OWME merchant ship captain. Passenger liners were the plum assignments, and colonization ships the next in the scale of desirability. OWME's small community of qualified ship captains saw cargo hulls as decidedly unglamorous.

But Captain Janice Benton cared not a bit about that. A command was a command, and OWME's space fleet wasn't growing nearly as fast as the number of qualified pilots and ship's officers. The *Cachalot* was big, ungainly, awkward and ugly, but it was a ship, and it was *her* ship.

Shifting, dancing and sparkling, the weird and unpredictable patterns of subspace flashed on the main viewer as the ship drove for Tarbos. Captain Benton, like the rest of her bridge crew, was strapped into her chair on the zero-gravity bridge; only the small passenger/crew quarters section of the ship was spun on the long axis to provide gravity.

And back in those passenger quarters, passage paid by the United States government, rode an unusual passenger indeed.

Six weeks in subspace, and they'd drop out into the normal space outside the orbit of Tarbos. Six weeks, and she'd be able to take one of the *Cachalot*'s small freight shuttles to the surface, to see another new planet with her own eyes. Tarbos would make six planets Jan Benton had seen first-hand.

*I do love this job*, she thought for the twentieth time that day.

# Ten

**Three weeks later, Tarbos, a maintenance warehouse, 2AM local time**

Tarbos nights were uniformly dark, since the planet's one tiny moon reflected almost no light. This made clandestine meetings all the easier.

"You brought the progress report?"

"Yes. The delegates are forming a Constitution. It looks like it will be based on the principles of at least three Earth nations."

"Never mind that. What about military forces?"

"There is a provision for a Navy. They've shown a design for an armed ship, a frigate. Larger ships are being designed."

"That's not going to go over well with my superiors."

"I didn't think it would. I'm just telling you what happened – do you want the truth, or do you want a bunch of song and dance?"

"You've done well." A package was passed over. "One week from tonight, same time, same place. Mind your security."

"I always do."

## Tarbos, the Main Conference Hall, the next morning

King Harold I of Corinthia leaned back in his chair, staring at the ceiling as Stefan Ebensburg of Caliban read off a listing of proposed amendments to the Confederate Constitution. Several attendants sat around him, their expressions alternating Deep Thought, Rapt Attention and Barely Conscious. In front of the King, Russia's Vice President Vladimir Tarakanov was paying close attention, jotting down notes in a flawless Cyrillic script. The UK's Prince Harry sat next to the Russian, turning now and then to exchange a whispered comment with his cousin, King Harold.

Mike Junior was finding them all pretty amusing. His father was doggedly trying to pay attention to the droning Ebensburg reading what was to become the Confederate Bill of Basic Rights.

Freedom of Religious Practice. The Right to Privacy. The Right to Bear Arms. The Right to Free Speech. The Right to a Trial by Jury. All the rights enumerated in the American Bill of Rights, but put in a bit more modern language; where America's Second Amendment read "A well-regulated militia, being necessary to the security of a free state, the right of the people to keep and bear arms, shall not be infringed," the Confederate Third Basic Right was drafted as "The right of no free citizen to bear arms in defense of home, community, or planet shall be called into question."

Mike liked what he'd heard so far. A very libertarian interstellar government seemed to be in the works.

## A janitorial closet, nearby

"Will this work?"

"Yes. Turn that dial – there – to thirty minutes. Push the big button."

A thunderous roar split the quiet of the morning.

## The Main Conference Room

The blast hurled Mike from his chair, slamming him against the floor with rib-cracking force. A choking blast of dust and grit washed over him, and the shock wave of the explosion rippled sickeningly through his body. The roar of explosives seemed to come almost as an afterthought, passing as quickly as it came, leaving only the tinkling of broken ceramics, glass and the crackling of flames somewhere. Mike looked up, eyes stinging, to a room filled with smoke and dust.

"Junior?" he called out.

"Dad?" Mike coughed instead of sighing in relief at the sound of the familiar voice. "Are you alright, Dad?"

"I'm fine. Look for the Vice President, Junior."

"He's over here, Dad. He's bleeding, but I think he'll be alright."

"Good." Mike stood up, stretching his arms and legs experimentally. "The blast came from the back, over there."

A pair of broad-shouldered OWME Security troops was already running in that direction. Another tall figure in the uniform of an OWME Security Lieutenant appeared in the dust and haze. "Ladies and gentlemen, let's get you all out of here. Quickly, people! Let's all get to a safe location!"

"And where might that be?" Mike wondered quietly. All but two of the delegates stood slowly, many wincing with the pain of injuries. Two at the back of the room did not stand; Mike shook off the arm of the Lieutenant to go over to the two prone figures.

He shouted for medical help as he went, but it was to be of little use.

New Albion's Angus MacPherson and Forrest Cox of Zed lay dead in the dust and rubble and with them, all hopes of a quick conclusion to the Convention.

The Lieutenant crossed to Mike's side, shaking his head at the sight of the two bodies. "Sir," he repeated, softly, "we really need to get you to a place of safety. There may be more explosives. We need to sweep the building."

"All right," Mike agreed. "Who would do something like this?"

"If we can figure that out, sir, I hope they give me five minutes alone with him," the Security Officer replied. He'd served four years as a U.K. Royal Marine on Earth, and the warrior mentality was ingrained in him. "I'd know just how to handle him."

"I hope you get your chance."

Fifteen minutes later, Mike found himself in a skimmer with his son and the Gutierrez family, racing south along the coastline. An OWME shuttle pilot had been impressed to run the skimmer; several other skimmers were accompanying them on the journey, carrying the delegates to safety.

Mike Junior leaned forward, poking his head over the seat into the driver's compartment. "Where are we going?"

"Twenty klicks south, the Tide Pool resort," the driver called over his shoulder, raising his voice so the other passengers could hear. "It's a pretty big place. OWME executives like to hold meetings there, but I don't reckon it's big enough for what you all are doing. Still, it's a hundred-room hotel."

"I bet they'll have a ring of security troops all around it, too," the younger Crider predicted, dropping back into his seat.

"We can't really continue the Convention, can we?" Mike Senior was watching the rolling surf whip past, fifty yards from the skimmer's window. "We've lost at least two delegates. We need to have someone from each of the settled worlds."

"We'll get new delegates, Mike." Hector Gutierrez was holding a blood-soaked bandage to the side of his head, but the cut was superficial. "This is too important. We're delayed, but we're not stopped."

"Of course," Mike agreed. "You're right. This is too important." He turned back to the window. "I wonder who else thinks stopping it is important – and why?"

# Eleven

**Tarbos, three weeks later**

A hyperphone message brought the first note of cheer to Bob Pritchard's life since the explosion. The Project Directors from New Albion and Zed were on the way to Tarbos personally to replace their slain assistants. It would be another month before they arrived, but at that point the Convention could at last proceed.

Lying alongside the hyperphone message was a report turned in two days after the blast by Tarbos' Security Chief, Colonel George Perkins. Pritchard picked it up again, reading the conclusion for the thousandth time:

> And so it would seem that the two conspirators were given an explosive device with what looked like a timer, but was actually a simple detonator switch. It is one of the oldest tricks in the terrorist book, getting rid of the saboteurs at the same time as the target. It tends to be pretty hard on the bombers, but it eliminates, in this case, two possible leads as to the identity of the responsible party or parties.

The surviving delegates were quartered in Tarbos' sole hotel, twenty kilometers down the coast, and under heavy guard by nearly half of the Company Security troops on the planet.

There was one exception. On the second day after the blast, the delegate from Forest had wheedled some field gear and a rifle from the Security troops and vanished into the unpopulated hills behind the hotel, re-appearing ten days later seemingly well-fed and grinning. This caused Colonel Perkins no small amount of consternation.

"Sir," the Colonel had complained, "We know there's a conspiracy to break up the Convention. We know there is someone out there somewhere willing to kill to prevent the forming of a government here. And now we've got this, what's his name, Crider, just walking off into the hills all alone for ten days? He's got to be first on the suspect list, sir, he's just got to be."

"I think you're barking up the wrong tree, George. Mike Crider's the Hero of Forest. He's not going to turn against his own kind. He's a pioneer; I imagine it's hard for him to keep cooped up. You know the type — we've still got a few pioneers here on Tarbos, don't we?"

"Be that as it may, sir."

And so the investigation was under way.


## The Tide Pool Hotel, Tarbos

Mike was getting restless again.

His ten-day adventure had been fascinating. The wilderness northwest of the Tide Pool was mostly rolling, grassy hills dotted with riverine woodlands, and once Mike had gotten used to the unfamiliar rifle and gear, he'd had a great time. The local wildlife was decidedly odd — sort of six-legged half-mammal, half something else, hairy creatures with strange, shelled carapaces, from mouse-sized up to the size of an Earth coyote.

Not bad eating, though, once you cracked the shell and cooked them.

Ten days in the wild had enabled Mike to stand the following nine days once again stuck in the hotel, but he was getting claustrophobic. Casinos and restaurants held no appeal for the aging pioneer, and certainly he had no reason like his son's blossoming friendship with Maria Gutierrez to keep him indoors.

On this twenty-second morning after the blast, Mike was contenting himself with a long walk down the beach, his son and the Vice President's daughter in tow. A trio of rifle-bearing Security troops followed, not too discreetly, fifty meters behind.

As he walked, devouring the distance with a typical pioneer's long, even stride, he stole the occasional glance back towards his son, walking hand in hand with Maria Gutierrez.

There was no doubt they made an attractive couple. Mike Junior was tall and lean like his father, blonde, blue-eyed, still dressed in his habitual jeans and blue cotton shirt. Maria was tall too, and slim, but her olive complexion and raven hair made an attractive contrast to Junior's fairness. She laughed easily, and her eyes shone when she looked at Mike Junior with a light that the older Crider recognized all too easily. *Well*, he told himself, *the boy could do a lot worse.*

*I wonder if she'd be happy living on a backwater like Forest?*

Five or six kilometers up the beach, Mike stopped suddenly at a large boulder, sticking out of the sand. He seated himself on the rock and stared out to sea. For all his travels, he'd only been to two other seashores, a day on the Pacific in Oregon as a boy and one trip to the Forest town of Edgewater.

"What's up, Dad?" Mike Junior and Maria strolled up, the Security troops following along behind.

"Nothing. Just thought I'd set and watch the water a spell."

"Alright – mind if we walk up a little farther?"

"Help yourself. Plenty of beach."

The young people walked off. One of the Security troops – a Sergeant, from the uniform – spoke to the other two in low tones, after which the two followed along after Mike Junior and Maria. The Security Sergeant walked over to where Mike perched on the rock.

"Mind if I join you, sir?" he asked.

"Sure thing," Mike replied. "And you can drop the 'sir.' I'm just Mike, OK? I'm not a politician or a Director, just a hunter and a pioneer."

The Sergeant took off his polymer helmet, revealing a surprisingly gray head. "I know," he grinned. "I know all about you. I was on the Security team in Settlement that night twenty-two years ago when you and your boys knocked out that broadcast power station." He seated himself beside Mike on the boulder, scratching his close-cropped head as he did so. He extended his hand. "Gerry Stiles." Mike took the proffered hand, shook it.

Sergeant Stiles went on. "I was in the Mercantile. Only twenty-one, a Private in OWME Security, and I was scared half out of my wits. Those silver spider-ships were buzzing overhead, green energy bolts flying everywhere – my best friend was cut in half by one of those things before we could get inside. I figured we were all dead."

He looked out at the rolling surf, reflectively. "Then, all of a sudden, we heard a girl's voice – your wife – shouting at us to come outside, that the aliens' power was out. Boy, I don't mind telling you, we kicked some ass when we heard that!"

"I'll bet you did," Mike replied, quietly. His own memories of that long-ago moment weren't too pleasant. A sudden memory came unbidden into his mind; a rainstorm, roaring thunder, green bolts and rockets crisscrossing in the dark, a brilliant young scientist working valiantly to save them all while his life drained away into the ferns. The Sergeant's voice snapped him back to the present.

"And if it weren't for you and those scouts, we'd have all been killed. They had us beat, Mike, and that's a fact."

"So, how'd you come to be on Tarbos? The company doesn't move people around too much, do they?" The cost of interstellar travel was still high enough to deter a lot of planet hopping.

"Well, sir, I'm a city boy. Born and raised in Chicago."

"Forest too quiet for you?" Mike grinned. It wasn't an uncommon sentiment.

"Something like that, yes. Three years after the Battle of Settlement, old Colonel Davies gathered a bunch of us young troops around, said Tarbos was growing fast and hurting for NCO candidates. It was a chance to move up, and a chance to move to a boom planet with a real city, so…"

"So, the pioneer's life isn't for everyone. That's good – if it was, there'd be too damn many of us."

"Something like that, yeah. What's Forest like these days, anyway?"

"Not much has changed since then," Mike answered. "There are more people, of course. Settlement's almost a real city now, forty thousand people. Outskirts is a good-sized town now, maybe eight thousand, and then there's Edgewater, up on the coast, maybe twenty thousand, and an honest-to-gosh harbor and shipyard. Still no Skyhook, though – we had to go up to the liner on an old orbital shuttle."

"This new government, it's really going to change things, isn't it?"

"Not without a lot of help from Earth."

"Well, I agree with one thing. We'll need a Navy. But one other thing, you know," Stiles added. Mike looked at him expectantly. "You can't just have ships, you need troops, too. I don't care how high-tech mankind gets; you can't have a military unless it's built around guys with rifles. They may be all home-based on starships, but that's how it has to be."

"Marines. You're talking about Marines."

"Aye aye, sir," Stiles joked. "Something to think about. There aren't any former military or Security types among those delegates, are there?"

"Not that I know of. I'm probably the closest there is," Mike said.

"Well, sir, there's plenty of Security troops here on Tarbos that can offer you advice, and most of the officers and senior NCO's have Earthside military experience. I don't – that's why I'm still a buck Sergeant at forty-three. Anyway, something to keep in mind."

"Thanks, I'll do that." Mike wasn't accustomed to thinking in terms of having advisors.

"One other thing you should know, Mr. Crider."

"It's Mike, remember. What's that?"

"Well, Mike, there's an investigation into that explosion back at the Conference Center in Mountain View."

"I should hope so!"

"You should also know that you're one of the chief suspects, Mike. I shouldn't really be telling you, but hell, I figure I owe you that much. For Forest, you know?"

"What? Me? How the hell can I be a suspect?"

Stiles looked at Mike. "You really don't know, do you? Your disappearance for ten days into the hills raised a lot of eyebrows, Mike. Think about it. There's an explosion, two people killed, two conspirators die in the blast, but everyone figures there's an organization and a leader somewhere. And then, a couple days later, you borrow a rifle and some gear and vanish for ten days."

"I was just doing a little hunting," Mike mused. "I guess I see what you mean, though. I never thought…"

"Best you be thinking about it now, sir." Stiles looked up the beach, where the figures of Mike Junior and Maria Gutierrez were coming back towards them. "Here come the kids back. They've been spending a lot of time together, haven't they?" He stood, putting his helmet back on. "Only thing that's holding them up is that you've got no motive, no reason to try to sabotage the Convention. But someone out there does, and right now the powers-that-be here are barking up the wrong tree."

"Thanks."

There would be no more hunting on this trip, Mike realized. At least not out in the hills. What he would be hunting would be as dangerous as any roc, though, and many times as clever.

Still, a hunt was a hunt, and Mike had been a hunter all his life. His mind was already starting to work.

# Twelve

**The _K-101_**

"Commander, incoming signal from the planet."

"Yes?"

"Text signal, sir, it reads 'Green File.'"

"Good. Inform the hangar bay to ready an infiltration pod, and have Senior Lieutenant Akillistrak stand by for orders. I will be in my quarters; I must update the Imperium."

"By your command." The bridge crew responded instantly; in a few moments, the cloaked Grugell frigate slowly began to slide inwards, towards the system's one inhabited planet.

"Sir," the SubLieutenant on the Scanning console called out, "A ship, in high orbit; scans indicate a heavy cargo ship."

Commander Kadastrattik walked over to examine the tactical display, recognizing at once the typical huge disk-shape of a human cargo hauler. "Fine. We'll leave it alone. They'll never know we're in the area."

"Yes, Commander."

Kadastrattik looked around his Bridge once more; the crewmen were all attending to their duties with typical Grugell scrupulousness. Nodding once in satisfaction, he left for his private stateroom to contact the Imperium.

## The Tide Pool

The alarm buzzer went off at 0600 local, as it had for the last two months since the explosion.

"Junior?" Mike called.

"Mrfff. Come on, Dad, I was out late." Mike Junior rolled over in his bed, across the suite from Mike's. "I took Maria out dancing, didn't get in 'till after two."

"We're going back to Mountain View today, son. Best get up and moving; the Convention is going to resume after lunch. The two new delegates got in last night."

Mike Junior buried his face in his pillow.

The older Mike showered and dressed quickly, donning his gray jacket from the first day of the Convention. From the bottom of his trunk, he pulled a small leather case. He opened it carefully, almost reverently, and inspected the contents minutely. Everything looked in order. He removed the rig from the case and belted it at his hip, where the hang of his jacket concealed it nicely.

*There*, he thought. *I guess I'm ready*.

He walked over to his bed, grabbed a pillow and chucked it at his son's head. "Come on, Junior, we're burning daylight."

## Mountain View, the Conference Center

While Bob Pritchard had expected the two Project Directors, another arrival due in a few more days from Earth - shipped on the cargo ship *Cachalot* – was the biggest surprise he'd been handed in some time. Still, the Conference Center was repaired, rewired, and ready; the Convention was to resume just after lunch today.

## Two kilometers down the coast

In the shade of a tall boulder that jutted from the grass behind the beachfront dunes, two figures met. One was tall, rail-thin, and the other shorter, stockier. They spoke in low tones, even though there wasn't another sentient creature within a kilometer. The clandestine nature of their joint enterprise and the risks inherent in the daylight meeting were not lost on either party.

"Are you sure this is a safe place to meet?"

"As safe as any. Are you ready to take the next step?"

"Yes, all my pieces are in place."

"Good. Don't do anything until you hear from me."

"All right, but this is a dangerous business. My expenses are running several times higher than I'd anticipated."

"Don't worry. You'll be compensated more than adequately."

"That's another thing, you know. When, exactly, am I going to be 'compensated?' I'm fronting a lot of the costs of this operation myself."

"Don't worry. You'll get everything that's coming to you, and soon."

"Soon, he says. Are you sure you want me to go ahead with this? These people aren't stupid, you know. It won't be hard to figure out that you people are behind all this."

"That's not your concern," the tall, thin figure said to the shorter one.

"It's damned well my concern if I get caught," the shorter figure replied.

"Then, I'd advise you to not be caught."

# Thirteen

**Caliban**

A really good Executive Secretary is a treasure to any executive.

Ingrid Holtz was an exceedingly good Executive Secretary.

Good enough, as it happened, to have been hired on by Off-World Mining & Exploration at Stefan Ebensburg's insistence, when he was hired away from Heidelberg Polytechnic, where he had been running a petroleum drilling operation. Ingrid was old enough to be Ebensburg's mother, indeed she should by rights have retired years before; but her sense of loyalty had brought her from Berlin to Heidelberg to the North Atlantic oil fields, and now to Tarbos, all as the secretary to one man.

And now, after all these years, she was about to earn her retirement pay, in spades.

Two hyperphone messages had arrived in the Director's office, in the space of one twenty-six-hour Caliban day.

The first was an account of the destruction of one of the lost cargo ships, the Beluga, from the ship's sole survivor. Crewman-First Giorg Konstantin survived six weeks in a tiny orbital shuttle before being picked up by an OWME passenger liner headed in the opposite direction.

The second message was from Earth, from an old friend of Herr Direktor Ebensburg's at Heidelberg Polytechnic. Doctor

Hans Richter was a physicist working on cataloging interstellar matter, gases and particle ratios, with the intent of improving the efficiencies of the Gellar drive tunnels used in OWME ships. His analysis of the sketchy reports gleaned from survivors of the stricken ships had uncovered something remarkable.

"*Mein Gott.*" Holtz copied both messages, set them to forward, and checked her note file for the locator address Herr Ebensburg was using on Tarbos. The messages would take a week or more to arrive. Hopefully *Herr Direktor* was checking his message cache regularly.

# Fourteen

**Tarbos, the Main Conference Center**

"Son, I'm going to take a walk around the building during the break," Mike announced. "I imagine I'll have one or two of those guards for company, but I need some air."

"OK, Dad. Maria and I are going to duck back to that snack bar they set up, get a drink."

"All right." Mike adjusted the hang of his jacket and walked ostentatiously out of the building and, as he'd expected, an OWME Security troop tagged along. Mike wasn't surprised to see Sergeant Gerry Stiles' face behind the polymer helmet face-shield.

He paused for a moment just outside the Conference Center's main doors to drink in the cool, humid evening air.

"Sounds like everything's moving along in there pretty well, Mike," the Sergeant observed, stepping ahead of Mike to make a show of scanning the surroundings.

"Yeah, I suppose. Did you get a chance to scout around the area?"

"You bet I did." Stiles took a step back. "There's only four buildings within a kilometer that are ever empty at any time of day or night, and one of those is a bank – it's got computer-run security cameras and stun panels on all the doors and windows. There are two big warehouses that are empty at night, one just north of here about a block, and another about half a klick to the east. Last one's a power station, it's got one night operator for about a square kilometer of station – that's as good as empty."

"I don't see how they could be pulling off something like this without someone on the inside," Mike said. "And they've got to be meeting somewhere around here, don't you think?" Stiles nodded agreement. Mike stood a moment, rubbing his chin with one hand.

"Let's think about this for a minute. They already tried to bomb the Convention, and it almost worked, didn't it? They killed two delegates. Now, the Convention is starting up again, and Bob Pritchard's tech people have cooked up explosives sniffers to cover every way in and out. Now, these people, if they've got someone on the inside, they'll know that. So, they'll try something else." Mike looked up at the Conference Center building. "Could a rifle bullet get through those windows?"

"Not likely, Mike. That polymer will deflect an artillery shell."

Mike examined the area with the trained eye of a hunter. "You know, though, if I had a good rifle, and I wanted to nail someone walking out these main doors, I think I'd set up right over there, just up that alley – see those trash bins? You've got a clear shot right at the doors, and the alley hooks off to the left. Good place to get away if things go wrong."

"You've thought about this some," Stiles observed.

"You don't hunt rocs twenty years without learning how to set up a stalk and a shot, and also how to get away in a hurry if you miss," Mike said. "I'd be roc-food by now if I didn't have an instinct for this sort of thing."

"Well, I can put a sensor in that alley, sure enough, and that'll tell us if anyone slips in there."

"Let's do that but keep it quiet. Nobody but you and me should know about it. If someone goes in there and hides, just come and tell me. OK?"

Stiles nodded. "If you say so."

## Inside the Convention Center

"Where'd your Dad go?"

"Outside, I guess," Mike Junior answered. He smiled broadly at Maria Gomez. "He can't stand being indoors too long. Back home on Forest, the biggest problem we have around the place is getting Dad to stay indoors for more than five minutes."

"You're not too good about that yourself, you know." Maria giggled as Mike Junior drew her into his arms, kissed her.

"I know. It's hard to get used to all the people here."

"You're doing better than your Dad."

"Yeah, Dad's hardcore. I didn't think he'd ever make it through that month down the coast."

Marie put her arms around the younger Crider's neck and stood on tiptoe to kiss him back. "You're hardcore yourself, you know. Just in a different way."

"They're coming back in. Guess the break's over."

Maria frowned prettily. "That was too short. Take me dancing again tonight?"

"Try to stop me."


## The *Cachalot*, in Tarbos orbit

"Captain, last shuttle to the Skyhook is leaving in ten minutes."

Captain Jan Benton of the *Cachalot* picked up the handset on the desk in her stateroom. "Very well. Please ask our guest to meet me in the hangar bay."

"Yes, Captain."

## The Convention Center

Free of speeches for the moment, the Convention Center was a buzz of conversation; knots of people stood discussing minutia of the forming government, sub-committees held caucuses around tables, and social plans for the evening were finalized with laughs and back-slapping. Amazingly, the Russian Vice President Tarakanov and the Chinese President Kee Chow An had struck up a fond friendship, despite centuries of tension between their Earthside nations that still lingered today. They and their wives spent most of their evenings together, touring Mountain View's shops and restaurants. *How fast things change in a new perspective*, Mike Crider told himself.

"Mike?" Mike looked up from his notes to see the American Vice President.

"Hector. What can I do for you?"

"We're about to wrap up for the evening. Will you come over to the Mountain View Skyhook with me? There's someone coming in from Earth to provide technical advice. I'd like you to go with me to meet him."

"All right. Who is it we're meeting?"

"Let's just say he's someone with a unique perspective."

Mike stood up, stretching out muscles unaccustomed to spending the days in a chair. One issue had been weighing on his mind most of the day, and he said so: "A lot of the delegates don't like the article about a right to bear arms in the Bill of Basic Rights."

"I know. I was hoping you'd speak to the Convention about that."

"Better you do it, Heck. You're a Libertarian politician, you know all the arguments."

"Yeah, Mike, but you've been there. If it wasn't for armed citizens, Forest would be a Grugell colony now."

Mike nodded. "And I'd be dead. Yeah, nothing like first-hand witnesses, is there? OK, I'll make some notes, and talk to Bob Pritchard about getting on the clock for a few minutes during opening remarks in a day or so."

"Thanks, Mike. I've got to go talk to Kee Chow An for a few minutes, then I'll be ready to go."

"OK, I'll go find Junior, tell him where I'm going. We're going to have a situation with these kids of ours, Heck."

The Vice President rolled his eyes and chuckled. "Don't I know it? All Maria talks about is 'Mike this, Mike that.' I suppose your son is the same."

"Pretty much." Mike looked doubtful. "I'll meet you at the main entrance in what, ten minutes?"

"Sounds good."

**One hour later, the Mountain View Skyhook**

"Here's the bus," Hector Gutierrez pointed up at the yellow indicator light above the bus walkway doors, which had just flashed on. He and Mike stood in the waiting area in front of the big disembarkation doors, which slid open a moment after the bus slid to a stop. Mike goggled at the tall figure that stepped out.

"*You!*"

Clomonastik III, once and former Group Commander in the Grugell Navy, now a Maryland restaurateur, strode forward, a wide grin on his narrow face. "Michael! What an honor it is to stand before you again, my respected friend!"

Mike couldn't quite forget that this tall, imposing alien had tried very hard to kill him and his Jenny at one point, but that had been a long time ago. He took the Grugell's proffered hand and shook it, carefully, allowing for the alien's delicate bone structure.

"You are well, my friend? You look fit!" Clomonastik looked exactly as he had twenty-two years earlier, but an obviously expensive tailored three-piece suit in dark gray silk had replaced the issue Grugell uniform and cloak. A narrow black silk necktie on a sparkling white shirt completed the outfit. While Clomonastik had adopted the dress of a successful Earthly entrepreneur, his fastidiousness had survived the years unchanged.

"I'm fine. You look like you're doing well on Earth."

"Very well indeed. I've grown quite fond of your home world, Michael. You must be Vice President Gutierrez," Clomonastik noted, extending his hand again. "It is my honor to meet you at last. Your President speaks very highly of you."

"Pleased to meet you, sir. Tony and I go way back. He told you what we're dealing with here?"

"Indeed, he did. I do hope my insights may be of some small assistance."

"I don't understand this," Mike said. "I know it's been a long time, but you're one of them! How do we know you're going to steer us straight?"

Clomonastik just smiled. "This must indeed seem very odd to you, my old friend. But the President understands my motivations for helping, and he finds me adequately trustworthy. You are so right to be cautious, Michael, but we have not the time for excesses of prejudgment just now."

"Let's head back to the hotel," Hector Gutierrez answered. "We'll fill you in on the way."

## The Truffle, a restaurant in Mountain View

While the service and the cuisine were impeccable in the Truffle, one of Tarbos' most exclusive – and expensive – restaurants, Corinthia's King Harold was less than happy with one aspect of the proposed Constitution and didn't hesitate to let his kin from Earth know about it.

"So, I'm to understand that I'm to put this to a vote of my subjects on Corinthia? A vote?" He slapped his wine glass down on the table, sloshing a bit of rich Tarbosian red on the sparking white tablecloth. The red stain widened, faded, disappeared into the polarized polymer thread woven into the cloth.

Prince Harry of the United Kingdom, Earth, paused with a forkful of steak halfway to his mouth. He laid the fork down, frowning. "A vote, cousin. You know, it's not such a bad thing, having a Parliament. Blighty's managed very well with one these last few hundred years, you know, and the Royal Family carries on." Prince Harry smiled at his cousin. "Would it really be so bad? You can't expect to hold onto a true monarchy for more than a generation, not in this day and age."

"I'll be forced to form a Parliament, the way this thing is worded." Harold held up a draft of the Constitution in one hand, slapping it with the fingertips of the other. "I didn't take my subjects a hundred and eighty light years from Earth to form just another rule-by-rabble!"

The British Prince scowled. "You know, Harold, you were an arrogant sod when you were a lad, and I'm afraid you haven't changed much. We've done very well on Earth, you know, with 'rule by rabble' across the globe now. We've fought very hard to make it that way. It's not realistic of you to think you can keep your world otherwise."

"And if we choose to go it alone? What need have I for this Confederacy? And the right to bear arms, what's the purpose of that? They may as well say the rabble has a right to overthrow their rulers!"

"Given the way you're carrying on, you're right to think that, you know. As for the first, you can bloody well answer that for yourself, cousin. There's a hostile race out there, in case you've forgotten, and part of this Confederacy involves forming a Navy to defend us all from attack."

"Well, I don't care for it, you know."

"Perhaps you don't," Harry chided his relative, "But you'd better accept it. Unless you want your precious Corinthia to be facing an alien occupation army with nothing to protect you but a couple of local cargo haulers and an orbital shuttle."

"I've half a mind to form my own Navy," Harold sniffed.

"Billions of dollars of your own money, cousin," the British Prince reminded him.

King Harold I of Corinthia lacked an answer for that. His own personal fortune, while unparalleled in human history, still wasn't up to forming a Navy. And he had three daughters to think of, three little girls whom he didn't want seeing an armed Grugell Occupation force landing on Corinthia. Still… "Well, I don't like that last bit. I'll vote against it."

"You must do as your conscience dictates, of course." Prince Harry said, smiling wryly at the intended irony.

# Fifteen

**High orbit over Tarbos**

The *Cachalot*'s Captain was not happy.

"Say again, Tarbos Ground," she barked into the wand mike on her command console.

"Permission to leave orbit is denied. You are to remain in your parking orbit until released by Tarbos Ground Control."

Control of all ship traffic in the Tarbos system was, by Company regulation, completely subject to the planetary ground control department, but this was an unexpected reach beyond the normal exercise of jurisdiction.

"Tarbos Ground, we are due back at Earth in six weeks. The Director better have a good reason for keeping us here."

"*Cachalot*, I cite OWME Shipping & Container Division's General Order Four."

That set Captain Benton back in her chair. General Order Four was quite simple:

> No OWME starship will leave a designated parking
> orbit when there is a clear and present danger to ship
> and/or crew.

Tarbos Ground Control's use of GE4 meant that they suspected a danger somewhere near the planet – somewhere close enough to be a risk before the *Cachalot* could travel far enough to jump to subspace.

And OWME had lost three ships in three years to unknown attackers, presumed to be the warlike and hostile Grugell.

"As you were, Helm," Captain Benton ordered. "All stations stand down from under-way status. We'll be staying in parking orbit for a while. Exec, get a shuttle ready – we're going to the Skyhook and down to talk to someone in the Director's office."

### The *K-101*, Fifty kilometers above and behind the *Cachalot*

"Homely ships, Commander, are they not?"

Kadastrattik XII opened his eyes lazily. The huge off-white disk of the human ship had dominated their main scanner screen for three revolutions of the planet below, and he'd gotten sick of looking at it. He ignored his Sub-Commander's remark.

"Have we received any more messages from the surface?"

His Signals watch officer didn't even look up. "No, Commander. Nothing since the initial code."

"He's taking his time, this renegade," Kadastrattik muttered. "Order an inspection and diagnostic routine on all weapons systems. We'd best be prepared for the second option."

### Tarbos, the Convention Center

Mike Crider stood once more at the podium, concluding his description of the Battle of Crider Meadow and the Battle of Settlement.

"That, delegates, is why the Bill of Basic Rights must contain a guarantee of the right to bear arms. When the Grugell came to

Forest, we fought them of with hunting rifles. Now I know, the main reason we're here, the main reason we're forming this association of free planets, is to raise and equip a Navy. Some of you are no doubt thinking, 'if we're to have a Navy, why do we need a Constitutional right to bear arms?' I'll tell you why. In fact, I'll give you three reasons why."

He paused for a moment, looking out over the assembled Convention. They were openly calling it a Constitutional Convention now, and the soon-to-be-born government had a name – the Confederated Free Planets, or simply the Confederacy.

Some of the expressions Mike was seeing were skeptical. Most were not. The Grugell invasion of Forest was too recent for that.

"One." Mike held up one finger. "Numbers. It's a big galaxy, and this Navy won't be able to be everywhere at once. It might be weeks before a ship or ships could get to a planet in trouble. Now every planet can and should have their own armed force, but let's look at Tarbos here for an example – Tarbos has four million residents, and only four thousand security troops. But based on figures I've been provided, roughly half of Tarbos' population owns at least one firearm – which yields a standing militia of two million.

"Two." He held up two fingers now. "It's not just about the Grugell. We don't like to talk about it, but you all read the news-screens. I've been reading them every morning in my room, before we come over to the day's sessions." He extracted a notepad from his pocket. "In the last ten days here in Mountain View, there have been three muggings, two armed robberies, one rape, and one attempted murder." He dropped the notepad back in his pocket and glared at the group. "That's a pretty low crime rate for a city of three million, like Mountain View, but it won't get better. It will get worse. The Company screened the emigrants from Earth pretty well, but they can't screen the people who are born on these

planets, and as the generations go on, the demographics will shift
to be more like Earth normal – and that means you'll have criminals. And we learned long ago on Earth, the best way to deter
criminals is an armed citizenry.

"Now, that brings me to three." He held up three fingers. "And
three is the biggest one of all."

Mike stood still for a moment, seemingly lost in thought.

"We all come from a place that has one thing in common. At
least it does now, after millions of people died fighting to make it
that way. That thing is a word, just one two-syllable word, but it's
an important one, because it stands for an idea. It's an idea that
eighty million people died for. That word, that idea, is freedom.

"There are two kinds of freedom. There is freedom to, and
freedom from. What we're talking about here deals with both
kinds. Free people, as I see it, should be free to do as they please,
as long as they don't hurt their neighbors. But when there are
people out there, and there will be, who will try to hurt their
neighbors, then free people should be free to defend themselves,
and free to own the means to do that. That's where we come to
the freedom from. Free people should be free from fear. Free from
subjugation. Free from invasion. There's only one way to guarantee,
absolutely guarantee, that a free people will remain free, and that
is to have the guarantee in our Constitution that every free citizen
who chooses to be armed shall be free to be so."

Without waiting to gauge the group, Mike stepped down.
Murmurs floated through the hall as he walked slowly back to his
seat. Hector Gutierrez was waiting for him.

"That was good stuff, Mike," the Vice President observed
sotto voce. Harvey's Project Director Annalee Fadzen was at
the podium, arranging her notes to speak on another issue. "Just
between you and me, I think the Right to Bear Arms will pass. I
make it twelve yes votes, three no, one I can't call."

"It would be nice if we had an odd number of delegates," Mike whispered back. "Think how confusing it will get with tie votes."

"We've been really lucky so far," Gutierrez agreed.

Mike frowned. "Doesn't it seem a little, well, odd, sixteen people deciding the form this interstellar government is going to take?"

"Wait until tomorrow. You'll feel a lot better about it."

## Tarbos Security Headquarters

The eyepieces of the human's microscope weren't adjustable for Clomonastik's narrow face, and so he was required to squint uncomfortably into the device with one eye or the other. Three technicians and Colonel Perkins waited impatiently for him to finish.

"Well." Clomonastik stood up straight, massaging the small of his skeletal back. "If only you'd put your benches a little higher, I'd be much more comfortable."

"Sir?" Colonel Perkins wasn't a man gifted with patience. "What do you think?"

"Colonel, I'll want to see the results of your metallurgical studies to be sure – mind you, that never was a specialty of mine. I went to Command School, not the science and engineering academy. But I know enough to give you an answer. On the surface, though, I'd say that you're looking at fragments from a Grugell device, yes." He gestured at the microscope with a thin, clawed hand. "The fragments are distinctive, and your analysis of the explosive residue is even more so. It's a Grugell high explosive. We called it," he chattered out an unintelligible Grugell word, "which, unfortunately, has no real translation."

"Any conclusions, sir?"

"I can only offer you my opinion, Colonel, with the quali-fication that what I offer is a uniquely informed opinion at this time and place. You have a cloaked Grugell frigate very near this planet, very likely in high orbit, and they are sending landing craft down to liaise with someone on the surface. The trick of fooling the conspirators using a bomb fused to detonate – that's an old, old trick, first documented in our history in an incident called the Night of Seven Blades. An assassination attempt was made on Emperor Ignostak III in the same manner. The Emperor survived, of course, but most of his family was killed in a series of incidents during that same night. The Emperor's reaction to those attempts led to the complete militarization of our culture." Clomonastik looked reflectively at the ceiling. "I would suspect, Colonel, that you have a student of history up there." He scratched his pointed chin. "You know…"

"Yes? What?"

"Colonel, do you think it would be possible to have a Grugell Navy uniform tailored for me, were I to provide the specifica-tions?"

"Certainly. Won't it be kind of an old uniform? You've been out of touch for twenty-some years."

Clomonastik laughed. "No. The Grugell officer's uniform has not changed in over three hundred Grugell years. We are not as – how shall I say it – capricious as you humans."

"Very well, sir. I'll look into it."

# Sixteen

**Later that evening**

There still weren't very many restaurants in Mountain View, but the Palace was one of the better ones, featuring beef from a Black Angus herd imported from Earth ten years earlier.

Seated between his father and an equally wide-eyed Maria Gutierrez, Mike Crider Junior couldn't keep his eyes off the tall, weird figure across the table.

It was an odd congregation around the dinner table, and one that brought more than a few stares from the dining room's other patrons. Mike Crider and his son, the American Vice President, his wife, daughter and son, and the alien former Commander of an occupation force bound to take over the planet Forest. Clomonastik was finishing off a large porterhouse steak with obvious enjoyment; his side dishes of potato and vegetables were left untouched.

Wiping his narrow mouth with satisfaction, Clomonastik laid down his napkin and smiled across the table at Mike Junior.

"You have heard your father's stories, no doubt, my young friend. I trust his tales did my handsome and commanding presence justice?" He chuckled, a thin, strange sound.

"I suppose so. You're my first alien," Mike Junior commented. Beside him, his father spluttered into his napkin, trying to hide his amusement.

"You're a young man yet," Clomonastik observed. "I trust I won't be the last. Michael - it's gratifying to see you have such a strong young son, my old friend. He is the very image of you as a young man. You should be very proud."

"I am. He has a sister, too, back on Forest with her mother." With the instinctual pride of a parent, Mike extracted a flat card from his jacket pocket, pressing a contact to display a 3-D holo of his family from a portrait taken a year earlier in Settlement. It seemed so odd to be showing a family portrait to this alien who had once tried very hard to kill him, but…

"Ahh." Clomonastik leaned forward to examine the holo closely. "Still only the one wife? I know, I know! I've lived among you for many years now, but some of your ways are still so peculiar to me. Why should a man such as yourself, a great warrior and a hero among his people, be so limited, and by force of law at that?"

"I'd be so 'limited' by choice, even if it weren't the law," Mike answered, "and the only reason I was ever a warrior, you may recall, is because you dropped in on my home with an Occupation force."

"And what an adventure that was for us both, Michael! And look tonight, this friendship that has sprung from that old conflict! Tell me now," he turned serious, "are you not in the slightest bit nostalgic for those exciting times? Do you not miss the excitement, the rush of battle, the surging of the blood?" He fixed Mike with an unfathomable glare from his jet-black, featureless eyes. "Did you not feel more alive then than at any other time in your life?"

"Well," Mike began, but Clomonastik cut him off with a wave of the hand.

"You need not temporize with me, my old friend. I know you in many ways, in some ways perhaps better than you know yourself. I come from a culture that deals in war and conflict as a matter of routine, you must remember. I know all too well the mind of a warrior-born. I know how the rush of battle gets into a man's blood. You specialize in hunting rocs, yes? Those giant bird-beasts of Forest, like the one that tore my arm that long-ago day?" Mike nodded. "And why?"

"Well, that's where the money is, and I've got a family to support."

"Please. Michael. You are a man of vast means, of vast talent and experience. You would earn a very good living hunting the harmless herbivores that roam the plains of that planet, and yet you hunt the most dangerous creatures extant, and you specialized in that since your arrival on Forest – when there was only yourself to feed and clothe. For the money? You hunt them for the excitement, Michael, do not try to convince me otherwise. Your son – how many rocs has he killed?"

"Three," Mike Junior answered for his father.

Clomonastik turned to address the young pioneer. "And you felt what, when you killed that first great beast?"

"Excited. Scared. Sick to my stomach afterwards, but only for a minute. I was really proud of myself, but Mom sure fussed at Dad for taking me out after a roc."

"You see, Michael?" Clomonastik turned back to the senior Crider. "Your son, he has it as well. All of you do. Vice President Gutierrez, you were a businessman before you were a politician, yes?"

"A contractor, but yes."

"You had competitors, yes?"

"Of course. Denver's a big city. There were times during the last big recession, competition for what few construction jobs there were got pretty tough. The kids were just little then, and I was working twelve, fourteen-hour days, Tony and I were busting our humps trying to keep our people working…" His voice trailed off.

Clomonastik was quick to jump on the opening. "Allow me to speculate. You competed ruthlessly. Your loyalty was to your people, your employees. You pursued your competition, you defeated them on price, on service, on quality, on every front, until they were bankrupt, and your own company was the premier construction company in Colorado." Clomonastik may not have been eligible to vote, but that didn't stop him from reading the political section in the news services.

"Yes."

"And in spite of all the hard work, the time away from your family, the uncertainty, the conflict, you remember those times with a certain satisfaction, do you not?"

"Well, yes."

"And your wife? Madame, how do you recollect those days?"

"It wasn't easy," Sandy Gutierrez reflected. "Heck was working all the time. Sometimes weeks went by when he only saw the kids asleep in their beds at night. It was worth it, don't misunderstand – it all paid off – but it was hard. We all pulled through it, though – as a family." She patted her husband's hand fondly, and the nostalgic smile on her face wasn't lost on the former Grugell officer.

"You see?" Clomonastik took a sip of the red table wine provided with dinner, made a face. "You thrive on conflict, all of you. Without it you become bored, complacent, lazy. I've seen it myself, in your own American city of Baltimore. Humans who have everything provided for them quickly grow fat, lazy, and useless. You need conflict, and yet you treasure peace. You co-operate and you compete all at once. You are violent, yet you avoid violence until it comes to your door."

"It hasn't always been that way," Hector Gutierrez noted. "Our history has been,"

"Warlike? Violent?"

"Yes. Yes, it has."

"Our societies are not so different, you see. And yet I think that ultimately, in this greatest of all conflicts that your race will prevail. Why?" He set his wine glass down. "One of your failings, of course, is this pale, tasteless water you call wine. But I digress. You humans will prevail due to your ability to co-operate."

"But surely your own Grugell military co-operates as well. Any organized structure, such as a military, requires intense co-operation to function." Hector Gutierrez hadn't known a thing about military organization a few years earlier, but he was a quick study.

"Co-operate, yes, but only to the extent necessary to complete a task. You see," Clomonastik continued, "my time among you has gifted me with perspectives into the similarities and differences between our peoples, but there is not yet one among you who has done the opposite. You must understand, the Grugell hierarchy is a vicious, intemperate competition – advancement by assassination is not unknown. I myself achieved my rank by ruthlessly under-cutting my Commander on my last ship assignment – I concealed from him a serious shortfall in weapons qualifications records, and revealed them to an Imperium Inspectorate officer on a routine inspection tour. My superior was disintegrated, and I moved into his role."

Clomonastik looked around the table at the staring faces of his human companions. "And so you see, the tendency of the indi-vidual Grugell often runs counter to the overall sense of mission. It is that tendency that we must use to our advantage."

"You know, one thing concerns me," Hector Gutierrez said. Clomonastik looked at him, an unspoken question on his narrow face.

"Based on all you've told us – especially that last bit – what reason do we have to think we can trust you? How do we know you won't try to find a way to turn this to your own advantage?"

"Mister Vice President – you do not."

Hector Gutierrez was a bit taken aback by the blunt but honest answer. "Why did you ask Colonel Perkins to have a Grugell uniform made for you?"

Clomonastik grinned, baring his predacious teeth. "Many years ago, when I was in command of a small weapons station on the planet Ghathaba, I had a very annoying subordinate. He took Grugell competitiveness to an unhealthy extreme – he was suspected in several assassinations and assassination attempts, including one on my own self. He fancied himself a student of history, you see – he had produced a long, quite boring scholarly work on an incident in our history known as the Night of Seven Blades." He explained for a few moments, as expressions around the table grew more thunderstruck by degrees.

"And if my former subordinate Kadastrattik XII is indeed up there in orbit," Clomonastik pointed up at the restaurant's ceiling, "I'd like to meet him again. Yes, I'd like that very much indeed."

"Do you think there's a chance he's the one that's up there?" Mike asked.

"Yes, my old and respected friend, I do think he may well be. I'm not certain, but that bomb; it had a certain… inelegance… that reminds me of my former subordinate. And if it is in fact, he who is in charge of this mission…"

"Then you'll know how to turn his own impulsiveness and ambition against him?"

Clomonastik laughed delightedly. "You see, my old friend? You and I, we are not nearly so different as you would like to believe."

Mike considered that thought for a moment. "I just hope you're right. We haven't had many breaks yet."

"There's an old Grugell aphorism that applies. Let me see if I can translate: 'When your enemy has you on your back, things are looking up.' Things may be looking up for us now."

# Seventeen

**Tarbos**

"Sandy, would you look at this?"

Sandy Gutierrez had been doing casual duty helping her
Vice President husband with note-taking and keeping track of
his schedule of committee meetings, working breakfasts, and the
various other functions taking place as the Convention worked
through the vagaries of forming a Galactic government. At the
moment, though, they were lunching in the courtyard outside
the Conference Center's main building, enjoying Tarbo's pleasant
summer sunshine.

A few meters away the Gutierrez's daughter, Maria, sat
sharing a bench with the younger Michael Crider. They faced each
other on the bench, noses almost touching, sharing a bowl of some
Tarbosian dish or other. Their eyes were locked together, wondering smiles on both their faces. As Sandy watched, Maria picked
up a napkin, dabbed something from the Crider boy's chin.

"Well, Heck, what do you expect? Maria's a grown woman
now. She's turned nineteen right here on Tarbos, remember?" For
her birthday, the Crider boy had presented her with a lovely green
silk shawl and hair cover fashioned from the fleece of an animal
native to Avalon. Maria had worn the lace about her shoulders
almost continually since.

"I know, and Mike's son is a great kid. He's honest, he's strong, he's open, he washes his face and keeps his fingernails trimmed – everything I'd expect in a suitor for Maria. But…"

"But what, Heck?"

"Sandy," Hector lowered his voice a notch. "He lives on Forest. That's – well, I don't know how far, but it's light-years from Earth. We're going back to Earth when this is over, Sandy, and he'll go with his father back to Forest! How's that going to affect those kids?"

Sandra Gutierrez sat down, laying her hand on her husband's knee. "Heck, look at them. Look at the way Maria looks at Mike. Look at the way he looks at her."

"That's what I'm saying, I…"

Sandra cut her husband off. "Heck, it wasn't that long ago you and I were young, remember." She smiled at her husband. "You know, you looked at me just like Mike looks at Maria. And you know, sometimes, when you're not being all Vice Presidential, you still do." She waved a hand at the young people. "You said it yourself – young Mike is like his father, he's honest, he's strong. He'd make a fine husband. And Maria's a grown woman, and she's been here on Tarbos for almost six months now, falling in love with that young man."

Hector Gutierrez looked helplessly at his wife, forced to the conclusion that he'd been subconsciously avoiding. Sandra, with the intuition borne of twenty-five years of marriage, read his mind for him. "Yes, Heck, I think we'd better accept the possibility that our daughter may be going to Forest when this is over, and not back to Earth with us."

"It's such a long way…"

"I know." Sandy kissed her husband, and her eyes were damp. "But you know, this is another side of what we're doing here. In the old days on Earth, you know, young people would go off to the

New World – like our ancestors did, Heck, yours from Spain and mine from England and Germany – and their families would most often never see them again. As this Confederacy you're building grows, this will happen to other families too, you know. And these kids aren't growing up thinking of just Earth. They're seeing a larger society. It's not just America, Russia, Europe, Brazil, and the other hotspots on Earth. With this new government, kids are going to look out to Tarbos, Caliban, Zed, and new worlds we haven't even found yet. History is starting all over again."

"It doesn't make it any easier knowing it's inevitable. And it's strange, but it doesn't even make it any easier knowing that she'd be getting a fine young man."

"I know." Sandra Gutierrez stood up. "And, my dear husband, I've got a committee meeting of my own to get to – we're designing a flag for this Confederacy of yours. We'll be looking for some agenda time later this week to present our design for a vote."

"A flag?" The Vice President looked surprised. "I don't think anyone thought about that."

"A nation has to have a flag, doesn't it?"

"A nation?"

"The Confederacy. It's a nation, isn't it? The nation of humanity?"

"It is, isn't it?" This gave Hector Gutierrez something new to think about. *I wish Tony were here. He always was better at seeing the big picture.*

"I'll see you later, then." Hector stood up, kissed his wife. He took one last look at his daughter, who was still lost in Mike Junior's eyes. He shook his head and headed for the Conference Center for a committee meeting of his own.

## Tarbos, OWME Engineering Design & Development

"How long will it take to build this?" Bob Pritchard wasn't generally a man of great urgency, but the hyperphone messages from Earth and Caliban had made him break his usual habit.

Frad Gilpin looked the plans over casually, wiping a bit of egg sandwich out of his mustache as he did so. A fat, sloppy and profane man, he was a master with electronics and computer technology – good enough to lead to a prestigious posting as Chief of Tech on a high-status planet like Tarbos. "Two days, three maybe."

Pritchard looked at his watch: Seven-thirty-four. "You've got until tomorrow afternoon. I want you ready to go to the Skyhook at fifteen tomorrow, to catch a shuttle to the *Cachalot*. You'll install the scanner on the ship."

"You want to spend a half a million dollars on hardware to stick on a freighter?"

"Just do it, Frad."

"You're the boss. You're signing off on my equipment expense vouchers, right?"

## Evening

Tarbos' short day made the sunsets sudden; in the space of a few minutes, the sun slipped into the ocean off Mountain View, and darkness fell. Several committees were still meeting in the Conference Center, and the delegates not in committee were in and outside the Center. OWME Security Sergeant Gerry Stiles walked into the building, his uniform allowing him to pass the security guards unchallenged. He didn't see the person he wanted to talk to, but he saw someone that would do almost as well.

"You're Mike Crider's son, right?"

"Yeah, that's me." The boy was hanging onto a tall, dark-haired girl Stiles didn't recognize.

"Your Dad around?"

"He went off looking for something to eat," the younger Crider answered. "Should be back in a little bit."

"Damn. I needed to talk to him."

"I could take you to him – I think I know where he went."

Stiles looked the young man over. "Sure, I guess."

"I'll just be a minute, sweetie – will you wait for me here?"

Maria Gutierrez nodded, kissing Mike Junior on the cheek. "I need to go talk to my Mom for a minute anyway."

They left the conference center together, angling around the corner of the building. "Dad's been eating at that place across the Plaza – we can cut through the trees right over here."

It was dark and still under the trees. Stiles was starting to sweat now. "Are you sure he went this way?"

"Pretty sure." The boy stopped suddenly. Stiles almost bumped into him in the dark. "Well, I think he did."

"You *think*?"

"He thinks right," a soft voice came from behind him.

Stiles reached reflexively into his jacket pocket, but three sharp clicks from the darkness stopped him. "I wouldn't," the voice advised. "Junior, light us up."

Mike Junior pulled a light-wand out of his pocket and snapped it, lighting up the area with a bright yellow glow. Stiles turned his head, carefully keeping his hands visible. Mike Crider Senior was leaning casually against a tree, an ancient – but no doubt fully functional – revolver in his hand, pointed at Stile's heart.

With his free hand, Mike tipped the brim of his big gray hat back a little. "You've never been a hunter, have you? It's all about setting up a stalk. Sometimes," Mike continued in a conversational tone, "you even use a lure. But the trick is to draw your game into the place of your choosing."

Pounding footsteps announced the arrival of a squad of Security troops, led by a lieutenant. "His right-hand jacket pocket," Mike advised.

Two of the troops pinioned Stile's arms while the Lieutenant searched him, quickly and efficiently. "A compressed-gas hypo," he reported.

"Let's get it analyzed. Be careful with that," Mike advised. "I'm sure it's dangerous as hell."

Mike had expected Sergeant Stiles to be defiant, but instead, he was subdued – almost deflated. Mike pulled his jacket back and holstered his antique Colt before stepping up to the captured traitor.

"Gerry, you've been just a little too anxious to help since this whole thing started, and you've been a little too anxious to get me suspicious of the rest of the group. I began to wonder why, and then it hit me. The people who set off that bomb had to have someone on the inside, someone who could get them past all the security stations around the Conference Center. And it occurred to me that I hadn't seen you that day; I checked with the Duty Sergeant and found out that you'd asked for the day off, and that nobody had seen or heard from you that whole time. And then it just sort of all came together, and it wasn't hard to figure out what your next move would be." Mike smiled; his hand still rested on the ivory grips of the ancient revolver. "You know, Bob Pritchard wanted to let his men handle this, but I wanted to be the one who caught you. I wanted to look you in the eyes when you knew you were caught. I can't imagine why you'd want to betray your own kind, but that's just what you're doing, isn't it? Somebody gave you orders to kill me, and that somebody was probably tall, skinny, and alien, weren't they?"

Stiles remained silent. Mike frowned at him.

"All I want to know is, why?"

Stiles looked Mike in the eye and set his jaw. "I'm not telling you anything."

"Oh, you will," the Lieutenant snorted. "Get him out of here," he ordered his men.

"Good work, Junior," Mike told his son. "Let's go get some supper."

"Sure thing, Dad. OK if Maria comes with us?" After having faced his first charging roc at age sixteen, the capture of a would-be murderer was tame stuff for the younger Crider.

## The Director's Office

"Those entryway scanners were a great deal," the Security Lieutenant told Bob Pritchard. "Whoever your guy is that cooked those up, he did a great job. They picked up Stile's hypo easily enough."

"Frad's a pain in the ass in a dozen different ways, but he's a hell of a technician. Thanks, Lieutenant, that'll be all for now. Why don't you head home? It's been a long night."

"I'll do that, sir, thanks." The Lieutenant spun on his heel and left.

"Has he told you anything yet?" Stefan Ebensburg asked from his chair near the window. Outside, the surf rolled in against the nighttime beach.

"No," Pritchard replied. "But it's pretty obvious where he's getting his orders, isn't it? There's a cloaked ship up there, and somehow, they're getting messages down to the surface without being detected. We'd have picked up a transmission or an orbital shuttle coming down."

"We don't know how their ship cloaks work," Ebensburg pointed out. "It's possible they can cloak a shuttle."

"Yeah, but according to these messages, we might be able to put something together to track it. I've put Frad on that, too."

"This is getting complicated. I'm sure Stiles wasn't the only person they have on the payroll."

"I'm sure he wasn't," Pritchard agreed. "There was Sergeant Stiles, and the two that were killed in the bombing. None of them were what you'd call take-charge types; the two bombers were just warehouse workers. There's someone running the show, someone with some authority. He's the one we've got to smoke out."

"*Jah*," Ebensburg agreed. "And now, *mein freund*, may I suggest you follow the advice you've given the *Leutnant*? You look as though you have not slept in several days."

"I managed about three hours last night," Pritchard chuckled, "but you're right, I'm not sleeping much. I want to get this thing started off right, Stefan."

"Then you must rest, Robert."

## The *Cachalot*, the next morning

After ten long, boring days watching Tarbos rotate uneventfully under her ship's hull, meeting a fat, sloppy technician from the surface didn't make Captain Benton's day. But that's precisely what she was doing. She and Gillian Furst, the *Cachalot*'s Executive Officer, were facing the man across a table in the freighter's tiny wardroom, which at least was in the section of the ship that was spun to provide gravity.

"Let me get this straight. You want to wire this gizmo into my main forward navigational scanner? And for what?"

Frad Gilpin tapped a pudgy forefinger on the display pad. "This here will enable you to track quantum anomalies and non-random distributions of normal spatial matter, both normal matter and dark matter."

"And that is important, why?"

"Well, Captain, if you wanted to track a ship that's not visible, that's a pretty good way to do it."

"So, you're saying I'll be able to track a cloaked ship with this? A cloaked Grugell ship?"

"That's the only kind of cloaked ship I know about." Gilpin was brilliant, but infuriatingly rude.

"So, what you're telling me is that Director Pritchard suspects that there's an armed and cloaked Grugell ship somewhere in orbit here? And we're just setting here big as life in plain sight of this thing?"

"I don't know anything about that," Gilpin demurred. "I'm just the techie, all right? Just the techie."

Jan Benton threw up her hands. "Great. What am I supposed to do when I detect it? This is a freighter, you know? I don't have any armament, no guns, no missiles – what am I supposed to do? Those things have already cut apart, what was it, four freighters in the last year? Freighters exactly like this one?"

"Captain, it's like I said, I'm just the techie, OK? Mr. Pritchard told me come up here and wire this thing in your ship, and since he's the local Project Director, what he says goes, like it or not. Plus, he's the guy who signs my paycheck, so I do what he tells me. So, by your leave, ma'am, I'm going to get to work."

"Sure, go ahead."

The fat man stood up and, bracing himself in the two-thirds gravity of the wardroom level, moved out into the passageway.

"What do you suppose the Company has in mind?"

"Well," the Exec answered her Captain, "I suppose, if the thing works, and we pick them up, we can always ram them."

"You're real funny, Gillian, that helps a lot, thanks."

**Meeting Room E, the Conference Center**

Maps of the area around Mountain View covered the conference table, all of them liberally marked up with scribbled notations. OWME Security Colonel Perkins was holding forth to the assembled group.

"We've had patrols out day and night, all around the area, within a day's march of the city, and of the Tide Pool resort up the coast. We've placed remote sensors, we've flown recon droids out farther than the patrols have gone, we've covered every damn inch of ground within fifty kilometers of the city. If somebody's infiltrating by orbital shuttle, they aren't doing it anywhere around here."

"Well, they sure aren't coming down the Skyhook," Bob Pritchard pointed out. "They've got to be coming down by shuttle, and someplace closer than we think."

"If you'll permit me, Mr. Pritchard?"

Pritchard nodded assent to the tall, weird figure at the end of the table. Clomonastik III stood up and rubbed his narrow jaw contemplatively.

"It's not at all uncommon, in exercises, you understand, for an audacious Commander to place his reconnaissance assets actually inside the enemy's perimeter wherever possible. That may well be the case here. You have searched the area outside the city, I am certain, with great efficiency, and as a result of that we may now rule out the likelihood of a landing site in the countryside. We therefore should begin to look inside the city itself."

"In the city? We've got enough radar coverage over this city to cook birds in flight," Colonel Perkins objected.

"Ah, yes, but radar has its limits, Colonel. How small a craft could your radar detect?"

"Well," Perkins said, "We don't have any military stuff; what we've got is traffic-control radar. Frad Gilpin has tweaked the frequencies to allow us to track ships down to six or seven meters long. That's smaller than any landing shuttle I've ever heard of."

"But not smaller than a Grugell infiltration pod." Clomonastik held up a sketch on a large notepad. "An infiltration pod is designed to do precisely what we are speculating happened here; namely, to land one operative safely in a heavily patrolled and guarded area. The pods are one-time devices; they can only descend to the planet's surface. There is no provision for them to return to orbit."

"So, the operative is expecting to be picked up by follow-on troops?"

"Or to die in the course of his mission," Clomonastik agreed.

"Nice," Colonel Perkins observed.

"Sometimes necessary," Clomonastik pointed out. "Your recent history makes it plain that your military members are expected to return from their missions, successful or not; you even plan campaigns to minimize losses when possible. The Empire knows no such scruples; an officer assigned a task is expected to succeed or die in the attempt. There is no return from failure. Which, of course, explains the initial reason for my own presence among you."

"So, what we have to do, is to find this pod…" Bob Pritchard began,

"…and we'll have a clue to finding our infiltrator…" Colonel Perkins added,

"...he may very well lead us to whoever he's working with," Clomonastik concluded with a sharp-toothed grin.

"Who's got the map of the city?" Colonel Perkins asked.

## Detention A

"Still isn't saying anything, is he?"

"Nope."

Two Security troops were detailed to watch the former Sergeant Gerry Stiles, currently Mountain View Detention A's sole resident. A vidcam inside the block covered Stile's cell, and since the prisoner was currently sleeping, the guards took the opportunity to grab a bite of lunch in the block's office.

"He's still crashed, is he?" The younger of the two guards was extracting a sandwich from his lunch pack.

"Yep," the other answered, glancing up at the video monitor as he chewed. "They had him up half the night, grilling him. Used drugs and everything. But he's not saying shit."

"Huh."

The guards ate their lunches and argued about the upcoming zero-gee football championships on Terra Station in high Earth orbit, and it was twenty minutes before they looked at the video monitor again.

"Holy shit!"

Plainly visible on the monitor was the bunk that, until just recently, prisoner Stiles had occupied. All that was left was a few charred bits of cloth and half-molten metal.

# Eighteen

**The Conference Center**

The Constitution was taking shape. Mike Crider was well pleased with how the document looked.

Two houses of legislators, the House of Selectmen, allocated according to a planet's population, and the Senate, with two Senators from each world. A High Court would interpret the laws passed by the Legislature, and the President's office would be responsible for enforcing those laws, as well as managing the security of the Confederacy as a whole.

Each world would support the Confederate government by a levy of a percentage of the Gross Planetary Product, and from that GPP tax would come funds for the Navy, the Confederate government – Mike was not surprised to see that the initial government base would be right here on Tarbos, since it was more or less centrally located – and the various functions that the Confederacy would fulfill in arbitrating interplanetary trade.

And best of all, Mike noted, was that the Constitution strictly limited the Confederacy's authority in planetary affairs – the free worlds were limited to freely elected, representative governments and to respect and abide by the Bill of Basic Rights, but other than that the Confederate government was barred from planetary affairs.

"Looks familiar, doesn't it?" Hector Gutierrez sat down next to Mike. Small knots of delegates and staff were seated here and there in the main Conference Hall, reading the final draft of the Constitution and making notes before the initial vote.

"Yeah, looks real familiar," Mike replied. "It's a lot like America's Constitution, but a bit tougher on Federal – I mean, Confederate interference in the state's affairs."

"Right. That's on purpose, and it will make ratification easier. The free worlds won't accept this if there's too much chance of the Confederacy getting too overbearing – we went through that in the States once, you know – and this pretty much precludes that. The President has the authority to intercede if a world fails to allow free elections or protect the individual rights that we've defined, but other than that, his responsibilities are to the Confederation alone."

"And each planet, to be part of this, will have to ratify by a simple majority of the electorate?"

"Two-thirds," Gutierrez corrected him. "And any new worlds opened up will have to vote to ratify or not when their population reaches half a million. If they don't ratify, of course, they aren't entitled to trade protection or Naval support in the event of attack."

"So, it's a pretty sure bet all thirteen worlds will ratify?"

"Eleven will. Corinthia, who knows? Their 'king' isn't going to be happy about putting it to a vote. Oddly enough, I'd expect Earth to be the other possible holdout."

Mike looked at the Vice President, his eyes wide. "Earth?"

"Earth. There's a lot of fuss in the US over how much we've spent on planetary defense, and since the United Nations collapsed, , there's really been no global international alliance or governing body to speak of. I don't know how Earth is going to manage a vote on ratification."

"I guess I never thought about that."

"Well, I sent Tony – that's the President – a hyperphone message. Maybe he'll be able to work something out."

Mike considered that for a moment. "You know, my son asked me something back on Forest once. There's an issue of citizenship – I'm an American citizen, but what about the kids born on the settled worlds? Junior asked if he's a citizen, and to tell the truth, I didn't know what to answer. And, after this, he'll be a citizen of Forest – and so will I, for that matter. I'll cast my vote for ratification on Forest, and so will Junior. Will we have dual citizenship?"

"Another problem to work out, Mike. I hadn't thought of that one, either."

"And, Heck, to be perfectly honest, it may be something that comes up in your family, too. You've seen those kids of ours together, right?"

The Vice President nodded. "Yeah. Sandy and I were talking about it yesterday."

## The Stardust Lounge

Late afternoon, and Mike Crider Junior had spirited a giggling Maria Gutierrez away from the Conference Center for an early dinner.

"I'm glad you could get away early," Maria confided. The young people say in a booth side by side, their discarded plates pushed across the table.

"I'm not really doing all that much," Mike answered. "Just taking notes and helping my Dad keep his paperwork organized."

"Why did he bring you, then?"

"He mostly just wanted the company, I guess." He frowned. "Dad doesn't make friends too easy. He's lived on Forest for twenty-three years, and you know I bet we don't get ten people a year out to the place to visit? I remember when I was a little kid old Colonel Davies used to come out for some hunting once in a while, and just before we left Dad had a visit from some of his old scouts from the Invasion, but that's about it."

"You're not like that, Mike." Maria squeezed Mike's hand in hers. He put his arm around her and squeezed.

"No, I'm not like Dad in that respect. I like being around people more than he does. Mom's afraid that once Dad gets older, it will be impossible to get him off the place at all – he only goes to town two or three times a year now."

"Your home sounds beautiful, though, Mike. The pictures you showed me sure are."

The young hunter/pioneer caressed Maria's satiny shoulder with his callused hand briefly. He turned toward her, his face very serious now. "I'd like you to see it, Maria. In fact, I've been thinking about that a lot. I'd like you to see our family place, I'd like to show you Outskirts – it's a really pretty little town now. I'd sure like you to come to Forest."

"I don't know, Mike." Maria smiled, ever so slightly. "Passage fare from Earth would be awfully expensive."

"I was kind of thinking of another arrangement."

"What arrangement?" Maria knew perfectly well what arrangement the young hunter had in mind, but she was woman enough to want him to say it.

"I was thinking of you coming back to Forest with Dad and me. If you and I were to…"

"To what?"

"To get married. That's what I'm trying to say. If you'll have me, that is." Inwardly, Mike Junior cursed his awkwardness.

Maria smiled broadly, pleased that her prediction was correct. She kissed him once, quickly. "Yes, Mike, I'll certainly have you. And I can't wait to see your home. I know I'll love Forest."

## Earth

President Gomez had anticipated the ratification issue.

The old United Nations building in New York still existed, but only as a shell. Since the Third World War, the UN had been all but disbanded, only a handful of Third World countries still meeting in a smaller headquarters in Belgium to debate resolutions that most of the world ignored. The old New York City building still existed, was still maintained at the expense of the United States' National Park Service, largely as a historical site. But now the President of the United States, Anthony Ignacio Gomez, had just become the first U.S. President to visit that building in several decades. Leaving the UN building with the Secretary of State by his side and the usual trail of Secret Service agents, the President was cautiously optimistic.

"The old building is still in pretty good shape," Secretary Stetson opined. "But as to whether anyone will show up to a forum at the UN after all this time is another story."

"It's the first thing that might actually be appropriate for the UN to talk over in almost a hundred years," President Gomez reminded her, "and all they have to do is go back to their respective countries and convince their legislative bodies to come up with a mechanism for a plebiscite. Remember, Claudia, there's no Constitutional provision right here in America for what we're going to try to do. Each State will have to have elections using their own system, and we'll combine the totals to the global count."

"You're that confident that the meeting on Tarbos will come up with a Constitution to ratify?"

"I am." Gomez looked up at the sky as he walked. "I read a lot of history when Heck and I decided to run for national office. I think it's inevitable. And, based on Earth's own history and the usual political bent of businessmen, I'm guessing it's going to be a fairly libertarian government, and that implies that it will have to be ratified by each planet. Earth's the only one that's carved up into separate nations, even though it's been dominated by one nation since before the Third World War." The famed circle of flags outside the old UN building was still maintained, like the rest of the site, by the National Park Service. A lot of the flags had changed since the UN had been founded following the Second World War: most of them, in fact. One had not. Gomez pointed at one flagpole where a familiar red, white and blue flag was flying – still flying – after three World Wars and the best efforts of generations of dictators and terrorists, *still* flying. "And the world will still listen to the United States. They'll complain, they'll kick and fuss, they'll whine and bitch, but in the end, they'll listen, because they know this has to happen. This is going to work. We're going to get that building back in shape, we're going to assemble ambassadors from every nation we can get to attend, and we're going to knock Earth's collective heads together. We'll have our plebiscite."

**The *Cachalot*, Tarbos orbit**

"Well, I'll be damned. It works."

The scanner readout was fuzzy; mostly just a rough indication of a course track, but it was there nonetheless, drawn in green on the *Cachalot*'s navigation readout. Captain Benton was impressed, in spite of herself.

"There, Captain, is your Grugell ship, running cloaked."

Captain Benton examined the readout closely. "This is just an estimate – the error here could be a kilometer or so either way."

"That will firm up as the system gathers data. The program algorithm will gather data on the individual track; once you've got the data, you should be able to pick this ship up anytime, given a few minutes scanning. You'll have a good enough fix in a few hours."

"Good enough to do what? Nobody's been able to tell me that, yet."

Frad Gilpin made a sour face. "I'm just the techie, Captain. That's a question for the bosses."

"Well, he's above and behind us, we can tell that now," First Officer Furst pointed out. "That doesn't give me a warm and fuzzy feeling."

"And I bet there's no way we can out-maneuver him – not with this big hog."

"How about if we dropped the cargo disk, and went after him with just the drive section?"

"Go after him for what?" Benton demanded. "The only thing we could do is ram him. You want to ram him with the drive section? The only way I'd want to try ramming him would be to clip him is with the edge of the cargo disk, and I'm not too crazy about that. At least we're mostly empty right now, and there's no crew in the disk, but we're still looking at shock damage, bulkheads sprung, all sorts of trouble."

"So, what are we going to do?"

"I'm going to talk to Pritchard, that's what I'm going to do." Jan Benton pulled herself across the zero-gee Bridge towards the Signals station. "Get me the Director's Office."

**An alley in Mountain View's warehouse district**

"Well?"

"It is a Grugell infiltration pod," Clomonastik said.

Colonel Perkins rapped on the opened, empty shell. "What's it made of?"

Clomonastik rattled out a series of high-pitched, squeaking syllables. "I don't know the English term," he smiled. "I imagine your engineers can determine the composition, yes?"

"Well, they'll sure try," Perkins agreed. "So this thing tells us we've got a Grugell agent here on the surface, then?"

Clomonastik scrutinized the Colonel's face closely. "Why, yes, obviously. I should think he would be a senior Lieutenant, probably well trained in infiltration tactics, probably fluent in English, and no doubt well-armed and well equipped."

Colonel Perkins tapped the pod casually with the toe of his boot. *Rather too casual about all this*, Clomonastik thought. *Rather too casual altogether.*

# Nineteen

**A warehouse on the edge of Mountain View**

His "contact" was tall, narrowly built and weird, and how he had learned English was anyone's guess. But learn it he had.

"I've been in contact with my superiors. We're not at all pleased with your progress. Having your man captured so stupidly…"

"I understand - that was a setback. But…"

"But nothing," the tall figure snapped. "It's already been taken care of. There will be no setback – my superiors will not tolerate it. Do you appreciate what I'm telling you? My superiors – will – not – tolerate – it."

"What exactly do you mean?"

"An orbital bombardment is not out of the question. We do possess the capability to reduce this planet to a smoking ruin, you know." They had nothing like that sort of firepower, but this human didn't need to know that. They had enough to destroy a good part of the city, and that would certainly do.

"There won't be any more problems, at least not if you keep your wits about you. They've found your infiltration pod, you know – you did a piss-poor job of hiding it. But I can cover that up, make sure they get sent off on a wild-goose chase somehow."

"A what? Wild *goose*? What purpose would that serve?"

"Never mind. I'm going to make sure nobody finds out what's going on – all right?"

"Very well. And this Grugell renegade that you say is among them?"

"I'll find a way for you to get him back, just like I said I would."

"Good. He has much to answer for. The Emperor Himself has requested that Clomonastik III be brought before him, before he is disintegrated."

They split up and left the area by different routes than they'd used to come in. The tall, skinny figure of the Grugell officer disappeared into a patch of woods, and the human went the other direction, pausing for a moment under a streetlight, where the white glow briefly revealed the form of Colonel George Perkins, Tarbos' Head of Security.

## The Conference Center, next morning

"I make the votes for the GPP tax fifteen aye, one nay. The motion is carried. Article IV will levy a twelve percent tax on the Gross Planetary Product of each member world." Not too surprisingly, Corinthia's King Harold had been the lone dissenter.

"We're within days of wrapping this thing up, Mike," Hector Gomez said in a low voice.

"Bill of Basic Rights passed yesterday, Articles I through IV this morning, five more to go, and we've got a Constitution," Mike agreed.

Best of all, the soon-to-be Confederacy had a flag now. The first Confederate flag hung now above the speaker's platform at the front of the main Conference Center.

The dark blue banner held thirteen four-pointed stars, twelve in a rough oval with one in the center. A light blue field at the upper left held a stylized representation of the Galaxy in white, with the single spiral arm containing all the settled worlds in red.

"How long do you suppose it will take to ratify?" Mike wondered.

"A year, maybe a year and a half. Who knows? Hyperphones are only about twenty percent faster than a ship, and every world will have to set up a system for an election."

"Well, that solves a question my son asked me once." Mike told the Vice President about the citizenship question Mike Junior had asked back on Forest.

"Well, as I understand it, your kids are American citizens, just as the kids of two citizens born in, say Europe are still citizens. They'll be citizens of Forest, now, though – I suppose they can claim dual citizenship. But in a couple generations, Mike, this is all going to be moot."

"We're changing everything, aren't we? We're setting the pattern for interstellar politics for generations to come."

"Good thing we know what we're doing, eh?" Gomez smiled, slapped Mike on the back.


**OWME Engineering Design & Development**

Another one of Frad Gilpin's gadgets was flashing and blinking away in his personal workspace. Gilpin sat watching the device's main panel like an expectant father timing his wife's contractions.

Twenty-eight slim antennae had been set up around the perimeter of Mountain View. Those antennae now cast the faintest, barely detectable web of a force field over the city. Feedback from any energy source penetrating the field would be reflected on the panel that Gilpin sat watching.

Every so often a sparkle would race across the panel's main display, and Gilpin would check it against the receipted traffic from Tarbos Main Signals station. Signals aimed at Tarbos Main Signals, he ignored. He was waiting for a beamed message that was being sent somewhere else.

He sat up suddenly, coughing a spray of sandwich crumbs. A signal had crossed the field, a tight-beam signal of some sort, aimed nowhere near the planet's Signals station. A handset was at his elbow; he grabbed it, punched in five digits.

**Near the edge of town**

Fifteen armed Security guards moved into the small copse of trees quietly. A special unit, they answered directly to Bob Pritchard; no one else knew their whereabouts.

The squad leader held a small hand-scanner. He held up one hand for the group to stop. A heat source showed on the scan, no more than ten meters to his front.

Senior Lieutenant Akillistrak XI didn't expect to evade capture forever, and his orders were that to happen were clear. But he hadn't expected to be found in his field shelter, a narrow, branch-lined pit covered with a film of opaque polymer. Hunched at one side of the pit, grimly re-reading the decoded message he'd received shortly before, he was taken completely by surprise.

The humans had slipped silently up to the edge of the shelter, led by the squad leader's scan. The polymer cover was visible at one edge, where the electronic image-enhanced camouflage had shorted out. An OWME Security troop took hold of the polymer and flipped it back, revealing the startled, upturned face of the

Grugell officer. Akillistrak had time only to let out a startled squawk before the squad leader clubbed him unconscious with a rock-hard fist.

"Call the Director. Tell him we've got our bad guy."

## Detention A

Consciousness returned slowly. Akillistrak opened his eyes at last, wincing at the pain of a mild concussion. He looked up – some sort of cage, with bare walls, a metal-barred window and the shimmering gleam of a force field at the one entrance.

Two figures stood in that entrance. One was a human, short as they all were, gray-haired. Akillistrak had received images of the primary human commanders on Tarbos; this was the planetary leader, Robert Pritchard. Beside him…

"Lieutenant, do you always recline in the presence of a superior?" The tall figure was a Grugell Group Commander. Akillistrak didn't recognize him, but his reactions were inbred by generations of militarized culture.

Akillistrak snapped to his feet. "Please accept my apology, Group Commander."

"Accepted, for the moment. Tell me, with what authority did your Commander send you down to this planet?"

"Group Commander, I assume – well, he acted with the authority of the Emperor, sir, as all Commanders do."

"I see. And did you see the order dispatch? Did you verify your orders, in accordance with Standing Order Ten?"

A stricken look from the Lieutenant in the cell was all the clue Clomonastik needed to proceed. "I see. You did not. And so now you are an accomplice to a serious violation of orders, and so are answerable to the Imperium directly. What have you to say for yourself, Lieutenant?"

"Nothing, Group Commander. Group Commander, Standing Order Ten likewise requires me to confirm your identity, does it not?" The Lieutenant looked suddenly suspicious.

"Indeed it does." Clomonastik volunteered nothing.

Akillistrak's initial disorientation, the result of his sudden and violent capture, was fading away now. "Group Commander, I do not think it necessary to ask. You are Clomonastik III, failed Occupation Commander, traitor and renegade."

"I *am* Clomonastik III, Lieutenant." Clomonastik was unperturbed by the Lieutenant's announcement. "You knew I was on this planet, obviously from the traitor in our own estate."

Akillistrak sat back down on the narrow bench in the detention cell, his jaw set.

"I should remind you, Lieutenant, that you find yourself now in similar straits as myself. You have failed in your mission, have you not? And what do you suppose awaits you, should we turn you over to your Commander?"

The Grugell Lieutenant remained silent, but a look of doubt swept across his narrow face for the briefest of moments – enough for Clomonastik.

"You do know, Lieutenant. You'll be disintegrated for your failure."

Akillistrak looked up briefly before turning his gaze on the polysteel floor.

"As I would have been disintegrated, Lieutenant. A harsh punishment, is it not, for a failure in the face of a capable – and honorable – foe, yes?"

"It is known to all…"

"Yes, and officers in the Imperial Navy are not encouraged to question the Imperium's policies, is it not so? No matter how harsh – no matter how counter-productive?"

"Counter-productive, Group Commander?"

"Indeed. You know it to be true, Lieutenant. Too many good officers have been wasted, through no fault of their own. Failure even in the face of insurmountable odds is dealt with in the same way – disintegration, and the reversion of the officer's Estate to the Emperor. The incentive is not to succeed at all costs, but rather to avoid risks." Clomonastik waved at Bob Pritchard, who stood behind him, trying in vain to follow the conversation. "These humans have learned better."

Akillistrak looked up again, his face a study in confusion.

"Now, if you would see another sunrise, you will tell me what you know. You will tell me of your purpose here, and why Commander Kadastrattik XII is orbiting this planet in a cloaked ship without orders. You are already dead to the Empire. Your only hope for life is here, as was mine after my defeat in the Occupation."

"Group Commander, the Commander has orders – I mean to say, he claimed to have orders, from the Imperium, to make contact with an agent here on Tarbos, to sabotage this convention by any means necessary, and to prevent the formation of a human interplanetary alliance."

Clomonastik nodded, inwardly pleased that he'd guessed correctly. "And who is your contact on this planet?" The Grugell Lieutenant told him.

Bob Pritchard, while he was unable to follow the high-pitched, chittering Grugell language, had no problem understanding the words "Colonel Perkins" even when spoken in a heavily inflected Grugell accent. He was turning away in rage when he felt Clomonastik grab his arm.

"Director Pritchard, what will you do?"

"I'm going to order Colonel Perkins arrested, for starters," he began, stopping when Clomonastik held up one hand. The tall Grugell pulled Pritchard out of the cell bay.

In Detention A's lobby, out of earshot of the cells, Clomonastik finally spoke. "It's safe to assume that our infiltrator speaks English, Director."

"What? How?"

"I'd imagine the Imperium has had cloaked ships monitoring your message traffic for several years now."

"Oh."

"In any case, Director, might I suggest you let your good Colonel remain a free man a while longer? He may be of more use to us free and active. As long as Kadastrattik XII thinks he still has an agent on the planet, he may overlook the death of his officer."

"But he's not dead," Pritchard protested.

"He no doubt has orders to be killed or to kill himself in the event of imminent capture, Director. He is dead to the Empire. We were very fortunate that your men were able to take him by surprise."

"So, his boss will assume he's dead," Pritchard said, "And he'll do what? Send another officer down?"

"He may. I suggest you prepare for that possibility. Now, Director, if you'll excuse me, I think I should continue my conversation with the young Lieutenant."

# Twenty

## The Chief of Security's Office

Things weren't going at all well for Colonel George Perkins.

Word of Akillistrak's capture had, of course, reached his office. Knowing it was only a matter of time before the captured Grugell officer revealed the name of his contact, Perkins was making some alternate arrangements.

In a locked compartment of his office desk were three complete sets of identification cards, complete and indistinguishable from OWME issue right down to the holographic ID image that sprang from the card at a touch of a contact. Also in the locked compartment was a sum of cash, sixteen thousand, two hundred and fifty American dollars and five thousand UK pounds; enough to see him back to Earth, where he had banked a considerably larger sum, gained from various activities over the years.

Finally, in the drawer, was the final piece of his intended retirement. He pulled the small black cube out of the desk, examined it for a moment before dropping it in his oversized briefcase along with the cash and ID cards.

"I've got a couple errands to run," he announced as he strode through the outer office. His aide and admin assistant both looked up from their desks, but offered no reply.

"Oh, and I'll be going over to Detention One to have a look at this Grugell prisoner, too. Don't look for me back until tomorrow."

Six blocks away was his apartment, and ten blocks from there was the Transit Office. A quick change of clothing and ID, a ticket purchase on next-available transit back to Earth, and then all that remained would be to fade away into the background until his ship arrived.

And the Chief of Security knew all the places to disappear.

## The *Cachalot*

Captain Jan Benton and First Officer Gillian Furst had just finished reading the orders from Tarbos Ground for the fifth time, their heads bent together over the message flimsy as they floated on the *Cachalot*'s claustrophobic, zero-gravity Bridge.

"I'm not sure I understand these orders."

Captain Benton nodded, agreeing with her First Officer; but in her nine years with OWME, she'd learned that the Company always had a reason for whatever it did. Anyway, the orders were clear. Benton began barking orders to her Bridge crew.

"Helm, bring us to one-fourteen, positive fifty, engage the main drive, all ahead two-thirds."

"Coming about, Captain, star drive engaged. Engineering answers ahead two-thirds." The massive cargo hull accelerated slowly, the drive sending an audible *thrummm* through the ship.

Captain Benton made her way to the Navigation station. "Lieutenant Karzai, plot a course to five AU's outside Tarbo's orbit; give me a trajectory that lands us in a parking orbit that keeps us with a line-of sight to Tarbos as much as possible. Relay the trajectory to Helm as soon as you have it."

"Won't be easy to keep a line-of site that far out, Captain. I'm not even sure if we can scan that far, visually or any other way."

"We don't need to. They'll contact us when the time's right."

"Contact us for what, Captain?"

"They haven't said."

The Bridge crew exchanged puzzled looks, but the expression on Captain Benton's face forestalled any further discussion. Silently, the *Cachalot*'s crew carried out the necessary tasks to place the ship in a parking orbit near the system's single gas giant.

## The Conference Center

Corinthia, as several delegates had suspected, was shaping up to be a problem. In particular, the King of Corinthia, who had emigrated hundreds of light years to set up an autocratic rule, was shaping up to be a real problem.

"We do not see why we need to have this ratified by a plebiscite on each world. The various planets sent delegates here, and to do what? To set up a system of interstellar government, and to raise a Navy. Fine and good, We say – We are more than willing to contribute the required percentage of Corinthia's product to build ships and train people to man them. But We consider the requirement for a plebiscite to be an unacceptable interference in Corinthia's internal affairs." The King pounded on the speaker's lectern with one hand as he spoke.

"Are not the several worlds to be sovereign entities unto themselves? What right, then, this Confederation, to dictate how We administer our own planet, a planet founded Our own self at Our own expense? A planet settled by Our loyal followers, dedicated as they are to serving their sovereign?"

In the audience, Mike Crider Senior was beginning to get annoyed at Harold I's constant use of the royal "we." He wasn't alone in that sentiment. The King continued on, oblivious.

"And so, We must say no, no to the presumption that The Confederation will run roughshod over the rights of free planets to determine their own destinies. We must say no to the ratification rule and no to conditional acceptance. If this is to be a limited partnership of sovereign worlds, let it be so. Let the Confederation levy its tax and raise its Navy, and interfere not with the internal affairs of the member worlds." With a final glare at the audience, King Harold relinquished the floor. In front of Mike, the United Kingdom's Prince Harry muttered to himself, "Stupid, cousin, very, very stupid."

Mike leaned forward. Around him voices were raised, many in anger. "Is he really your cousin?"

Prince Harry turned around in his seat. "I'm sorry to say, yes, he is. He was never considered one of the brightest of the Royal Family, you know. His father was very clever indeed, and he made a tremendous fortune developing land in Africa following the wars and resulting famine. Harold – you know, at times I'm sorry I share a name with the blighter – always was an arrogant bastard, even as a lad, and you see now where that's led him. The moment he inherited his father's money, off he went, and the family was quite frankly happy to see him go."

"He sort of just blasted his own argument apart," Mike commented. "Letting the 'free planets determine their own destinies?' Isn't that the whole purpose behind this plebiscite requirement?"

"Indeed. You understand that, and I understand that. But Harold will never understand that. As far as he's concerned, he *is* Corinthia. The man, unfortunately, cannot see past the end of his own nose."

"He's not making any friends here. He seems to have just ignored the last few hundred years of Earth's history."

"Oh, he excels at ignoring inconvenient facts, I assure you."

## Director Pritchard's office, the next day

The Grugell didn't know or understand the human concept of nostalgia, and so Clomonastik was perfectly happy to shed the replica of the uniform he'd once worn with pride. He had replaced it with a tailored, dark blue silk suit with his usual sparkling white shirt and tie. Fastidiousness was customary among the Grugell, and Clomonastik was no exception.

"Well, Director Pritchard, it seems my initial guess was correct. The Lieutenant – his name, by the way, is Akillistrak XI– informs me that his Commander is indeed on a mission to interfere with any attempt by humanity to form an interstellar government, to include the use of force if necessary. I'm convinced that my old subordinate would attempt an orbital bombardment, if he thought he would gain the Emperor's favor in so doing; he always was an ambitious sort. So, are we all, though, yes? But Kadastrattik XII possesses ambition in an unhealthy extreme."

"Do they have the power to do so?"

"Almost certainly yes. The weapons on even a small frigate could certainly destroy a good part of the city. Twenty-two years ago, a frigate mounted several different weapons systems, including an energy weapon that is quite capable of penetrating the atmosphere to do considerable damage. The Imperium may well have developed more effective weapons since then, although the Navy's scientists and engineers do not work with the – how shall I say this – abandon that your own technical people display? Innovation is slower in the Empire."

"People work harder for a personal carrot than a communal stick," Pritchard noted.

"So I've learned, Director. At any rate, I'm certain Kadastrattik XII would not shrink from bombarding the planet if he thought it necessary; however, his orders would seem to state that such force is to be a last resort. Unusual," he mused, "that the Emperor would be so circumspect. I would have expected him to send a fleet to Tarbos and reduce the planet to a smoking ruin. Interesting – perhaps the Empire is not as strong as we suspected it to be? Some internal problem, perhaps?"

"We have no way of knowing that," Pritchard pointed out. "We can only proceed on what we know, and try to anticipate what this Kadastrattik will do next."

"Indeed. And I may have some insight there as well." Clomonastik continued for several minutes.

Pritchard drummed on his desk, thinking rapidly. "Would these Grugell ships use radio for short-range communications, like we do?"

"They would indeed, Director."

"Good." Pritchard stood up and walked out of the office without further explanation. Clomonastik watched him go, shrugged philosophically, and followed him out.

# Twenty-One

**The *K-101***

Kadastrattik XII was beginning to become impatient. He'd taken time for a meal in his quarters, and now bounded back onto his Bridge, barking at his Signals officer. "Signals, has there been any word from Lieutenant Akillistrak?"

"No, Commander. No word from the surface."

"He's been killed," Kadastrattik muttered.

"It's soon to assume that, Commander," the frigate's Subcommander pointed out.

"It's not," Kadastrattik disagreed. "He's three cycles overdue, and he's never been so much as a millicycle overdue in reporting before. No, he's been found and killed by the humans. They will know now that the Empire is involved. We'll proceed with our second option. Subcommander, see to the preparation of the Weapons station."

"By your command."

**Central Signals, Tarbos**

While the main radio tower for the Mountain View area was on the same hilltop as the base of the Skyhook, Central Signals was in the same building as Director Pritchard's office. Three video and ten audio channels provided news and entertainment for the settlers on Tarbos, but the station also had the ability to transmit on a wide range of frequencies – including the list of likely frequencies provided by Clomonastik.

"Send a standard hail on all these freqs," Pritchard ordered, handing the list to a technician. "Use all the power you've got."

"You want a directional signal, sir?"

"Yeah, if you can. Focus on about a twenty-degree arc centered on a geosynchronous orbit over Mountain View. That's where our target is likely to be."

"A moment, please, Director?" Nearby, Clomonastik was jotting something down on a notepad he'd picked up from a desk. "Send the following, if you would, in binary code," he told the technician, handing over a notepad page with a series of ones and zeros. "It's a standard fleet hailing code; their computers will recognize it."

"Yes, sir." The technician programmed a quick multi-frequency standard hailing code and punched to transmit.

"Sending now, sir."

It took a few minutes, but after that time a message-return indicator blinked on the technician's terminal screen. Clomonastik leaned over to look at the code. "Send this in reply," he handed over another notepad page. "This requests voice communication."

Two minutes passed, then three, before the message-return indicator blinked again. A tap of the key and the technician reported, "Sir, you're on a voice channel." Pritchard picked up a headset, motioned Clomonastik to do likewise. "I'll probably need you to translate."

"Unidentified ship, this is Tarbos Ground. Please identify yourself." Beside the Director, Clomonastik translated into the chittering Grugell language. In a moment, the high-pitched, rattling reply came, also in the Grugell tongue. Clomonastik translated again: "If you are calling us, then you already know who we are. Who are you?"

"This is Director Bob Pritchard. I'm in command down here on the planet." That wasn't a perfectly accurate description of Pritchard's level of authority, but he correctly assumed that it would be something the militaristic Grugell would understand. Again, Clomonastik handled the translation:

"Indeed. This is the Commander of the Grugell Imperial Navy warship in orbit. What is it you want?"

"I require you to drop your cloak, and to leave orbit and depart this system without further delay."

"Or you will do what?" Clomonastik's translation couldn't quite disguise the contempt in the reply.

"You are in violation of Tarbos space," Pritchard evaded.

"We are, Director? And exactly by what authority," the voice replied, "do you claim right to control passage through this space? What governing body do you represent?"

Pritchard paused for a moment, confused. Clomonastik scribbled another note and handed to him, whispering, "you should pronounce the names 'Kad-ah-strat-ick' and 'Ah-kill-ah-strahck.' It's the closest approximation you'll make in English." Pritchard examined the note, nodded.

"Commander Kadastrattik," he barked into the headset's mike. Beside him, Clomonastik translated in a voice that was strangely calm and composed. "Your agent Lieutenant Akillistrak is in our custody. He has told us what your intention is and who you are. You are currently under the surveillance of our defensive systems." Which was true, as far as it went. "I ask you a final time, you will drop your cloaking field and leave this system at once."

"I think I will not comply, Director," Clomonastik translated in reply.

"Sir, the signal has been terminated at the source," the Signals technician announced.

"Well. I wonder if I could have screwed that up any worse," Pritchard groused.

"You have done better than you think, Director," Clomonastik assured him. "Kadastrattik has been handed a piece of information that will surely make him uncomfortable. He now knows that we know something, which he assumed we would not. This will cause him to consider his next action carefully; we have succeeded, for the moment at least, to force him to react to us, instead of the opposite. We should take advantage of that."

## The *Cachalot*

The *Cachalot*'s duty helmsman called out, "Captain, we're on station as ordered." The deep rumble of the drive faded away quickly to nothing.

"Good. All stop. Hold station here. Navigation, are you still able to track that ship?"

"No, Captain – too far away. We lost him about a hundred thousand kilometers out."

"Great. Just great. How fast do you think you'd be able to pick him up if we move back?"

"No idea, Captain. This is kind of a makeshift rig; you know?"

Janice Benton muttered a curse under her breath. "The whole situation is rapidly going from bad to worse."

"I have a really bad feeling about this," her Executive Officer agreed.

# Twenty-Two

**The *K-101***

Kadastrattik sat quietly, his hand still on the cutoff switch for the communication wand on the arm of his Bridge chair. He thought very rapidly for a few moments, and then stood up.

"Tactical, are any forms of energy emissions directed at us from the planet's surface?"

The Tactical officer examined all of his readouts carefully. "No, Commander. No unusual energy sources from the planet's surface. The communications signal has stopped. There are the usual electromagnetic communications transmissions, and one and one-half cycles ago there was a subspace transmission from the transmitter on their low-orbit docking tower. All traffic appears routine."

"Give me a global scan of the area."

"Scanning now, Commander. Space scans clear for one hundred thousand kilos around the ship. The human cargo ship left orbit six cycles ago, Commander. There is no other detectable ship traffic."

"And as far as we know, they can't cloak a ship," Kadastrattik mused. "Weapons, status."

"Commander, anti-proton projectors are warmed, charged and ready. Torpedo bays report loaded and ready, all weapons are on-line."

"Excellent." Kadastrattik crossed over to the Weapons station. "Since they know we are here, perhaps it is time to send a more stringent message. Tie in the targeting computer of the number one forward anti-proton projector to the main scanner and pick up the antennae for the subspace transmitter. Very carefully, now - target the antennae only, not the power source or the tower itself. We shall cut off their ability to communicate with their fellows on other worlds, and now that the cargo ship has departed, there will be no way for them to call for assistance. Then," Kadastrattik grinned wickedly, "Perhaps this Director Pritchard and I will speak again."

The whole process took less than fifteen seconds. "Commander, target is acquired, I am ready to fire."

"You may proceed," Kadastrattik replied.

## The Tarbos Skyhook

From outside, were there anyone to see, the sight would have been impressive. Seemingly from empty space, a slight green glow brightened suddenly, building within a second to a blinding green glare that disgorged an emerald energy bolt down to the planet's surface.

The hyperphone transmitter's antennae on the top of the Tarbos Skyhook consisted of a stout titanium and gallium pole, a meter thick at the base, thirty-five meters high, tapering to only ten centimeters at the tip. Various wiring, relays, molecular switches, and a massive power transformer filled the interior of the transmitter; at the heart of the mechanism was a tiny magnetic bottle holding, in separate eddies of a powerfully driven field, a tiny particle of dark matter and another of anti-germanium.

The bolt of emerald-green anti-protons, traveling at about a third of the speed of light, hit before anyone could even notice them coming. The bolt smashed into the antennae three meters from the base.

The anti-protons converted the titanium and gallium layers of the antennae wall to plasma, which flashed outward, cutting through the rest of the antennae base. Before the top portion could begin to fall, the follow-on antiparticles in the bolt penetrated into the magnetic containment bottle holding the particles of dark matter and anti-germanium, exposing both to the surrounding environment. Both materials exploded violently, and only the tiny quantities involved prevented an enormous catastrophe. As it happened, the upper portion of the antennae was shattered into several pieces, which were shot into space by the force of the blast.

Three technicians were working in the monitoring station below the antennae. The explosion immolated all three before they had the chance to know anything was wrong. The next level below the monitoring station was taken up with an automated weather monitoring radar and various mechanical elements of the shuttle docking stations, which absorbed most of the rest of the blast. The next level down contained offices and a small cafeteria for the Skyhook staff, which survived with minor damage. Decompression alarms began hooting as the Skyhook's self-repair droids immediately deployed to close several small breaches in the level's pressure hull.

Three seconds after the anti-proton bolt hit, alarms were clanging up and down the Skyhook, and an emergency message was flashed to the Director's office even before the emergency evacuation of the Skyhook's staff began.

The Conference Center

The blast from the Skyhook was only a faint rumble when it reached the courtyard in the back of the Conference Center, where roughly half of the delegates were enjoying the balmy afternoon. Mike Crider looked up curiously, scanning the sky for thunderclouds with an outdoorsman's instinct, but the sky was clear.

"Dad," his son called from a bench a few meters away. "Did you hear that?"

"Sounded like thunder. No clouds, though…" Around them, the ebb and flow of conversation went on as before, until a contingent of Security troops burst into the courtyard.

"Ladies, gentlemen, please follow me at once," the Sergeant leading the detail shouted.

"What is this?" "What's going on?" Several delegates, assistants and various hangers-on began asking questions at once. The Sergeant cut them all off with the swipe of one hand. "There's no time for questions now, people. I need you all to follow me out of here right now."

"Come on, then," Mike called out, and got up to follow the Sergeant out of the courtyard. The rest of the groups slowly followed them to the street side of the Center, where three skimmer-buses were pulling up. People from inside the Center were already filing aboard the first bus.

"What's this all about?" Mike asked the Sergeant.

"Don't know, sir, I've just got orders to get you all in the bus and get moving. We'll get destination orders once we're under way."

"Fair enough," Mike acceded.

The buses whipped away from the curb the moment the last passenger's foot left the pavement. The Sergeant had boarded the bus Mike was on; as soon as the skimmer-bus was moving in the light mid-afternoon traffic, he stood up at the front and removed his polymer helmet.

"OK, folks," he announced, "I'm Sergeant Paul Kroger, and here's what we know so far." He turned to look out the front windscreen before continuing.

"There's been an explosion and a fire at the top of the Tarbos Skyhook. We don't have all the details yet, but the hyperphone transmitter was knocked out. Initial indications are that the tower was hit by an energy beam or particle beam of some sort, fired from an orbiting ship."

Mike Junior and Maria Gutierrez had taken the seat just behind Mike; the younger Crider now leaned forward. "Grugell ship, Dad?"

"Yep. Pipe down and listen, Junior."

At the front of the bus, Sergeant Kroger was still talking. "…at this point, we know that three technicians have been killed, and several people in the office/cafeteria level were injured. The Skyhook is being evacuated right now, and the Director has ordered all of the delegates and conference attendees be taken to a safe place. Where that safe place is, I don't yet know. When I know, so will all of you."

The bus shot through traffic, dodging the few private skimmers and larger cargo haulers as it sped for the outskirts of Mountain View.

## Central Signals

Bob Pritchard was back in Central ten minutes after the explosion, trailed again by Clomonastik. "Get me that Grugell son of a bitch on the line again," he barked at the technician on duty.

Two and a half minutes later, the technician reported, "I have a reply, sir."

Pritchard heard a string of high-pitched, chittering Grugell in his headphones, reminding him of the calls of bats. Almost instantly, Clomonastik smoothly translated.

"Is this Director Pritchard? What is it you want?"

"You know what I want, you bastard," Pritchard barked. (Clomonastik, after a pause, translated the last word as "one without honor.") "You fired on our Skyhook. That's an act of war."

"Against whom, I ask again, Director? What government do you represent?"

"I'm speaking as a representative of the Confederated Free Planets," Pritchard replied, using the term publicly for the first time. "I'll warn you one more time, Commander, you have been ordered to leave Confederate space at once."

"I think I will oblige you to force me, Director."

Clomonastik removed his headset. "Director, I strongly recommend you terminate communications at once and recall your cargo ship. Kadastrattik's ship must be destroyed at once."

"What? Why?"

"He knows more than you suspect, Director. He has already destroyed your hyperphone transmitter, effectively cutting off your communications with the rest of humanity. Were I in his situation, I would now be back-scanning your location from the radio transmitter signal to discover your location, and we will know when he has succeeded when he fires on this location. Decapitation," Clomonastik explained, "Has long been a common tactic against a competent enemy." Despite his prediction, Pritchard noticed the Clomonastik was quite calm and seemed unconcerned for his own safety. "You should remove yourself from this place at once, Director," the tall alien urged. "He may already have a close approximation of your location."

"Cut the signal off," Pritchard ordered. "All right, let's get out of here."

"A wise decision, Director. Where shall we go?"

"The Conference delegates. We'll join them."

Clomonastik nodded and bent from the waist in a half-bow, motioning for the Director to precede him from the chamber. "Evacuate this building," Pritchard snapped at the Signals staff as he left. "Everybody out."

# Twenty-Three

**Fifteen kilometers inland**

The setting was beautiful.

Fifteen kilometers from the outskirts of Mountain View was the tiny community of Rangely, a farming and ranching town of about two thousand. And just outside of that community was the Rangely Retreat, a resort and vacation area still under construction in the timbered hills. The main lodge was built on the edge of a thick stand of native broadleaf trees that resembled, somehow, giant gingkoes. Facing a huge meadow of grasses and forbs, the lodge's enormous porch was within rock-throwing distance of a burbling stream. The air was filled with the twittering of several species of bat-winged, flying creatures that ran from sparrow to crow-sized; most of them hadn't yet been named, but they added to the ambience of the setting nonetheless.

"The main lodge is pretty much finished," Sergeant Kroger was explaining to the assembled delegates as Pritchard and Clomonastik climbed out of Pritchard's personal skimmer. "The guest cabins back there in the trees are a little rough, but we're bringing in a few crews from Mountain View to make them as comfortable as possible. The problem right now is power; the hookups from the main station in Mountain View aren't finished yet, so we're flying in a Torch to rig up power for the time being." In fact, the small portable fusion reactor was less than ten minutes away, sling-loaded under a retrieval droid. "The area around the resort is secured by a company of Security troops. So, for the time being, I'd ask you all to stay in the immediate area – you'll be stopped by the troops if you go too far – and have a look around. We should have power in a half-hour or so."

The delegates began to fan out around the area, most of them heading inside the main lodge. Mike Crider watched his son and Maria Gutierrez wander nonchalantly off towards the guest cabins before he went looking for Hector Gutierrez.

He found the Vice President talking with Bob Pritchard and Clomonastik III near a picnic table on the edge of the meadow a few meters from the stream.

"It's past time," Pritchard was saying as Mike walked up. Clomonastik was nodding agreement. The Director noticed Mike's questioning look and answered before Mike could ask: "I've ordered Colonel Perkins arrested; he's in custody and on his way to Detention One as we speak. I figured that particular jig was up; no point in letting him pass any more information on."

"Like the location of this place," Hector Gutierrez added.

"Exactly."

"So, what now?" Mike wanted to know.

"We're about to wrap this thing up," Pritchard replied. "What have we got, two more votes? Let's get it done, printed, signed, and 'phoned off to the other worlds for ratification. What those people in orbit don't know is that we've got a backup to the Skyhook hyperphone antenna. I can have it back in operation in three days, with another day or two to repair some mechanical and structural damage. Let's get our Constitution voted up and sent out for ratification."

"You're in a bit of a hurry, Bob," Hector Gutierrez noted, examining Pritchard closely.

"Well," Pritchard confessed, "I jumped the gun a little. I just ordered the Grugell Commander to leave the Tarbos system, in the name of the Confederated Free Planets."

Mike laughed. "Well, what was his answer?"

"Basically, it was 'make me,'" Pritchard replied. "That's in the works now."

## The *Cachalot*

"Incoming message from Tarbos Ground, Captain."

Jan Benton released the buckle of the web belt that held her in her Bridge chair and floated to the Signals console. "Well?" she demanded. The Signals tech pointed at her screen.

"The hell…" Captain Benton was a fast reader. Spinning in the zero-gee Bridge, she tossed herself back at her chair and began strapping in. "All decks, secure for maneuvers," she barked into her wand mike, her voice booming out across the ship. "Navigation, get me trajectory back to Tarbos orbit, maximum sub-C speed. No breaking into subspace this trip. Helm, bring us about, one-eighty by zero. Ahead full."

"Coming about, Captain, Engineering answers ahead full."

"Keep her under the Subspace transit," Benton reminded the helmsman. "Scanning, get that gadget on-line, I want a course track on that cloaked ship as soon as we're in range."

## The *K-101*

Kadastrattik turned away from the smoking ruin of a body that still slumped on the deck in front of the Scanning station, his personal weapon still in his hand. "Have this wreckage removed at once," he snapped. "And I will repeat my policy; failure on this ship is not tolerated! If this fool had moved a millicycle faster, we'd have had the human's Commander located, and this would be over!"

The Bridge crew was silent. "Weapons! Get me a target. Any target. A major population center will do nicely."

"Tying into the Scanning console now, Commander," the Weapons officer answered in a querulous voice. "Commander, the center of the city below seems to have a marketplace, or at least some center of activity. Scans show heavy traffic in that sector. I am currently tracking vehicle and foot traffic. Number One anti-proton projector is locked."

"Very good. Weapons, hold on that target. I will allow them two cycles to think. When that time is up, we shall see if we can raise that fool Pritchard again."

## The Rangely Retreat

The buzzing of his personal comm-link shouldn't have startled Bob Pritchard, but he was. He pulled the tiny gray card from his shirt pocket and tapped the blue oval on the front to activate it. "This is Pritchard," he answered.

"Director," a disembodied voice came from the card, "This is Central Signals. I've got a call in that alien language. We weren't sure what to do about it, so we're prepared to forward it to you, sir."

"Go ahead," Pritchard answered, throwing a glance at Clomonastik. A stream of chittering Grugell came from the comm-link.

"It's Kadastrattik," Clomonastik answered. "Director, keep your transmission short; speak to him for no more than a minute or he will trace you. He's demanding that the Convention disband, or he'll destroy Mountain View."

Pritchard thought very hard about that. "Any chance he's bluffing?"

"Virtually none, Director."

"Neither am I," Pritchard replied. He switched the comm-link to another channel, and spoke a code into the tiny mike. "How far out is the *Cachalot*?"

"Six minutes, Director," came the reply.

Pritchard switched back to the first channel. "This is your last chance, Commander. Decloak and leave my system now." Beside him, Clomonastik translated into chattering Grugell; as soon as he finished, Pritchard killed the signal.

"Let's see what happens," he said. "In about five and a half minutes, we'll know."


## The *K-101*

Kadastrattik listened to the hiss of static for a moment before turning to his Weapons officer. "Very well, Director, it seems we must do this the hard way. SubLieutenant, you may fire when ready."

"By your command."

In space, the faint green glow appeared again, brightened, turned into a spear of anti-protons that lanced for the surface of Tarbos.

## Downtown Mountain View

In the middle of downtown Mountain View was the Main Street Mall, a pedestrian-only avenue lined with shops, cafeterias, and lounges. On a weekday afternoon, in a Company town, it was mercifully an hour before the end-of-workday shopping rush. There were only a few hundred people in the Mall when the anti-proton bolt arrived, smashing through the Synergy Bar & Grille and exploding outward into the street. Four employees and sixteen patrons of the Synergy were incinerated instantly, and five others badly burned from the heat flare from the searing conversion of elementary particles. Nine people walking on the Mall were burned, and one killed by flying debris. As the roar of the explosion settled, panic set in, and customers and employees alike began to run from the area.

Overhead, another bolt of emerald lightning shot down, obliterating the OWME Mercantile Furniture & Appliances branch and killing sixteen people. Twenty-eight more were badly injured.


## The *K-101*

"Cease fire, SubLieutenant," Kadastrattik ordered. "Find another target. Find another concentration of humans."

"Scanning now, Commander. There is something…"

"Something? What do you mean, something?"

"There is a concentration of humans here, Commander," the Weapons officer said, pointing at a blue fleck on the display, "outside of their main city. There is a small settlement here," he pointed again, "And then this concentration of human readings here, just a few kilos away. There's nothing else in the area."

"That's it, Kadastrattik. That's where their gathering is – I'd wager a year's wine ration on it. Target that concentration, make ready to fire!"

"By your command – locking number one anti-proton projector now."

## The *Cachalot*

"There he is, Captain. One hundred sixteen kilometers out and closing."

The *Cachalot* had been decelerating hard for a minute and ten seconds, slowing from the run in to scan for the alien warship. Janice Benton was at the Navigation station in a single bound. A faint green track showed on the screen, off the freighter's port bow.

"All right, we've got him. Now let's see if we can make this work." She turned to the Helm. "OK, all ahead flank, come left to one-sixteen degrees, negative ten. All decks prepare for evasive maneuvers."

"Captain, all decks report secured for evasive maneuvering. Engineering answers ahead flank, coming about to new course one-sixteen by neg ten."

"Very well. Navigation, plot an intercept course, feed adjustments to Helm as necessary."

"Adjusting now, Captain."

Beneath them, the deepening *thrummm* of the star drive increased in pitch as the huge cargo hull accelerated.

"Helm, come right three degrees," the Navigation officer advised.

"Coming right three."

The Navigation display showed the faint green track coming in closer, closer.

"Helm, hold on the source of that track," Captain Benton ordered. "See how it's flattening out? When we get within two hundred meters, angle us so the starboard edge of the cargo disk intercepts the leading edge of this trace. Give me about ten meters of overlap. Understand?"

"Captain, you're ordering a ramming."

"That's right." Benton looked down at the track again. "All ahead emergency."

"Ahead emergency, aye. Engine room answers ahead emergency, Captain. Six minutes to subspace transit. Ninety-eight seconds to impact on current course."

"Stay on that course, Helm."

Beneath the deck the engine sound deepened to a dull roar.


**The Rangely Retreat**

"Let's get everyone into the main lodge," Bob Pritchard called out. "Let's all get inside. We've still got business to take care of, everyone."

In the stress of the moment, Pritchard forgot that he had laid his comm-link on the picnic table; in the stress of the moment, he didn't notice Clomonastik III casually wandering past the table and picking it up.


**The *K-101***

Kadastrattik looked up as the Signals officer called out. "Incoming signal from the surface, Commander."

"Weapons officer, hold your fire. Put it through to my head-set," Kadastrattik ordered. He pulled a slim silver headset from the arm of his command chair, and placed the earpieces on his head.

"This is the Commander Kadastrattik," he answered the messaging tone. "Is this Director Pritchard again?" His eyes widened in shock as a familiar voice answered, speaking not in the human's language but in his own.

"It is not Director Pritchard, Commander. You know who this is, do you not?"

Kadastrattik's voice dripped with contempt when he finally answered. "I do. This would be the traitor and renegade Clomo-nastik III, yes?"

"Yes. Commander, I presume you are still scanning the planet's surface?"

"You know that we are, renegade," Kadastrattik snapped. "You are all too aware of Imperial Navy policy while in orbit above a possibly hostile planet. And what interesting things we are scanning, renegade! Gatherings of humans far outside the city – almost as though they were hiding! Hiding what, I wonder?"

"Yes, I am aware of Imperial policy, Kadastrattik, and your strict adherence to it does you no credit now. You were always a shallow thinker; you were so when you served as my inferior, and I'm gratified to see you have not changed."

"What? What do you mean?"

"Tell me something, my rigidly ambitious one-time inferior. You fancy yourself a student of Grugell history, yes? Yes, of course you do, how well I remember the boring lectures you would deliver after several servings of wine. Tell me what happened to the conspirators involved in the Night of Seven Blades."

"They were captured and executed," Kadastrattik answered, remembering the history all too well. He waved a hand at the

Tactical station. The officer at that post was already at work tracing the transmission's source.

"And you've attempted to retrace the steps of those conspirators, have you not? Perhaps not against the Emperor, no, but against several of your contemporaries and, indeed, a former Commander. It seems only fitting, then, that the fate of those conspirators be retraced as well."

"Speak plainly, renegade," Kadastrattik barked. "What is it you want?"

"Only to ensure that, before you die, you know who it was that told them how to find you," Clomonastik lied. "A final joke to play on my would-be assassin. You are tracing this transmission, yes? It will avail you nothing. You are still my inferior, Kadastrattik, in so many ways." Clomonastik cut off the transmission.

"What?" The signal died in Kadastrattik's ears. He snapped to his feet, turning to the Tactical station. "Tactical officer, stand down on your surface scan, give me a global scan of the area immediately! Weapons, lock that target and fire at once!"

## The *Cachalot*

"Captain, energy emissions from the source of that track."

"It's a scanning beam," Benton guessed. "Too late. We've got him."

"Forty seconds to impact, Captain."

Benton pulled herself back to her bridge chair and fasted her emergency safety harness. Around her, the rest of the Bridge crew followed suit.

"Thirty seconds."

Benton grabbed the wand mike off the arm of her Bridge chair, pressing the PAGE stud. "All hands, brace for collision. All hands, brace for collision." She shouted to the Signals station, "Sound the collision alarm."

"Fifteen seconds. Captain, there's something happening on the visual channel."

Captain Benton switched her personal Bridge chair flip-up viewer to the forward scanner's visual channel. Out there in space, growing closer rapidly, a faint green glow was appearing out of nowhere, growing rapidly brighter.

The rumble of the engine was still increasing in pitch.

## The *K-101*

"Commander, *enemy ship approaching at high speed!*"

Kadastrattik shouted, "Turn hard right, drives ahead full! Weapons, power down!"

They'd been caught looking the wrong way. Kadastrattik looked at the Tactical readout display on his personal viewer, noting the huge shape of the human cargo ship racing in at them from behind. The *K-101* responded quickly to its helm, but it was plain to see that they were too late…

"Sound the impact alarm!"

## The *Cachalot*

"Captain, the track is changing aspect. Track source is turning, I have a bearing change, they are turning to starboard. Won't do them any good, Captain. We'll clip them with the edge of the cargo disk, just like you planned."

"Five seconds. Four. Three. Two. One. IMPACT!"

The ship gave a mighty lurch and spun to the side. Hooting alarms began to sound, and a calm synthetic voice intoned, "HULL BREACH ON CARGO DISK, DECKS THREE AND FOUR, SECTIONS FOUR, FIVE, AND SIX."

"Seal off those sections!" Benton barked. "All stop! Bring us around to face that ship, Helm. Stand by on navigation thrusters."

"All stop. Coming left to one-zero-nine pos three. Standing by on navigation thrusters."

"Are those damaged sections sealed off?"

"Already done, Captain. Damage control systems have activated," the Signals tech reported.

"Get me a forward scanner on the main screen!"

The main viewer sparkled with interference, but gradually resolved. At the lower edge of the display, Tarbos rotated serenely, but at the upper, a silver orb with two slender arms wallowed in space, trailing a sparkling cloud of gas from a serious hull breach. As they watched, one of the yellow drive pods disintegrated in a spray of bright metal and sparks.

"There they are, Captain," the Navigator pointed out.

"No shit," Benton answered. "See if you can raise them on ship-to-ship. And get me a damage report!"

## The Rangely Retreat

Clomonastik III came striding into the lodge, an odd grin on his face. He handed Bob Pritchard his comm-link card. "You left this on that table, Director," he said with a strange, smug tone. "I believe you have a call. I heard it beeping."

Pritchard took the card and tapped the contact. "Director Pritchard."

"Director, this is Tarbos Ground. We have monitored a collision in orbit. High-resolution radar is showing the *Cachalot* and an unknown ship, sir. The unknown just appeared."

"You don't say," Pritchard smiled. "What's happening now?"

"Sir, it looks like the smaller ship – the unknown – is badly damaged. It seems to be out of control. Sir, is that the ship that fired on the Skyhook and downtown?"

"Yes, it is."

"Director, it looks a lot like the cargo ship rammed the unknown deliberately."

"Yes, that's right. They did."

"Good."


**The *Cachalot***


"No reply to ship-to-ship, Captain."

Janice Benton wasn't too surprised. Still… "Keep trying. Let's close on them a little. We should be able to use one of our landing shuttles to render assistance, if…" A flash of light from the main viewer cut her sentence short.

"*All hands brace for impact!*" she shouted, watching as the blast front from the Grugell ship's thermonuclear self-destruct mechanism raced towards them.

The *Cachalot* rang again, and again the damage-control alarms hooted, but their distance – and the attenuated shock front from the explosion in the vacuum of space – saved them from major damage.

"That had to be a scuttling charge, Captain." Benton looked up to see First Officer Gillian Furst floating through the Bridge hatchway. "Damage parties are shoring up shock damage on the port side of the cargo disk. Chief Wilson says forty-eight hours,

and he'll have the damage secured enough to return to Earth."
Furst's face was blackened with soot, her uniform blouse torn, but
she looked unhurt.

"I didn't think they'd blow themselves up," Benton replied.

"I guess they had something to hide," Furst snorted.

"Ma'am," the Scanning console operator called. "I've got five
small objects on radar – they look like escape pods of some kind."

"Get a landing shuttle out there," Benton ordered, "and pick
'em up. And Signals? Get me the Director."

"Working on it, Captain."

# Twenty-Four

**The Rangely Retreat**

Director Pritchard pocketed his comm-link, a satisfied grin on his face. "All right," he announced, holding up his hands to gain the attention of the delegates assembled in the main lodge. "That was Captain Jan Benton, commanding the *Cachalot*, an OWME cargo ship now in orbit overhead." He waited for the group to quiet down before continuing. "The *Cachalot*, on my orders, rammed and badly damaged the unidentified ship that fired on the Skyhook, and on downtown Mountain View."

A cheer rose up from the assembled delegates. Pritchard stood, grinning, until the noise subsided.

"We have now determined that the unidentified ship was a Grugell warship. The ship self-destructed shortly after the ramming, but the *Cachalot* has recovered several escape pods containing survivors, including the Grugell Captain. They will be brought to Mountain View by shuttle for questioning."

"Hang 'em!" came a shout from the crowd.

"No, I don't think so," Pritchard answered. "We've tried very hard to create a society where everyone – everyone – has basic rights. We've tried to create a civilized society, a government of laws, a civilized society that lives under the rule of law. The Grugell don't understand that – as our new friend Clomonastik here tells me, they live as a lot of people on Earth once did, under the fist of a dictator. Well, we're going to face them one day, as free people on Earth had to face the despots and dictators there, and fight to make all people free. We won that fight, and we'll win this one, too. And in that fight, we'll hold to our principles. The Grugell survivors will be questioned, but then any that wish will be returned to their home society, and any who wish asylum are welcome to stay here on Tarbos."

Hector Gutierrez led the applause, which rapidly swelled to fill the lodge. Director Pritchard, grinning from ear to ear now, shouted over the noise: "Now, let's get these last two items voted on!"

Vice President Gutierrez turned, still smiling, to see the junior Crider and his daughter approaching him, hand in hand.

"Mr. Vice President?" Crider the Younger was slightly nervous, but only slightly. "There's something I'd like to talk to you about."

The smile faded from Hector Gutierrez's face, and for the moment he ceased being the Vice President of the United States and a delegate to the Constitutional Convention for the Confederated Free Planets. For the moment, he was just a father.

"I have a feeling I know what about. Maria? I presume you've already answered?"

"Yes, Daddy. Yes."

"Mike, I don't suppose you'll be interested in moving to Earth?"

"Actually, sir, we were thinking of living on Forest."

"I thought you might be. You've got too much of your father in you, Mike. I don't think you'd be happy on Earth." He stopped and looked at both of the young people critically. "Well, I can't say this is unexpected. Mike, I think you'll make a fine husband for Maria. Maria, your Mom and I will miss you, but I can see already that you're going to be quite happy on Forest."

Behind him, he heard the elder Crider's voice. "What's going on here?" Mike Senior asked.

Mike the elder was surprised to hear Hector Gutierrez burst out in laughter. "Come on, bro," the Vice President chuckled, slapping Mike on the back. "Let's let the others get this thing organized. We've got something else to plan for at the moment."

**Two days later**

The votes were taken, all measures passed, and the draft Constitution hyperphoned to the several worlds of the nascent Confederacy for ratification. Seated once more around a table in Mountain View's Palace restaurant, both Criders and Gutierrezes had cause now to celebrate rather than deliberate. And once more, at Mike Senior's insistence, Clomonastik III joined in the gathering. While the Grugell restaurateur was still amused at the human tradition of monogamy, he was more flattered than he cared to admit by the invitation.

"Well, I sent a hyperphone message to Jenny and Andrea on Forest with the good news," Mike said, in between sips of a Tarbosian beer he'd grown to like. "So, in about six weeks, they'll know what's going on. And of course, it'll be a done deal by then."

"Not soon enough," the younger Crider quipped. Maria, blushing, punched him in the shoulder.

"See? They're acting married already."

Sandra Gutierrez raised her glass. "Well, here's to all of you who got this Constitution written and done. Now, we'll have a government, we'll have a Navy, and we'll have some security."

Clomonastik looked up from his plate at that. "Dear lady, do not be so quick to think all is well now. There was a history-making thing done here these past months, yes; but this Confederacy of yours is but the beginning of Galactic history, not the end."

Hector Gutierrez had been thinking along the same lines. "You think the Grugell Empire won't stop at trying to break up the Convention."

"Indeed, I do not. We – and I do not use 'we,' lightly, my trusted friends – we have one rather large advantage. The Empire knows the location of Tarbos, but since there has been no detectable traffic in the area of Earth, we can presume that they have not located humanity's home world yet. I assure you, that will change, in time."

"Do you think they'll strike at Earth itself?"

"Yes, Michael, my old friend, I am as certain of it as I am certain of the table before me. From my 'conversations' with my former inferior Kadastrattik, I have discovered that the Empire is currently operating under the presumption that Tarbos is the center of human operations – a presumption that we have just corrected for them – and I can assure you that they will be back here again, as well. It is only a matter of time, my friends. Relax not your vigilance yet."

"We don't intend to." The Vice President of the United States tapped on the table with a finger as he spoke. "And we've gained ground ourselves; Bob Pritchard tells me that his technical wizards here are pretty close to figuring out the gravity field generators in the floor plates we salvaged from that Grugell ship, for one thing. It won't be in time for the first generation of our Navy ships, but it will be soon enough. It's just too bad we couldn't recover whatever device they use to make the ships undetectable – a stealth device like that could be really valuable."

"And difficult at best to obtain," Clomonastik countered. "They are well-shielded from scanning, and rigged to self-destroy if they are tampered with."

"You're full of good news," Mike Senior grouched.

"Only the truth, my trusted friend. But," the Grugell inclined his head gracefully, "I must apologize to our young couple. This evening is a celebration in their honor, and I have sullied it with talk of conflict. We must speak no more of these things this evening. On the morrow, you two are to be wedded – and I, myself, am pleased and honored to have been invited to witness this ritual." He chuckled, a strangely high-pitched chittering sound. "It is ironic, is it not, that a former shipmate and fellow Grugell Imperial Navy officer has ended up my enemy, his ship destroyed, and the survivors of his crew imprisoned, and all due to my aid. And here I sit, across the table from a former enemy who once tried as hard to kill me as I did him, and tonight I am so fortunate as to claim this man, his family and his associates as my friends!"

"And we're fortunate to have you as our friend, as well," Hector Gutierrez agreed. "Without you, we would have had a lot more trouble with that Grugell warship."

"It was my privilege to do so," Clomonastik responded with great solemnity.

# Twenty-Five

**Mountain View Central Legal Center**

Oddly enough, after all the preparation, the ceremony was brief.

A small chamber to the side of the main courtroom was used for marriages. Mike Junior stood at the front of the room in front of Tarbos' Chief Magistrate. The few guests and family members filed in and stood waiting until the faint tones of music from some unseen speaker announced the arrival of the bride. A vision in a simple white silk sheathe of a dress imported from Earth, Maria glided in to the room on the arm of her beaming father. Next to Mike Senior, Sandra Gutierrez sniffled and dabbed at her eyes while Manuel Gutierrez actually ceased fidgeting for a moment to watch.

The Magistrate read the stock marriage ceremony from the OWME Legal Ceremonies Manual, Mike Junior kissed his bride, and the marriage was official.

*Except for the nice clothes, that could be Jenny and me back on Forest twenty-three years ago*, Mike Senior thought. Maria Gutierrez – Maria Crider, now – was tall and raven-haired instead of petite and blonde like his wife Jenny, but the important part was the same. The look the two young people shared, standing in front of the smiling Magistrate, lost in each other's eyes, was just the same. *As long as they keep that*, Mike thought, *they'll be all right.*

"Well, Mike, it's customary to look at these things as 'not losing a daughter, but gaining a son,'" Hector Gutierrez noted, "But I confess, it's going to be hard on Sandy and I having Maria go off to Forest. But there's sure a pretty good compensation, and that's your son. We couldn't ask for a better young man for Maria."

"I'm pretty pleased, too," Mike answered. "It's a good match, Heck." He watched, entranced, as Clomonastik approached his son and shook his hand. The tall alien then faced Maria and, with a broad smile, placed both hands on her head, her shoulders, and then he traced the outline of an oval in front of her torso with one clawed finger, chittering in Grugell all the while. "A fertility blessing," he heard the alien tell Maria. "You will now have many children!"

Hector Gutierrez spoke again. "I hear the *Bay of Biscay* has dropped out of subspace, Mike. They'll be in high orbit and ready for boarding in four days. I've arranged three days' honeymoon for the kids down at the Tide Pool. You have any plans?"

Mike thought about that for a moment. The events of the last few weeks had been so overwhelming, and now that the Confederate Constitution was submitted to the planets for ratification, he had no plans other than getting home as quickly as possible. "I don't know, Heck. Maybe I'll slip out of town, do some hunting."

"Hunting, eh? Well, I'd rather join you than follow along on Sandy's round of socializing, shopping and restaurants – but I'd just slow you down." He slapped Mike on the back. "You'll be glad to get home, I bet."

"I never expected to leave Forest," Mike said. "And I never expect to leave again. I'm glad I was here, but I tell you what – I'm sure glad it's over. I'm more than ready to go home."

"Me too, bro. Me too." The Vice President paused, thoughtfully. "We've made history here, man. Real, kids-reading-about-it-in-school-for-a-hundred-years kind of history."

Mike considered that for a moment. "That's fine. Let them write their books. History geeks a hundred years from now can judge whether what we've done here was worthwhile or not. All I'm worrying about from here on is hunting meat for the Settlement Mercantile."

"I'm going to have to come to Forest and hunt with you one of these days. Your stories of those rocs are really something! I may stick with something safer, though."

"You'd be welcome, Heck, anytime. Everyone in Settlement knows how to find our place."

"You know," Gutierrez leaned to speak conspiratorially in Mike's ear, "after the reception out at the Retreat, the kids are going to be heading down to the Tide Pool, and Sandy and Manuel both want to go back to the hotel in Mountain View to get some rest. But I noticed a neat little bar and grille a few blocks from the hotel that we haven't tried out yet. I think that maybe you and I ought to slip out later, have a steak and a few beers. One last celebration to put this thing to rest."

Mike laughed. "You know, that doesn't sound like a bad idea." *A 'guy's night out'*, he thought. *That's something I've never done before.* "No, it doesn't sound like a bad idea at all."

# Twenty-Six

**Grugell**

A valuable ship lost.
A mission failed.
A plan proven futile.
And an enemy grown stronger.
The Emperor was not happy.
His principal advisor, Kaxatrisk II, along with the Admirals
Pokatak IX and Gilgakat XII, were now scattered vapor in the thin
Grugell atmosphere, drifting slowly downwind from the Imperi-
um's disintegration chambers.

Attended now by four of his favored wives, Ignostak XI
reclined on a lounge chair in his personal chambers. Before him
floated a hologram of Pokatak IX's replacement as Fleet Commander, Kodatrax II. The Emperor watched, for the fourth time
this evening, the replay of the new Fleet Commander's report:

> Our conclusions are as follows:

> First, the humans have formed an alliance of sorts, not
> a central authority after the manner of our Empire but
> an alliance of their settled worlds. Second, they have
> devised a means of tracking our cloaked ships. Third,
> we have managed to decode message traffic that indi-

cates they will begin building armed ships themselves, at a location we have not yet been able to discover.

To that end, Your Majesty, we have increased patrols in their main traffic lanes, but all Commanders have been ordered to not fire upon any human ships unless hostile action is directed against them. We must more carefully analyze their trade routes and attempt to discover the source world of the species. That is, without doubt, where their shipbuilding activities will take place.

Also, Imperial Shipwrights are working on improving our cloaking devices. We have discovered that the passage of a cloaked ship leaves a disturbance in trace normal matter patterns and in the dark matter matrix. It is possible that the humans have discovered this as well, a hypothesis that is supported by the destruction of our ship orbiting the human world Tarbos. My predecessor was less then prudent in his decision to send only one ship to monitor the human's activity; in the future, all ships will travel in groups of no less than two.

Finally, Your Majesty, we propose to step up production of our own armed frigates, and with your permission of course, to begin construction of larger, more heavily armed vessels with improved defenses. It will take several years to assemble the Fleet we will need to decisively engage the human planets, but with patience and planning, our best estimates indicate we will be prepared in the space of twenty years.

Finally, it would be advisable in the meantime to open
communications with the humans. Were we to project
the appearance of abandoning aggression in order
to seek peaceful relations, our actions may seem less
threatening, and the humans may decide to slow or
even cease building their armed fleet. To that end we
suggest that Your Majesty appoint an envoy to proceed
to the human world Tarbos to open discussions with
this 'Confederacy.'

This concludes the report as of this date, the ninth
day of G'risth, Sixteenth Year of Ignostak XI. I remain
Your Majesty's most humble servant.

The hologram fizzled and went out.

Ignostak sat up and clapped his hands once. His four wives
disappeared; a servant slipped quietly in from an anteroom,
bowing once, quickly.

"You. You will take a message to Admiral Kodatrax II at the
Imperium Headquarters. Tell him, 'Proceed.'"

"Is there anything else, Your Majesty?"

"No. Why are you still here?"

The aide flinched visibly and bowed his way out of the room.

Ignostak stood up and strode to the huge windows in the
curving outer wall of his chamber. Far below him, the central
city of the Grugell Empire sprawled out across the yellow sands.
Shining silver spires and domes cluttered the landscape, and in
the traffic lanes a few vehicles moved, some power vehicles, others
drawn by a large herbivorous animal common to the west of the
city. In the distance, the endless rolling dunes of the Empire's
home world stretched out to the horizon. Somewhere to the south
was the Imperial Retreat, another gleaming silver spire rising from

the scrub along the ocean. Tomorrow he would take his wives, servants and other assorted household members and go there; his spirit was raw, his demeanor irritable, and he was in need of time away from the city and the court.

A movement caught the Emperor's eye. In the medium distance, a small Imperium Security flyer floated idly over the city, its scanners no doubt recording activity below, its crew analyzing for any sign of dissent.

*One day, Imperium flyers like that will watch over every world now occupied by the mongrel race, 'human.' I vow it to be so.*

# Twenty-Seven

**Settlement, fourteen months later**

As Bob Pritchard had predicted, ratification was swift. On a specified Standard Date, the new blue banners of the Confederacy were being raised on all thirteen worlds, not excluding Earth; the old United Nations building in New York City had been refurbished to serve as the Confederate headquarters on the home world. Fourteen months, a little over one Forest year later after the Confederate Constitution was submitted for ratification, the new Confederate flag was raised from a spanking-new flagpole in front of the old Main Mercantile in Settlement.

Mike and Jenny were there to see the new blue flag go up. With them were Mike Junior and his wife Maria, now heavily pregnant with their first child. Andrea Crider was absent, having accepted a commission to the new Confederate Navy Academy on Tarbos.

A swell of pride filled Mike as he stood on the red dust of the old Common watching the new flag snap in the stiff breeze off the river. He stood with one arm around Jenny's slim shoulders, smiling at the new banner he'd been instrumental in bringing to life.

"Everything's going to be different now, you know, Dad?"

"I know, Junior. It's a good thing we got things started off right."

"I remember something from history classes in school," Jenny observed quietly. "After America's Constitutional Convention, one of the Founders – I think it was old Ben Franklin – told somebody, 'we've given you a republic, if you can keep it.' We've got a republic now. I hope we can keep it. I'll admit, with Bob Pritchard as our first President, I think we're off to a pretty good start."

"We'll keep it." Mike looked very confident. "We'll keep it."

"You sound awfully sure, Dad."

"I'm as sure as I can be, Junior. I think Mankind has finally learned how to govern itself. We saw that in the ratifications – the narrowest vote was on Corinthia, and there it still passed almost 70-30." *And I bet old 'King' Harold is hopping mad about it*, he thought. "Look at what Earth went through before everyone on the rock lived free. Three World Wars, and who knows how many smaller battles. Humanity won in the end, and you're seeing the result there now. And we won a newer battle here on Forest all those years ago, and another on Tarbos just last year. We're tougher than the Grugell give us credit for." He placed one hand unconsciously on the ancient Colt, still holstered at his hip, and with the other motioned towards the blue flag. "Someone once said that America was the last, best hope for mankind. I think there's another bright, shining hope now, the Confederated Free Planets, and we based it on the same principles. Yes, Junior, I am confident."

"You should be my speechwriter if I do decide to run for Selectman, Dad."

"Not me," Mike laughed. "There are still rocs and bosers out there to hunt, and the colony still needs meat. I'm going back to being a hunter and pioneer, and that's all."

He looked up once more at the bright blue flag, whipping in the freshening wind. "That's all," Mike repeated, quietly. *That's enough. I've done enough. I'm home, and I'm staying home.*

Wrapping his arm more tightly around Jenny's slim shoulders, Mike turned to walk back to where the skimmer waited for the trip back to their mountain meadow.

Book Three
# The Orleans Incident

# The First Galactic War

Rear Admiral Isaac Gauss, Commander, Task Group One, Confederate Navy, is overseeing a Fleet exercise near the Confederate world New Albion. The Confederate battle cruiser CSS *Orleans*, Gauss' flagship, is under way at sublight speed when several Grugell ships are detected dropping out of subspace. In the ensuing engagement, the *Orleans* is crippled, and several ships destroyed, in exchange for two Grugell warships. The Confederate Task Group escapes into subspace, fleeing in disarray.

Nearly three years of fighting ensue. Planetary bombardments and invasion forces render the Confederate world of New Albion nearly sterile. Fleets of starships engage in running battles.

Meanwhile, on Tarbos, the Confederate Senate and House of Selectmen debate expanding the role of the Confederate government to strengthen the Navy, while maintaining the sovereignty of the individual planets. The Senator from Forest, Michael Crider Jr., leads the fight to secure funding for a new class of warships, even as his sister Andrea leads her squadron of strike fighters into battle. To further save precious funds, the Confederate Navy Department authorizes the use of privateer ships – armed, privately owned starships that fight in several engagements. One privateer, the Starship *Shade Tree*, succeeds in destroying a Grugell Occupation ship.

The *Shade Tree* was also present at the second Battle of Fortune, and recovered data taken from the main computer of a Grugell frigate the alerted the Confederate Navy of the Grugell's plans to attack Earth directly. The final engagement comes in the Battle of Rally Point Alpha, where the new class of Confederate ships – the *Dreadnought* class – makes its debut.

*—Morris/Handel, "A History of the First Galactic Confederacy," University Publications, 2804CE*

# One
# January 2251

*Above all, we must realize that no arsenal, or no weapon
in the arsenals of the world are so formidable as the will
and moral and courage of free men and women. It is a
weapon adversaries in today's world do not have*

—*Ronald Reagan, President of the United States, 1981-
1989*

**Grugell, the Imperial Palace**

Emperor Ignostak XI was enjoying the attentions of his five
favored wives when the door to his private apartments crashed
open. Eyes narrowed in rage, he looked up to see his chief military
advisor, Admiral Apportamattid XIII. The Admiral was flanked
by two armed soldiers, and in his right hand, the silver tube of a
blaster was leveled at the Emperor's head.

"What's the meaning of this?" the Emperor demanded as his
wives scattered.

"Meaning, Your Highness? The meaning of the twenty years
I've spent working so carefully to become at last your most trusted
advisor?" Apportamattid's voice was conversational, but the aimed
blaster belied his calm tone. "The meaning of *my* action, Your
Highness, is obvious. Indeed, our soon-to-be late Emperor, I
might well be the one to ask the meaning of *your* actions. Those

actions include, of course, your orders to hold only a weak status quo against the human encroachments on our space. Your orders to leave unsettled the dispute over the planet Forest, where my younger brother died in payment for a lost battle over nothing. Nothing, Emperor!"

"Forest? What planet is that?"

"You don't even remember, do you? Well, it matters not a bit. The Empire needs a stronger hand at the helm in this time of crisis, Highness, and since you've no son to contest a claim of succession, and since I control the loyalty of the Navy…" Without further ado, Apportamattid fired his blaster.

"Remove that," the former Admiral, now claimant to the throne, pointed at the smoking corpse of Ignostak XI. The two soldiers hurried to obey.

"You wives of the former Emperor, executed traitor to the Grugell Empire, you must choose. Join the Estate of the new Emperor or join the former Emperor in death." He leveled his blaster again at the huddled forms of Ignostak's five wives.

The oldest of the five stood up slowly, her hands shaking as she extended them to the new Emperor. "Your weapon is not necessary, Lord. Our allegiance is to the Empire. You are the Empire. Your Estate is ours now."

"You have chosen wisely," Apportamattid assured them as he holstered his weapon.

**Tarbos, the Confederate Senate Office Building**

The gleaming red time/date readout gleamed softly from mid-air, above the polished black desktop.

2058:31/12/2250

Senator Michael Crider Jr. pressed a stud, and the display faded away. He rubbed his eyes and yawned.

*Another year gone*, he thought. *Another year.*

Two minutes until midnight on Tarbos' twenty-one-hour clock, and Tarbos Standard would tick over to Standard Year 2251. New Year's Eve was about to tick over to New Year's Day. Outside, in the streets of the Confederate capital city of Mountain View, the citizens were shouting, drinking, and embracing each other in a typically balmy Mountain View summer night.

*Two terms*, he reminded himself. *Twelve years away from Forest. Twelve years away from home.*

At thirty-seven, the Senator was still tall and straight as he had been when he first saw Tarbos as a twenty-year old boy accompanying his father to the Constitutional Convention that had established the Confederacy. His eyes still glittered ice blue, but he wore his straw-blonde hair close-cropped now in the fashion popular on Tarbos. Dressed in his habitual conservative dark, tailored suit, he passed among the denizens of Mountain View with little notice.

Michael Crider Jr, Senator to the Confederacy from the Sovereign World of Forest, was no ordinary man. And the year to come, the fateful Standard Year of 2251 C.E., was to be no ordinary year.

He picked up a printout from his office hyperphone terminal. His sister Andrea had 'phoned with two pieces of good news – her promotion to Lieutenant Commander, and her long-awaited assignment to VS-66, a strike fighter wing assigned to the new fighter carrier CSS *Mountain View*. The first in its class, the *Mountain View* would be departing the orbital shipyards on Earth in another six weeks to join up with a task group forming to secure the Grugell frontier. Senator Crider had co-sponsored the legislation that had funded the ship and named it after the capital of a growing Confederacy.

*Interesting times*, the Senator reminded himself. The *Mountain View* would be joining another new ship, the battle cruiser CSS *Orleans*, to form the foundations of Task Force One, home-ported at Fleet Headquarters on Tarbos.

Sixteen years after the forming of the Confederacy, and the Navy had a grand total of twenty-six ships. The Fleet consisted of the *Orleans*, the *Mountain View*, four light cruisers, ten destroyers, and ten frigates. This was the genesis of the First Fleet of the newly birthed Confederate Navy.

It wasn't much of a force to cover a border that spanned thousands of light years. Senator Crider's father had fought the Grugell first-hand almost forty years earlier, and the Criders knew the alien race for an implacable foe. They needed more ships, and more than that, they needed the political will to finance and build them.

But the still-young Confederacy was having a crisis of political will. While Tarbos and Halifax were quickly developing shipbuilding capacities, and Earth already had them, the balance of the sixteen Confederate Free Planets were balking at spending almost half of the Confederacy's Gross Confederate Product on building a Navy.

Senator Crider tapped on the top of his desk twice, bringing up a query note on his desktop computer terminal. "Replay Senate debate on Funding Bill 2250:125A, 1400-1415," he announced. The computer obediently replayed that portion of the debate, where the senior Senator for Corinthia, Lord James Galloway the Third, held the floor:

> Forty-five percent, my friends. Forty-five percent of
> the output of sixteen settled worlds. Forty-five percent

of a tithe paid to the Confederate government on Tarbos by the hard-working people of the sixteen free planets. And for what?

The usually bombastic Lord Galloway was in rare form. He pounded the podium with his fist as he spoke.

Pretty new toys for the Navy. And there are pretty new barges for a new Fleet Admiral to move about the skies, most expensive of all a shiny new battle cruiser. And to build these pretty toys, there are now pretty new shipyards at Tarbos and Halifax. And for what? Where are these feared enemies, these 'Grugell' we hear so much about?

A shout rose from the floor, but at the speaking microphone, Lord Galloway's voice thundered out unchecked.

No! Don't answer! I'll tell you! One of these feared aliens is living a comfortable retirement on Earth – and twelve others were returned peacefully to their own society twenty years ago from right here on Tarbos! And only this year, the Grugell Empire has sent an envoy to open diplomatic relations. Diplomatic relations! Does an Empire bent on conquest open diplomatic relations, I ask you? No! Is this massive expenditure on a Navy required to defend us against this non-existent threat? No! Is there any evidence – even one scrap of empirical evidence that the Grugell pose a threat to this Confederacy? No!

I'll tell you, honored members of this Senate, what
poses a threat. The threat is to the livelihoods of the
citizens of the free worlds who bear the financial
burden for this…

"Stop replay." He'd seen enough.

Every bit of the funding the Confederate House of Selectmen
and Senate had been able to get for the Navy had come at the
cost of endless bickering, endless debate on the floor, endless
conference sessions in back rooms, endless testimony by a handful
of new Admirals with no fleet to command. Six years earlier the
Confederate Congress had managed a funding package to build
the basis of a fleet, a task group really, based on the wing carrier
*Mountain View*. Four years ago, the funding package for the
*Orleans* and three more frigates had passed by a narrow margin.

And in the meantime, Senator Crider and a handful of others
had funded a few other, smaller projects. Black projects, projects
intended to get more 'bang for the buck' than conventional forces.

A polite cough from the doorway drew the Senator's eyes
upwards from his desk to see his Chief of Staff, Anton Silva,
standing there.

"It's awfully late, Senator. Why don't you go out and catch a
drink or something? It is New Year's Eve, you know."

"I know. It *is* late, isn't it?"

Silva nodded.

"You know; I think I'll pass on the festivities. You go on ahead
and bring in the New Year for me, Tony. I think I'll just head
home."

*Home*, he thought. *Not much of a home anymore.* Senator Crider's wife, Maria, had taken their teenage son Nelson and left for
Earth six months earlier, filing divorce proceedings by hyperphone
from Denver.

*And she may have been right*, he told himself. *I am too wrapped up in the job. Maybe after this term, I'll go to Earth, see if we can patch things up.*

*Maybe.*

In the meantime, though, several big jobs remained. And Tony Silva was still standing there, watching him expectantly.

Slowly, Senator Crider of Forest got up, stretched, and put on his suit jacket. "All right, Tony, you win. I'll see you in the morning."

## March 2251: Earth, the International Space Station

Rear Admiral Isaac Gauss viewed his new charge with a quiet pride.

The *Orleans* was the Confederate Navy's crowning achievement. A kilometer and a half long and five hundred meters across, built around the newest revision of the standard Gellar Star Drive, the first space-going battle cruiser built by human hands. She was powerful enough to fight any three ships known to be run by the opposing Grugell, and fast enough to catch them if they ran. And best of all, the *Orleans* was to be the flagship for Admiral Gauss' new command, Task Force One. The Confederate Navy Department, in love with long-winded titles, had gifted Rear Admiral Gauss with the official title of Commander, Task Force One, or COMTASKFORONE.

"She's a beauty, Admiral. She's a fitting flagship for the first Task Force Commander in the Confederate Navy."

The newly appointed COMTASKFORONE turned away from the viewport to see his aide, Captain Jerry Jensen. "Jerry. Are we ready to move the flag aboard?"

"Two hours from your say-so, sir."

"Good. We'll be moving to the new Fleet spacedock at Tarbos to meet up with the rest of the Task Force, and then…"

"Yes, sir?"

"I'm thinking exercises around the New Albion system."

"Right near the frontier, sir?" Two systems lay uncomfortably close to the Confederacy's border with the Grugell Empire, New Albion and Fortune. New Albion was half a parsec closer to the red line than was Fortune.

"Might as well show the flag. You know they'll be watching."

"Yes sir, I know they'll see us. It's us seeing them that I'm worried about." Jensen was, obviously, referring the Grugell's ability to conceal their smaller ships with cloaking fields. So far, the Confederacy had been utterly unable to duplicate the technology.

Admiral Gauss grinned at his aide. "Oh, come on, Jerry, you joined up for the excitement, right? Remember Colorado Springs?" Both men were graduates of the United States Air Force Academy; two years earlier, Rear Admiral Gauss had been Colonel Isaac Gauss, United States Air Force.

"First Flight, *sir*," Captain Jensen answered, remembering an old class motto. That same two years previously, he had been Lieutenant Colonel (Promotable) in the selfsame USAF. A much larger gulf in rank now separated the two men, but they had worked together in the past, and each knew the other well.

"First Flight is right, Jerry. We're the first flight for this whole Navy. There's only so many inhabitable planets out there, Jerry, and the Grugell are going to try to take another one from us sooner or later."

"Let's hope for later. We could use five or six more like the *Orleans* before that happens. We've got a really thin green line, sir," Jensen observed, referring to the newly designed Navy service uniform.

"We'll just have to draw it in where it counts, Jerry," Gauss answered. "Remember old Napoleon. If you can't be strong everywhere, you have to pick one spot and be strong there, and just hope it's the right spot."

"Yes, sir."

"Let's move aboard tomorrow morning, Jerry. Oh-nine-hundred, I think. I'll inform Fleet Admiral Kosake that we're going to put to space tomorrow. Let the *Orleans'* Captain know we're coming, will you? Oh, and send a hyperphone message to the *Mountain View* at Tarbos, let them know we'll be jumping for Tarbos late tomorrow. Give them our ETA; tell them to be ready for exercises. Best get them in the gate early, right?"

"Roger that, sir. If you don't have anything else for me, sir, I'll get going."

"Go ahead, Jerry. I'll head back to that broom closet of a temporary office they gave us. We've both got a lot to do before tomorrow."

At 0900 hours the next morning, the *Orleans'* shipboard announcing system bellowed "COMTASKFORONE, arriving," as Rear Admiral Gauss and his staff came aboard the new battle cruiser. The Navy's first operational Task Force was ready to get under way at last.

# Two
# March 2251

**On the Frontier**

Light years away, on the Grugell frontier, one of the less publicly known bits of Senator Crider's funding agenda was at work.

The Star Ship *Shade Tree* was a privately owned vessel, but in spite of its small complement – three officers and twenty-one crew – it was faster and better armed than most of the light ships in the fledgling Confederate Navy. A reading of history had prompted the Senator to quietly seek out the adventurous sorts that would be amenable to a re-creation of a bit of Earth's seafaring history, and the concept of the privateer had been born anew. Mounting six ship-to-ship missiles and three particle beam projectors, the small, agile and fast *Shade Tree* was quietly doing a bit of intelligence gathering along the frontier.

"Bring her right a few degrees," the *Shade Tree*'s Captain Jean Barrett ordered. "Give me a scan on that big asteroid there – yeah, that one." She pointed at a blue speck on the main viewscreen.

The flat black finish on the ship's radar-transparent polymer hull reflected not a bit of light as the craft turned, slowly, only the slightest glow from its oversized Gellar drive tunnel giving it away.

"Returns coming now, Captain," the crewman at the Scanning station replied. "Nickel-iron asteroid, nothing unusual. No hitchhikers, no indications of any mining or any other activity.

Trajectory indicates it's in an irregular orbit around that type G star a half light-year to our stern."

"Very well. Helm, return to base course. Let's see if we can pick up the trail of that Grugell cruiser that passed through here. It might be interesting to see where they're going. That system aft of us, it's in Confederate space, no habitable worlds but lots of iron-rich asteroids. I bet they're looking it over."

"I'm getting a slight ripple in the dark matter matrix for this region, like a big Grugell drive field just went through," Crewman Iolanth Simmons reported from Scanning. "I've seen it before, anyway."

"Good," Captain Barrett answered. "Cross-link the data to Helm. Let's drop in behind them and trail a while. If they're unescorted, we'll follow along and listen to them chatter. Bring us to pursuit course, ahead two-thirds."

"Coming about now, Captain."

"Stay clear of that asteroid, Helm. It may have some trailers. I can't afford any more repairs this quarter."

"Yes, Captain. We'll pass about a kilometer starboard of the rock. Search radar showing no trailers."

"Good. Secure radar and rig for EMCON. No more emissions of any kind until I say otherwise. Passive sensors only." *I need to find a good First Officer*, she thought wryly. The lack of a good Second-in-Command had Captain Barrett on her own Bridge an average of fourteen hours every twenty-four-hour shipboard 'day.'

She looked at her watch. "Change of watch in fifteen minutes. I'm going to take a nap. Wake me in three hours."

Sliding silently through space, the *Shade Tree* turned to follow the unknown ship into unknown territory.

Only about ten steps and one ladder separated the *Shade Tree*'s Bridge from Captain Barrett's stateroom. Her ship was only a year in commission; new enough to have installed the first generation of gravity-generating deck plates copied from the wreckage of a Grugell ship destroyed twenty years earlier over Tarbos. None but the newest of the Navy's ships had those yet; most of the Navy crews had to make do with spinning outside sections for gravity, and zero-gee Bridges and Navigation suites. But the legacy of her grandfather's early investment in Off-World Mining & Exploration had left her a considerable fortune, enough to build and equip the *Shade Tree*. A grant from the Confederacy paid her crew, and she hoped that any salvaged weapons and equipment from any Grugell ships taken unawares might actually bring her a profit.

She closed her stateroom door behind her. Never much of a one for uniforms, she wore only black canvas fatigue pants and a black t-shirt; most of her crew followed her style. The five former Marines she kept as a boarding party and security force had combat armor on board, but generally went about the ship in well-worn black workout outfits.

It had been three months since she – or any of her crew – had bathed with water, or eaten anything more appetizing than dehydrated Combat Ration Alpha-Packs, the acronym for which well suited the taste. With a frown at her tiny static-jet shower, Barrett stepped to her tiny sink. Pressing the hot water button gave her a five-second ration of tepid water, which she splashed on her face before examining herself critically in the mirror.

She carried her thirty-six years well. Her curly strawberry-blonde hair was cropped short for shipboard life, but she liked the way it framed her fair-skinned, slightly freckled face. Her eyes sparkled bright green, befitting her Irish ancestry; while her father had been a London businessman, her mother had grown up mere blocks from the River Liffey in Dublin.

With a skill born of practice at dressing and undressing in the tiny space, Barrett kicked off her shipboard sandals, skinned off her fatigue pants and removed her t-shirt before turning her attention once more to the mirror. *Still looking good, girl*, she told herself. *For all the good it does you. Only four single men on this bucket, and the Captain sure as hell can't get caught in the sack with one of the crew.* Still, her fair skin was smooth and unblemished, her stomach flat, her breasts small but shapely. A petite woman, she would never have the long legs that some men drooled over, but her legs were still strong, straight, and tightly muscled.

*Maybe I should have joined the Navy after all.*

Shrugging off the thought, she turned to her tiny foldout bunk to catch her nap.

## Three parsecs away

The border between Grugell and Confederate space was not well defined. A vague area between three of the more recently settled Confederate worlds and two identified Grugell colonies formed the "frontier" between the two civilizations.

It was this frontier now that a trio of invisible Grugell frigates was crossing. A quarter of a light-year behind them was a force composed of two larger, uncloakable ships. Gleaming silver orbs trailed by four drive pods each, the two Grugell cruisers followed their reconnaissance screen on a mission to probe Confederate responses in the area.

On a command from the flagship, the frigates fanned out into a line abreast formation, roughly a hundred thousand kilometers wide, and made a course for the nearest known Confederate world, New Albion. The cruisers fell in behind them as all five ships leaped into subspace to transit, hopefully undetected, into Confederate space.

## The *Shade Tree*

"Bridge to Captain Barrett." The voice page was followed by a chiming tone that battered its way into Jean Barrett's sleeping mind. With a muttered curse, she reached over her head to tap the intercom button on the bulkhead. *That was never three hours,* she thought angrily. A glance at her desktop display clock told her she'd been asleep forty-five minutes.

"What is it?"

"Sensor ghosts, Captain, three of them."

"All right. Give me a minute."

Tugging on her fatigue pants and t-shirt, Barrett picked up her sandals and walked barefoot the few steps to the Bridge. "What is it?"

At the minuscule Scanning station was one of Barrett's prize "finds," Indira Krishnavarna. Once a PhD candidate at the Massachusetts Institute of Technology on Earth, Krishnavarna had been involved in an "experiment" involving a quarter-gram of anti-matter, a magnetic bottle rigged to a remote switch, and the luggage truck of the visiting Yale University football team. Expelled for her part in the prank, Krishnavarna had eschewed the discipline of the Navy in favor of a five-year contract with a privateer, and Jean Barrett had made her the best offer.

"Captain," Krishnavarna called, "I had you paged. I'm reading three sensor ghost tracks, fading rapidly."

"And that means what?" Barrett's testiness betrayed her fatigue, but she was interested.

"It might be three subspace transits."

"You can't track ships in subspace," Barrett snapped. She sat in her bridge chair and lifted her right foot to put on a sandal.

"That's what the Navy and the brain trust at Off-World thinks, yes," Krishnavarna replied. "But I think you can, if you calibrate for it."

"And how do you do that?" Barrett shifted in her seat to put on her left sandal.

"It's a matter of adjusting the dark-matter scan to… Captain, I'm not sure how to explain it. Unless you want to study physics for about five years first."

"All right, what makes you think it's a subspace transit?"

"Because I tried it when we were leaving Caliban last month after our provisioning stop. Remember when we were in the traffic pattern behind that big OWME liner? I tracked it when it kicked in its drive, and followed it up to the subspace transit. We were accelerating in the lane right behind it, so I was able to analyze the track for about four minutes after it jumped into subspace before we broke in ourselves. And just like I figured, there was this sensor ghost trail, right along the liner's last bearing. And now I'm tracking three sensor ghost tracks right now, running parallel, heading in to the Confederacy from Grugell space."

"I don't suppose you'll be able to track them if we jump into subspace ourselves, will you?"

"No, I don't think so. I mean, our scanners work in subspace, but the data stream is gibberish. Nobody's figured out yet how to interpret it."

"You'd think, after all these years… All right. Record everything you can on those sensor ghosts. Feed the trajectory to Navigation. Navs, I want a plot of every inhabited system on that projected trajectory. As soon as you've got that, get Helm a course to the nearest one."

"You got it, Captain."

"Helm, the minute you get that course, I want us headed for that system at best possible speed." Captain Barrett stood up, yawning. "Indira, you just keep right on experimenting. You know, I'm not going to be able to afford you one of these days."

Indira Krishnavarna grinned at her Captain. "I'll settle for a nice bonus this trip, Captain."

"So would I. You find out where those ships are headed, and we may just both get our wish."

"Captain, the first settled system along that track is New Albion. There's really nothing much else on that track; about twenty degrees above and to the left relative to the Galactic ecliptic is Corinthia, but it's another three hundred and eighty light years past New Albion. Smart money says they're heading for New Albion, ma'am."

"Good work. Helm, get us under way. Haul ass."

"Coming about already, Captain. Course plotted; engine is ahead full."

"Fine. Now, since we're almost an hour into the third watch, do you think I might finish my nap now?"

The Bridge crew – all three of them – shared a laugh as Captain Barrett left the compartment, once more, for her stateroom.

# Three
# June 2251

**The Confederate Star Ship *Mountain View*, Tarbos high orbit**

The *Mountain View*'s hangar bay was truly cavernous, but it wasn't hard for Lieutenant Commander Andrea Crider to find her personal A-66 attack fighter. Her squadron, VS-66, Hunter Squadron, was assigned to the parking area nearest the starboard forward elevator. As Squadron Executive Officer, her bird was second closest to the hangar bay doors, next to the Commander's bird.

The fighter was stubby, short, and humpbacked in profile, a laminate polysteel bubble canopy enhancing the profile. Stub wings with hard points for Shrike missiles stuck out to the sides, and a 30mm rotary cannon hung under the bulbous nose, which was home to a powerful search and fire-control radar. The whole thing was built around an enormous ion drive, capable of pushing the fighter to a good half a C. The A-66 was a tactical craft, and any beauty it possessed existed only in the eyes of its pilots. But Lieutenant Commander Crider did find the bird beautiful.

VS-66's birds were painted dark gray with blood-red stripes on the stub wings. Crider's bird had her call-sign, "Angel," painted on the right side of the fuselage below the canopy. She was just climbing the crew ladder to the cockpit when she heard that call-sign shouted out behind her.

"Angel!" She turned on the ladder to see her wingman, Lieutenant Junior Grade Horace Hamilton, who by the accident of his first name was tagged with a call sign that was all too obvious.

"What's up, Horse?"

"VS-42 wants to have a bet on today's flight exercise," the gangly youth called.

Crider took her flight helmet off, ruffling her short strawberry-blonde hair with one hand. "What's the bet?"

"Case of Scotch. From Earth. Seems that there's a shipment of twelve-year old single malt in from Earth on the last supply freighter."

"Oh, geez, that won't be expensive, will it?"

"Figure five hundred bucks, maybe a little over."

"Great. Is your LCS system checked out, Horse?" she asked, referring to the Laser Combat Simulation system installed now on her squadron's birds – and on VS-42's as well.

"Perfect, Angel. One hundred percent." Horse, confident in his skill, was grinning broadly.

"All right, then. Tell 'em they're on." Crider put her helmet back on. "Let's saddle up."

Four birds from each squadron were scheduled for this morning's combat exercise. The frigate CSS *Ian Mac Vie* would serve as the target; VS-66 was to simulate an attack run, against the defenders from VS-42.

Andrea Crider climbed into her fighter and strapped in tight. Plugging her helmet's leads into the control panel, she snapped on her ship-to-ship comm system as she activated the fighter's computer and flight control systems. On the deck to her left front, the Chief Petty Officer who served as her Crew Chief – and who really 'owned' the fighter – shot her a thumbs-up. Crider toggled her ship-to-ship. "Hunter Flight, this is Hunter Lead. Report, over."

"Hunter Two, ready to fly," Horse called back.

"Angel, Three is primed and ready."

"Four, ready to fly."

"*Mountain View* Flight Control, Hunter Flight requesting departure clearance."

The terse answer came back in Crider's headphones. "Hunter Lead, you are cleared for departure on Runway One. Set transponder code one-four-seven."

"Roger that, Flight Control. Hunter Flight is rolling."

Advancing the throttle gave Lieutenant Commander Crider the familiar kick in the back she had grown so fond of as her A-66 shot forward, her wingman's fighter tucked in ten meters off her starboard wing. Hunter Three and Four shot off just behind them, the flight of four clearing the runway and racing out the open hangar doors. The force field over the front of the hangar bay shimmered for a moment as the fighters shot through.

"Hunter Flight," Crider called, "Close up tight. Follow me up. We're going a few thousand kilometers sunward, to get the light behind us. The *Ian Mac Vie* will be trying to hide in a low orbit. We aren't going to let them get away with it."

"Roger that, Hunter Lead."

The four fighters stayed on full thrust, riding the tips of blue spears of energy from their ion drives. Turning on their internal gyros, they angled towards Tarbos' sun.

Behind them, the four fighters of VS-42 rocketed out of the *Mountain View*'s hangar and angled downward towards Tarbos.

"Two thousand kilometers, Lead," Hunter Three called.

"Good enough. Three, Four, go five hundred meters negative. Horse, stay on my wing. Turn in now."

Crider lit up her search radar, knowing that doing so would invite an attack, relying on the speed and maneuverability of the A-66 to avoid it. "Radiating now. Heads up, Hunter Flight."

Three returns showed up: the *Mountain View*, and three hundred kilometers away the *Reuben James*, another frigate doing escort duty on the carrier. And a few thousand meters to the left, and a thousand meters closer to the surface, another ship appeared:

"There's the *Ian Mac Vie*. All right, Three, Four, arm Shrikes and start your run. Two and I will cover you. Heads up for fighters."

The A-66's control panel beeped suddenly. "Fire control radar warning; it's from the target. Evasive Pattern Three, people. Let's hit it." Three and Four peeled off, diving after the frigate.

"I'm getting radar hits, Angel. Jammers activated."

"Loosen up some, Horse. They'll focus on Three and Four in a second."

"Yeah. I'm showing the *Ian Mac Vie* trying for a lock on Four. They've got a lock – no, Four broke it."

A sudden screech in Crider's headphones made her blood run cold. "Horse, break left!"

"MISSILE GUIDANCE RADAR LOCK," Crider's onboard computer calmly warned. "I know," she groused, looping her fighter over. "RADAR LOCK LOST."

Two pale blue shapes shot past; it was two fighters from VS-42. Crider pulled a five-gee turn to follow. "Horse, you with me?"

"Got you, Angel. There's two more to your two o'clock high, going after Three and Four."

"I see 'em. Horse, you take those two. I'm going after Frick and Frack here. Break off now!"

Horse spun his fighter away. "Angel, watch your six."

"You got it, Horse. I'm on one of them now."

Spinning in on the other fighter's tail, Andrea Crider called out "Fox Three!" and hit her the 'guns' button on her stick. If the attack had been for-real, a stream of depleted uranium slugs would have lanced out from her 30mm cannon, shattering the 'enemy' fighter into a cloud of wreckage. But since this was an exercise, the button instead sent a burst from the infrared laser slaved to the main weapons hard point under her fuselage. The IR laser hit the VS-42 ship squarely, activating the combat damage simulator. The 'enemy' fighter's engine died, and the gyros locked, sending the ship spinning out of control. "That's one!" Angel hooted.

*Screeeeeeee!* Her threat receiver screamed a warning as a scattered burst of laser fire struck her fighter a glancing blow. "YOUR STARBOARD STUB WING IS DAMAGED," the computer intoned. "THERE IS AN ENEMY FIGHTER ATTEMPTING MISSILE LOCK TO YOUR SIX O'CLOCK."

"Gee, you think?" Crider slammed her fighter left, right, looped and spun, but the pilot from VS-42 matched her moves.

"MISSILE LAUNCH WARNING."

Crider slammed her throttle back into full reverse, gasping as she pulled a full eight negative gees. Her seat straps cut into her viciously as her vision went red for long moments. Dimly, she saw the other fighter flash past, his drive flaring into reverse as he tried to stop in time.

"Too late, sucker. Fox three, Fox three for a kill!" Slamming her throttle forward, she hit her guns switch and 'killed' the other fighter.

"Horse, I'm clear," she called. "Where are you?"

"Three kilometers to your three o'clock and low," Horse called. "I could use a hand here, Angel."

"On my way. Where's Three and Four?"

"Tangled up with one of their own, Angel. Hound is trying to keep one off of Sleaze so she can launch on the frigate."

"All right, I'm coming in hot on your nine, high. Heads up, Horse."

"I'm taking hits, Angel."

The pilot from VS-42 was concentrating too hard on his quarry. Crider closed, lining up her target optically, shouted "Fox three" and hit 'guns' for a kill.

"You're clear, Horse. How you doing?"

"Partial drive failure, weapons are down. I'm done, Angel."

"Hit your SAR beacon and stand by. Sleaze, Hound, I've got you on radar. Talk to me."

"Angel!" Lieutenant Elizabeth Fitzsimons, 'Sleaze,' called. "He's on my six, he's on my six!" A burst of static was followed by a hoot of triumph on the open channel. "One of yours down, Angel," the VS-42 pilot called.

"Where are *your* buddies, asshole?"

"What?"

Crider dove after the one remaining VS-42 fighter, her search radar emitting. "TARGET LOCK," her computer announced as a red circle appeared on her heads-up display.

"*Fox One*," Crider called. She hit her missile launch button.

Instead of launching a missile, a tight-beam transmission shot from her fighter to the VS-42 fighter. The two onboard computers compared range, trajectory, and velocity data, and in less time than it would have taken for the Shrike to actually have covered the distance, the 'enemy' fighter's computer decided that the missile was lethal.

"Damn it, Angel!" The VS-42 pilot slammed his fists on his suddenly inactive controls as Angel's fighter flashed past, rolling slowly, her laughter percolating over the open channel. "That's a case of Scotch you owe us, dickhead!" Her voice rang with triumph. "Hound, you with me?"

"Coming in on your wing now, Angel."

"Let's go get that frigate."

The *Ian Mac Vie* wasn't about to make herself an easy target. Showing up as ghostly white trails in her heads-up, harmless IR laser fire simulated far more deadly particle beam projectors as they played in sweeps and arcs across space.

"Weave!" Crider called. The two fighters began looping and weaving in a wild corkscrew pattern. It was two thousand meters to Shrike range.

"Damn it! I've lost primary gyros!" Hound called.

"Use your thrusters. Drop in to my seven o'clock."

One thousand meters.

"YOUR CANOPY IS DAMAGED. ACTIVATE EMERGEN-CY SUIT SEALS." Crider dropped her face shield, sealed it, went to suit pressure.

Five hundred meters.

"Angel, I'm hit again, my port wing is gone."

"Stay with me, Hound, you hear? You stay with me!"

Two hundred meters. One hundred.

"Range! Fox One, Fox One!"

"Fox One," Hound screamed into his mike. Three simulated Shrikes were racing for the frigate now, as the ghostly traces of laser fire continued…

…and suddenly stopped.

"God damn it," a new voice came over the channel. "You just killed my ship. Who's flying lead out there?"

"*Ian Mac Vie*, this is Hunter Lead. Beers are on you tonight!" Laughter sounded from several different transmitters.

On the *Ian Mac Vie*'s Bridge, Commander Minoru Tosaki stood looking at lights flashing red on the several control stations around the compartment. "Damn fighter jocks." He grinned at his Bridge staff. "Well, people, looks like we're going to have to run some extra fire control drills the next few days."

"Hunter Flight, Jockey Flight, *Ian Mac Vie*," a new voice called. "Exercise is concluded. Hunter Flight, Jockey Flight, return to the carrier at once for debrief." On all the 'killed' and 'damaged' fighters and on the frigate, systems suddenly flashed back to life.

"Good job, Hunter Flight. Form up on me. Let's go home."

"And collect our Scotch, Angel. Don't forget that," Horse added helpfully.

## Near New Albion

Sliding invisibly through space, a pair of cloaked Grugell frigates took up positions near the system's Jupiter-type gas giant, counting on the mass of the planet to mask them from any sensors. On command, the sensor suites of both ships began tracking radio transmissions and tracking ship traffic. Burst transmissions relayed the data to a massive Colonization ship, parked in deep space a quarter-parsec away, guarded by two cruisers.

Group Commander Gorbamatchik IX watched as the data from his frigates began to arrive. The humans had a substantial population on the planet, numbering in the tens of thousands, but there appeared to be no military ships in orbit, and little if any armed forces on the planet itself. "An easy game," Gorbamatchik remarked to his SubCommander, Itschtistk IV. "We'll watch carefully for some time. One Group Commander Tortallastik has disabled their Fleet, we'll move on the planet unopposed."

Less than half a light year away, Group Commander Tortallastik III was assembling a considerable force of ships to do exactly that.

#### Four
# July 2251

**Tarbos, six weeks later**

"Gawd almighty, would you look at that?" Horace Hamilton gaped at the sight.

The *Mountain View*'s Pilot Lounge offered a good view of space to the starboard side of the ship, and it was there that the newest ship in the Fleet was coasting slowly into the Fleet's new orbital spacedock. The battle cruiser *Orleans* was the first in its class, fifteen hundred meters of dark metal around a huge Gellar tunnel. Bumps on the giant cylinder housed particle beam emitters and missile pods.

"Would you look at all those guns? God, there must be thirty, forty emitters. And I can see six missile bays just on this side. What a monster!"

"Settle down, Horse."

"Angel, you want to make any bets against running a simulated attack on *that*?"

Lieutenant Commander Andrea Crider looked at her wingman. "It's just another ship, Horse. They've all got their weak spots."

"This one ain't got very many, Angel."

"If the Grugell ever come storming in with a fleet, you'd better hope you're right."

## The *Orleans*

Admiral Gauss looked up from his desk when the panel door to his Flag stateroom opened. "Jerry. Have we docked yet?"

"We're about to, sir," Captain Jensen replied. "I thought you'd want to come watch."

"I'll pass. I've seen ships dock before."

"Yes, sir."

"What I need you to do, Jerry, is get in contact with the *Mountain View*, the *Reuben James*, the *Ian Mac Vie*, the *Robert Pritchard*, and the *Cairo*. Set up an assembly formation in the *Mountain View*'s Hangar Bay. I want ship Captains, XO's, squadron leaders and XO's, Chief Engineers, Chief Medical Officers, and whoever else the ship's Captains think are essential personnel. Arrange to have the address piped over to all personnel standing watch on the ships. With the Flag here now, this is officially a Task Group. Time to let 'em know what we're going to be doing."

"I'll get to it, sir. Anything else?"

"Yeah. Find out where the best place is to get a steak down in Mountain View. I've had my fill of shipboard food. I bet you have too."

Captain Jensen chuckled. "I'll get right on that, sir."

"Jerry?"

"Yes, sir?"

"Your wife and kids, have you got them passage from Earth to Tarbos?"

"They'll be in on the *Adirondack* in eight weeks, sir."

"We should be back from exercises by then. You'll be here to meet your family, Jerry."

"Nobody ever said this was supposed to be easy duty, sir."

**The *Shade Tree***

"Coming out of subspace in three, two, one, *out now*."

The *Shade Tree* lurched slightly as it dropped into normal space. Dead ahead was the orb of a type G star.

"Running spectrographic analysis now," Indira Krishnavarna called from Scanning. "Data confirms that's New Albion's sun. We're about two days travel standard sublight drive. No other traffic detected in the area."

"Good. Ahead one-third. Navs, arrange for and plot a standard parking orbit for New Albion as soon as you can pick up the planet. Anybody remember if New Albion has a Skyhook?"

"One, Captain, about sixty kilometers from the port," Krishnavarna answered. "Kinross is the port town, and about two hundred kilometers from that is *Glengarry*, that's the capital."

"Good. We should let someone down there know that they're going to have company. Indira, get that tracking system of yours set up, start scanning for transit tracks."

"Already doing it, Captain. There's nothing showing right now. I don't know how long a track will show after a transit, though."

"Something else we'll have to find out."

**The *Mountain View*'s Hangar deck**

"Officers and crew of Task Force One. The Task Force Commander."

The assembled personnel in the Hangar snapped to attention to the clatter of folding metal chairs. Rear Admiral Isaac Gauss, the newly arrived Commander in Chief, Task Force One, strode the central aisle of the room to the podium at the front. "Take your seats," he barked.

"Before I left Earth," he began, "Fleet Admiral Kosake charged me – charged us – with the task of securing the frontier. Now, for those of you who haven't really thought about that, let me tell you exactly what that means.

"We've got eight ships. The new battle cruiser CSS *Orleans*, and the carrier *Mountain View*, both the first and only ships in their classes. We have the light cruisers *Dallas* and *Settlement*, and the frigates *Ian Mac Vie*, *Reuben James*, *Robert Pritchard* and *Farragut*. Eight ships, two wings of A-66 attack fighters, and one of A-70 strike fighters."

Gauss tapped a contact on the podium, and a giant holographic map of the Confederacy swam into view over the assembled officers and crewmembers. Along one side of Confederate space, outward in the spiral arm, the border was traced in red; this was the Grugell frontier.

"That red line is what concerns me. On the other side of that red line is a hostile, totalitarian, militarized dictatorship that threatens our very existence. Our eight ships have been charged with securing this border, which for your information is just over sixty thousand light years by almost a million light years in the plane of the ecliptic.

"That's a lot of ground to cover, people. That's one hundred and eighty *billion* square light years of border. With eight ships. How are we to guard one hundred and eighty billion light years with eight ships? We face the same problem Napoleon faced on old Earth – too much border. Old Bony told his generals 'you can't be strong everywhere, so pick one spot and be strong there, and hope it's the right spot.' Well, we have a plan for that, and when we leave tomorrow for Fleet exercises in the New Albion system – the system nearest that border – you'll know what that plan is. But for today, I want you to know what my thoughts and intentions for the Task Force we are forming here right now.

"What concerns me, people, is what's going on across that red line. Back on Earth, we have had all too much historical precedence that tells us what to expect from military dictatorships. What we can expect is that this dictatorship, this 'Empire,' will not be able to co-exist peacefully with a free society. We can expect a fight, and probably sooner rather than later. Time works for us, not for them, and they have to know that.

"Which brings me to my next concern. They know more about us than we do them. You've all seen the briefing data. The Grugell have cloaked ships, and they've routinely run reconnaissance missions into the Confederacy. They know the locations of our major settled worlds, and they know our traffic lanes. We know nothing about them. We need to start an active reconnaissance program to learn their transit lanes, their standard jump points, and their primary settled worlds.

"But most of all, people – most of all, you all have my word, this Task Force will be ready when that fight comes. Now down there on Tarbos, some of the politicians are nattering about finding some sort of 'common ground,' with the Grugell. They want to 'negotiate,' when we're the ones negotiating from a weaker position. Well, I'm here to tell you that their position is pure, unadulterated *bullshit*." He paused to let the profanity sink in; most of the assembled audience weren't used to hearing Flag officers swear in public. "When the fight comes, and it will come, the only way we'll achieve a peace is to win that fight. And we will win it decisively, finally, overwhelmingly.

"It's going to be hard. Training for this fight is going to be hard. We'll be in space for months at a time. There will be long nights with no sleep, there will be drills after drills after drills. We'll run exercises until we're about to drop, and then *we'll run them again.*

"Some of you won't be able to take it. When that happens, we'll drop you down there on Tarbos next time we make port; you'll turn in your uniforms and find yourself some other occupation. But those of you that do, and by God that will be most of you, we'll be the finest fighting force in the Galaxy. And that's because we're fighting *for* something.

"And that's the biggest thing of all. Look around you, all of you, to your left and right. The politicians in the wrangling down there on the surface, they make a lot of noise about freedom and liberty, but that's a distant thing when you're boarding an enemy ship with a pistol in your hand, or when you're dodging particle beam fire in a fighter, trying to get in missile-launch range. When the fight comes, you'll be fighting alongside the people around you now, and you'll be fighting for them, and for the Navy, for the honor and pride of the Navy. Because without the Navy, there won't *be* any Confederacy, and there won't be any freedom and liberty. There will only be the smoking ruins of our cities, and the iron fist of an Empire over the Galaxy. And I swear before you this day, I will fight alongside any one of you myself to prevent that from happening.

"There's just one thing I want you to remember when this fight comes. A long time ago, on Earth during the Second World War, a general addressed his troops before a battle just as I'm doing now. He told them that no battle was ever won by going out to die for your country – battles are won by making the other poor dumb bastards die for *their* country. Good words to remember.

"We'll leave the Tarbos system at eight-hundred local time tomorrow with the *Orleans*, the *Mountain View*, the *Dallas*, and the *Ian Mac Vie*, *Reuben James*, and the *Farragut*. We'll be headed for the New Albion system to perform our first Fleet exercise. The details of that exercise, which we're calling Prescient Force, are awaiting you in your ship's Signals sections as I speak. You – every one of you – will carry out your tasks to the best of your ability. Either that, or you'll be finding a new line of work. I want you to make sure that everyone on every one of your ships out there," he pointed to the ceiling, "Understands that as well."

"That is all," the Admiral concluded. As he stepped back from the podium and turned to walk down the main aisle out of the hangar, a grizzled Master Chief Petty Officer shouted, "Atten-tion!"

A roar rose from the room as the assembled Navy officers and crew snapped to their feet. "First Flight, *sir!*" was the thunderous exhortation, shouted simultaneously by over a thousand people.

Gauss swept down the main aisle between rows of officers standing at rigid attention, his aide following closely. "You're responsible for that, aren't you Jerry?" he asked, *sotto voce*.

"I don't know what you're talking about, sir," Captain Jensen replied, his expression carefully neutral.

At the rear of the room, a gray-haired, stern-looking man in the green uniform of a Master Chief Petty Officer waited for them. Service hash marks ran most of the way from his elbow to his wrist, each representing three years of service; the Navy had allowed transfers from the various armed services on Earth to include their former time as time-in-service in the new Confederate force. Judging by his left sleeve, Gauss estimated that the hoary old Master Chief had seen better than thirty years in uniform.

As Admiral Gauss approached, the gray-haired old Master Chief stepped forward and saluted.

"Admiral Gauss," he announced, his voice gravelly and rough. "I'm Master Chief Bosun's Mate Paul Ortega. I'm the Division Master Chief." That title announced him as the senior non-commissioned officer in the Task Group and its support units. As such, Master Chief Ortega would be as much the Admiral's right-hand man as his ubiquitous Chief of Staff.

"Pleased to meet you, Master Chief," Gauss replied, returning the man's salute and then shaking his hand. "This is my Chief of Staff, Captain Jensen."

"Sir." Master Chief Ortega acknowledged the Captain politely.

"What's on your mind, Master Chief?"

"Just making my welcome, sir. We've got something in common, I understand. You came to the Navy from the U.S. Air Force, is that right?"

"Yes. And you did too, right?"

"Yes sir. I was a Master Sergeant; last posting was at Petersen Air Force Base in Colorado Springs. I signed up with the Navy the year they opened up offices on Earth."

"Where's your office, Master Chief?"

"I've been here on the *Mountain View*, sir. That's what I wanted to talk to you about. I figured you'll be using the *Orleans* as your flagship, so I was planning to move my office and staff over there."

"Of course. Can you get that done yet today?"

"It's already happening, sir."

"Is your family here?"

"Yessir. We've got Base housing, in fact, down in Mountain View. Bumped a Chief Gunner's Mate. He wasn't too happy about it, but you know what they say about the bricks falling in."

"I do," Gauss chuckled at the ancient Service idiom. "Good. I'll see you on board, then, Master Chief."

The grizzled old NCO rubbed his chin thoughtfully. "That was a good speech you gave there, sir. Nice to see an Admiral that really gets what we're trying to do out here. Wish you could kick some of that up a little higher. Well. I'd best get on back to my office, make sure my people are hustling. I'll see you at port call, sir."

"Very well, Master Chief," Gauss answered, returning the Master Chief's salute.

The two officers turned into a branching corridor leading to the carrier's starboard docking port, where a shuttle waited to take them back to the *Orleans*.

"Jerry," Admiral Gauss said after a few moments of thought, "What do you suppose the Master Chief meant by that last comment?"

"I suppose, sir, that Fleet Admiral Kosake's reputation precedes him – even out here."

"His reputation?"

"He's rumored to be – well, sir, I suppose *timid* is the word I'd use."

"I've never met him. I sure hope that's not true, Jerry – I hope to God that's not true. We've got no hope if the guy in the top chair doesn't have it where it counts."

"Yes, sir." Captain Jensen looked doubtful. Gauss let it drop.

# Five
# August 2251

**The *Orleans* Combat Information Center**

"Oh, that's very clever," Admiral Gauss pointed at two new images that suddenly appeared in the holographic 'tank' displaying the exercise. "Captain Wallace brought his task group out of subspace sixteen hundred kilometers *above* the *Mountain View* group. Do you see now, people? That's what I've been talking about – that kind of planet bound, two-dimensional thinking is going to get people killed. Now Captain Wallace, he gets it…" The Admiral's voice trailed off. He was staring across the tank at the Ensign manning the Master Scanning board.

"Ensign Lesk, what is it?"

"Admiral, sir, these aren't Gellar drives generating this signature. There's something here I've never seen before."

"What?" Captain Igor Ivanov, the Orlean's commander, leaped to the scanning console. "They're Grugell! Three, no, four of the bastards just popped out! ` *Der'mo!*" In his agitation, Ivanov slipped back to his native Russian for a moment before catching himself. "Call General Quarters!"

Commander Tak Ordell was serving as Tactical Officer for the exercise. Cursing colorfully, he ran to the Signals board. "Raid warning Red! All ships, this is *Orleans*, four possible hostiles at one seven one positive ninety! This is no drill, say again this is no drill - all ships turn as necessary to unmask main batteries!"

Admiral Gauss' shout drowned out the Task Group Tactical Officer. "Tell them not to fire unless fired on!"

The Task Force Commander's order was rendered moot by a sudden blast that shook the *Orleans* like a rat in a terrier's jaws. The Tactical Officer was still shouting into the mike. "All ships, weapons free, say again weapons are free!" Commander Ordell dropped the mike, turned to the Admiral. "I think that's it, sir."

"I think you're right, Commander."

"Three inbounds, sir!" Ensign Lesk had somehow managed to stay on his feet at the Scanning console. "Missiles of some kind, I can't tell what…"

Admiral Gauss barked at the Group Tactical Officer. "I want projectors targeting those inbounds."

"Working on it, sir."

"Admiral, I've got to get to my Bridge," Captain Ivanov called as another blast shook the battle cruiser. "Go!" Gauss shouted back.


## The *Mountain View*

The sudden burst from the Hangar deck announcer almost bowled over the pilots, most of who were pre-flighting their strike fighters.

"ALL FIGHTERS SCRAMBLE, SAY AGAIN, SCRAMBLE. ENGAGE AND DESTROY GRUGELL SHIPS ATTACKING FROM THE NORTH." North meant "up" relative to the *Mountain View*'s orientation. Coordinating the mass movement of ships in three dimensions had resulted in a whole new set of conventions.

Andrea Crider leaped into the cockpit of her A-66 in a single bound. Before her Crew Chief was able to roll the crew ladder away, her drive was engaged and the fighter rolling towards the runway. "Hunter Flight, this is Hunter Lead, scramble plan Alpha," the call came into her headphones as she frantically pulled her seat straps tight.

"Horse, where are you?" she called.

"I'm number four in line, Angel, I'll form up with you outside."

A sudden lurch came to Crider through the fighter; the carrier was going through some pretty strenuous evasive maneuvers. *Evading what?* The question popped into her mind and was almost instantly answered: *Grugell. It's for-real now.*

"Hunter Flight, Lead is rolling."

"Two is rolling," Crider called into her mike as she slammed her throttle forward. "We've got no Shrikes, boss, we're prepped for an exercise flight."

"Once you're out, jettison the laser pod," the squadron commander answered. "We've all got full loads of thirty mike-mike, that's going to have to do."

Behind Lieutenant Commander Crider, the rest of the flight called out as they roared down the carrier's Runway One, through the shimmering force screen and out into space.

"Hunter Flight, this is Lead. We have four bandits, one at three-five-five pos twenty, two and three-oh-one pos fifty, one at zero-one-zero neg ten. Angel, Horse, you take the one at oh-one-oh. Sleaze, Hound, go for three-five-five. Burger, you and me, Rocks and Taffie, take the two at three-oh-one. Heads up for friendlies, VS-24's launching too."

"The more the merrier, Goose," Crider called back to the Squadron commander.

"Goose, is it just me, or am I getting more bandits popping through?" Sleaze's normally soft voice was raised an octave in surprise.

"Looks like it. Stay loose, people. Wingmen, stay with your leads; watch your fuel states and ammo levels. In two-ship elements, take 'em! Charge!"

## The *Orleans*

Two Grugell ships, cruisers from their size, were raking the *Orleans* with bursts of emerald anti-proton fire.

On the Bridge, Captain Ivanov was barking orders while holding a blood-soaked bandage on his temple; he'd been thrown against a bulkhead when a Grugell torpedo had crashed into the ship's shields.

"Come about to two-seven-zero. Ahead full. Weapons, get me a target solution on that big one on our port."

"Working now, Captain. Just a moment… There! Ready on missile bays three and four, weapons checked and ready in all respects!"

"Fire!"

Six Lancer missiles, larger and faster than the Shrikes carried by the smaller ships, leaped from the *Orleans'* flank and raced after the Grugell cruiser. Drive pods flaring bright orange, the enemy ship tried to evade, but to no avail. Thirty-eight seconds after the missile launch, the enemy ship vanished in a flash of thermonuclear flame.

"That's a kill! Helm, take us up, bearing steady, north ninety. Get us out from between these two others."

"Captain, force field shields are failing on the aft port quarter."

"Belay that last. Turn us into them, head-on," Ivanov ordered.

"I'm showing fighters coming in, Captain, two of them. They're A-66's from the *Mountain View*."

**Hunter Flight**

"We won't make much of a difference with no missiles, Horse," Andrea Crider called, "So target any gun turrets you see, any projectors, anything that looks like a weapon."

"Roger that, Angel."

"Follow me in. I'm going to take a run on this big one that's firing on the flagship."

Crider dove her fighter directly at the gleaming silver orb of the Grugell ship, and to her surprise there was no fire coming her way. *Do you suppose they can't detect something as small as a fighter?*

She hit the ranging button on her stick; the readout blinked on her Heads-Up Display, three thousand seven hundred meters. While theoretically, cannon shells would fly forever in the gravity-neutral vacuum of space, her targeting radar was limited but the strength of the return signal.

Two thousand meters, and still no fire came her way.

"Angel, they aren't shooting at us."

"I noticed, Horse. Hunter Lead, this is Two, these ships, they don't seem to be able to see us."

"I noticed, Angel."

One thousand meters. "Fox-Three," Crider called, triggering her cannon. Her slugs glanced off the Grugell cruiser's force screen, striking a shower of orange sparks but doing no damage at all. "Shit," she cursed under her breath. "Lead, if someone can bring these shields down, we can do some damage here. Otherwise, we may as well be throwing spitballs."

"Working on it, Angel. Hunter Flight, this is Lead, hold fire, say again hold fire. Don't waste your shells yet."

**The *Orleans***

A haze of smoke hung in the Combat Information Center. The *Orleans* was under full drive now, but a hit through the side of her Gellar tunnel was reducing drive efficiency by a fourth. Wallowing like a pig, the battle cruiser was trying unsuccessfully to evade the fire of two Grugell cruisers.

"Admiral Gauss, call from the *Mountain View*!"

"What? What the hell do they want?"

"They want you, sir."

Gauss grabbed the headset away from the Signals officer. "Gauss. What the hell is it?" He listened intently for several seconds before shouting new orders.

"Tactical Action, tell the Bridge to concentrate all fire on that cruiser at our seven o'clock. Bring the *Ian Mac Vie* and the *Dallas* in on their sixes, tell them to target missiles. We need to break down their force screens."

"We've been trying that, Admiral. Particle beams aren't getting through. Missiles can, but we don't have enough of them. We're not carrying our full Basic Load."

"They can't see the fighters," Gauss snapped. "They must be too small. But the fighters aren't packing anything that can get through their screens. We've got to try something else. Signals, contact the *Mountain View*. Order them to recall half of the fighters, re-arm them with Shrikes. Do it now!"

"Sir, negative reply from the *Ian Mac Vie*. I think the Mac Vie is gone, sir, I'm not getting a radar return from their last known bearing."

"Shit. Is the *Dallas* moving?"

"Yes sir!"

## Hunter Flight

"Angel, Horse, Sleaze, Hound, return to base for re-arm," Hunter Lead called.

"Goose, say again that last," Andrea Crider called.

"Damn it, Angel, you heard me. Go back to the goddamn carrier for some Shrikes! We aren't doing any good out here!"

"Goose, it'll be too late by the time we re-arm!"

"Get moving, Angel, or I'll have you flying a desk!"

Swearing like a Marine, Andrea Crider looped her fighter away from the Grugell frigate she'd been stalking to race back to the *Mountain View.*

## The *Farragut*

The *Farragut*'s Bridge was as yet undamaged, but a hull breach on Deck Six leaked a cloud of gas into space as the oldest of the Navy's armed ships dove at the silver form of a Grugell frigate.

"Come left three degrees. Ahead two-thirds. Weapons, get me a missile firing solution, all four forward bays."

"Solution set and locked, Captain, missiles are checked and ready in all respects."

"Fire!"

"*Missiles away,*" the Weapons officer screeched. "All birds are hot and tracking."

"Ahead full, come right to zero-nine-zero."

A sudden blow shook the ship. "Captain, main drive failure, main drive failure! We're coasting, Cap…"

The Engineering officer's call was cut off as the *Farragut* vanished in a flash of flame, expanding gases and wreckage.

## The *Orleans*

"There goes the *Farragut*!" Admiral Gauss was raging at the display on the holographic tank. "Damn it, we're getting our asses kicked here!"

"Admiral," the Tactical Action officer called out. "*Orleans* is out of missiles, we're down to particle beams. Drive efficiency is down to two-thirds; shields are failing in the port rear quarter. The *Reuben James* reports no damage, but she's out of Lancers. The *Dallas* has taken three torpedo hits, she's trying to evade and get her targeting radars back online. The *Mountain View* has eight fighters re-arming with Shrikes, but she's taken one hit, their targeting radar and navigation radars are down."

"How can we be out of birds that quick?"

"We were only carrying a minimal load, Admiral. Standard load-out for exercises. Orders direct from Fleet."

"Shit – SHIT! That changes as of now, assuming we survive this goat-screw."

## The *Mountain View*

Four fighters of VS-66 shot once more out of the Hangar deck, armed now with four Shrike missiles each. "Horse, you keep my six clear. Sleaze, Hound, both of you go high, take that bad guy up there that's bleeding air. Horse, let's go after the big boy that's firing on the *Orleans*. He looks like their Flag – let's take him out. That ought to mess them up some."

"I'm with you, Angel."

The fighters separated, racing after their intended targets.

"Horse, listen up. It might take all my Shrikes to break through this thing's shields. Follow me in on my seven o'clock; I'll launch and break right. As soon as I break clear, pickle off your Shrikes and follow me out. I'm not sure where we'll go from there, so just hang on my seven."

"Roger that, Angel."

"Full throttle, Horse, let's get 'em."

## The *Orleans*

"Bloody hell," Captain Jensen muttered. His left arm hung crookedly; his shoulder has been dislocated when a torpedo hit had hurled him to the deck.

"You all right, Jerry? Tactical, pass to all ships, break to subspace, say again break for subspace, regroup at Point Alpha." Admiral Gauss' face was bleeding from some unseen wound.

"Sir, we're *running*?"

"We've got *no goddam choice*, Commander, you understand that? We're getting creamed here!"

The Commander stared at the Admiral for a moment. "Yes sir." He turned to the Tactical Action console, picked up a handset. "All ships, withdraw, best possible speed to subspace transit. Regroup at Point Alpha."

"Let's get as many of these ships back to Tarbos as we can," Gauss said to no one in particular.

A buzz sounded on the Signals Panel. "CIC, Bridge. Unless someone can scrape that cruiser off of us, we'll never make transit," Captain Ivanov's voice sounded tinnily from the speaker.

## Hunter Flight

"Horse, loosen her up some, you're about to bump me. Two thousand meters."

"Roger, Angel. Shrikes are armed."

"Twelve hundred meters. One thousand. Let's fire at five hundred, they won't have a chance to dodge even if they can detect them."

"Gotcha."

"Range! Fox One, Fox One, missiles away! *Breaking right now*," Crider called.

"Fox One, Fox One for a kill!" Horse loosed his four Shrikes and pulled into a five-gee turn to follow his flight leader.

Behind them, the first four Shrikes arrived at once, shattering the Grugell cruiser's shields and blasting four decks open to space. Seconds later the second volley of four impacted, blasting through to the ship's interior, shattering the cruiser's main hull into several pieces. The Grugell ship rocked with secondary explosions, and one of the two drive pods broke free, cartwheeling into space trailing a sparkling stream of electrical discharges and gas.

"That's a kill, Horse, that's a kill," Crider called.

"VS-66, VS-42, return to base immediately, acknowledge."

"*Mountain View* Flight Control, this is Hunter Two, roger that," Crider answered. "I wonder what's up now?"

"We're out of missiles anyway, Angel," Horse pointed out.


## The *Orleans*

"Captain Jensen, I want you to find out who was flying those two fighters. They just saved our miserable asses," Admiral Gauss said through gritted teeth. "Commander, how long to transit?"

"Forty-eight minutes, Captain. We may be able to shade that by five minutes, max, if Engineering can moderate the disruption in the conversion matrix from the breach in the mass tunnel. *Reuben James* has already gone into subspace. *Dallas* is two minutes from subspace. *Mountain View* is recovering fighters now; they report fifteen minutes to complete recovery and then nine more minutes to subspace transit."

"There's still enemy ships out there," Gauss growled.

"Nothing within a thousand kilometers on the screen at the moment, Admiral. But that doesn't mean they aren't there, does it?"

"God, what a debacle." Gauss sat down in the first chair he saw. "What a total, unmitigated fuck-up."

"Sir, call from the *Dallas*, they're asking if we require an escort to transit."

"No. Tell them to get the hell out of here. Line up our trajectory to cover the *Mountain View* with whatever damned weapons we still have until they make subspace. We can't afford to lose the carrier."

"We can't afford to lose the flagship either," Captain Jensen pointed out.

"We've lost two frigates already, and we couldn't afford that. We're down from eight ships to six, now. And three of those are badly damaged. If those Grugell bastards wanted to hit us hard, they sure as hell have." Gauss grimaced, rubbed his temple. "God, my head hurts."

# Six
# September 2251

**Tarbos, Fleet Spacedock**

Four ships, the last remnants of a beat-up Task Force, sat smoking and battered in the Tarbos Fleet spacedock. The *Orleans* was the last to arrive, and the first man off the battered ship was Rear Admiral Isaac Gauss, on his way to brief an unhappy Fleet Admiral.

He had the unhappy feeling that his career was in much the same condition as his flagship.

The Dock debarking level was sixteen decks outward, 'below' the Fleet headquarters. Since the Dock still depended on the rotation of the massive main disk to provide gravity, Gauss and his aide had to find a lift to take them up to Deck Four, where the Fleet Headquarters staff worked in a comfortable two-thirds gee. When the lift arrived, Captain Jensen waited for the Admiral to enter, as protocol required, before stepping in and pushing the contact for Deck Four. Both men stood watching the numbers over the door slide slowly upwards towards Four as the lift as-cended.

"This isn't going to be pretty, Jerry."

"Probably not, sir."

Admiral Gauss rocked back and forth on his heels, silently, strangely calm, as he had been since shortly after the battle.

"There we are, Deck Four. Ready to face the wolves, Captain Jensen?"

"I've got your six, sir. Let's do it."

"You're a good man, Jerry."

The two officers strode into the Flag office as though they were boarding an enemy ship. Admiral Gauss walked directly to the Chief Petty Officer manning the front desk and announced, "Rear Admiral Gauss and Captain Jensen to see Fleet Admiral Kosake."

The gray-haired CPO looked up at Gauss' stern visage and said in a low voice, "Go on in, sir, I'll buzz you through."

A tone sounded, and a panel door behind the desk slid open. Gauss strode through the door, followed closely by his aide.

Fleet Admiral Minoru Kosake sat behind an expansive desk of polished Tarbosian blackwood. On the wall behind him was a map of the Confederacy, and on his desk a small, polished metal model of the *Orleans*. The office was large, but Spartan in its appointments, and with good reason; the office of Fleet Admiral had been created less than a year earlier.

"Rear Admiral Isaac Gauss reports as ordered, *sir*." Gauss stood at attention, saluted. Still seated, the Fleet Admiral returned the salute, a little too casually. Gauss' mouth turned down in a slight frown.

"Sit down, Admiral Gauss. Captain, you too, have a seat." The two officers sat down. Fleet Admiral Kosake ruffled through some papers, took off his glasses and cleaned them, and stared at his desktop for a moment before speaking again.

"Well, gentlemen. We've had a hard time these last few weeks, haven't we? Yes, a very hard time indeed." Kosake stood up and turned to face the wall map. Gauss turned to give Captain Jensen a puzzled look; his lips silently traced a question: *We?*

Jensen just shook his head.

"It would appear that the New Albion system is in some contention," Admiral Kosake continued. "The presence of our armed ships in the area may have provoked the attack."

"Provoked, sir?" Admiral Gauss' mouth hung open.

"Yes, that's the question at hand. Senator Galloway claims that New Albion is too close to the Grugell border; he thinks we should limit our expansion in that direction, perhaps abandon that colony."

"Abandon New Albion?"

"Yes, possibly. Unless we can negotiate something with the Grugell. I understand that Senator Galloway is pushing to open diplomatic relations with…"

Gauss came halfway out of his chair, unable to contain himself any longer. "With all due respect, *sir*, what the fuck are you talking about? Negotiate? Abandon a colony? One of the original thirteen Confederate worlds? I'll be God-damned if we abandon a colony – we've got over five hundred killed and twice that many wounded from an unprovoked attack, and Senator Galloway wants to *surrender a planet* to those bastards?"

"Admiral Gauss!" Kosake snapped, finally showing a little animation. "Do I have to remind you that we do not make policy? The President and the Congress make policy; we only carry it out. You know that, do you not?"

"I know that, sir, sure as I know that the President listens to her Fleet officers. You most of all, sir. Please don't tell me you're buying into this appeasement horseshit?"

"Mind your tone, Admiral. I'm not buying into or advocating anything. I'm merely discussing alternative views. Now, as to the attack on your Task Group, I would hope we have learned some valuable lessons in that engagement. I've read your report, but I'd like to hear your impressions directly."

"Well, sir, my direct impression is that we were not prepared, and we had our asses handed to us. Captain Jensen, if you would?"

Captain Jensen extracted a small silver disk from his jacket pocket and pressed a stud; a holographic display of the deployed *Orleans* Task Force swam into midair.

"Sir," Jensen narrated the unfolding display in a monotone, "You can see that here, at the beginning of the exercise, the *Orleans* was here, escorted by the *Ian Mac Vie*. The *Mountain View* and the *Farragut* were a hundred and eighty kilometers below the flagship's keel. The *Dallas* and the *Reuben James* popped out of subspace here," he pointed at three new blue symbols beneath the *Mountain View*, "to simulate an attack. Less than ten seconds later, before the flagship even detected them, four Grugell ships – a heavy cruiser, a light cruiser, and two frigates, from the sizes – popped through above the flagship on this axis." Four red symbols appeared. "Four more came through to the flagship's stern, this group with two light cruisers and two frigates. It was this cruiser that fired first on the flagship…" As the hologram unfolded, Captain Jensen calmly explained every detail of the debacle.

*Great jumping Christ. The whole thing lasted less than thirty minutes.* Gauss had seen the run-through four times, and the same thought occurred to him each time.

"…and the *Orleans* was the last ship to transit to subspace. That concludes our available data." He sat down.

"Well." Admiral Kosake sat down, picked up a piece of paper, stared at it for a moment. "Yes. Well, that was certainly a bad day for the Navy. Admiral Gauss, what recommendations have you to prevent a repeat of this incident?"

"Sir, I'll tell you exactly what we need to do. First of all, full combat load-outs for all ships. We ran out of missiles too soon in that engagement, and we've learned that particle beams aren't enough when you're dealing with capital ships. Second, we need to put standing patrols near the border planets, New Albion especially. The *Mountain View* and at least one other ship should be tasked to that system; we already know that the Grugell are operating in that area, and the one advantage we have is that they don't seem to be able to track something as small as a strike fighter. That won't last long, though. They lost one ship to Shrikes launched from the *Mountain View*'s fighters, and they won't take long figuring a way to counter that threat.

"Finally, sir, we need more ships. We could use ten more like the *Orleans*."

Admiral Kosake sat staring at the ceiling.

Gauss looked at Captain Jensen. Jensen shrugged.

"Thank you for coming in, Admiral Gauss," the Fleet Admiral said at last. "I'll review all of the data you've provided and speak to you again. I'm sure you've got plenty to do, so I won't keep you any longer. Dismissed."

In the elevator, bound once more for the Dock levels, Captain Jensen finally broke the silence. "Sir, is it just me, or was that about the strangest ass-chewing I've ever sat through?"

"It sure as hell wasn't what I expected, Jerry, but I only know Admiral Kosake by what little reputation he had in the Japanese Defense Force. I do know one thing – we've got another problem that might hurt us as much as the Grugell fleet."

"What's that, sir?"

"A damned leadership vacuum, Jerry. A Fleet Admiral that is a complete non-entity. That big chair up there may as well be empty for all the good he'll do us."

"That's what I was thinking, sir, not to disparage a Flag officer, but…"

"I know, Jerry. Keep it under your hat for now. Fleet Admiral Kosake seems to be in this Senator Galloway's pocket, but I know there's at least one Senator that *is* on our side."

## Seven
# September 2251

**Tarbos, the Senate Main Chamber**

President Cochet had only once addressed the Senate directly in full session, and that was three days after her inauguration. That had been a hopeful occasion, marked with good will and good cheer.

Not so this time.

She strode to the polished black podium at the front of the Senate chamber, a tiny silver disk barely visible in her hand. The silver disk fit into a tiny recess on the podium top, displaying her speech in tiny, red holographic text a few centimeters off the podium top, invisible to the audience and the recording videos from a hundred different media outlets.

"Senators, Selectmen, ladies and gentlemen, my fellow Confederation citizens.

"Sixteen days ago, our Confederation suffered an attack. This was an unprovoked attack, an attack directly on the ships and the brave men and women who have volunteered to defend our way of life. This attack was aimed deliberately at our capacity to defend ourselves, at our ability to protect our rights to live as free people.

"This attack was launched by agents of a hostile race, by the military forces of a tyrannical culture bent on conquest. Let us make no mistake; the Grugell Empire have no interest in 'dialogue,' or in 'peaceful co-existence.' The incident of the attack on the *Orleans* Task Group proves that to be true. This incident, the *Orleans* incident, marks the first known instance of an act of war committed in space.

"A free people, to remain free, must on occasion fight to preserve their freedom. We acknowledge that necessity, even as we seek to prevent it. To that second purpose, we will meet tomorrow with a special envoy from the Grugell Empire, whose ship is in orbit about this planet as I speak to you. The envoy will land tomorrow for a meeting with myself, selected members of the House and Senate, and selected members of my Cabinet.

"To the first purpose, should it come to a fight, I have request-ed the Senate to authorize increased funds for Naval construction and personnel. Details of that funding request are being provided to all House and Senate members and to the media now.

"To the Grugell I can say only this. In the long history of humanity, we have learned many lessons, but the greatest lesson of our history is this: A free people, fighting to preserve their freedom, will bear any hardship, overcome any obstacle, face any danger, to defeat those who threaten our way of life. Think well on that.

"Thank you." President Cochet spun on her heel and strode from the room, ignoring the shouted questions of reporters.

## The Confederate Senate Office Building

"I'm glad you came to see me, Admiral." Senator Crider poured a cup of coffee, handed it over to Admiral Gauss. As he poured a second cup for the Admiral's ever-present aide, he examined the pair closely. He liked what he saw.

"Thank you, sir," Gauss replied. He sipped the coffee, and his eyebrows shot up. It was considerably different than the stuff served on the Fleet spacedock far above Mountain View.

"Forestian coffee," the Senator explained. "Here, Captain, a cup for you. I import it for my office. Our soil is remarkably fertile; we can grow just about anything. I've never found coffee like it anywhere."

"I'd like to have some for my flagship, once it gets out of dock, anyway."

"I think I can probably arrange for a few cans." The Senator sat down at his desk and poured a cup for himself. "But I get the feeling you didn't come all the way down here to talk about coffee, Admiral. So, what can I do for you this morning?"

"Sir," Gauss began, setting his cup down on the arm of his chair. "You saw the President's speech last night, right? I don't know about you, sir, but that read to me like a virtual declaration of war. We *are* at war, sir, in case the Congress hasn't figured it out yet."

"I can't speak for the whole Congress, or even the Senate. But I have figured that out myself, Admiral. In fact, my whole family has. My sister is in your command. She's an A-66 pilot on the *Mountain View*."

Admiral Gauss surprised the Senator by suddenly snapping his fingers. "Crider. That's right! I thought I recognized the name. I should have put it together sooner – it's not a common name. Your sister is the reason I'm sitting here today, sir. How much has she told you about the battle we were in?"

"Not much. I only spoke to her for a few minutes after the carrier docked. She just wanted to let me know she was all right."

"I'll say she's all right. Senator, your sister is in for a Distinguished Flying Cross, and at my request. She and her wingman saved the *Orleans* from being completely destroyed. They attacked and blew away a Grugell cruiser that was beating us to pieces. We would never have made it to the subspace transit if they hadn't taken that ship out."

Senator Crider leaned back in his office chair, his coffee cup cradled in his hands. He brought the cup to his face, inhaling the aroma of the coffee, a reflective expression on his face. "Well," he said quietly. "That would be my sister. She always was a little wild. I could tell you stories… But I digress." He set his coffee down untasted. "You wanted to talk to me about funding for the Fleet, am I right?"

"That's right, sir. How'd you know?"

"Admiral, you're an admirable tactician, but I can tell you're not a politician." Crider grinned. "I'm the Chairman of the Senate Budget Committee, and the Navy's Appropriation bill is in front of my committee right now. It's not that hard to figure out, is it?"

The two men locked eyes for a moment. Each recognized the other as an equal, in strength, in skill, in determination.

"Sir," Admiral Gauss said at last, "No, I'm not a politician, and I'd have to say I'm glad I'm not. On the other hand, sir, I'd have to say I'm glad *you* are. The Navy needs a few friends in Congress right now. Everybody else seems to be a bit too worried about bean-counting, and a not worried at all about protecting the Confederacy from a hostile outside force."

"I'm glad you're not a politician, too, Admiral. You're doing very well where you are. You did well in getting as much of your Task Group back as you did. That was no mean feat, you know – I looked at the telemetry, and you were outnumbered and out-gunned. I don't know what Fleet Admiral Kosake told you" – the politically astute Crider didn't miss the sudden frown that flashed across Admiral Gauss' face – "but I'll tell you that I'm pretty impressed."

"Thanks, sir."

"Admiral, I want the same thing you want. I want this Navy properly funded and equipped. If this is going to be a war, I want to win it. We *have* to win it."

"I wish more people saw it that way, sir."

"If they'd been raised by Mike Crider, hearing the stories of the Grugell invasion of Forest, they might. Admiral, I'd like you to come testify to the Budget Committee meeting tomorrow morning. Can you stay down in Mountain View until ten-hundred tomorrow?"

"You bet, sir. Captain Jensen and I can get transient quarters at the Fleet logistics base on the edge of town."

"Good. It's settled, then. More coffee?"

# Eight
# September 2251

The *Shade Tree*

Captain Barrett had almost gotten used to the gut-wrenching feeling of dropping out of subspace. Suddenly the weird shifting lightshow of subspace gave way to a normal starfield, and immediately…

"Captain, multiple radar returns, scattered metallic objects – looks like a debris field."

"Where are we? How far out from New Albion?"

"That's New Albion's sun, Captain, that big bright dot to the upper right of the screen. We're about a day and a half out." The Navigation tech was on the ball.

"Indira, get scanning on all bands, I want to know what this debris field is."

"Working on it. We're getting short-range and medium-range radar and spectrographic returns now. Lots of metal, some semi-transparent stuff that look like plastic, and about six hundred meters off to our starboard bow, looks like organic matter."

Barrett's eyebrows shot up. "Organic? What do you mean?"

"Resolving… Looks like bodies, Captain. Three of them, right near a concentration of debris. I'm guessing that we're looking at the remnants of a starship that was destroyed."

"Wonderful. Signals, get on the hyperphone to New Albion Ground, give them our ETA, request a parking orbit, and find out what the hell went on out here."

"Right away." The Signals tech immediately began programming a burst transmission to New Albion Ground, which would take about three hours to reach the planet and get a reply back.

Indira Krishnavarna looked up from her readouts, a frown on her face. "Captain, something's under power about six hundred klicks to our nine o'clock low, looks like Grugell drive field at about quarter power."

"That explains a lot," Barrett snapped. "Let's get them. Helm; get us on an intercept course. Ahead three-quarters. Weapons, as soon as we're in range get me a particle beam lock on their drive pods. Someone wake up the Marines, we're going to have a job for them here in a minute."

"They're on the way to the lander now, Captain." One of the *Shade Tree*'s latest modifications had been the addition of a tiny clampon lander, a smaller version of the sort carried aboard Navy frigates.

"Four hundred kilometers and closing," Helm reported.

"I'll be able to get a lock at a hundred klicks," Weapons chimed in, "but I recommend holding fire until ten to get a precise shot."

"Very well," Barrett agreed. "Continue to close."

Two levels down, Barrett's four ex-Marines were climbing into the claustrophobic lander, clad in full battle armor and toting submachine guns firing frangible polymer slugs.

"Coming in now, Captain, I'm firing braking thrusters now to cut our overtake speed. Sixty kilometers. Forty. Twenty. Slowing down… Ten klicks."

"Fire particle beam." Captain Barrett's voice was strangely calm, with an undercurrent of repressed tension.

"They've got two of four drive pods functioning, targeting the left-hand side – there it goes, cut loose from the ship. Targeting the right-hand side – target!" The Weapons tech hooted. "They're dead in space, Captain, only retained velocity."

Barrett uncoiled out of her Bridge chair. "*Away boarders!*"

The book-shaped clampon lander shot away from the *Shade Tree*, thrusters firing to drive it towards the wallowing Grugell ship.

"No signs of weapons powering, Captain, no signs of hostile activity," Indira Krishnavarna reported.

"Too bad. They're intruding on Confederate space, and I bet they've got something to do with that wreckage back there."

"Look – the lander's making contact now."

On the main screen, the lander swiveled to face the enemy ship, opened, and slammed against the gleaming silver hull. Several interminable moments passed before the Signals tech spoke up.

"Captain, call from the boarding party."

"Put it on speaker," Barrett answered. She got up to pace nervously about the ship.

"Go ahead, boarding party," the tech called.

The reply came over a hiss of static. "Five prisoners, *Shade Tree*, we've had sixteen enemy killed in action. Sorokin has a bad burn on his arm, but he should be OK. These things are no damn good at hand-to-hand. You want we should bring the prisoners back to the *Shade Tree* or what?"

*Prisoners, shit*! Barrett was more than a little angry she hadn't considered the possibility. Her claustrophobic ship had no brig, no facilities for prisoners. "Boarding party, this is Captain Barrett. Negative on that, keep them where they are. One of you come back with the lander, now that the ship is secure, I want a couple of the techs to come over and see if there's anything we can take with us that the Navy might be interested in."

"Roger that, Captain. Anything else?"

"No. Just send back the lander. *Shade Tree* out."

On the Grugell frigate, a former Lieutenant of Marines grinned at the other three boarding party members, one of whom guarded a despondent gaggle of prisoners. "Klept, take the lander back to the ship for passengers. Captain wants to send over a looting party." They all shared a laugh.

## New Albion

They had turned the Grugell survivors and what remained of the ship – minus a few objects that Captain Barrett deemed to be of obvious monetary value - over to the authorities on New Albion on Tuesday. It was now Thursday.

The *Shade Tree*'s Captain and crew were anxious to get back to open space, the tiny, claustrophobic ship notwithstanding. New Albion, the world in whose system the *Orleans* Incident had taken place, was clearly on a war footing.

"Another call from New Albion Ground, Captain."

At least the Guest Quarters on the tiny New Albion Militia base were comfortable. More so than her quarters on the ship, certainly. Captain Barrett, Indira Krishnavarna and the two ex-Marines that had escorted them to the surface had been assigned a four-room suite.

"I'm coming." Jean Barrett called through the door. She stretched and climbed off the narrow bed in the high-ceilinged room she had appropriated for herself. Six steps – three times the number that it took to cross her stateroom in the *Shade Tree* – took her to the door. In the main room, she took the handset offered by a bored Crewman Krishnavarna.

"This is Captain Barrett," she barked into the handset.

She listened intently for a few moments.

"All right. We'll be leaving orbit within the hour."

She broke contact and laid the handset down on a nearby table. Three pairs of wide eyes were turned on her as she looked up.

"Back to the ship, everyone, as fast as we can go. There's a Grugell Occupation group headed our way. New Albion Ground recommends we get the hell out of here as fast as we can. I concur. The smart thing for us right now is to get the hell out."

"Captain," one of the Marines protested, "we're the only armed ship in the area! We can't just leave New Albion undefended, can we?"

"I said we'd be leaving orbit within the hour, John, and so we will," Barrett snapped. "Did you hear me say where we were going?"

"No," the Marine answered, a thoughtful look on his broad face.

"Good. Now, if nobody else has any objections, all of you get your gear together, right now. Indira, call down to the desk, get us a cab over to the Skyhook. New Albion's about to be occupied, the Governor is ordering all the citizens into the hills, and we can't stop them by ourselves. We're out of here."

# Nine
# December 2251

**Tarbos**

"All we can do, for now, is wage a hit and run campaign. We have but two advantages. According to the prisoners that the privateer brought in to New Albion, they don't know where Earth is, and they don't know about the shipyards on Halifax. So, hopefully, we can build more ships without them knowing where they're coming from. At least not right away."

"Admiral Gauss," one Senator stood up. Gauss' eyes narrowed; it was "Lord" James Galloway from Corinthia, leader of the appeasement lobby. "Might I ask who it is that's going to pay for all these ships?"

"The free worlds of the Confederacy will pay for them, I presume, Senator," Gauss replied, deliberately refusing to use the term "Lord." Galloway preferred the latter form of address, which to Gauss was reason enough to refuse it. "Our survival is at stake, sir."

"Indeed it is, Admiral. The sovereignty of our worlds is at stake. Our financial well-being is at stake."

"Senator," President Cochet chimed in from her place at the front of the Senate Briefing center. "One world has already been occupied. Maybe you think that the Grugell will be content to stop there, but I don't believe they will. Now, Senator, will you allow the Admiral to finish his briefing?"

Galloway sat down, frowning, and smarting internally from the browbeating delivered by the President.

At the front of the high-ceilinged chamber, Admiral Gauss allowed himself a tight, crisp grin. "As I was saying, at the moment we have the *Orleans* almost ready to put back to space; the *Mountain View* is in a parking orbit in an undisclosed location, along with the cruisers *Cairo* and *Dallas*. The frigates *Reuben James* and *Bob Pritchard* are in another location, within a day's travel of the *Mountain View* task group. I have the destroyers *MacKee* and *Perry* on the way from Earth now to join Task Force One. The rest of the Navy's frigates and destroyers are being deployed to protect Earth, Tarbos and Halifax."

A Senator in the front row waved her hand. "Why those three planets?"

"That's where the shipyards are, ma'am," Gauss replied. "We need to build more ships. We can't afford to lose that capacity. The *Seattle*, a twin to the *Orleans*, will be coming off the ways at the Halifax orbital yard in another six weeks, and there are more ships already in the planning stages."

The Senator frowned but didn't offer any comment. Gauss belatedly recognized her as the junior Senator from New Albion, stranded now on Tarbos for the duration – or maybe forever, unless the Navy could take the planet back.

"When will you be ready to put back to space, Admiral?" Gauss blinked; President Cochet hadn't said much during the briefing, her verbal slap to the Senator from Corinthia notwithstanding.

"Forty-eight hours, ma'am. I'll move my flag back aboard the *Mountain View* at eight-hundred Friday morning, and I expect to leave the system by noon."

"Good." President Cochet turned her attention back to her notes.

"That, ladies and gentlemen, concludes my briefing." There was a rumble of conversation, and the sound of chairs being pushed back. Captain Jensen helped Gauss gather his notes and holo-projector, and the two officers left the room.

"There hasn't been a formal declaration of war yet, Jerry."

"No, sir, there hasn't."

"The vote is tomorrow. No matter what I said back there, we can't put to space without that."

"No sir."

"Cross your fingers, Jerry. Either we go find them out there, or they'll find us here. And they already know how to get here."

## New Albion

Springtime on New Albion's large southern continent, eighty kilometers north of the capital city *Glengarry*, and the prairie flowers set the grasslands alive with a riot of color.

But Jason MacFeeters' band of guerrillas had no time for enjoying the view.

The Bent Fork River ran south out of the Crow Ridge Mountains towards *Glengarry*, and in the stretch before MacFeeters now, the river ran through a rather deep valley. MacFeeters was dug into a narrow hole in the side of the valley wall, covered with a light lid of plastic covered with sod; the hole he occupied was of the type known as a "spider-hole," for reasons MacFeeters had never known. But he knew how to employ the tactic, and he had shared that knowledge with the eight other members of his militia group now dug into similar holes to his left, right and front.

A whirring sound was growing slowly louder. Approaching from the south, from the abandoned city, a Grugell scout vehicle was approaching the valley, using the river as a transit reference.

MacFeeters had noted that the Grugell occupation force tended to use waterways to navigate in undeveloped terrain. Today he would make that a costly habit.

Crouched in the stuffy hole, he shifted sweaty hands on a portable heat-seeking missile. Three of his guerrillas held similar units, another a light machine gun, while the rest held hunting rifles much like the Ordnance Specialties 500K that leaned against the side of MacFeeters' hole.

A click came over the short-range radio headset MacFeeters wore under his narrow garrison cap. He lifted the front edge of the spider hole cover, very slightly, and stole a look. The gleaming silver insect-shape of the scout was floating into view, slowly, making its way up the valley, turning from side to side as it scanned the valley walls.

"Hold your fire," MacFeeters whispered into his throat mike.

The plan was simple. MacFeeters would fire first; the rest of the precious missiles would remain unlaunched unless the first failed to bring the scout down. Peering out of the hole, Mac-Feeters let the scout move closer.

It was a warm day. The spider-hole smelled of dirt, plant roots, and sweat. A trickle of sweat ran into the guerrilla leader's eyes, and he wiped it away with the back of his hand. His heart was hammering in his chest, but he forced himself to wait just a few seconds longer...

"*Execute!*" At the barked command, nine spider-holes popped open. MacFeeters stood up, his head and shoulders out of the hole. The scout turned slightly at the movement, but before the Grugell could react, MacFeeters shouldered the launcher, depressed the launch stud, and dropped back into the hole, leaving the empty launcher on the ground outside.

The missile screeched towards the scout, covering the hundred-meter distance in less than a second. It impacted on one of the insect-leg drive units and detonated, knocking the scout craft spinning wildly to the valley floor.

A volley of rifle shots brought MacFeeters up and out of his hole, his rifle in his hands. The scout was lying broken and smoking a couple hundred meters away. Rifle fire crackled from the opposite side of the valley; MacFeeters could already see three alien invaders down in the grass near the wreck.

His eye was drawn to a slight movement. A Grugell peered cautiously from a hatch in the side of the wrecked scout. The guerrilla leader dropped to one knee, brought his rifle up, sighted carefully through the scope, and fired one round. The alien collapsed into the spring wildflowers.

"Move in, be careful, be quick," MacFeeters announced into the throat mike.

Ten minutes later the wreck was stripped of anything useful and portable. By the time another scout craft flew up the valley in response to the distress call, the guerilla band had faded into the endless prairie, taking six Grugell plasma rifles and two packs of explosives with them.


## The *Shade Tree*


*Tarbos again at last*, Captain Jean Barrett thought to herself. The pale blue and white orb of the Confederate capital world was growing slowly large on the main screen as the *Shade Tree* decelerated slowly in to their assigned trajectory. A berth in the Navy's orbital dock awaited the ship, and the bars and hotels of Mountain View awaited Barrett's leave-hungry crew.

And a Senator, the Senator who made the *Shade Tree*'s excursions profitable, was waiting to speak to Jean Barrett.

There were plans to make, supplies to buy, and two crewmembers to hire to replace the two who'd announced their intentions to join the Navy. Fortunately, Indira Krishnavarna wasn't one of them.

And out there on the edge of Confederate space, there was a planet to take back, and Captain Barrett had a feeling that the Privateer SS *Shade Tree* would play a part in that.

In fact, she looked forward to it.

# Ten
# January 2252

**Mountain View**

Senator Crider had only met the privateer captain Jean Barrett once, on board her ship in its berth in the Fleet spacedock, a year ago. That day he'd spoken with her briefly on her Bridge, and had a five-minute tour of her cramped, claustrophobic ship. Captain Barrett, clad in her habitual black fatigue pants and shirt, had threaded through corridors stacked with ration boxes and water cans to show the Senator the tiny engine room, the crew's quarters, the central astrogation computer and the weapons bays.

It was a very different Captain Barrett that had just entered the Road House, the downtown restaurant where the Senator had arranged a dinner meeting away from the Senate Office building.

She had just walked into the dining room, dressed simply in a light gray cotton spaghetti-strap dress, cut just above knee-length in the current fashion, and gray heeled Roman-laced sandals. The Senator caught himself gaping for a moment but controlled himself with the discipline of a practiced politician before waving at the privateer captain. Jean Barrett spotted him and made her way to the table, smiling slightly.

"Good evening, Captain." He stood up as Barrett approached the table.

"Senator," she replied. She sat down, and Mike noticed her brisk economy of movement; no doubt a habit born of long months aboard her tiny ship. "Thank you for offering me a dinner. I've been eating CRAP so long; I don't know if I remember what real food tastes like."

Senator Crider almost dropped his napkin. "Crap?"

Barrett laughed. "Combat Ration Alpha-Packs. Dehydrated shipboard rations, one pack feeds one person for one twenty-four-hour period. Trouble with them is that they take a lot of water, and even with a good recycling system, that's what limits our deployment – we can only carry enough water to stay out about three months without a planet fall, unless we can snag a comet and whack off a chunk of ice to distill for water. And they're bloody monotonous, too."

"I'll see if I can set up a meeting with the Navy Commissary department for you," the Senator said. "Maybe they've got something that will work better." It was difficult not to stare, even for a seasoned politician; Mike was having a hard time reconciling the woman before him with the hard, curt professional he'd met aboard the *Shade Tree* a year earlier. Her russet curls bobbed in an engaging way when she laughed, and her green eyes sparkled. He shook his head quickly, once. "I read the report you hyperphoned from New Albion. I imagine that the Grugell have their prisoners back by now, but you'll be pleased to know we did learn a few things from them before the planet fell."

"Oh?" Their waiter appeared, hovered over the table. Captain Barrett ordered Forestian pale ale. The Senator followed suit. "What exactly?"

"As we suspected, they're planning to occupy our space, one planet at a time. They knew the *Orleans* Task Group was going to be in the area, and they hit it deliberately – and within a week of driving the Navy clean out of the sector, they moved on New Albion. They dropped troops right into the middle of *Glengarry* in the middle of the night, but the Governor had already had all but a few Security troops out of the city and into the woods and prairies north of the city. There have been some skirmishes; I guess at least one group of guerrilla fighters is operating. I grant you the reports we're getting are pretty sketchy."

"I imagine so. We did a quick flash-by of their Occupation group as we left the system – they took a couple of shots at us, but I've got a pretty good Helmsman, and we were coming at them head-on, so the engagement speed was too high for either of us to do much. I'll tell you one thing, their Occupation ships are big damn things – their drive fields screw up the dark matter matrix for a couple thousand kilometers all around. It was a rough ride there for a few seconds." The waiter appeared again, setting frosted glasses of ale before them. She picked up her glass and sipped the cold ale. "I thought about turning in behind them and taking a shot or two, but there were too many ships in the area – we were getting all sorts of alarms in our scanner tanks. So, we just beat feet out of the system, aiming north out of the Ecliptic before turning for Tarbos."

"You'll get your chance, Captain," the Senator began. Barrett reached across the table and touched the back of his hand.

"Jean," she said.

"Oh. Of course. And please, call me Mike." He was suddenly, unaccountably, flustered.

"All right, Mike," she smiled, removing her hand. "What do you have in mind?"

"Well, Jean," Mike replied, grinning, "Let me start by asking you a question. Do you think you can slip back into the New Albion system with a Navy drop boat attached to your sally port?"

"Probably. I'll want to talk to my Tactical people first. I'd have to leave my clampon lander here at the dock to take on the drop boat, but I have a feeling I won't need it this trip, will I?"

"No, I shouldn't think so. You're going to drop a couple of people and some equipment in to help out those guerillas. What you do after that is up to you, but indications are that there's a fairly heavily armed fleet in the area. If you can get back to Tarbos, I'm sure there will be more work for you and your ship."

"Standard contract?" The privateer's eyes glittered like polished jade at the mention of money.

"Standard contract. Twenty percent bonus if you're successful, and back here on Tarbos six weeks from today."

"That's fast," Barrett mused, "But I think I can do that."

They shook hands.

"Now, Senator," Barrett smiled, "Tell me, is there a decent nightclub within a few minutes' walk? Better yet, let's eat, and then you can *show* me. I've been cramped up on my ship too long."

**Three days later - the *Orleans***

A slight shudder announced the jump to subspace. Admiral Gauss stood in the flagship's Combat Information Center, watching the scanning displays turn to unintelligible gibberish. The *Orleans* and two other ships would rendezvous with the *Mountain View*, before proceeding on a plan of the Admiral's making. He was sure it would prove to be an interesting trip.

**The *Shade Tree***

*I should be ashamed of myself*, Captain Barrett told herself with a touch of anger. *Flirting with a Senator like some addle-brained schoolgirl. And that bloody dress! What was I thinking? I'm amazed he was still willing to give us the job after that performance.*

She glanced at the Navigation scanner display. The walls of the Tarbos spacedock still curved protectively around the tiny gray ship. "Is that drop boat secured?"

"Yes, Captain," someone replied. She didn't look up from her Bridge chair to see who had answered. "Good. Clear all moorings, navigation thrusters back one-third. Get us out of here. Navs, I want a course taking us high out of the ecliptic, loop over and bring us into New Albion from a direction the Grugell won't suspect. It's a big damn sky, they can't watch all of it."

"You got it, Captain."

"Are we clear of that dock yet? Bring us about, one-eighty by fifteen. Thrusters ahead full. Go to full main drive as soon as we're at the space beacon. I'm going to go talk to our guests – call me when we jump to subspace." She kicked her feet back into her sandals and left the Bridge.


## The Confederate Senate Office Building


Senator Crider had been trying all morning to keep himself from looking up at the sky. Not that he expected to see anything; the Fleet spacedock was only visible at night, and then only with a good pair of binoculars or a cheap telescope.

But he knew that, up there, right now, Captain Jean Barrett was going into harm's way again, at his request, and on the Confederacy's payroll.

The feel of her small, tightly muscled body in his arms on the dance floor of the Tiger Den nightclub was burned into his mind. And the image of her laughing green eyes haunted him.

*I hope she gets back safely.*

## Eleven
# April 2252

**New Albion**

Mostly hidden in the tall grass, an open Navy drop boat stood empty under the stars. A faint trail, visible only to a trained tracker, led away to the north. At the end of the trail, already six kilometers away from the empty boat, three figures trotted north. The heavy packs on their backs slowed them not at all.

Leading the group was Master Gunnery Sergeant Gregory Smith, Confederate Marines. Following him was Gunnery Sergeant Tinker Morris, a recent transfer from the United Kingdom's Special Air Service, and in the rear ran First Lieutenant Mark Jerrold, Honors Graduate of the first class of the Confederate Marines Force Recon School.

"Ell-tee," 'Gunny' Smith called over his shoulder. "Brightening up some. Reckon sunrise in about half an hour."

The lieutenant pulled a tiny device from the cargo pocket of his fatigue pants, pressed a contact. "There should be a stream about half a klick ahead. We'll stop there and belly-up until nightfall."

"Good deal, sir."

The guerrillas they were to contact could only be in the thin strip of forest at the edge of the Crow Ridge range. The Marines planned to find cover and hide until the next evening, and cover the rest of the distance to the mountains the following night. How they would find the guerrillas after that remained to be seen.


## The *Orleans* Task Group

"Message for you, Admiral." A young Ensign handed Admiral Gauss a message form. He took the plastic pad, placed his thumbprint on the edge, and read the scrolling text quickly.

"Humph." He turned to the Combat Information Center Tactical Action Officer. "Commander, send to all ships, prepare for formation subspace jump in ten minutes." He walked over to the Tactical holo-display. "Set up standard battle group formation, with the *Mountain View* sixty klicks behind the flagship, the *Cairo*, *Reuben James* and *Perry* stay with the carrier. I want the *Dallas*, the *Bob Pritchard* and the *MacKee* sixty klicks to our front in a standard pyramid formation with the cruiser at the twelve o'clock."

"Course, sir?"

The Admiral punched up a display of the Fortune system. Fortune was a new world, only opened to colonization three years earlier, but it was a prize indeed, rich in minerals, petroleum products, and plant life, a pleasant world of open forests, beaches, and temperate oceans.

"Right here," the Admiral pointed at the symbol representing Fortune. "A Grugell Occupation ship escorted by three cruisers just entered the Fortune system. A listening droid on an asteroid six AU's out from Fortune orbit picked them up as they entered the system's ecliptic, and they'll make orbit in about sixteen hours. We should be there about ten hours after that." He punched up a course track. "We'll come in from south of the ecliptic, and use the system's big gas giant as cover. They won't know we're around until we're already on their sixes."

"I'll get the course plots out to the Task Group." The Commander grinned. "Payback's a bitch, ain't it sir?"

## The *Shade Tree*

A quick pass to the edge of New Albion's atmosphere had disposed of the drop boat, after which the *Shade Tree* retreated to the shelter of the system's sole gas giant.

"Give me a weapons count," Captain Barrett snapped, for the third time that morning.

"Six Shrikes, Captain, two magnetic mines, particle beam projectors charged and operational." The Bridge crew was under enormous stress; the sensor suite gave almost constant warnings as Grugell drive fields crisscrossed the system.

"Where's that big Occupation ship?"

"Still orbiting New Albion, Captain," Indira Krishnavarna called out. "I don't expect it will be going anywhere, will it? I should think it is providing logistical support for their troops on the planet." Krishnavarna was using a new toy, added on to the *Shade Tree* in the Tarbos spacedock. Three tiny, unmanned reconnaissance drones – the Navy called them 'proxies' – were serving as the *Shade Tree*'s eyes and ears closer to the inhabited planet.

"It would sure help those people on the planet if we could take out that Occupation ship, wouldn't it?"

The Weapons tech, Orlando Taylor, spoke up. "It would that, Captain, but I don't see how we'll get close enough without them detecting us – and I'm not sure six Shrikes will be enough, anyway. That's one hell of a big ship."

"One of those mines might. Those are 1-megatonne nukes." The Navy didn't know the *Shade Tree* had those, and Captain Barrett wasn't about to reveal her source for that sort of hardware.

"But we'd have to get it into New Albion orbit."

"Yeah." Barrett snapped her fingers. "Didn't we hear something about the *Orleans* engagement, something about the tactical fighters being too small for the Grugell to pick up?"

"Yes," Krishnavarna confirmed. "But we're a lot bigger than an A-66, Captain. And I wouldn't be surprised if they've recalibrated their scanners to pick up small craft now – they lost a cruiser to fighters from the *Mountain View* that time."

"We still have a spare parts kit for that drop boat, don't we?"

"We do indeed, Captain." Weapons tech Taylor frowned. "But what…"

"There are spare solid-fuel maneuvering thrusters in that kit, right?"

"There are, Captain," Taylor replied, grinning widely now.

"Indira, are you still monitoring that type II comet that's inbound?"

"Yes, Captain, but it's going to pass way away from New Albion – it's really pretty in the night sky right now, but that's about all."

"That's enough. We're going to use it. We've got three days before we have to head back to Tarbos, if we want to get our bonus. Let's make use of it to do something besides hide behind this damn gas giant and record drive signatures. Indira, recall one of your proxies; you'll have to make do with two until we get back to Tarbos. Orlando, call your relief to the Bridge. You and I are going to modify one of those mines."

"Yes, *ma'am*," the Weapons tech replied.

## The *Orleans* Task Group

One of the *Orleans'* quirks was a slight, ship-wide flutter when it was decelerating out of subspace. The flutter always caused Admiral Gauss an uncomfortable feeling in the pit of his stomach, and never more so than now, when they were expecting to emerge only a few kilometers away from a Grugell task group. And with any luck, the Grugell would have their attention on the planet Fortune.

"Approaching subspace now," Captain Jensen intoned. "All stations report battle stations manned and ready." The Admiral had called the task group to General Quarters a half-hour earlier. Around the Admiral and his ever –present Chief of Staff, the flagship's CIC was quiet as a tomb, essential conversations were carried out in anticipatory whispers. "Entering normal space in five, four, three, two, one – normal space!"

A thousand or so kilometers away, there hung the three-kilometer, gleaming silver bulb of a Grugell Occupation ship, looming rapidly larger as the *Orleans* closed.

"Launch Lancers!" the Tactical Officer barked.

Four six-meter Lancer missiles burst from bays on the *Orleans'* flank. The flagship was decelerating hard, the *thrum* of the Gellar drive rumbling underfoot as the mass tunnel fought to slow the ship. The missiles accelerated away, homing on the unsuspecting Occupation ship.

Larger, faster and longer-ranged than the fighter-borne Shrikes, each Lancer carried a fifty-kiloton fission warhead. The first pair hit the Occupation ship at the very aft portion of the main hull, blossoming into sun-bright bursts even as the second pair flashed through to burst against the forward portion of the Grugell ship, obliterating it in a flash of nuclear flame.

"That's a *kill*," someone shouted on the *Orleans'* CIC.

"Settle down!" Admiral Gauss barked. "Did you think we couldn't hit something that big? Tactical, where are the rest of them?"

"Searching now, sir. Something at two o'clock high… Looks like a Grugell cruiser, sir, showing turn to starboard, he's turning in towards us, range sixteen hundred kilometers and closing. Another ship at three o'clock – belay that, sir, three ships at three o'clock, five more at eleven o'clock low, in lower orbit."

"Send the *Dallas* group that way, tell them to engage with missiles. Watch for fire from cloaked ships. Signals, start the Task Group on a one-minute countdown, I want all ships to be ready to accelerate back to subspace at one minute from this mark."

"Sir, the *Mountain View*?"

"Tell them not to launch fighters. Not yet. We took out the Occupation ship, but we're outnumbered eight ways to hell. Hit and run time, folks."

The *Orleans* shook once, hard. "Incoming fire, sir, unknown source. Tracking back now."

"Targeting particle beams," Tactical called out.

"Targeting on what, exactly?" The Admiral's voice was deceptively calm.

"Source of the fire, sir, you can detect them for just a moment when they power weapons… *There! There! Target that emission and fire!*"

A shimmering line of force shot from the *Orleans* port forward emitter, playing in an arc around the detected location of an anti-proton projector. A flash of sparks and a puff of flame announced a hit.

"He's moving off – trailing gases and plasma."

"Let him go," the Tactical Officer ordered. "Secure emitter. Scanning, keep your attention forward. Forty seconds left."

Beneath their feet, the rumble of the Gellar drive increased as the battle cruiser accelerated again, straining for the Subspace transit.

"Admiral, you'll want to look at this. The *Dallas* group is romping and stomping, sir."

Gauss leaned to look over a Chief Petty Officer's shoulder at a scanner tank. The *Dallas* and her two accompanying frigates had romped into the vanguard of a Grugell formation consisting of two cruisers and a frigate and launched no fewer than ten Lancer missiles; the Grugell ships were exploding like milkweed pods on a windy day back in Admiral Gauss' native Iowa.

"Sir, the carrier and her escorts are gone back into subspace, ten seconds early. *Reuben James* shows minor damage. *Dallas* group is jumping… And there we go," the Scanning station petty announced, watching his display turn to hash as the battle cruiser leaped back into the surreal world of subspace.

"Well," Admiral Gauss observed. "That was a hell of a show. Now, let's get to our rally point. We've got another hit to prepare for."

**New Albion**

"OK, we're coming in right behind the comet," Indira Krishnavarna pointed out, unnecessarily – the *Shade Tree*'s entire Bridge watch was watching on the ship's main screen.

What the screen showed was a faint luminous glow; the cannibalized proxy scanner now riding the front of a thermonuclear mine relayed the image. A nudge now and then from a pair of solid fuel maneuvering thruster made course corrections as needed, but Indira Krishnavarna's initial trajectory calculation had been close enough to require little correction.

"Ten minutes to targeting burn," the Scanning tech announced. Jean Barrett glanced at the Bridge chronometer, trying to force the numbers to click past faster by force of will.

"Five minutes."

Barrett shifted in her Bridge chair, kicking off her sandals and curling both legs under her. She frowned at the screen. The glow had brightened somewhat as the mine gained on the comet.

"This just might work," the Weapons tech announced. He was looking at a small screen on his panel tuned to one of the remaining intact proxies, which was keeping an eye on the Occupation ship. "The bad guy is motoring along just as he has been for the last two days, regular high orbit."

"It'll work," Captain Barrett muttered.

"One minute. Initiating gyro realignment."

"Go, baby, go," Barrett whispered. On the big screen, the view changed as the mine rotated slowly; through the faint, hazy glow the massive form of the Grugell Occupation ship moved into view.

"Cruiser behind them," Barrett noted.

"Time. Initiating burn." Krishnavarna's hand stabbed down on a stud. A few seconds later, the haze disappeared as the mine moved out of the comet's tail and accelerated.

"No reaction from the target. Mine is on course. Sixteen minutes."

Captain Barrett went back to scowling at the chronometer. The minutes ticked away with agonizing sloth as, on the screen, the image of the Occupation ship swelled to dominate the screen.

"Five minutes."

Barrett got up and began to pace.

"Two minutes. Still no reaction from the target. The cruiser's just tooling along about five hundred meters to their aft port side — even money says the nuke gets them both."

"One minute."

"If you start counting seconds, I may just blow you out the sally port," Barrett snapped. The crew exchanged grins.

"And there we go!" The main screen flashed to a scattered pattern of random interference.

"Switch to the proxy," Barrett ordered. The image on the main screen fluttered once, finally resolving on a view of an expanding cloud of gas and rubble. At the top of the screen, the Grugell cruiser wallowed, trying to regain drive control with one drive pod knocked off. A trail of gas sparkled in the light from New Albion's sun.

"We didn't quite kill the cruiser, but that Occupation ship is history."

"More's the pity," Barrett said. "Still. That ought to give the people on the ground a break, anyway. Indira, recall your proxy. Helm, bring us about, head south out of the system's ecliptic, ahead full. Navs, get us a course to Tarbos. We've still got to collect our bonus."

# Twelve
# May 2252

**Tarbos**

Admiral Isaac Gauss was uncharacteristically cheerful. Seated in Senator Mike Crider's office with another cup of Forestian coffee, he was grinning ear to ear at the news from the privateer *Shade Tree*.

"I'm not sure I understand your obvious satisfaction." The Senator was just a bit confused. "You just destroyed several ships yourself, including an Occupation ship. Why is the *Shade Tree*'s kill so special?"

"It's simple, Senator," Gauss exulted. His energy was such that he couldn't remain seated; he bounced to his feet and gestured with his coffee cup as he spoke, "You see, those skinny bastards hit us hard right off. They probably have a pretty good idea of our strength, and they probably know we don't have a very good idea of theirs. They thought they had us by the short and curlies. Well, we showed them different at Fortune; we showed them that we could plan and execute an ambush just as well as they can. But the *Shade Tree* did us one better."

"How?"

"The way they snuck that mine in right under their noses! That was a work of art, Senator, a goddamn work of art. I wish I'd thought of it myself! But they did more than destroy an Occupation ship, and they did more than remove the main source of support for their troops down on the surface at New Albion. The Grugell lost a ship and had another badly damaged, and they don't know how or why. All they know is that a nuke went off right against the hull of an Occupation ship, wiping it out of space and banging up a cruiser. Don't you see? *They don't know what happened.* They'll start to doubt themselves now, to doubt their capacities, to wonder what they're overlooking. I can *use* that, Senator. Now's the time to press ahead, to bear down on those bastards, to make that doubt grow stronger."

"Well, that may not be so easy. The Senate has cut your funding bill down by almost twenty percent. We're trying to push through a series of amendments to get some projects funded piecemeal, but it's not looking good."

Admiral Gauss thought about that for a moment. "Damn. You know, Senator, if we lose this war, it won't be for lack of fighting spirit, or brains, or guts. It will be because Congress tried to pinch pennies. We can *do* this if you'll give us the ships and the supplies!"

"I'm working on it, Admiral." Crider didn't look too convinced. "In the meantime, we'll have to make best use of what resources we've got."

The 'we' wasn't lost on Admiral Gauss. "Well, that privateer sure helped us out at New Albion," he replied.

**New Albion**

Night on the outskirts of *Glengarry*, a small band of men moved silently through the tall grasses towards the city. Lacking a hyperphone, the guerillas had no idea why the Grugell seemed to be in disarray; regular patrols were no longer regular, and enemy forces had been pulled back into the city.

The Marines led the party carefully into the outskirts of *Glengarry*, past abandoned houses, apartment blocks, and warehouses. Slipping silently from shadow to shadow, the raiders moved carefully towards Off-World Mining's main office building.

Three nights previously, Sergeant Tinker Morris and Jason MacFeeters had reconnoitered the building. In several hours of creeping and darting from shadow to shadow, the two had planted a number of remote sensors, thimble-sized devices that stuck to walls to send timed burst pulse transmissions to a shoebox-sized receiver. That receiver had been left behind at a hidden guerilla camp in a cave network in the Crow Ridge Mountains, but the data gathered had revealed the Grugell's main headquarters to be the Off-World building.

Pausing at the corner of a deserted supermarket a block from Off-World, Lieutenant Jerrold took a small object from his pocket, twisted a tiny dial on the top, and laid it on the concrete of the darkened alleyway. A tiny red light glowed on the top of the ten-centimeter-wide oval; eight thin mechanical legs unfolded from the sides of the device with a faint clicking sound. Rising up on its legs, the mechanical spider scuttled off around the corner towards the Grugell Occupation headquarters.

"Cover me," Lieutenant Jerrold whispered. Behind him, Jason MacFeeters raised one fist and snapped his fingers open. The other guerillas melted into the shadows, weapons at the ready.

Jerrold dropped to one knee, fished around in a capacious cargo pocket in his jacket, extracted a device that looked like a pair of very dark sunglasses connected by a cable to a small pad and joystick. Donning the virtual reality glasses, he picked up the control and prepared to guide the spider-droid to its goal.

The tiny droid scuttled forward, its half-millimeter eyespot sending a low-powered transmission back to the Marine controlling it. In the VR glasses, the Lieutenant could see what the droid saw; with the control pad, he could tell it what to do, where to go.

Scuttling much like a real arachnid, the droid slipped between the booted feet of a Grugell guard at the main door, who noticed the scuttling object but had no idea that it didn't resemble any life form indigenous to New Albion. The door swung open for a moment as the guard's section leader stepped out to speak to him, and the tiny droid slipped in.

Across the main foyer, down a hallway, the droid ran along the edge of a wall until it came to a polysteel fire door. "That ought to be the fire stairs," Jerrold whispered to himself. He pressed a contact on the control pad, and a fine spray of a powerful acid shot from the droid's slightly pointed nose. A moment later, the machine scuttled through the hole eaten in the door. At the top of the stairs, the droid took to the wall, needle-pointed feet gripping as the tiny machine ran around the circular stairwell to the building's lower level.

At the bottom of the stairs, Jerrold paused the tiny machine and looked around. As he turned his head, the eye-spot on the droid turned to mimic his motion.

"There." Off-World's blueprints for the office building had listed two large hydrogen fuel cells, backup power for the crucial computer systems of the Company's largest office on the planet. Jerrold moved the stick again; inside the building, the droid scuttled under one of the tanks.

One button on the control pad was set a little apart from the others. Jerrold removed the VR glasses, stowed them in a pocket, replaced the tiny comlink headset in his ear. Courtesy of the Confederate Marines, all the guerrillas wore similar comlink sets.

The Marine Lieutenant whispered into the tiny boom mike, "Fire in the hole." He pressed the final button.

Inside the tiny droid, a tiny swirl of magnetic force held a tenth of a gram of anti-matter in an eddy of energy, encased in a bubble of vacuum. When Lieutenant Jerrold pressed the button, the magnetic field dropped, exposing the anti-matter particle to the ordinary matter of the droid's interior.

The resulting explosion was impressive, amplified as it was by the hydrogen in the emergency cells. A loud *crump* sounded inside the building, and on the lower four levels all of the windows were blown outward a split second before the building sagged, slumped, and finally collapsed in on itself.

Only one Grugell escaped. At the sound of the first dull roar, the guard at the door sprinted into the street, only to be dropped by a single rifle shot from the alley across from the supermarket. Three minutes after the explosion, two silver Grugell scout craft turned up, scanning the area with all sensors, but the guerilla band had faded into the night, leaving most of the Grugell Occupation leadership dead behind them.

# Thirteen
# July 2252

**Earth**

Earth's high orbital graving dock had once belonged to Off-World Mining & Exploration, but the Confederate government had appropriated it for the duration of the war. OWME executives spent much of their time calculating the profits from the burst of shipbuilding.

Three ships occupied the three construction docks. The first, Project 955, was a twin to the *Orleans*. The second was a carrier, similar to the *Mountain View* but sixty meters longer and twenty wider through the beam. And the third was a frigate of the same class as the destroyed *Ian Mac Vie*.

An identical orbital graving dock at the planet Halifax was busily turning out two frigates and a light cruiser, while the smaller dock at Tarbos was preparing to build two heavy cruisers.

Denver, Colorado was home to OWME's shipbuilding division, in fact the block-wide, gleaming stainless steel and glass OWME Shipyards building was a feature of the Mile-High City's Denver Tech Center district. From the computer drafting desks of spaceship architects on Inverness Place East, designs for newer, faster, more heavily armed ships were hyperphoned to the space-borne graving docks.

The most hotly contested of those designs was the work of Arnold Emory, PhD, a pale, thin man with no family, few friends,

and no interests other than spaceship design. Emory's design –
given the planning number One Thousand, and known as the One
Thousand Project – was generally considered a monstrosity.

Emory, on the other hand, considered it the possible salvation
of the Confederacy.

Sixteen hundred meters long by five hundred wide, built
around the most massive Gellar tunnel yet conceived of, the One
Thousand ship would mount twenty batteries of particle beam
projectors, sixteen Lancer missile bays, and ten bays for the new,
larger, faster Hawk missiles. Arrays of force field generators and
the latest design in inertial dampers would generate protection
against anything up to a one-hundred kiloton nuclear warhead.

But Emory's design – he called it the *Dreadnought* class after
a British battleship of the First World War – had yet to make it
past the Confederate Senate's Appropriations committee. Emory
was certain that it would take a major crisis to force passage of the
necessary funding to build his ship.

He had no way of knowing that just such a crisis was only a
few months away.


**Grugell**


To say that Emperor Apportamattid XIII was angry at the
reports from the Imperial Navy was the grossest of understate-
ments. Three Admirals had rotated through the posting of Fleet
Commander, and all three had since found their way into the
Imperium's disintegration suite.

The Emperor did not suffer failure lightly.

Before the Imperial Throne now stood the fourth in a line of
Fleet Commanders. Tillistik IX was young for the role, but his
performance as the Commander of the task force involved in the

rout of Confederate forces at New Albion recommended him for the job.

"Your predecessors," the Emperor pointed out, "failed me at Fortune. They failed to follow up on the advantage you left them at New Albion." (The Emperor used the Grugell names for both planets.)

"Indeed, Majesty."

"What I require of you, Admiral, is simply this. Hunt down the Confederate fleet and destroy them."

"I intend to, Majesty. If I may say so, the Confederates show a decided reluctance to become decisively engaged. They hit and run, strike from ambush, disappearing into subspace before we can bring the weight of our ships to bear."

"Go on." The Emperor was interested.

"At present, I have six cloaked ships in Confederate space. Their task is to use their long-range sensor suites to discover in which system the Confederate home world is located. Once that is determined, there will be an overwhelming strike carried out at once."

"Have we not already done so? We know where their seat of government lies, yes?"

"We do, Highness. But that world is too recently developed, too sparsely populated, to be their home world. No, Highness, we need to look further." Tillistik went on for some time. By the time he finished, the Emperor was more pleased with his new Fleet Commander than he would have thought possible.


**Fortune**

The gleaming silver form of a Grugell frigate swam into view briefly in high orbit over the Confederate world. It was the work of a few minutes to gather long-range scanner data that would enable them to reconstruct the debacle that had occurred there days earlier.

More importantly, the known presence of the Confederate Navy at Fortune, New Albion and other points would enable the Imperium to calculate likely systems that the human fleet would be using as rally points, as well as further understanding Confederate shipping and travel patterns.

Sensor sweeps complete, the Grugell ship turned out of orbit and, as it accelerated, shimmered and vanished.

## Tarbos

Reports continued to trickle in from the field, and President Janine Cochet made a point of reading, personally, each and every one. From her office a stream of correspondence went out by hyperphone and by ground mail to Tarbos addresses, to the families of Navy personnel killed in the fighting as well as to Congress members embroiled in the ongoing budget crisis.

On the evening of December 31, 2251CE, President Cochet was in her office, ostensibly observing the New Year, but in reality, mooning over a growing list of casualty reports.

"Fortune, at least, has held up," she observed to John Fund, her Vice President. "Two orbital bombardments, but the planetary government is holed up in an underground complex. It looks like it's going to be a while before we can get New Albion back, though."

"We've got three teams of Marines operating there now, training and supporting the guerrillas," Fund pointed out. "Thanks to two different privateer ships, we've landed three Force Recon teams and six more drop boats of hardware, arms and ammunition."

"Which privateer ships?"

"*Shade Tree*, from Earth, and *Red Witch*, from Halifax." The Vice President had a head for details.

"Make sure they get paid on time," Cochet snapped. "Those people are carrying a lot of water for us."

"I'm not sure I like the idea of employing mercenaries."

"They're only mercenaries in the strictest sense, John. The concept of the privateer isn't exactly new, you know."

"So Senator Crider tells me. But the privateers in the eighteenth century were pirates, given a letter of marquee by a king to prey on enemy commerce. These people aren't really pirates, I'll grant you that, but they are carrying out military operations, and we're paying them for it."

"What exactly is it that bothers you about that, John? Are you afraid that they'll change sides if the Grugell make them a better offer? They've got ships to supply and crews to pay – or do you expect the ship owners to feed their crews a diet of patriotic cant and inspirational songs? The Navy has too many tasks, not enough ships, and the privateers have been screened and approved by Fleet Admiral Kosake. What more do you want?"

"Why not simply conscript them?" The Vice President was losing his point, and he knew it.

"There's no provision for conscription in the Constitution," Cochet pointed out, "And Article Ten expressly prohibits us from carrying out any actions not specifically authorized. The individual planets can conscript troops for their own defense if their individual governments approve it, but the Confederate government cannot. So that's not even an option, John, and you know it."

Throwing up his hands, Fund conceded. "Well, I can't argue with the results. Their mission success rates are higher than the Navy's, and with no casualties to date."

Cochet smiled, for the first time in several days. "That's why I'm asking Admiral Kosake to approve two more privateer ships to begin operations next month." She held up two dossiers. "The *Cape Fear* and the *Pilgrim* are offering their services; both are armed ships very similar to the three already operating, the *Shade Tree*, the *Red Witch*, and the *Titan*. I intend to take in as many privateers and can be confirmed as fit for raiding duty."

Fund smiled and bowed his head. "You're the Commander in Chief," he agreed.

"Yes, I am. And I may have to remind Fleet Admiral Kosake of that fact once in a while."

# Fourteen
# January 2253

**New Albion**

*Glengarry* was now reduced to a smoking ruin; the Grugell had briefly withdrawn from the surface, and three days later bombarded the city with five fission bombs. The guerillas continued to operate in the Crow Ridge mountains, while the Grugell countered by establishing a new Occupation base three thousand miles away on the small island continent west of the main landmass, and conducting an extensive air offensive against the human camps. Two temporary camps had been attacked and destroyed, and Jason MacFeeters' guerrillas had only two downed Grugell scout craft to show for it.

Marine Lieutenant Mark Jerrold was hoping to change all that.

On the ninth of June, in the middle of a chilly autumn New Albion night, the Lieutenant – he had in fact been promoted to Captain but had no way of knowing it – convened a meeting of his NCOs and the chief guerilla leaders.

"It sure would be nice to get some help from the Navy, here," Jason MacFeeters grouched as the group gathered around a tiny, cheerless campfire.

"Their Occupation ship is gone. I'll take that for starters, even if a privateer did it and not the Navy." Lieutenant Jerrold had gotten some news from another Force Recon team that had dropped in three months earlier.

"Bloody nice, that. But it does damn all to help us deal with the Grugell already down here, you know. They're over there across a couple thousand miles of bloody ocean, and we're stuck to the ground with a couple hundred fighters scurrying around in these damnable hills, hiding our families in caves and dodging fire from whatever scout ships decide to fly over and take shots at us."

"That's what I mean to solve," Jerrold grinned. "Sergeant Morris, if you would?"

Gunnery Sergeant Tinker Morris, late of the Special Air Service, scraped a patch of sandy soil clear with his battered boot and began sketching out a diagram.

"Gentlemen. Twenty kilometers south of here, the West Branch River flows through a steep canyon. Two weeks ago, Master Gunnery Sergeant Smith and I went on a wee stroll and planted remote sensors in this canyon to test a theory we had developed after seeing two Grugell scout ships descend below the canyon walls as we watched from the savannah above. The sensors have since confirmed what we suspected."

"And that would be?" The Marines had come to know that MacFeeters' supply of patience was short.

"There's a sharp bend in the canyon about one kilometer down from its start," Morris continued. "On the inside of that bend, where the canyon widens out a bit, there's a large spit of flat land, grown up with a few small trees and some grass. Our friends the Grugell have been using it as a bit of a picnic area. Scout ships passing that way, a minimum of one per week, generally stop there, set down, and let their troops wander around a bit and eat their lunches near the river. One would suppose they find it a safe and protected area."

"Leave it to a Welshman to take forever to get to the bloody point," MacFeeters observed.

"Patience, *Mister* MacFeeters, is a virtue in planning military operations." The jibe wasn't lost on the surly Scot, and while his temper bridled a bit, he held his tongue as Morris continued.

"Now, there is bloody little cover in the canyon bend, but there is deeper soil back amongst the trees where we could place a few spider-holes, and here across the river there are two large caves. The upstream one isn't very useful for our purposes, but the downstream one has a large, open mouth that faces directly towards the Grugell's favored landing spot. As it happens, the West Branch runs over a shingly spot just there, and it's only a few inches deep right now at the end of the dry season."

"There has to be easier ways to destroy a little scout ship," one of the guerilla fighters piped up from the back of the gathered group.

"We aren't planning to destroy one, mate," Morris replied. "We are planning to capture one."

A burst of surprised murmuring went around the group before Lieutenant Jerrold held up his hand for silence.

"We know three things about the Grugell operations on this planet as of right now," the Lieutenant pointed out, "One. They didn't like us blowing up half their leadership several months ago in *Glengarry*. Two. They know we have no transport other than our feet, so they've cleverly – they think – moved their base to a place that's impossible for us to reach, so they can hurt us, but we can't hurt them. Three. They don't expect we ever will be able to reach that base, so they aren't posting any guards around the place – no guns, no guard towers, nothing. The last drop boat in here six weeks ago contained a few orbital shots of the place taken by the privateer that dropped in the supplies." Reaching into his right-side cargo pocket, Jerrold withdrew several prints. "You can see here, there's no perimeter, no guards, no arms – just a landing field, with buildings lined up neatly on either side, and a large construction over here that we presume is their headquarters building." He passed the prints around. "Now, you may remember that one of the items in that last drop boat was a large, heavy object in a sealed titanium case."

"Damned right," someone in the darkness complained. "I had to help carry the bloody thing a good twenty kilometers up here."

"That 'bloody thing,' gentlemen, is a ten-kiloton fission device. Now I intend to capture a Grugell scout ship, and I intend to use it to deliver this device to the largely unguarded Grugell headquarters. The details are what we are here to work out."

There was silence for ten seconds, fifteen, before Jason Mac-Feeters stood up and reached to shake Lieutenant Jerrold's hand. "Consider my earlier complaints retracted, old man," he grinned. "Sounds like a hell of a plan. Let's do it."


**Tarbos, Fleet Headquarters**

"Things aren't going all that well."

The President's comment raised the hairs on the back of Fleet Admiral Kosake's neck. He knew that the war with the Grugell Empire was barely being held short of a disaster.

"We expected to fight a holding action for the first few months, Madam President," Kosake demurred. "It takes time to bring new ships online."

"Why have you declined to approve any new privateer ships? We have two more that are capable of beginning operations immediately. The least of them packs the firepower of a scout ship, and the larger one is almost the equivalent of a frigate."

Kosake looked uncomfortable. "I'm not sure about approving untrained crews and ships. We don't know where they've come from, how they're organized…" He stopped as the President's glare stabbed across the desk.

"Admiral Kosake, you know damned well that the performance of the privateers to date has been sterling – on a par in every way with our Navy ships. The *Shade Tree*'s operations around New Albion have been nothing less than brilliant, and the *Red Witch* has been returning invaluable intelligence from the frontier around Fortune. We can't afford to refuse the use of armed ships and crews, Admiral. We've lost New Albion, we may yet lose Fortune, and while Admiral Gauss has been running an admirable hit-and-run campaign, he's down to the carrier, two cruisers, and three frigates." Three ships, including the *Orleans*, were in the Fleet dock at Halifax undergoing major repairs. "He can't keep that up for very long." She stood up suddenly, taking the Fleet Admiral and her bevy of Secret Service guardians by surprise. Pointing a long finger across Kosake's desk, she issued her pronouncement: "Fleet Admiral Kosake, you have on your desk applications to approve two more privateer ships for operations in the contested systems. You will review those applications by this time tomorrow. If you fail to approve even one of them, I'll expect a detailed explanation why. Do we understand each other?"

"Yes, Madam President," the Admiral whispered. The Commander in Chief had spoken, and he could offer no argument.

"Very well. Let me make this plain, Admiral Kosake. I mean to see this war fought well and won. If you can't make that happen, I'll find someone who can."

## Deep Space, near Fortune

"Admiral, *Reuben James* reports her repairs are complete."

Gauss looked up from the chair he now habitually occupied in the *Mountain View*'s Combat Information Center. He rubbed his eyes, trying to shake off a chronic lack of sleep. Captain Jensen was no better off; Gauss noted dark circles under his aide's eyes. "What's the flagship's status?"

"Shields at eighty percent. Two particle beam emitters are down, and can't be fixed until we get to a Fleet dock. Fighter wings are at seventy percent strength."

"It will have to do, won't it?" Gauss stood up and walked over to the Navigation tank. "OK, let's see what we've got. Any word from that pirate hovering out there off Fortune?"

"Not in the last twelve hours." The *Red Witch* had provided intelligence on Grugell operations near Fortune for the last twelve days that had Gauss thinking that the enemy might try another move on that world.

"We may have to pull out of this sector." Missile inventories were down, and all ships were operating on less than full capacity. "We've got to re-arm, and get these ships up to par. That means hitting the docks at either Tarbos or Halifax. Unless we want to go to Earth."

"That means abandoning Fortune to the Grugell," Captain Jensen pointed out.

"Maybe not. Do you think that the *Red Witch* could slip in and out of the system undetected?"

"I imagine so. He's been doing very well at staying undetected so far, and he's managed to take out a Grugell frigate in the process."

"Good. Let's head up to Signals. I've got an idea."

## The *Shade Tree*

Faint glints of New Albion's sun struck off the *Shade Tree*'s matte black hull as the privateer swung into a trail position behind a Grugell cruiser.

"Shrikes one and three checked and ready in all respects," the Weapons tech called out.

"Scanning?" Captain Jean Barrett was getting nervous; the *Shade Tree* had left the shelter of a large asteroid only moments before as the Grugell cruiser passed.

"He's showing turn to starboard. He's picked us up."

"I figured he would. Weapons, launch now-now-now! Helm, come to new course ninety by forty, ahead full. Get us to transit as fast as you can…" her barked orders were cut short by an impact that threw her out of her Bridge chair. "Evasive maneuvers! Weapons, get a lock on the source of that blast and engage with particle beams. Helm, get us the hell out of here!" She climbed to her feet, wincing at a sprained ankle, and got back into her chair, taking a moment to fasten the restraint belt.

Behind the privateer, a Grugell frigate decloaked, the silver shape swimming into view even as a torpedo leaped from the silver hull and raced towards the *Shade Tree*.

"Evading," the Helmsman called out. "Torpedo is homing. We're gaining speed – three minutes to transit."

"Both Shrikes have hit the cruiser," Weapons shouted. "Some visible damage – cruiser is still maneuvering."

"Damn. They suckered us in," Barrett snapped. "Get me data on that torpedo!"

"Missed us on the first pass, Captain. It's turning for another try. Coming in from our ten o'clock."

"Helm, come to one-fifteen by ten. Weapons, engage that torpedo with the aft projector."

From the rear of the *Shade Tree*'s cylindrical hull, a line of almost invisible force shimmered out, seeking the racing torpedo and finding it only a hundred meters short of the ship's hull. The resulting explosion rocked the privateer mercilessly.

"Are we still here?" Barrett asked a moment later, blinking at the haze of smoke that filled the Bridge. "Anyone hurt?"

Nobody was seriously injured. "Captain, there's been some damage to the drive, but we're still going to make subspace – about a minute fifteen." Barrett's Helmsman had a smear of blood on the side of his head where he's been thrown to the deck, but he was back at his station and functioning.

"Aft particle beam projector's busted, Captain," Weapons reported.

"Come about, bring us right at them," Barrett ordered. "Weapons, stand by forward projectors."

"Forward projectors charged and ready in all respects."

The ship turned sluggishly. Bolts of green from the pursuing frigate shot past, and one hit, tearing into the privateer's Engineering section, ripping two compartments open to space.

"Forty seconds to transit!"

Both forward particle beams spat their defiance at the Grugell frigate as the *Shade Tree* accelerated, but the beams glanced off the gleaming silver ship's shields. "We may as well be throwing spitballs," Barrett muttered.

The Scanning tech let out a scream at her station, "Torpedo launch astern!" Behind them, the damaged Grugell cruiser had managed to come about, and launched two torpedoes. "We should make transit in time to shake them. We're already pulling away."

"Teach them to launch from dead astern," Barrett observed. The only way a sub-light missile or torpedo could catch a ship accelerating towards subspace was to be launched from the forward quarter to intercept the faster ship.

Two more anti-proton bolts smashed into the *Shade Tree*'s shields before the ship escaped into subspace. The moment the main display jumped from a normal star field to the weird, shifting patterns of subspace, Captain Barrett was barking orders.

"All right," she snapped, "I'll be needing damage reports from all stations. Weps, give me a full weapons inventory, if we've got anything left at all. Navs, I want best possible trajectory to Tarbos."

"I didn't get a chance for a hard position and bearing fix before we jumped, Captain – we'll have to drop out of subspace for a few seconds."

"Fine, set it up – Helm, fifteen minutes from now, program in a deceleration curve that will drop us out of subspace for fifteen seconds, and then accelerate us right back again. Navs, you'll have that fifteen seconds to get your readings and program your trajectory."

"I can do that, Captain."

"You'll have to. OK, I'm going aft to see how bad that frigate tore us up." *Good thing my insurance is paid up*, she thought wryly.

The tiny Engineering section was a shambles. The two broken sections had been sealed automatically as the bulkhead doors slammed shut, but Captain Barrett got the bad news from the junior engineering tech the moment she walked into the smoke-filled Environmental compartment:

"Chief Wilson was in there, ma'am." He pointed at the ruptured compartment. The *Shade Tree*'s Chief Engineer, Geri Wilson, was scattered somewhere in space back in the New Albion system. With her went any hope of comprehensive repairs until the ship reached Tarbos.

# Fifteen
# March 2253

**Tarbos, the Confederate Senate**

Three times the funding bill for the One Thousand Project had been brought up before the Senate. Three times it had been filibustered by the Senators from Corinthia and Zed, with the votes of most of the Democratic-Republican members on their side. Three times Senator Crider had returned to his office in a blind rage; he and the other Libertarian Party members all supported the bill, but lacked the votes to invoke cloture.

Now, it was time for a fourth attempt, this time after a blistering bully-pulpit speech by President Cochet. Thirty Senators – the full Senate – were seated and prepared to vote on cloture, necessary to end debate on the funding package; then the Senate could vote to approve or decline the bill already approved by the House of Selectmen. To end debate, eighteen Senators had to vote 'yes.'

So far, all Senator Crider had been able to swing to his side was seventeen. Seventeen Senators were convinced that the One Thousand Project – the Navy's proposed *Dreadnought* class – was essential to the war effort. Seventeen 'yes' votes were enough to pass the appropriations bill, but not enough to break the filibuster.

Senator Allesandra Catalona, DR-Hecate, would be the key. The senior Senator from Hecate, she wavered on the edge of ending debate.

Senator Crider spent most of President Cochet's speech watching Catalona. Her face was normally held in careful neutrality, but Mike had certainly seen a flash of doubt when President Cochet had thundered, "the future of the Confederacy is at stake," and that the Senate should "hold a fair and open vote on this issue once and for all."

Senator Gordon Blanchett, L-New Albion, stranded here on Tarbos for the duration but still representing the people of that conquered world, opened the issue as part of his role as Senate Majority Leader.

"Under the previous order," Blanchett formally intoned, "the clerk will report the motion to invoke cloture on S.B. 405-9."

The Senate clerk, a thin, pale woman whose name Mike could not recall, stood up and read the motion. "We the undersigned Senators, in accordance with the provisions of rule IX of the Standing Rules of the Senate, do hereby move to bring to a close debate on Senate Bill 405-9, a bill to enhance security of Confederate Free Planets worlds, to authorize appropriations for the Department of the Navy for Fiscal Year 2253, and for other purposes." She read the name of the Senators, and Mike blinked when she announced, "Senator Michael Crider, Forest," at the beginning of the list. He blinked harder when the name "Senator Allesandra Catalona, Hecate." A grin crossed his face; Senator Catalona's endorsement added to the motion indicated a change of heart.

"The question is this: Is it the sense of the Senate that debate on Senate Bill 405-9 shall be brought to a close?" Senator Blanchett continued. "The yeas and nays are required under this rule. The clerk will call the roll."

The vote took nine minutes, and the tension in the room was palpable.

"The yeas and nays resulted--yeas nineteen, nays eleven, as follows," the clerk finally announced, proceeding through the list of names for the official record.

"On this vote, the yeas are nineteen, the nays are eleven. Three-fifths of the Senators duly chosen and sworn having voted in the affirmative, the motion is agreed to."

A round of applause followed, and the remaining issue – the formal vote to approve or disapprove – was a foregone conclusion.

As soon as the final vote was concluded, Mike left for his office, to hyperphone Arnold Emory on Earth and let him know his project was a go.


**Deep space, near Fortune**

The *Red Witch* was a large ship for a privateer, and heavily armed, but its Captain was a cautious sort. While he had accounted for one Grugell ship already, Johann Hess was loath to risk his ship without a good chance at success – and a clean escape.

Nevertheless, he had been returning good intelligence from the Fortune system for several months now, lurking at the fringes of the system's Kuiper belt, moving sunward when necessary, in the shadow of the one big gas giant to evade Grugell scanners.

And now, the intelligence forwarded by the Captain of the big, blood-red armed yacht was bearing fruit.

"That bastard sure is a secretive old shit, isn't he?" Admiral Gauss was pleased with the data, less than pleased with the brusque wording of the pulse-transmission message.

"Can't argue with the results, though." The *Mountain View*'s Captain Thomas Olney was reading over the Admiral's shoulder. "Looks like another Occupation ship has moved into the system, but this time they've got four cruisers backing them up. And you can bet there's a half-dozen of those damn little invisible frigates going back and forth, too."

"If the *Shade Tree* really has figured a way to track them in subspace, that ought to help deal with that problem for a while," Gauss observed, "at least until they figure another counter. Remember, it didn't take them long to find a way to hide their dark matter wake. They're mean, but they sure aren't stupid."

"Are we going to try to hit that Occupation ship?"

Gauss thought about that. The enormous Grugell Occupation ships were prime targets for several reasons, primary among them that they were the main support for Grugell troops investing a planet.

"The whole thing smells, doesn't it?" Gauss was in one of his rare cautious moods. "They already lost one Occupation ship at Fortune, and they probably aren't too sure how they lost another at New Albion. They know that it was the Navy at Fortune, though; it seems odd that they'd move another one in only a few months later. How many of them could they have? Three, four? The damned things are as big as a good-sized moon," he exaggerated.

"It's very likely they're trying to land troops again, sir," Captain Jensen answered. "There hasn't been any activity that they know of since we hit them six months ago. It's a valuable planet."

"Four cruisers, figure six to eight frigates escorting," Gauss mused. "Even with the carrier's fighter wings, that's too much for us to take on in a straight fight." He sat up and snapped his fingers. "How is the *Red Witch* armed?"

Captain Jensen stepped to the CIC Records station and tapped keys for a few moments. "Sir, they have two particle beam emitters, fore and aft. There are two bays for Lancers, with stowage for four missiles. They expended one on that frigate, so figure they've got three working weapons."

"Not enough to do too much. Too bad they can't work something like the *Shade Tree* pulled with that magnetic mine."

"Not bloody likely," Captain Olney snorted. "You can bet they've adjusted their scanner's resolution down to pick up anything larger than a football now."

"A football?" Admiral Gauss' eyebrows went up.

"Yes, sir..."

"A football." Gauss leaned back in his chair. "A *football*. I wonder..." The Admiral surprised everyone by leaping to his feet, striding across the compartment to the Astrogation tank.

"Here's Fortune," he said, pointing at the holographic image of the Fortune system he'd punched up, "And here's the big gas giant sixteen AU's out from Fortune. The Occupation ships tend to go into a high orbit more or less around the equator, and Fortune's spin is pretty much in line with the ecliptic, right? That jibes with what that old pirate Hess has told us. Now look here," he continued, and the other officers gathered around. "See, here's Fortune's moon – a little bitty rock, about the size of Phobos. You've all heard about that trick the *Shade Tree* pulled with the proxy head, right?" A chorus of nods. "OK, how many proxies are we carrying in the Task Group?"

"About a hundred and sixty, sir."

"Good. How many do we have deployed at once?"

"Each ship in the Task Group is running a standard spread of six."

"So, we're carrying plenty of spares."

Captain Olney was looking increasingly perplexed. "Yes, sir, because we lose a few of them every now and then. We started out with what would have been about two hundred, but we've had a few malfunction in use, and that one time last May when we had to do an emergency jump to subspace we lost the full spread – no time to recover them."

"Fine, fine. So right now, we've easily got a hundred proxies we could put up at once?"

"No, sir, not really – each ship only has the capability to control eight or ten. The frigates can only handle six, in fact, through their CIC suites. The cruisers can handle eight, and they do when they're in an inhabited system. The carrier can run ten. It mostly has to do with signal bandwidth and processing capacity."

"But the proxies all have a hands-off recon capacity. We can program them to make an unpiloted run on a set course, gathering data as they go, and we download the data when we recover them."

"I'm not sure I'm following you, Admiral."

"Listen. Those proxies are a lot smaller than a Lancer, but head-on, the radar cross-section isn't that much different. Suppose we launch a wave of proxies into the Fortune system, programmed to run past the planet's orbit right on the equator – and hide about six Lancers in the formation, programmed to go into hunt-and-kill mode right as they reach high orbit level? The damned Grugell won't be able to hit all of them – there's a good chance at least two or three of the Lancers will get through, and two or three fifty-kiloton nukes will knock that big ship right into next week. In old Earth football they called it a 'blitz' – bury the opposition's ball carrier under your side's players. If we can make this little trick work, we'll be burying that Occupation ship and its escorts in targets. Little, fast targets. Proxies and missiles are supposed to be hard to detect and hit – they're made that way – and with that many of them to shoot at…"

"You know, sir, you've got a nasty, devious mind," Captain Olney chuckled.

"Great, isn't it? Go down and talk to your Technical people, Tom, and see how long it will take to set this up. One of the cruisers – the *Dallas*, I think, her skipper's a nasty, devious sort like me – can drop out of subspace right near Fortune's moon just long enough to launch the proxies and the Lancers. That ought to take no more than five or six minutes, and then they can scoot back into subspace before the Grugell can get a bead on them."

"And bury the Occupation ship in the blitz," Olney laughed. "I love it. I'm on my way down to Engineering now, sir."

## Tarbos

"Senator, Captain Jean Barrett is here to see you."

The sudden announcement over the inter-office com caught Senator Crider by surprise – he hadn't even known the *Shade Tree* was in the Tarbos system. "Send her right in," he answered.

His office door slid open, and there stood Jean Barrett, still in her shipboard black fatigue pants and shirt. Dark circles of weariness showed under her eyes.

"Jean," Mike breathed. He stood up and walked around the desk.

"Mike." There was nothing else for it; she walked forward and let Mike fold her into his arms. They stayed like that for some time.

Finally, Mike spoke. "Are you all right?"

"We took an anti-proton hit off New Albion. That and a near-miss from a torpedo. Wrecked my Engineering suite and killed my Chief Engineer. We got the ship back all right, but repairs are going to take a while."

"What happened?"

"They ambushed us. There was a light cruiser, trailing along all by itself, with at least two cloaked frigates a few kilometers behind. We closed in on the cruiser's six, launched two Shrikes, and the frigates popped out behind us, just had us dead to rights. We were lucky to get away at all. And the Shrikes didn't do much, either – the Grugell seem to have punched up their shield strength some."

"We'll have to see about getting you in to tell Navy Intelligence about all this."

"Yeah, I thought about that. Not today, though?"

"No, not today." Suddenly self-conscious, Mike released the privateer captain. "You look like you could use some rest. How about your crew?"

"About a third of them live here on Tarbos – they've gone home. The rest are berthed in the Navy's Transient Quarters over on the main base here in Mountain View. I gave them all five days leave before we have to start thinking about hammering the ship back together again."

"So, you'll be here for a few days, then?"

"More like a few weeks."

"Coffee?" The Senator indicated the ever-present coffee service set up behind his desk.

"Please." Captain Barrett dropped into one of Mike's office chairs with an exhausted sigh. "I haven't had a decent meal or a cup of coffee in weeks."

As he poured a cup of rich dark Forestian coffee, Mike wanted to ask where Barrett was staying, but didn't. "Could I interest you in another steak at the Road House this evening?"

"You sure could. What is it now, ten o'clock? Almost lunchtime, anyway. I could use a shower and a nap. How about I meet you there at six?"

"Sounds fine."

Mike handed her the steaming cup and poured himself one before seating himself at his desk. "Have you heard anything on the news from Tarbos?"

"Not really. We just made dock about three hours ago."

"We finally approved the Navy's Appropriations bill a few days ago. We managed to get funding for a new class of ships included. Of course, it will be a year or so before the first one is ready for space, but the framework's already being set up in the shipyard on Halifax for the *Arcadia*. That's the first of the One Thousand project ships – the architect that designed them calls them the *Dreadnought* class."

"Well, that ought to give the Grugell something to chew on," Barrett snorted. She took a sip of the hot coffee and leaned back in the plush chair, eyes closed. "You know, Mike, they're damned smart. They've got good tactical sense. If they've got a weakness, it's logistics – they support their occupations with those giant supply ships. We've taken out two of them, but they're starting to protect them pretty closely. It's not smart to put all your logistical eggs in one basket, though."

"That's what Admiral Gauss said."

Barrett's eyes went wide. "You've talked to the good Admiral, then?" Her surprise brought her Irish brogue out more strongly, which made the Senator smile.

"Regularly – whenever he's in dock here at Tarbos, anyway."

"Well, that's interesting. He's about the only commander the Navy has that's got any guts."

"He's doing a pretty fair job of keeping the Grugell guessing, and he's only got a few light ships and the one carrier to do it with."

"Aye, he's done that. We've got one Occupation ship to our credit, too."

"So I'm told."

They sat in silence for a time, each sipping at the steaming hot coffee, each contemplating their own thoughts.

"I should be on my way," Barrett said at last.

"Six o'clock, then?"

"Aye, Senator," Barrett said, a slight twinkle showing through the fatigue in her eyes. "I'll be there." She kissed Mike on the cheek before leaving.

An hour later, the Senator had cause to leave the office for a caucus meeting. He walked briskly through the office, whistling, a spring in his stride. His staff exchanged knowing looks as the door slid shut behind him.

"About time," his Chief of Staff muttered.


**New Albion**


Jason MacFeeters watched the Grugell scout ship settle gently to the ground next to the stream.

The team had been waiting in the caves for three days, during which they'd almost concluded that the Grugell were no longer patrolling this watercourse. MacFeeters had been on the late-afternoon watch when the whine of the scout ship's drivers had echoed up the canyon from downstream; the teams had barely gotten in place in time. The three Marines were now hidden in spider holes only a few meters from the grounded ship, while MacFeeters' guerillas took positions across the shallow river.

As the guerillas held their collective breath, a panel door swung open and three Grugell stepped out.

Two clicks came over MacFeeters' earpiece. The Marines were ready. He clicked his push-to-talk switch once in reply.

One of the Grugell drew his holster weapon, walked a meter or two, and looked around. Holstering his weapon again, he turned to the scout and called out something in a high-pitched, chittering burst of Grugell; a moment later, a fourth appeared.

Three clicks popped over the earpieces.

Sixty meters from MacFeeters, the four Grugell walked to the edge of the stream. One of them bent to fill a small container of some sort. The other three sat down on the bank. Two of them extracted some kind of foodstuff from tunic pockets.

It was MacFeeters' job to signal the beginning of the ambush. He did so by sighting carefully through his riflescope, centering the crosshairs on the chest of the one Grugell still standing, and firing a single shot.

Before his target fell face-down in the river, a volley of rifle shots echoed off the walls of the canyon. The remaining three Grugell hit the ground dead. Across the river, the Marines sprinted for the grounded, silent ship and ducked inside. Within a few seconds, Sergeant Tinker Morris' head popped out of the panel door.

"All clear!" His shout brought the remaining guerillas across the river at a run. Two of them struggled with a large, heavy titanium container, which was loaded into the ship. The Grugell bodies were searched, quickly and efficiently, and then abandoned.

Ten minutes later, Sergeant Morris – aided by a crash course in written and spoken Grugell on Earth – lifted the ship off the riverbank. The guerillas seated themselves in a spacious rear compartment, all of them keeping a wary eye on the nuclear device strapped to the floor in the center of the ship. The scout's drivers whined as the silver ship lifted out of the canyon and headed west.

**Tarbos, the Road House**

An eerie sense of *déjà vu* notwithstanding, Mike once more had a hard time keeping his eyes from the transformed Jean Barrett.

The gray dress had been replaced with a similar style in deep maroon, but the bright green eyes, the gamin smile, the strawberry-blonde curls were the same as their previous dinner.

Mike looked down at the empty plate in front of him. "The Road House puts up a good steak, don't they?"

"They do." Barrett looked strangely uncomfortable.

"You still look tired, Jean."

"I had a good nap, but I'll admit, I don't feel much like dancing tonight." She took a long pull at her wineglass. "I've never lost a crewmember before, Mike. I didn't like it. Geri was a good engineer, a good sort all-around. She kept her shop tight, and she got along with everyone – and on a tiny little ship like the *Shade Tree*, that counts for a lot. She has a daughter here on Tarbos, in Mountain View University. I'll have to go by and see her, I suppose."

"Jean, I can't imagine. I know it's a war and I know we've lost people all over. The Navy's lost ships, there have been people killed on New Albion and Fortune. But it doesn't make it any easier on you."

"No. But you're right, Mike, it's a war. We've been awfully lucky to this point." She looked up, her eyes shining, and smiled. "What I've got to do now is get my ship put back together, recruit another Chief Engineer and get back out there. There are quite a few scores to settle."

"Lots of people feel that way. Admiral Gauss, for one."

"Tell me something, Mike. Why isn't Admiral Gauss the Fleet Admiral instead of Admiral Kosake?"

"You'd have to ask the President that," Mike snorted. "Just between you and I, I'd like to know the answer to that myself. I do know that Admiral Kosake hasn't left the Fleet spacedock since this whole thing started. Admiral Gauss has been out with the Fleet since the word go."

The privateer captain drained the last of her wine. "Mike," she said softly, looking down at her empty plate. "Mike, I don't want to be alone tonight." She looked up, her eyes glowing green in the dim light of the restaurant. "I've got a really crappy, cheap, shoddy room in the Navy's Transient Quarters. I'd really rather not stay down there."

"Would you rather… That is, if you'd…" Mike's mouth had suddenly gone dry.

"I would much rather stay *with* you, Mike."

"I do have the spare bedroom in my condo, it's not very far…"

Jean Barrett reached across the table to take Mike's hand. "Spare bedroom? No, Mike. I said I would rather stay with you."

"All right…" Mike wasn't often at a loss for words.

"I'm not usually this forward," Jean breathed. Here green eyes glimmered, shining like polished jade in the dim light. "Maybe it's because it's wartime. Mike, could we leave now?"

"Let me get the check," the Senator replied.

## Sixteen
# March 2253

**Next morning**

Mike Crider Junior woke up slowly, blinking at the bright morning light glancing in through the blinds. His condominium apartment was on the sixteenth floor of a building only a kilometer from his Senate offices; the morning sun hit the higher floors early.

But not that early. He'd forgotten to set his alarm.

He looked down to find a slender, feminine arm across his chest. A mop of strawberry-blonde curls lay on his shoulder. He lay very still and tried to breath gently, like people do when they're trying to hold very still, but after a moment Jean Barrett opened her sparkling green eyes and looked up.

"Morning already?"

"Yes. I should be at the office by now. My staff is probably wondering where I am."

"Should you call in?"

"I suppose. I don't really feel like moving, though."

She placed a kiss on his chest. "I don't either. At least my crew isn't expecting me today – I should think most of them spent last night in much the same way." She laughed once, quickly.

Years later, the four days that followed would stand out in Mike's mind as some of the happiest in his life, an oasis of joy in the middle of the chaos of a Galactic capital at war. He spent as little time in his office as possible. At Jean Barrett's urging, he even found time to visit Mountain View's picturesque beaches – for only the second time in all his years in the Confederate capital.

On the morning of the fifth day, Captain Barrett departed to ascend the Mountain View Skyhook to see to her ship's repairs.

"I expect to be back in space in two weeks," she told Mike on that morning on her way out. "I'll be back down the Skyhook before we leave – say, the night before we leave dock?" She leaned against Mike, her face turned up to his. "I could leave for the Skyhook in the morning."

"I'll buy you a steak," Mike grinned.

She leaned up and kissed him once, hard. And then she was gone.


## New Albion

It hadn't proved hard to decipher the controls of the Grugell scout, once Sergeant Morris had located what passed for manuals on the ship – an odd set of round leaves of some sort of plastic, bound at the top – and to the guerilla's delight, the scout had a home-on-base feature. The ship was parked now in a tiny clearing in the woods, high in the Crow Ridge Mountains.

"So," Lieutenant Jerrold was just wrapping up a half-hour planning session around a tiny campfire, "We've got everything rigged right, then? The nuke is tripped by a pressure switch that is activated when the ship lands, which with any luck will be right on the Grugell base over on the other side of the ocean."

"Aye, sir," Sergeant Morris replied. "The Occupation troops over there are in for a ten-kiloton headache."

"Ground burst is going to be dirty, isn't it?" Jason MacFeeters had adopted his usual, sour expression again. "We're the ones that have got to live on this bloody planet after this is over, you know."

"Well, since the Grugell have already nuked *Glengarry*, this little device is a drop in the bucket – and unless we can kick the Grugell off this rock, I'll remind you, there won't be any humans living here at all."

MacFeeters shrugged. "Aye, well, I'm just thinkin' out loud, you know. After *Glengarry* I'm all for killing them."

"Anyone see any reason to delay?"

"Best it were done quickly, sir," Morris answered. "Before they start to wonder where the hell their ship is."

"Very well. Go ahead and launch."

Launching was the tricky bit. The controls had to be activated, and then Sergeant Morris had about fifteen seconds to bail out the rear hatch before the ship gained speed and height. The rear hatch would remain open through the flight, but there was no helping that.

For all that, the launch went flawlessly. The ship's drivers began to whine, and the silver form lifted slowly from the meadow grass. A moment later, Sergeant Morris appeared in the open hatch, looking down to gauge the speed and altitude of the ship. He jumped, tucking into a roll as he landed. The others ran to where he'd hit.

"Sprained my bloody ankle," he groused as Lieutenant Jerrold bent over him. "Over two hundred bloody para jumps with no injuries, and I sprain my bloody ankle jumping five meters from a bloody alien ship."

"Come on," Jerrold said, extending a hand. "Let's get back into the trees. We should put some ground between us and the launch point."

"Aye, sir," Morris ground out through clenched teeth. "I can walk, if just one of the lads can lend me a shoulder."

"Good. Let's get moving, everyone."

The unmanned Grugell scout ship climbed to four thousand meters before it picked up the homing signal from the landing field some fourteen thousand kilometers distant. Turning towards its base, it covered the distance in about five hours.

Four Grugell ground control operators were in the improvised control tower on the landing field. The incoming scout had been on their screens for several minutes with none of the normal communications.

"They don't answer calls, and there are no incoming messages," one of the controllers observed.

"Maybe their transmitters are damaged," the senior controller said.

"Perhaps. They appear to be auto-homing. We should call the perimeter guards and tell them there is a damaged ship coming in."

A moment later, six armed perimeter guards appeared on the landing field, just in time to see the damaged ship appear over the trees on its final descent. The silver form turned to face the tower and settled to the grass before the device detonated.

The landing field was on one edge of the Grugell compound, which was about six kilometers by four. The blast obliterated most of the compound, destroying all of the scouts and orbital shuttles as well as wiping the surface command structure off the face of the planet. One shuttle survived, having launched for orbit a few minutes earlier; despite some electromagnetic damage, it managed to clear the planet's atmosphere to reach a heavy cruiser in low orbit.

The Grugell Occupation leadership on the planet had been eliminated at a stroke, and with no Occupation ship to support them, the Grugell in orbit had no way to send more troops down to the surface or support them once they were there.

## The *Mountain View*

An addition to Admiral Gauss' initial plan had been suggested by the *Mountain View*'s Fighter Group Commander, and after some discussion, the Admiral had authorized the revision to the 'blitz' tactic. As a part of that plan, Lieutenant Commander Andrea Crider was now carefully piloting her fighter into the attack behind a cloud of proxies and Lancer missiles.

"Hunter Flight, Hunter Flight, be advised; the first wave of proxies is under fire." The call from the carrier confirmed what Fleet Intelligence had feared; the Grugell had adjusted their sensors to pick up small craft.

"Roger that, Hunter Base. Hunter Flight, Hunter Lead, heads up for incoming fire."

"Lead, I've got six bogies launching from the cruiser." One of the forward fighters, 'Sleaze' Fitzsimons, called out the contact report.

Andrea flipped on her search radar. "I've got them too, Lead, they aren't missiles, small craft of some sort."

"Heads up, people," Lead called out. "Sleaze, talk to me."

"Definitely not missiles, Lead. They're under control, they're engaging the lead proxies – *whoa*, there goes a Lancer." Everyone in the flight saw the burst of the missile's nuclear warhead. "Dammit, Base, are those things armed in flight?"

"Hound, tuck in tight," Crider called out.

"I got your six, Angel."

Ahead of them, the planet was growing into a blue-green disk.

"Lead, those are fighters, say again those are fighters – they're engaging the proxies!" Sleaze's shout almost blew off Crider's earphones. "I've got another flight of six launching from that cruiser."

"Hunter Flight, this is Hunter Base, engage those fighters, weapons are free. Say again weapons are free."

Hunter Lead's voice crackled in next. "OK, Flight let's get 'em."

"Horse, stay with me." Crider slammed her engine to full throttle. "Let's get that cruiser before they can launch any more fighters."

"Roger that."

Crider reached down and armed her four Shrike missiles. "Horse, two fighters coming at us from ten o'clock."

"I see them, Angel."

Three bolts of green shot past, missing narrowly. "OK, you son of a bitch," Crider muttered. "Horse, I'm taking the one in front. You get the one in the back."

"Roger that!"

The Grugell fighters were long, cigar-shaped, with one of the ubiquitous Grugell drive-pods mounted on the rear of the fuselage. Crider wondered, irrelevantly, for a moment just how the odd-shaped drive pods worked. Shaking her head, she got back to the business at hand.

A flip of a switch armed the big thirty-millimeter rotary cannon on the front of her fighter. She nudged the stick right, turning the fighter slowly on its big internal gyro to line up with the oncoming Grugell. "You want to play chicken?" she snarled at the Grugell ships.

The A-66's heads-up display gave the range of the oncoming fighters. Two thousand meters, one thousand… "Horse, break right now!"

Both Confederate fighters snapped to the right, catching the Grugell flatfooted. As the two cigar-shaped craft shot past, the agile A-66's flashed around, coming in behind them.

"I've got you," Crider breathed, watching the Grugell fighter grow in her sighting recticle. "Fox-Three, Fox-Three!" She stabbed her forefinger down on the trigger on her stick, and a burst of thirty-millimeter shells blasted the enemy fighter into wreckage.

"Angel, two more on your six," Horse called out. "Fox Three for a kill!" Crider snapped her head around to see a puff of flame and flying wreckage; Horse had turned around on his fighter and scored with his cannon.

Flashes of green flame shot past her canopy, and one glanced off the side of the A-66.

"DAMAGE TO PORT SIDE MANUEVERING THRUSTER," the on-board computer announced in a flat, metallic voice.

"Crap." A glance at the global radar told her that two Grugell fighters were hanging on her 'six,' less than a kilometer out. And behind them:

"Fox-Three, Fox-Three!" The new voice was "Sleaze" Fitzsimons, and as she called out, one of the Grugell fighters shed a cloud of wreckage from one side and spun out of control. The other yanked hard left and pulled away, abandoning the three-to-one engagement.

"Thanks, Sleaze. Where's Lead?"

"Lost him in the furball. They've got to be forty-fifty fighters out there."

"Great." Crider tested her stick; the A-66 reacted sluggishly. The gyro would do for mild maneuvering, but combat required using the thrusters. "Hunter Base, this is Hunter Two, get me a fresh bird ready, I am RTB with damage."

"Roger that, Hunter Two, we'll have a bird prepped."

"Hunter Lead, this is Hunter Two," she called next.

There was no reply.

"Goose, this is Angel, talk to me, over," she called.

No answer.

"Hunter Flight, this is Hunter Two, call in, by the numbers."

"Three."

"Five."

"Six."

"Nine."

There had been ten fighters launched. *Time to go*, Crider told herself.

"Hunter Flight, this is Two, everyone, break off and RTB, acknowledge." The four remaining fighters acknowledged, and the flight turned back towards the carrier under full drive, ducking through the cloud of proxies and turning north out of the ecliptic.

Behind them, the cloud of proxies managed to conceal two of the Lancers, which went into hunt-and-kill mode just inside the orbit of Fortune's moon. Both of them locked on the giant Occupation ship. One was destroyed in a crossing spray of anti-proton fire from two Grugell cruisers, but the other flew straight and true, impacting sixty meters forward of the giant support ship's port drive pod and bursting into sun-bright nuclear flame. The Occupation ship tilted, began a slow spin to the right, and fell away towards Fortune's atmosphere, where a fiery death awaited it.

Six minutes after Lieutenant Commander Crider landed her damaged fighter in the *Mountain View*'s Hangar Deck, she burst into the carrier's Combat Information Center. Admiral Gauss was there, looking over the playback of the proxies' broadcasts.

"Commander," he acknowledged her warily; the hangar deck had called ahead to report that the pilot had engaged the duty Flight Controller in a shouting match over search-and-rescue.

"Sir." She came to attention, saluted. "Sir, we've got five birds out there. Request permission to begin search-and-rescue."

"Negative. There are Grugell fighters all over the damn place in there, not to mention four cruisers. I'm ordering the Task Group the hell out of here."

Lieutenant Commander Crider's face flushed with anger. "Admiral Gauss, *sir*, we've got five birds still out there – they may be damaged and waiting for search and rescue! We can't just…"

Gauss roared across the CIC. "*You think I don't know that?*" He slammed his hand down on the tank display with a sound like a cannon shot. "Goddamn it, you think I don't know? Might I remind you, *Commander*, that this carrier is the only capital ship we have left, and we might want to hang onto it a little longer?"

"Sir, that's my flight out there! We can't just leave them!"

Gauss' voice lowered, and when he spoke next it was in a quiet and dangerous tone. "We can and we will, Commander. Goddamn it, you were told when you put that uniform on that it might be a dangerous job – if you're having second thoughts about that, then I suggest you turn in your wings *right the hell now*."

Andrea looked at the deck, her face brick red, and her posture eloquently revealing her struggle to contain herself.

"Commander, I don't do this lightly. But it's a dangerous business. The time we spend looking for five fighters that are probably blown to hell might cost us the carrier. I'm not taking that chance."

"Yes, sir." The pilot spun on her hell and walked out of the compartment. Gauss watched her go, and then turned to the *Mountain View*'s Flight Group Commander.

"Captain – I want her promoted to full Commander and given command of V-66."

"Sir?"

"You heard me. That girl has guts, and she's willing to face me down to protect her people. She's just the kind of commander we need."

"Aye aye, sir."

Under their feet, the carrier's drive rumbled under maximum acceleration. Within three minutes, the Task Group had jumped into subspace, bound for Tarbos.

# Seventeen
# April 2253

**Halifax**

It was fitting that a planet with a heavy surplus of metal ores would become a major shipbuilding center, and that is precisely what had happened on Halifax, admitted into the Confederacy only two years earlier. The massive orbital graving dock had already turned out both commercial freighters and liners, three of the Navy's cruisers and one frigate. But the task before Graving Dock Three and its crew of construction technicians, engineers, and architects was of a different order entirely.

They had the plans for the *Arcadia*, which was to be the first of the massive *Dreadnought* class ships, and only the four-kilometer Graving Dock Three was large enough to accommodate it. Now, the task of translating the plans into a real fighting ship was underway.

Dr. Arnold Emory was on hand to supervise the construction, having been sped to Halifax from Earth aboard a Navy transport. He looked now through a view port out to where pressure-suited techs were supervising construction droids in the laying of the framework for an almost two-kilometer mass tunnel. Within the week, construction was set to begin on another four-kilometer graving dock, which would contain the second One Thousand series ship, the *Ranger*.

In Emory's pocket was the printout of a hyperphone message he had personally received from Rear Admiral Gauss:

TO: DR EMORY

RE: ARCADIA/ONE THOUSAND PROJECT:

FAST IS GOOD. FASTER IS BETTER.

GAUSS

Doctor Emory had seen the news. The *Arcadia* was now officially a rush project.

## Tarbos

The Confederate Marines, until recently, had remained a small and elite force of specialists. With the invasion and occupation of New Albion and the narrowly averted occupation of Fortune, that was rapidly changing.

Camp Instruction was a large, sprawling complex of buildings and field training areas in the hills west of Mountain View. Ten thousand new Marines from across the Confederacy were now in training in the Basic and Advanced Combat schools; a select few were battering their way through the brutally rugged Force Recon School.

As was usual for large gatherings of troops throughout humanity's history, rumors were rampant throughout Camp Instruction, but most of them centered on one topic: New Albion.

The rumors were amplified by the arrival of a chartered OWME passenger liner, the *Santa Maria*, in Tarbos orbit. Typical of the rumor mills was the barracks bay of First Platoon, Charlie Company, 3rd Marine Regiment.

"Hey, check it out, guys." Lance Corporal Gerald Rosenberg pointed to his collar as he burst into the squad bay. He wore his new rank with pride; promoted a good six weeks ahead of his Advanced Infantry class, he was a shoe-in for a fire team leader slot when his company deployed.

Rosenberg's friends in Second Squad gathered around to admire the newly minted Lance Corporal. "You the man," one of them commented.

"Next stop, New Albion," Rosenberg grinned. He panto-mimed firing an issue M-22 carbine. "Time for First Platoon to *get some*."

His friends responded with a shout traditional to Marines since time immemorial:

"*Uuuuh-rah!*"


**Tarbos**

For only the second time since the war started, the carrier *Mountain View* was easing into the Fleet space dock at the capital. Admiral Gauss stood on the Bridge, trying to stay out of the way as the carrier's crew went through the docking evolution.

"We're looking at two weeks for repairs, re-arming and provisioning." Captain Jensen was at the Admiral's side, as always. He was examining data readouts on a terminal at an unoccupied station. "The good news, Admiral, is that the *Orleans* will be repaired and ready to put to space again in eighteen days. That's four more days at Tarbos, but we can take the field again with the battle cruiser."

"That's good." Gauss frowned at the main screen, where the display showed the interior of the huge docking berth. He stepped to the Signals station. "Signal all ship commanders to authorize as much leave as they can consistent with conducting repairs and rearming. I want all ship commanders to assemble here on the flagship at nineteen tonight."

"Yes, sir," the Petty Officer at the Signals station replied, and immediately began sending the word out to the Task Group ships, just now settling into their own docking berths.

The conference was held over dinner in the *Mountain View*'s spacious Wardroom. At Admiral Gauss' orders, each ship's Captain, XO and senior Master Chief attended.

"Ladies and gentlemen," the Admiral announced when the group was assembled, dress white uniform jackets sparkling in the bright lights of the carrier's Wardroom. He stood up and raised his glass. "We have an honored guest with us tonight. Senator, would you stand up, please?"

All eyes turned to the man in the dark civilian suit and tie. The Admiral continued: "Officers of Task Group One, this is one of the people who is fighting so hard in the halls of our esteemed Congress to make sure we have beans and bullets for these expensive boats of ours. Ladies and gentlemen, Senator Michael Crider of Forest."

Mike stood up slowly, his wineglass in his hand. He took a moment to look at the faces turned expectantly towards him. They were hard, professional faces, strangely calm, composed and confident. Most of the assembled company had some gray hair; Mike remembered that most of them, as senior officers in the Confederacy's new Navy, had originally come from one of Earth's various armed forces, as Admiral Gauss and his aide had come from the United States Air Force.

*How different they are than the faces I see in Congress*, he thought. *Those faces would be flustered, blustering, calculating and thinking three steps ahead to their next angle. They wouldn't be waiting to listen to what I had to say, as these are; they'd be thinking ahead to what they wanted to say. These people – they've seen the elephant.*

*That's the difference.* Suddenly it occurred to Mike where he'd seen such expressions before, many years earlier: *They look just like Dad and his old scout buddies when they were talking about the Grugell invasion back on Forest.*

An irrelevant feeling of unworthiness swept over him at the thought of his own presence in such company.

"Ladies and gentlemen of the Confederate Navy," he began, somewhat awkwardly. He gave himself a mental shake.

"I came here tonight to look for myself on the faces of the people who are fighting this war," he announced. "I came to congratulate you on the job you all have done so far, and to grieve with all of you for the troops we've lost.

"But most of all, I've come bearing some good news. Last month, the Senate managed to spring loose the Appropriations bill that authorizes the construction of two ships of a new class. They have officially been called the One Thousand series while in development, but the engineer in charge of the design team has called them the *Dreadnought* class, and the first ship – which is already under construction – will be called the *Arcadia*.

"I won't try to explain the details of the *Arcadia*'s size, design or armaments; I'll leave that to people who understand such things better than I." A few chuckles went around the room. "Let it suffice to say that they're damned impressive."

His instincts as a well-trained politician were re-asserting themselves now; he paused a moment for effect.

"It will be a year or more before the *Arcadia* is ready for space trials. I'm told that it will be three months more after that before the second ship in the series, the *Ranger*, is also ready. I'm sure Admiral Gauss, and all of you, will make good use of the additional firepower when the time comes. Until then," he raised his glass, "I know you'll stay the course. You've already made wonderful use of the materials we've provided you, you've done incredible things with limited resources, and I know you'll do more. I salute you all. You're on the sharp end of the stick, and the rest of the Confederacy is forever in your debt."

A conservative smatter of applause went around the room, and then stewards began bringing in the salads.

"Well said, Senator," Admiral Gauss commented quietly.

"Thanks. You know, Admiral, while I'm on board…"

Gauss grinned, a forkful of lettuce poised at his mouth. "I've arranged for your sister to be free for the evening, Senator. She'll be in the Terminal lounge waiting for you when we're done here."

"Thank you, Admiral," Mike replied, somewhat surprised. He hadn't expected the notoriously hard-bitten Admiral to be that thoughtful.

Dinner was excellent. Three hours later, a trifle woozy from three glasses of wine, Senator Crider shook Admiral Gauss' hand and took his leave, departing the *Mountain View* through the docking umbilical and proceeding to the lounge in the dock's Main Terminal, to there find his sister waiting for him.

After exchanging hugs, Andrea Crider surprised her brother by pulling a tiny holo-cube out of the pocket of her Navy green uniform jacket. "Here," she explained, "The folks sent me this a few weeks ago."

Mike pressed the tiny blue contact-spot on the cube, and a three-dimensional image of his parents appeared in mid-air.

"Dad thought it was pretty neat," Andrea explained. "They had it done down in Settlement a few months back. Dad says he's sending you one, too – I guess you haven't got it yet?"

"The war's got mail pretty screwed up," Mike replied. "Mail going out to the Fleet has priority, and that's as it should be."

Mike looked closely at the holo, realizing after a moment that he was homesick. The images of his indefatigably cheerful mother, who his sister resembled so acutely, and his thin, unsmiling father with his rock-hard arms folded stiffly across his chest, all made him realize how much he'd like to be pursuing rocs out on the fern prairies of Forest with the old pioneer.

"Dad says the rocs are thinning out some, but the bosettes up on the high benches above the cabin are as thick as rats," Andrea said, remembering the short, terse note that had accompanied the holo, "oh, and he went out for six weeks hunting loggers with that little Russian fellow who was at the house that one time."

"I bet they had a rare time," Mike said softly. "Here's Dad in his sixties, and he's still out hunting the biggest, meanest things around."

"He's not happy unless there's something big to take on," Andrea laughed. "I guess that's the Crider family curse, isn't it?"

"It must be. Congratulations on your promotion, by the way." Mike nodded at the silver oak leaves of a full Commander that now graced his sister's collar.

"I seem to have gotten somebody's attention," she laughed. "Squashing a Grugell flagship or two will do that for you. I'm now the Squadron Commander, to boot. There's nothing like a promotion, a command and a Distinguished Flying Cross to make your day. So, what about you, big brother? What monsters have you been hunting down lately?"

"Finding a few dollars for the Fleet," he replied. "We all have our monsters to deal with. Yours fly in silver starships; mine wear suits and rant and rave about all the money the Navy needs for ships and crews. Yes, we Criders really do have our share of monsters to fight."

"Don't I know it," replied the fighter pilot with three kills to her credit.

# Eighteen
# June 2253

**Near New Albion**

"We may have to withdraw from this system, Commander."

The destruction of the Grugell's last remaining ground base on the planet had been a major blow, and there wasn't another Occupation ship available to take up the duties of the one mysteriously destroyed some time ago. Occupation Commander Kiddastachik XI was seeing his career – and possibly his life – go down the drain before his eyes. Only a stroke of good fortune had placed him on an inspection tour on the heavy cruiser P-19 when the Occupation ship was destroyed, his offices and staff along with it.

The rest of the war with the human Confederation had settled into a high-tech stalemate. A series of border skirmishes bled both sides slowly, while low-intensity fighting on the planet below had been steadily diminishing what little force Kiddastachik was able to put down on the surface. For one entire solar orbit of the planet below, the Occupation Commander had sat in his new flagship and watched his Occupation go down the drain.

There had to be a way out. Withdrawal of Grugell forces from the system could only be seen as an admission of failure, and the new Emperor's policy on failure was harsh and unforgiving.

"No," the Commander said at last. "We won't withdraw. There are only a few hundred humans down there fighting us. We are warriors of the Grugell Empire, not food animals! Get me a tactical display of the planet's surface." His sole remaining aide bowed and withdrew from the Commander's private quarters.

"We won't withdraw," he repeated, quietly, to himself. "There's only a few hundred of them down there. We've got the resources to wipe the planet clean."

## New Albion, the Crow Ridge Mountains

It began at the far eastern end of the range, hundred-kiloton nuclear bursts walking up the Crow Ridge Mountains.

Jason MacFeeters' guerillas saw and heard the bursts in the distance, but there was little that could be done. A hundred or so families were sheltered in deep caves in the extreme west end of the range, but other than that, the guerillas and fugitives were scattered out in a few dozen small camps in the deep forest. Hide tents and huts of rough planks were no shelter at all.

The nuclear fireballs marched relentlessly up the spine of the mountain range. As they proceeded, trees were flattened, huts and tents incinerated along with their contents before being swept away by the repeated blast fronts.

Twenty minutes after the first warhead dropped out of orbit, the human presence on New Albion was all but extinct; fewer than a hundred people were left in the cave shelters, and over sixty of them were children.

For the time being, New Albion belonged to the Grugell.

## The *Orleans*

"Maybe we're going about this the wrong way."

Heads turned in the *Orleans* Combat Information Center. Admiral Gauss stood up to look over a main scanning tank at Master Chief Petty Officer Paul Ortega. "What's on your mind, Master Chief?"

"Well, sir, we've made some progress with the hit-and-run tactics. We've taken out two Occupation ships and a few cruisers and frigates. But you know, sir, this whole thing is going to fall into a war of attrition if we keep this up. We can't win a war like that; not with our logistics headaches."

"He's got a point, sir," Captain Jensen observed. "The Grugell can just order more ships built and damn the cost. We've got to wait for Congress to decide to get off their asses."

"We do have the *Arcadia* on its way to us now," Gauss mused. "And the *Ranger* will be off the ways in another three weeks. What are you thinking, Master Chief?" Gauss had learned to trust the veteran NCO as he trusted few others.

"Well, sir, look at it this way. I did some boxing when I was younger – held the Inter-Service middleweight belt for three years. First thing I learned was that you don't get a TKO by going for your opponent's arms and legs. You had to hit him in the head and body, sir, you know what I'm saying?"

"Aim for their higher command structure? On their side of the line, invade *their* space, is that what you're getting at?"

"Not by half, sir," Ortega nodded. "Look here." The grizzled NCO stepped up to the scanner tank and, tapping swiftly on a keyboard, brought up a display of the Galactic arm. "See here, sir, is Confederate space." A portion of the starfield turned faintly blue. "And this is what we've identified of the frontier with Grugell space." A portion of the blue area glowed red on one side. "Now, look at that. Look at the topography of that, sir."

"They're all on the outer portion of the arm," Captain Jenkins said softly.

"Yeah. Makes sense, doesn't it?"

"Get to the point, Master Chief. Why does it make sense?" Admiral Gauss was intrigued but his patience wasn't limitless.

"Sir," Master Chief Ortega pointed at the red border, "I been doing some reading. The stars and systems out here on the edges of the arm are lighter in heavy elements, the suns are smaller, and their systems are smaller. We know the Grugell come from a low-gravity world, right? They sure have a hard time in our gravity. That means a planet that's low in minerals and metals – power metals especially, I figure. Well, sir, what they want and need is more sources of strategic minerals, and that means moving in closer to the main run of the arm."

"Right into us," Gauss breathed.

"Roger that, sir. Well, all this time we've been fighting them in our space, on our side of that line. Sir, it seems to me that their logistic situation probably is more like ours than we think. It seems to me we should be looking for and breaking them up at their own logistical sources on *their* side of that line."

"Cut them off at the knees – is that what you're thinking?"

"You got it, sir. And then deal with their Fleet once we've cut off their support from home."

"Master Chief, I think you've got something here," Gauss grinned. "Captain Jensen, call in all the primary staff and get the Crisis Action Team up and running. You've got twenty-four hours to plan; I want at least three options for a reconnaissance in force into Grugell space, followed by a deep strike mission." He looked around the room. "We're going to go for broke, people."

**Tarbos**

"Seventeen Confederate planets, now," President Cochet said to herself.

Seated at her huge oak desk, the Confederacy's fifth President was engaged in her usual morning routine of scanning a condensation of the major network news screens, thoughtfully compiled and organized for her by her staff.

Vice President Fund's head popped up where he sat in a large chair on the other side of the desk. "The plebiscite passed, eh?"

"Yes, by over eighty percent of the vote. Mars is now the seventeenth Confederate world, instead of a Company planet run by Off-World Mining."

"It may be the *sixteenth* after all," Fund replied.

"I won't accept that. Not even after the bombing. New Albion is *our* planet, and we're going to take it back, even if we take it back as a radioactive cinder. There's a message to send here, John."

"Admiral Kosake disagrees. He's ordering the Fleet to move closer in towards Tarbos, to form a defensive line against any more incursions."

"I know." President Cochet grinned tightly. "Admiral Kosake isn't Commander in Chief, though, John – I am. I told him once, if he couldn't win this war on the terms I wanted, I'd find someone who could."

Vice President Fund narrowed his eyes. "I'd guess you already have."

"And you'd be right."

"Admiral Gauss?"

"No other." Cochet's frown disappeared. "He's planned every successful operation the Navy has carried out since this fracas began. And on top of that, he's commanded each of those operations from either the *Orleans* or the *Mountain View*. He's commanding from the front, and I like that."

"Keeps his headquarters in the saddle, so to speak."

Cochet nodded. "He'll have to." She smiled humorlessly. "His first job is going to be taking back New Albion."

## Grugell

The news hit the Imperium, and the Emperor Himself, like a rockslide. Apportamattid wasted no time in calling his senior advisors together to discuss a discovery made by a cloaked frigate, the K-221, that had been deep in Confederate space analyzing traffic patterns.

"And so, Highness, we followed the tracks to their source. Our analysis of the traffic patterns led us to a nexus in a sector we'd not explored before; our error previously was in assuming that the humans spread out more or less evenly, globally in fact, from their original planet. That has not been the case. The nexus we sought was here," Group Commander Traskellid IV pointed at a bright blue spot on a holographic map of the spiral arm, "and here we found the human home world. It's a large, heavy world, as are most of the worlds favored by humans, and like most of their worlds it's rich in mineral and other resources. But more importantly, Highness, it is vastly more developed than any of the other human worlds we've found; there is a massive orbital city and shipyard, and the human population runs into the billions, many times that of the other worlds. It's lightly defended by a series of armed satellites and two small human ships, slightly larger than our frigates."

"They do not suspect we've found their home world, then," the Emperor mused.

"The data suggests not," Traskellid agreed, "Else they would not leave the planet so lightly defended."

Apportamattid snapped his fingers. "Suggestions. Comments."

"Strike at once," Admiral Dakterrid XII snapped. "We can quickly recall the major ships we have operating near the Confederate frontier now, re-arm and re-supply them for a strike on the human home world. I suggest an orbital bombardment of major cities, followed by a reinforced Occupation."

"Are you willing to leave much of our frontier undefended, then?" The Emperor's voice was soft, but his tone was clear: *You'd better be right; your life is the price of failure.*

"I am, Highness."

"Discuss."

The discussion was heated and went on for some time; several of the Imperium officers disagreed on the course of action. But the outcome was never truly in doubt.

The Grugell Navy was going to move on Earth, in force.

# Nineteen
# September 2253

**The *Orleans*, sometime later**

The message caused Admiral Gauss a mild shock when it arrived in his Flag office on the *Orleans*, brought there by a Signals rating and handed to the Admiral at his desk. Admiral Gauss read the hyperphone message for the fifth time, still not quite sure whether to believe it or not.

> REAR ADMIRAL ISAAC GAUSS, COMTASKFORONE
> SENDS: CHIEF OF STAFF, NAVY DEPARTMENT
> YOU ARE PROMOTED TO FLEET ADMIRAL WITH
> RANK EFFECTIVE JULY THIRD. ASSUME FLEET
> COMMAND AS OF RECEIPT OF THIS MESSAGE.
> PRIMARY TASK IS RECLAMATION OF NEW ALBION.
> PRESIDENT COCHET SENDS PERSONAL
> CONGRATULATIONS AND CONFIDENCE.

"I wonder what happened to Admiral Kosake," Captain Jensen said, reading over the Admiral's shoulder.

"Retired," Gauss guessed, correctly as it happened. "And President Cochet has passed the ball to me, well well." He laid the printout carefully aside. He looked down at his Navy green collar, where the two tiny silver stars of a Rear Admiral glittered. "I suppose I'll have to wait until I'm at the Fleet dock again to pick up a new set of rank, Jerry."

"The President probably expects you to come back to Tarbos to the Fleet Headquarters," Captain Jensen observed.

"Nope," Gauss snapped. "Not a damned chance. Two stars or five, you can't lead combat operations from a cushy office in the Fleet spacedock on Tarbos, and I won't try. If the President expects me to squat behind a desk like Admiral Kosake did, she'll be disappointed. Besides, we can't spare a ship for the six weeks or so it would take to get me there. What's the ETA on the *Arcadia*?"

"Three weeks, sir. Six more after that for the *Ranger*. We'll have two more light cruisers, the *Glengarry* and the *Pretoria*, in four weeks."

"Good enough."

The new Fleet Admiral drummed his fingers on his desk, a habit he had when mulling over new information.

"Call the *Mountain View*. We'll transfer our flag over there for the time being. The President informs me that our main job is taking back New Albion. Well, I'm not going to give up on Master Chief Ortega's idea; we've devoted too much time and planning to it. We'll form Task Group 1.1 on the *Arcadia*, along with the *Seattle*, the *Orleans* and four or five of the frigates and destroyers. That's enough firepower to kick the hell out of any Grugell force they're liable to bump into. The rest of Task Group One heads for New Albion, along with the Marine division. I'll want the carrier to support landing operations there."

"Divide forces, sir?"

"That's what I said. Go wake up the staff, tell them I want to be briefed on their plan in twelve hours. The objectives are the liberation of New Albion, and a diversionary deep strike into Grugell space with the objective of destroying at least one major supply source."

"Yes, sir." Captain Jensen walked briskly out of the Flag office, sliding the door shut behind him and leaving the new Fleet Admiral alone with his thoughts.

## New Albion

An entire legion of Grugell infantry garrisoned the newly reduced New Albion. Avoiding the nuked belt of the main continent, they established a base in an archipelago of islands in the planet's southern hemisphere, where the warm tropical climate made up for the oppressively heavy gravity of the mineral-rich world.

Occupation Commander Kiddastachik XI hated the planet. He hated the scrubby brush of the large island where his headquarters was set up; he hated the heavy gravity that sapped his strength, he hated the occasional ash fall from the volcano at the heart of the island, he hated the white sand beach along the oceanfront, he hated the incessant calling of the four-winged, leathery flyers that clustered along the shore to feed on dead sea life.

Still, the posting was a plum, a jewel, and an essential step towards greater things in the Grugell Navy. Kiddastachik wasn't about to mess it up.

Roving patrols over the mountains of the northern continent revealed no signs of human activity. No human ships had been sighted in the area. The Imperium had no Occupation ship to support his operations, but three cruisers had been sent to the area, along with a flight of small landing shuttles to ferry necessary supplies down the gravity well to his troops.

Kiddastachik's orders were to hold this planet at all costs. He didn't have the courage to fail.

## Tarbos

"He's not coming back to Tarbos, you know."

President Janine Cochet looked up to see the Chief of Staff of the Confederate Navy Department, James Gallagher, standing in the office doorway.

"Did you think he would?"

"No. I suppose that's what makes him the right man for the job."

"If he's not," the President replied, "I'll find someone else. I think he'll do, though. Sit down, Jim." She gestured towards a chair across from her massive desk.

Gallagher was a small man, birdlike, quick in his movements and speech, and a former Special Air Service commando from the United Kingdom on Earth. He sat on the edge of the chair, filled as he usually was with nervous energy.

"I've looked into Admiral Gauss' dossier," he began. "He graduated, you know, from the United States Air Force Academy. His career has been impressive, although he's known in the Service as something of a maverick, a difficult man to work with."

"I'm an old American myself, by birth, Jim. You know how we Yankees love our cowboys." The President turned on one of her election-stump-speech smiles.

"Indeed. I'm not questioning the choice, Madam President. In fact, I approve. Admiral Gauss left the U.S. Air Force as a Colonel, and entered the Confederate Navy as a Rear Admiral – and now, in less than four years, he's in command of the Navy as a whole. Much of the Navy's senior leadership is in similar circumstances; almost all of the senior officers and the non-commissioned officer corps have been pulled out of the various armed services on Earth. A few of them joined from Off-World Mining's Security corps, but none of them have formal military training. Ma'am, we're asking a lot of these people."

"What's on your mind, Jim?"

"Training, Madam President. We've established Camp Instruction here to train Marines, and we've got the new Navy Academy, but we need to build more training bases for enlisted personnel, preferably scattered about the Confederacy. I'd also like to see a program similar to the old Reserve Officer Training Corps in your country to train Navy officers in the various universities on the several worlds."

"You've been watching the news commentaries, haven't you?"

"You cannot deny that it's a good idea, Madam President."

"No, I can't. But building ships has funding priority at the moment. The Confederate Treasury isn't a money tree, James."

"Yes, true indeed."

President Cochet flipped a couple of papers over. "So, what's become of former Fleet Admiral Kosake?"

"He turned down reassignment. Instead, he has accepted early retirement, and plans to return to Earth."

"Good." President Cochet had no desire to punish the rather timid officer, only to remove him. "Regulations allow the Navy to pay his travel to his choice of retirement location, don't they? See that he gets a ticket as soon as possible. I'd rather have him on Earth than Tarbos."

**Forty kilometers away, Camp Instruction**

Four regiments of Marines were now trained and ready at Camp Instruction. Inbound from Earth now, the well-worn OWME passenger liner *Santa Maria* would take the Marines to the Fleet.

The First Confederate Marine Expeditionary Force Commander, Major General Austin Anderson, knew their destination. So did his Deputy Commander, and within a day the Regimental commanders would know as well.

Nobody else would know until they were en route to New Albion.

**Halifax**

Months ahead of schedule, the *Dreadnought Arcadia* was backing slowly out of Graving Dock One.

Arnold Emory was present to see it leave. The massive ship was leaving with a minimal crew, and would be carrying out a minimal shakedown before reporting to the Fleet; but Emory was supremely confident in his design, and in the Navy personnel that was taking the ship out.

Backing slowly out of the berth with puffs of maneuvering thrusters, the slate-blue bulk of the ship was studded with particle beam projectors and missile bays. Projectors for a massive force-field scoop at the front augmented the now-quiet maw of the Gellar tunnel; the ship would be faster than any other ship currently in active service.

As the ship cleared the berth and began to turn for departure, Emory looked up across the scaffolding of the graving dock. Five kilometers up from where he stood was Graving Dock Three; in that dock, the second *Dreadnought Ranger* was nearing completion. The *Ranger* would leave in three more weeks.

The shipbuilder shook his head. He'd have bet a year's pay that the yard couldn't have finished both ships in time.

## An unmarked rally point near Fortune

For the first time since the war began, three privateer ships met to conduct a joint operation. Jean Barrett's *Shade Tree*, Johann Hess' *Red Witch*, and David Jones' *Cape Fear* were assembled at a randomly selected rally point, and their Captains met aboard the *Cape Fear* to plan their next move.

The *Cape Fear*, out of Halifax, was a larger ship than either *Shade Tree* or the *Red Witch*, which was why the Captains met there, in the *Cape Fear*'s Wardroom. As Indira Krishnavarna ran through the sensor calibrations she'd developed for tracking subspace transits, Barrett surreptitiously studied her two fellow captains.

David Jones was English by birth, like Barrett herself, but had left Earth for Caliban in the company of his parents when only three years old. Tall and slim, Jones carried the long equine jaw and pale eyes of northern England. He spoke confidently although not often, and the safety of his ship and crew seemed his primary concern.

Johann Hess was another matter. While Hess was taller still than Jones, he was not slim but skinny, with bony white arms protruding from the sleeves of a baggy black pea-jacket. Hands like claws lay on the Wardroom table, and he stared at Indira Krishnavarna from rheumy yellow eyes. Most surprising of all was his age; he seemed at least sixty, perhaps older. A shock of white hair sprang outward in all directions from his narrow, high-templed head.

Hess had brought three of his ship's officers with him to the meeting. Barrett had seen them before they'd trooped off with Jones' second-in-command for a tour of the *Cape Fear*. While they seemed intelligent, they were a strangely feral-looking trio; Barrett had the impression they'd be hell on wheels in a boarding party.

"Well," Hess said when Krishnavarna finished her spiel, "I trust my technicians will understand that better than I." He smiled, baring oddly pointed, yellow teeth. "Captain Barrett, I congratulate you on a fine and intelligent technician you have serving aboard the *Shade Tree*. Are all of your crew so bright?"

"Pretty much," Barrett replied.

"We're back where we started," Jones growled, dragging the discussion back to its original agenda. "Captain Barrett, your tech found five or more sensor tracks aimed at Fortune. We are to assume that the Grugell are moving again on Fortune, and while we've sent a hyperphone message to the Navy, they're too far away at present to do anything about it. We find that, excepting two frigates near Fortune somewhere, we're the only three armed ships in the area."

"That's right. The *Robert Pritchard* and the *Giles Davies* are at Fortune, as of three weeks ago at any rate," Hess agreed.

"What are we going to do?"

"Set formation course for Fortune," Barrett said. "We can coordinate our subspace entry and exits to coincide; the Navy does formation jumps all the time. I downloaded the programming they use when we were in the Tarbos spacedock two months ago, but I've never had reason to use it until now."

"Can you cross-link the software over to us?"

"Yes," Barrett replied, meeting Captain Hess' eerie gaze.

"Then it seems we have a plan of action."

"We'd best move quickly," Jones added. "With only five or six ships, it won't be an Occupation force, probably just a scouting expedition. We'll want to move smartly."

"Agreed. The Navy won't be able to do much to hold Fortune with two frigates."

# Twenty
## October 2253

**Fortune**

The three privateers broke through barely in time, and only one was able to bring weapons to bear. The *Shade Tree* launched two Shrike missiles and engaged the fleeing Grugell with their forward particle beam, damaging one frigate before the enemy disappeared into subspace.

"Damn," Captain Jean Barrett muttered, watching the last two enemy ships disappear from the *Shade Tree*'s main screen. "I thought we had that one. Scanning, are the *Red Witch* and the *Cape Fear* still with us?"

"Still there, ma'am. The *Witch* is breaking off to the port, high, looks like they're moving out of the debris cloud. The *Cape Fear* is on our eight o'clock, moving to the starboard. They just launched a lander, Captain – looks like it's moving towards what's left of the *Pritchard*. The *Giles Davies* is dead in space at our ten o'clock high, she's bleeding air, no engine signature, looks like life support is on emergency."

"Call the Marines, have them, Doctor Adams, and Chief Smith meet me at the lander. How big a crew does a Navy frigate have?"

"About a hundred and fifty," someone piped up.

"Let's hope there's some survivors."

It was the work of ten minutes to bring the *Shade Tree* along-side the wrecked frigate; the clampon lander puffed across the fifty-meter gap between the ships and docked on the *Giles Davies'* undamaged portside docking point. While the Marines and the Chief Engineer went to look for survivors, Captain Barrett went directly to the Bridge.

The twin door panels to the frigate's Bridge were bent out-wards and scarred by an explosion, but that at least told Barrett that there was still atmosphere inside.

"Gomp," she spoke softly into her throat mike, "any sign of Grugell boarders?"

"No, Captain," the reply crackled into her earpiece. "No signs of any burn-ins. I'm in the main Weapons storage now, and nothing's been disturbed except by shock damage. Chief Smith says the computer is damaged but hasn't been hacked, all security codes are clean."

"All right. I'm at the Bridge now."

She placed a hand thoughtfully on her pistol and decided to leave it holstered but kept her hand on the comforting plastic of the grip as she stepped carefully through the smoking doorway.

The Bridge was well and truly wrecked. One major panel had exploded, and the compartment was strewn with shards and splinters of metal and plastic, splashes of blood, and worse. The Bridge crew was cut to pieces.

Just then, a low moan came from the floor behind a fallen ceiling panel. Barrett stepped over the panel to find a burned, blasted figure in the remnants of a Navy uniform, the one side of his collar that remained bore the silver leaf of a Commander.

She knelt beside the man as his eyes fluttered open. "Can you hear me?"

He looked at her, squinting. "Who are you? Not Navy…"

"No. I'm Captain Jean Barrett of the privateer starship *Shade Tree*. I'm sorry we didn't get here sooner."

"Nothing… you could have done," he gasped. "There must have been a dozen ships… I'm Commander James McAllister, commanding the *Giles D*."

"What were a dozen Grugell ships doing at Fortune? We thought they'd given up on this system."

"It looked like a rally point." McAllister spoke with great difficulty, and his face was growing paler by the moment. Beneath him, a pool of sticky red was growing, puddling on the deck.

"Doc," Barrett barked into her mike, "Get up here to the Bridge."

"Give me two minutes," the reply came back.

"No time," McAllister breathed. "We caught a frigate scouting the rally point yesterday before their main body showed up, boarded it, took eight prisoners, and hacked their main computer before blowing it up." He reached into a pocket, produced a tiny object, and held it out. "This is a phoebe," Captain McAllister explained. "It's got thirty terabytes of data encoded in it."

"Thirty terabytes? In this?" Barrett took the tiny device, examined it; it was a three-centimeter chip of plastic with a tiny metal plug on one end for a standard data port.

"It will hold fifty," McAllister breathed. His life was hemorrhaging away along with the blood that puddled on the deck beneath him, and the knowledge of the impending death showed in his eyes. "But this one has the plans for the Grugell Fleet's plan to move on Earth. Co-ordinates, subspace jump points, rally points, everything. Lots more, besides. We destroyed the frigate before the main body showed up; they don't know we have this information. Get it to Admiral Gauss…"

"You bet I will," Barrett agreed. *With this kind of info, we could hit the Grugell unawares at a rally point. It's the perfect chance to hammer their fleet hard, maybe finish this thing for keeps… After almost three years, what if we could actually finish this war? It would be worth anything.*

Captain Barrett looked away from the tiny plastic phoebe to where Commander McAllister lay bleeding on the deck of his shattered ship, but his eyes stared back lifelessly.

"Shit," she breathed. "All *Shade Tree* boarders, return to the lander immediately. Say again, all *Shade Tree* boarders, back to the lander at once. Acknowledge."

"CheifEng, roger that."

"Gomp, acknowledged."

"Doc, heading back now with three survivors."

*Three survivors – out of a crew of a hundred and fifty.* Jean Barrett scowled at the Phoebe. *Damn right I'll get this to Admiral Gauss, or I'll die trying.*

Ten minutes later the tiny lander clamped on to the *Shade Tree*'s sally port, and one minute after that, Jean Barrett bounded onto the Bridge.

"Come about to one-eighty by zero, ahead flank. Navigation, get a course for Tarbos. Helm, lock in that course and bring us to subspace transit as fast as you can get there. Weapons, lock a Shrike on what's left of the *Giles Davies*. We can't afford to leave any clues behind."

"Ma'am, technically that's still destroying Confederation property; that's a Class One felony."

"Thanks, Weps, but I think Admiral Gauss will forgive us this once."

"Subspace transit in three minutes, Captain."

"Good. Get that course laid in."

As the ship accelerated away from the scene of the battle, a single Shrike missile leaped from the starboard stub wing, angling back to obliterate what remained of the CSS *Giles Davies*.

"How long will it take us to get to Tarbos?"

"Four weeks, Captain, if we're a bit lucky," Navigator Geoff Peters answered. "Hell, twenty years ago it would have taken four months. Be glad OWME keeps developing refinements in the drive systems."

"All right. Indira, doesn't one of the Marines speak a little Grugell?"

"Yes, Captain, Sergeant Gomp does." Indira Krishnavarna had, in fact, been spending a lot of time with former Marine Sergeant Hector Gomp, an event almost impossible not to notice on a ship as small as the *Shade Tree*. "He took a course in it on Earth, when he was still in the Corps."

"Have him meet me in the mess room. I want him to look at the data on this Phoebe. We still have that computer terminal, right?"

"In the mess room, Captain. We've been using it to write mail."

"Good enough."

It took two hours; the data was not encoded, but Hector Gomp's training in written Grugell had been six years before, and his skills were rusty. What he understood wasn't comforting.

"Captain," he said at last, looking up from the computer screen with red-rimmed eyes, "If I'm getting this right, the Grugell have found Earth."

"Shit."

"Chin-deep, Cap'n. But there's more. This here," he pointed at the screen, "is an operations order. There's a lot of other crap here – ship specs, personnel orders, even officer's mess menus – the

Intelligence people on Tarbos will love this stuff, but the op-ord is where it's at. The Emperor – I hope that's the right word – has ordered their fleet to mass at a rally point to attack Earth. I can't make sense of their coordinate system, it's probably based on their home world as a start point, but it sure as hell reads like they know where they're going. There's a whole star map of their territory here, and if I'm right it goes into Confederate space too – a good astrogator should be able to unravel the whole thing."

"Wait a minute – back up. You said that their coordinate system probably uses their home planet as a start point. Wouldn't that mean that we could figure out where to look for their planet based on this?"

"Maybe. You might want to stick one of your ship geniuses on it; I'm just an old broke-dick jarhead."

"Maybe. Go on."

"Well, Captain, the op-ord here has their rally point, jump points, and even an interim rally point; if we can figure out for sure where it is. But if their target point is Earth, and we can figure out where their home world is and plug that in, we should be able to plot out their whole route…"

"And ambush them at a rally point."

"Something like that, yeah."

"Good work, Gomp. You just earned yourself a bonus for this trip. Now, why don't you get some sack time? Between the landing and this, you look like you've about had it. You're going to be pretty busy the next few days – I want you working on translating this stuff for Indira Krishnavarna and Geoff Peters."

"Captain, all due respect, but you're looking pretty dogged out yourself. You were on the landing party too, you know."

"I know, and thanks. Soon, OK? Do me a favor, shout up to the Bridge and have Indira and Geoff come down." She leaned back in her chair, thinking hard.

"Roger that, Captain." The former Marine stood, gave Barrett an informal, one-fingered salute of sorts, and left.

*If we can figure out their course, and get word to the Navy... And if we can figure out where their home world is...I wonder if we could pull that comet trick again.*

*I'm too tired for deep thinking just now.*

Her eyes were trying to close of their own accord when the Scanning tech and Navigator walked in. She fixed them with a bleary eye as they took seats, trying to conceal their curiosity.

"You two, you two have got one hell of a job to do. Geoff, given two known points on a star map using unknown units of measure, could you translate the data to be usable in our own Navigation console?"

"I think so," he said, frowning. "I'd have to work out the data on a copy of the standard Galactic chart, and then plot the data into the console."

"Good. The data's in Grugell; Gomp is going to help you with translations. Indira, I want you to work on another little idea with me..." She went on for about ten minutes.

"I think we can do it, Captain," Krishnavarna said at last, her eyes wide. "If you're sure you want to try it. All on our own, I mean."

"Just our cup of tea, Indira. Are we on course, everything normal? Good. I'm going to crash. You two call your relief to the Bridge; you're both off-duty for twelve hours. Get some rest; at noon tomorrow, I want you here in the mess room, working with Gomp on making this happen."

"Shit," Peters observed. Barrett grinned at him and left the chamber.

# Twenty-One
# November 2253

**Task Group One, 0112 hours**

Isaac Gauss blinked hard as the overhead light in his Flag
stateroom went on suddenly. He turned his head slightly, prepared
to unleash his Jovian wrath at whoever invaded the Flag quarters.
He relaxed slightly on seeing Captain Jensen standing there,
wrapped in a worn Air Force Academy bathrobe.

"What's up, Jerry?" Gauss sat up, yawned, and rubbed his eyes.

"Sir," Jensen said, his voice noticeably tense, "There's a privateer ship just popped through, they want to send a lander over to
the flagship. The Captain wants to talk to you personally."

"Which ship?"

"The *Shade Tree*, sir, out of Earth."

"Good ship. They're the ones that took out that Occupation
ship. All right, signal them to send their lander over in thirty
minutes. We'll meet them in the Flag office."

Jensen nodded. "Yes sir. I'll have some coffee and sandwiches
sent up."

"Good idea."

Jensen left, leaving the light on.

Gauss stood up slowly, stretching out his sleep-tightened
muscles. *Little after zero-one*, he thought, staring at his wall clock.
*I really am getting too old for this shit.*

A static-jet shower, a shave, and a clean uniform took him twenty minutes. He used the remaining ten minutes before the *Shade Tree* Captain's arrival to review the data the Navy had on the privateer.

The ship had been commissioned at Earth's shipyards only three years earlier. Smaller than the Navy's *Pritchard*-class frigates, the privateer carried a crew of twenty-five, and mounted particle beams and Shrike missiles. Captain Jean Barrett had also purchased two almost ninety-year-old thermonuclear magnetic mines, Navy Intelligence had learned; Gauss had personally discouraged further action on the illegal purchase after the privateer had used one of the mines to knock out one of the Grugell's Leviathanic Occupation ships.

Mounting one of the newest marks of the Gellar Star Drive along with a rather unique, charcoal black polymer hull, the *Shade Tree* would be fast and stealthy, although rather cramped for her crew. *The Navy could use a few like those*, Gauss told himself.

The clock clicked over to 0142. Gauss stood up, straightened his green shipboard uniform jacket, and headed for the *Mountain View*'s Wardroom.

Captain Barrett was a surprise. She was young, no more than forty. Gauss thought that very young for a starship Captain – even for a privateer. Gauss remembered a rumor he'd heard on Tarbos that Captain Barrett was involved with his own friend and the Navy's patron in the Confederate Senate, Michael Crider (L-Forest.)

Barrett stood as Gauss walked in. He smiled disarmingly at her, shook her offered hand – he was tempted to bow over it; Captain Barrett was undeniably attractive – and motioned for her to sit as he took a chair at the side of the table. "Pleasure to meet you, Captain Barrett. Good work you're doing out there. What can the Navy do for you this morning?"

Jean Barrett was as impressed by Admiral Gauss as she'd expected to be, but she didn't let that distract her. "Admiral, I've got something you need to see." She tossed a small plastic chip on the table.

"A phoebe," Gauss said, picking up the tiny data chip. "Where'd you get this? The Navy's only been using them a few months."

"I got it from the wreck of the *Giles Davies*, Admiral. I've got their survivors aboard the *Shade Tree* now – my lander should be on its way back there now to transfer them over here to the carrier. The *Bob Pritchard* was already a total loss when we got there; the *Giles Davies* was dead in space. We boarded it…"

"The *Giles D*'s Captain – what about him?" Gauss snapped the question.

"Dead, sir. He gave me this phoebe before he died."

Gauss frowned. He'd known Jim McAllister from the old USAF days. "All right. Go on."

"Sir, the *Giles D* had hacked the main computer of a wrecked Grugell frigate the day before they were hit by a Grugell Task Group. The chip contains the data they retrieved, plus our interpretation and analysis of some of that data – sir, the big thing is that the Grugell have located Earth. There's an operations order in there detailing their plan to strike at Earth with the better portion of their Fleet. It's got rally points, jump coordinates, everything. My Navigator was able to convert most of their course – we've got it there on a standard Confederate star-map, along with the original data so your own people can double-check his work."

"Good God," Gauss breathed. "They're ambitious bastards; if they could do to Earth what they did to New Albion, that would pretty much take us out of business. But if we can ambush them at a rally point…"

"You could take out the better part of their Fleet."

"Jerry," Gauss barked. He tossed the phoebe to his ever-present aide. "Take this up to Intelligence. I want a full analysis by noon. Get them going." Jensen caught the chip and left.

"Captain Barrett, I have to thank you for this. You may have just single-handedly won this damnable war. You know," Gauss said, "I could use another ship on this ambush. Frankly the Navy can use every ship it can find. If you're willing to put yourself under the Navy's tactical control, I'd be pleased to have you come with us."

"I'm flattered, Admiral, but I'll have to decline," Barrett said gravely. "I've got a plan of my own, one that I'm just in the middle of. Once we're done with the task at hand, I'll make best time to join up with the Fleet, but not until."

"Very well. May I ask what it is you're up to?"

"You may ask," Barrett grinned. "But I'm afraid I'll have to keep it to myself for now."

"Suit yourself. Just the same, I'd like you to talk to my Intel watch staff about your finding our two frigates; we didn't even know anything was wrong with them until a couple days ago, when they missed a routine transmission. You've brought the first news."

"I will be glad to, sir, preferably quickly. I do need to get back to my ship."

"I'll walk you up there right now."

**A rally point in space, near the Grugell/Confederate border**

Group Commander Kaddaschik II looked carefully over the holographic representation of the Fleet in his flagship's main scanner tank. Almost eight ships in ten were being sent to join the strike on the Confederate's home world, leaving behind only a few small ships for local defense of key planets and installations.

In what amounted to another Grugell month, the attack force would be assembled, and the Fleet would jump for their target.

## Twenty-Two
# January 2254

**Task Group One**

A hastily rewritten plan split the Fleet along uneven lines. The light cruisers *Cairo* and *Dallas* and three destroyers were already on their way, escorting the Marine division to New Albion.

The balance of the Fleet, including the newly arrived *Arcadia* and her sister ship the *Ranger*, expected within forty-eight hours, would jump for the calculated location of the primary Grugell rally point, where the enemy was expected to regroup after their initial flight into Confederate space. The rally point seemed to be a randomly chosen spot in open space; exactly what Admiral Gauss would have chosen. It was a random coordinate-set in deep space, near no occupied system, deep in a sector of space normally transited only by ships traveling in subspace.

The task of calculating the trajectory required to drop the Fleet in on the unsuspecting Grugell had taken only a day, once all the locations were plotted. Assembling the Fleet had taken longer, and in this they had been aided only by the fact that the Grugell faced the same handicap.

When all was ready, Captain Jerry Jensen brought the finalized timetable to Fleet Admiral Gauss as he sat in his habitual chair in the *Mountain View*'s Combat Information Center.

Gauss studied the timetable carefully, and then looked up at the big time display on the wall. The Fleet would cross the Line of Departure in sixty-three hours and twelve minutes.

"Any word from New Albion yet?" he asked no one in particular.

"No sir," the Signals watch officer replied. "Shouldn't expect anything for a few days."

## New Albion

The cruisers and destroyers popped out of subspace within a whisker of normal orbit, a risky move but one deemed acceptable by Captain Kirk Oliver, commanding Task Group 1.1. Two Grugell cruisers and a smaller ship opened fire almost instantly, damaging the *Cairo* before both cruisers vanished in puffs of flame from several Lancer missile hits. The smaller ship, one drive pod sheared off by particle beam fire from the destroyer *Charles Daly*, fled into subspace, leaving the garrison below abandoned.

Landing operations commenced two days later, on arrival of the old OWME liner *Santa Maria*. By that time, the Grugell garrison on the surface had been meticulously mapped by the cruiser's scanning suites; detailed maps were passed out to all the Marines down to the Squad Leader level.

One platoon descended in each of the *Santa Maria*'s old landing shuttles, enduring the jolting ride down through New Albion's gravity well to find a dispirited defense waiting them on the surface. Abandoned by the Fleet, the Grugell infantry on the surface were more inclined to surrender than fight, with one notable exception.

Dug in around the Command compound for the Grugell Occupation was a battalion of the Fifth Imperial Guards, a unit noted for fanaticism. The Commander of the Fifth, Stekakrattik III, had issued orders: Fight to the death. No human troops to pass their perimeter. The Occupation Commander's compound to be preserved at all costs, in the name of the Emperor. Armed to the teeth and dug deep into heavily fortified positions, the Fifth would be the toughest nut for the Confederate Marines to crack.

The first Confederate troops down near the Fifth's perimeter was the shuttle carrying First Platoon, Charlie Company, 3rd Marines. Corporal Gerald Rosenberg led his squad off the shuttle with a roared, "Second Squad, all the way! *Follow meeee!*"

The eight Marines of Second Squad, First Platoon charged towards a high wire fence containing a number of low buildings. Green bolts of Grugell fire swept the field, killing two squad members and driving the rest to earth. Around them, Corporal Rosenberg heard shouts, screams, and the popping of M22 carbines as the rest of First Platoon tried in vain to find cover.

Two bunkers on the other side of the fence were laying down a fan of green flame over the field. Rosenberg stuck his head up; risking decapitation from the blast of energy weapons fire, he carefully marked the locations of the bunkers. Rolling into a tiny depression in the brown dirt of the field, he fumbled for his radio.

"Charlie Six, this is Charlie One Two. Request orbital particle beam fire on coordinates one four six five, six five three six and one four six six, six five three eight, over."

"Charlie One Two, this is Charlie Six. Negative on your request," the crackling answer came back. "Orbital emitters are busy elsewhere; unable to comply for one zero mikes. How copy, over."

"Six, One Two. Roger that. We'll all be dead in ten minutes. Over."

"One Two, this is Six. Use your goddamn head and take out your targets. Over."

Rosenberg swore at the unseen radio operator on the other end of the radio net. "Roger that, Six. One Two out."

The young Marine risked another quick look. The two bunkers were still firing away with abandon; a scream to his left let him know another Marine had been hit. He picked up his mike again. "One Two Two, where you at?"

"To your left, One Two, about thirty meters," the reply came back.

"You still got the Volcano?"

"Roger that. You want to dig a hole?" The Volcano was a cratering charge, which used a tiny particle of anti-matter to destroy landing fields by blasting a fifty-meter semi-circle of earth into vapor.

"Something like that. You see where I am? Make your way over here pronto. Bring anyone else from Second Squad you can find."

"On my way." Three breathless minutes later, Lance Corporal Jonah James arrived with three other Marines. He wordlessly handed the golf-ball sized Volcano explosive to his squad leader.

"OK, here's the plan. Mickey, you and Pete lay down fire on that bunker to the right. Harry, you roll a little to the left, fire on the firing slit of that other one. Jonah, you come with me." Low-crawling in the best style they'd been taught by the screaming, foul-mouthed Drill Instructors at Camp Instruction, the Marines wriggled off towards the right-hand bunker. After a minute or so of wriggling through the choking dust, they arrived at a small depression forty meters from the bunker.

"How you doing?" James asked the corporal.

"I'm fucking amazed we made it. How's your arm?" Rosenberg rolled to grin at James, his white teeth standing out against his camouflaged, dust-covered face.

"You did better than me in grenade practice," James replied.

"I'll give it a try. Horseshoes and hand grenades, right?"

He rolled on his back, holding the Volcano in his right hand. His thumb pressed a contact; the Volcano began to whine softly. He counted to five, half-rolled, rose to his knees, and threw the Volcano with all his strength at the bunker.

A bolt of green clipped his shoulder, but the explosive was already on his way. Rosenberg dropped to the dust, teeth gritted against the burn, and buried his face in the dust as a massive blast erupted only eighty meters away. The shock wave rippled sickeningly through both Marines.

"Gerry," James spat a mouthful of dust out. "Gerry? You ok, dude?"

"Think so. Burned my shoulder, but it'll be all right. No bleeding, anyway."

"Bunker's *gone*, dude. Sorry, I mean Corporal."

"Don't sweat it. What about that other one?"

"Still shooting, but taking a lot of fire back. WHOA!" Fired from Second Platoon's positions, a Kestrel anti-armor missile slammed into the other bunker, obliterating it. The path into the Grugell Command compound was open.

The mop-up of the main compound was over in two more hours. With the capture of the Grugell Occupation Commander and the destruction of the last of the Fifth Imperial Guards, the Grugell resistance evaporated.

On the third day after the firing stopped, a thin, bedraggled, and thoroughly exhausted Jason MacFeeters led a hundred and six survivors out of what remained of the Crow Ridge Mountains. He reported to the Marine outpost near the ruins of *Glengarry* as the commander of the "First New Albion Highlander Volunteers," and requested orders. He was told to stand down.

New Albion belonged to the Confederacy again.

<h1 style="text-align:center">Twenty-Three<br>January 2254</h1>

## At the main Grugell rally point

Fleet Commander Tillistik IX was in personal command of the mission.

He watched the holographic display as it showed the Fleet assembling as ordered; in less than one Grugell day, the last stragglers from the initial subspace jump into the Confederacy would be back in formation, and the Fleet would jump to the human's home world. The cruisers were heavily loaded with atomic bombardment canisters. "The human home world will be reduced to radioactive dust," he whispered to himself.

"Fleet Commander," a technician's voice intruded on his thoughts. "There is a disturbance in the center of the formation."

"What? What kind of disturbance?"

## Task Group One

The trajectory plot was perfect. Six Confederate frigates dropped out of subspace in the middle of the Grugell formation, and before the Grugell could react, the Confederates had radar lock to engage with particle beam fire and missiles. Lances of barely visible, shimmering force shot through space, and three

Grugell frigates and two heavy cruisers boiled into expanding clouds of gas and rubble.

A radio command barked from the lead Confederate frigate, issued by the Task Group Commander, Rear Admiral Igor Perchik. "Hitchhikers away! Engage at will. Weapons free, all ships maneuver as necessary. Watch for cloaking enemy frigates!"

The Hitchhikers were A-66 attack fighters from VS-66, VS-42 and VS-90, attached to the Confederate frigates with magnetic grapples, four to each frigate. On a command from Captain Andrea Crider, they released their grapples and engaged their main drives, darting away from their host ships. Twenty-four fast, agile, and heavily armed strike craft were now loose in the middle of the still stunned Grugell fleet. They immediately began engaging with anti-ship missiles and cannon fire.

Captain Andrea Crider drove her fighter head-on at the largest of the Grugell ships, presumably the flagship. "Hunter Three, this is Hunter Lead. Follow me in, Horse. We're going for the flag."

"Got your six, Angel," her wingman called back. As one, they kicked their strike fighters to full throttle, diving after the Grugell ship. Bolts of green flame shot out at them, narrowing the gap as they raced closer.

"That's getting close, Angel," Horse called. His voice sounded nervous. "That's a lot of damn fire coming up."

"Hang on, Horse. Six kilometers to Shrike range. Go to Evasive Pattern Three." Both fighters began looping, spinning, dodging as they continued to close the Grugell ship. "Three kilometers. Two. Arm your Shrikes, Horse."

"Armed and ready, Lead."

"Hunter Lead, Hunter Lead, be advised, enemy fighters launching, enemy fighters launching, sixty kilometers to your left rear." The call from one of the attacking frigates made Andrea glance at her tactical display for an instant; a Grugell cruiser was launching a wave of fighters. *They're too far away to stop us*, she thought. The Grugell flagship swelled in her front viewer.

"Range! Fox One, Fox One! Evade! Follow me out, Horse!" She pickled off her four Shrikes, breaking for open space as Horse launched his Shrikes and turned to follow.

Her wingman didn't make the turn. An emerald bolt from the Grugell flagship shattered his fighter into a thousand pieces seconds before all eight Shrike missiles struck, smashing through the ship's shields and obliterating the massive silver form. With the Grugell flagship died Fleet Commander Tillistik IX, and any hope the Grugell had of regaining control of the situation. Captain Crider, though, noted only the loss of her wingman.

"Horse!" There was no time for grief; at least ten Grugell fighters were arcing towards her on an intercept course. She glanced at her tactical display, frowning to see no friendly fighters within a hundred kilometers. The rest of the wing had struck forward into the Grugell fleet's leading elements.

"Hunter Flight, this is Hunter Lead, I could use some help here."

"Tied up, Hunter Lead."

"I'm engaged, Hunter Lead."

"I've got three of my own, Angel."

Several terse replies amounted to *everyone's already busy*.

She twisted the stick, swinging the fighter to drive directly at the oncoming Grugell fighters. *I'm faster than they are, but they're tougher. I can turn tighter. If I can dodge through them, I'll be out of range and headed back towards the rest of the Flight before they can turn and get a lock on me.*

*Or, I can turn and get on their sixes.*

*Well, let's see how these skinny bastards like playing chicken.*

A touch of her thumb to the right contact on the stick armed her 30mm rotary cannon. A blast of green shot past her cockpit, making her flinch. "Come on, you bastards," she muttered. She hit the emergency boost, punching up every bit of speed the fighter had. She stole another quick look at her tactical display.

A hundred and twenty-one kilometers away, a Confederate frigate wallowed, trailing sparks and gas from three hull ruptures. A Grugell cruiser stalked it from the rear, closing slowly, peppering the ship with anti-proton fire. The frigate was about ten degrees off her present course.

*Close enough.*

She hit the ranging button on her stick. The lead Grugell fighter was within a thousand meters. She hit the cannon button on the stick, sending a thirty-round burst of 30mm shells at the darting silver shape. She missed narrowly as the Grugell yanked his fighter hard right, but the shells tagged another fighter fifty or sixty meters farther back. That ship puffed into a cloud of flying parts and gas.

Two green bolts, three, shot past Commander Crider's A-66 jinked hard, back and forth, spiraling and rolling to throw off the Grugell's firing solutions. She yanked the stick right, then left. The red circle in her heads-up display flashed from red to green for a moment, and she triggered another burst to disintegrate another Grugell fighter. And then she was past them, two of the cigar-shaped silver craft flashing by almost close enough to touch. A bolt of green smashed into her starboard stub wing as she broke through.

Her onboard computer's flat metallic voice sounded in her earpieces. "WARNING. YOUR STARBOARD STUB WING IS DAMAGED."

"I know," she growled. "I didn't need it anyway. My missiles are gone."

Behind her, the eight remaining Grugell fighters arced across space, dropping towards pursuit positions. Crider arced towards the Grugell cruiser, using her speed advantage to stay well ahead of the pursuing fighters. Her cannon would be no more effective than spitballs against the cruiser. She reached across the stick with her thumb to arm her one remaining weapon attached to the underside of the fighter's fuselage.

The Grugell fighters were still shooting. A green bolt clipped her fighter on the port side. "WARNING. YOU ARE LOSING CABIN PRESSURE. ACTIVATE EMERGENCY SUIT SEALS AT ONCE." She pulled down her helmet's face shield, activated her suit's environmental system, shut down the cabin air system. "YOU ARE LOSING POWER. YOU ARE LOSING POWER. ESTI- MATE THREE MINUTES UNTIL MAIN DRIVE FAILURE," the computer reported belatedly.

Another bolt clipped the fighter. "Damn. Their shooting is improving."

"YOUR AFT MANEUVERING THRUSTERS ARE DAM- AGED. NAVIGATION FUNCTIONAL WITH GYROS ONLY."

"Shit." The Grugell cruiser was just ahead now. The enemy fighters stopped shooting, probably for fear of hitting their cruiser. "Perfect," Captain Crider muttered. "Follow me in, boys!"

"ESTIMATE TWO MINUTES UNTIL MAIN DRIVE FAILURE," the computer commented. The fighter was starting to feel a little sluggish. The Grugell cruiser had taken notice of her; a gunner on the enemy ship's silver humpback was trying to engage her with an anti-proton projector. *Too slow*, she thought. She flashed past the cruiser, touching a contact on the stick as she passed fifty meters from the enemy ship, trailing a half-dozen Grugell fighters a few hundred meters in her wake – and a ther- monuclear magnetic mine.

The mine, attracted to the largest ferrous mass in the area, fired tiny maneuvering jets, looping around in space, following and finally catching the Grugell cruiser. In her fighter, Captain Crider closed her eyes tight, pulling the fighter for clear space, wringing every bit of speed she could out of her failing main drive.

A new sun blossomed briefly in space behind her. The Grugell fighters vanished in puffs of flame, swallowed in the nuclear fireball. The cruiser was obliterated.

"WARNING, SHIP HAS SUFFERED ELECTROMAGNETIC DAMAGE. MAIN DRIVE SHUTDOWN IN FIFTEEN SECONDS. FOURTEEN. THIRTEEN."

Crider stabbed a contact, silencing the computer. She shut down her main drive manually and used her gyro on battery power to align the ship so she could see 'ahead' – in the direction of travel. No Confederate or Grugell ships were in view. She touched the radio button.

"Strike Commander, this is Hunter Lead. Main drive is out, maneuvering is out. Rescue beacon is activated. Request SAR."

"Hunter Lead, this is Hunter Base. Stand by for tractor beam pickup."

Andrea Crider snapped her head around, searching space for the source of the new voice – and there it was, the carrier *Mountain View*, accompanied by two cruisers and three frigates, popping out of subspace even as she watched to take the Grugell fleet in the rear. Her fighter rattled momentarily as the tractor beam took hold, yanking her fighter roughly into the ship's hangar – there was no time to be gentle. Four minutes later she was climbing out of the smoking, battered fighter in the familiar hangar deck, feeling like she'd just come home. No less than Fleet Admiral Gauss himself stood at the base of her crew ladder.

"That was some pretty impressive flying, Captain."

Andrea dropped off the ladder, came to attention, saluted. "Thanks, sir, but my flight's still out there, and…"

"I understand." Gauss turned to shout an order. "Someone get the Captain to another fighter!" He watched as the petite form of Captain Crider raced to follow a Chief Petty Officer to a freshly armed and fueled A-66. "There's a Medal of Honor in the works there, Jerry," he commented to his aide. "That's the second Grugell flagship she's taken out."

"Sir," Captain Jensen reported, reading a message pad he held in one hand. "The *Arcadia* group just dropped out of subspace, just as planned, five hundred kilometers in front of the Grugell lead elements. They're engaging now."

"Well, let's get back to CIC. Hard pounding, this," he said, quoting the Duke of Wellington. "Let's see who pounds longest."

They arrived in CIC to find that the *Arcadia* task group had dropped out of subspace neatly in front of the Grugell fleet.

The massive Confederate *dreadnought*s *Arcadia* and *Ranger* dove majestically into the midst of the shocked Grugell ships. Particle beam and Hawk missile fire poured from the great ships at an incredible rate, while Grugell torpedoes and anti-proton fire slammed into their shields with little or no effect.

"Have you got any proxies towards the front of the Grugell battle group?" Gauss' barked words brought quick results, as a Senior Chief Petty Officer quickly switched a large scanner tank to receive the take of a proxy overseeing the forward edge of the battle.

The *Ranger* had taken two torpedo hits, but showed no signs of ill effect other than a slight scorching of her hull plates near the outlet of her massive Gellar tunnel. A flight of Grugell fighters dove towards the vast ship, launching torpedoes as they went, but particle beam projectors on the *Ranger*'s hull engaged them with computer-controlled precision, playing arcs of fire across space, shattering torpedoes and fighters alike. A Grugell battle cruiser tried to engage the mighty ship, but failed utterly as particle beams from the *dreadnought* shattered its drive pods seconds before six Hawk missiles arrived to swallow the Grugell ship in a sun-bright burst of atomic flame.

Eighteen hundred meters away, the *Arcadia* had less luck, as a Grugell light cruiser rammed her amidships. Trailing gases and sparks, the second Confederate *dreadnought* turned slowly away from the main battle area, still firing away with main particle beam batteries as she went. A frigate attempting a repeat of the ramming maneuver met with crossed particle beam fire and was exploded only a hundred meters from the *dreadnought*, causing fragment and electromagnetic damage to the massive ship. With her shields down to minimum and weapons power reduced dramatically, the *Arcadia* went to full power and arced north to leave the area.

To the rear of the enemy formation, the carrier *Mountain View* launched another wave of fighters while the frigates and cruisers redeployed. The Grugell flagship was destroyed, and the lack of leadership made the Grugell ships easy targets as they tried in vain to evade, and the Confederate ships split up to hunt individual targets in what was rapidly degenerating into a shooting gallery.

Within the hour it was all but over.

Admiral Gauss stood looking at the huge tactical display in the *Mountain View*'s Combat Information Center. Three Confederate cruisers, six frigates and the *dreadnought Ranger* pursued the remnants of the Grugell Fleet, now obviously in a panicked withdrawal. Proxies from the *Mountain View* followed them until they jumped into subspace. Only one light cruiser and three frigates, out of the bulk of the Grugell attack force, made it to subspace. Gauss imagined that, once they got back to their home planet, there would be hell to pay.

"Captain Jensen," he called across the CIC. "Remember old Wellington after Waterloo?"

"Sir?" Jensen looked puzzled. He wasn't a student of military history.

"They came in the same old way, and you know, we beat them, in the same old way," the Admiral quoted. "We kicked their asses, Jerry. We kicked their skinny asses. Come on, let's head down to Signals. I've got a hyperphone message to send."

## Twenty-Four
# February 2254

**Six Astronomical Units outside the orbit of Grugell**

Word of the crushing defeat of the Grugell Navy had not yet reached the home world of the militaristic race, according to the stream of chatter interpreted by the *Shade Tree*'s Signals section. Parked behind a Mt. Everest-size asteroid inside the orbit of the system's first gas giant, the privateer ship was engaged in what Captain Barrett called "Operation Fastball."

Two days of calculation had preceded the fitting of five proxy maneuvering thrusters to an asteroid the size of a small village in Barrett's native England. On command from Indira Krishnavarna, the thrusters fired, aiming the asteroid on a plunging orbit that would result in an impact on the Grugell home world's northern hemisphere, roughly five hundred kilometers west of the largest city. Five days later, the asteroid impacted as planned, and the impact and the results of that impact were recorded by the *Shade Tree*. The privateer ship jumped into subspace for Tarbos ten hours after the strike, undetected by the remnants of the Grugell's planetary defenses.

**Tarbos, sixteen days later**

"A report, Senator, from Fleet Admiral Gauss."

"Yes? What is it? Did the battle come off as he'd expected?"

"I'd say so, sir." An uncharacteristically cheerful Anton Silva handed Senator Crider the printout, obviously just taken from the hyperphone printer. The terse message contained exactly three words:

WE WON.

GAUSS.

"A man of few words, our Admiral Gauss," Senator Crider laughed.

Another bit of news had come the previous day in the form of a video stream of what the privateer ship *Shade Tree* claimed was the Grugell home world; Crider sat down and replayed the ultimate portion again, for the fifth time, since he'd received a copy from the Navy Department.

The Grugell home planet was a small, Mars-sized world, which was not surprising given what the Confederacy knew of the alien species' tolerance for Earth-level gravity. The nighttime view showed one large city in the northern hemisphere of the small, desiccated planet parked about half again as far from its large, blue-white sun as Earth from Sol, and as Mike watched, a flash revealed what the Navy Department agreed was the impact of a very large asteroid. The Grugell home world was devastated by the impact; shock waves had leveled much of the capital city, and the aftereffects would wreak havoc on the planet for at least a generation.

*Add that to the wrecking of their Fleet*, Mike thought, *and the Grugell aren't a factor for a few years.*

Five days later, a Grugell ship appeared in near Tarbos orbit, preceded by a radio beacon requesting parlay in badly translated English. The Grugell Emperor was seeking a truce.

## Twenty-Five
# April 2254

**Honshu, a small mining colony near the Grugell Frontier**

President Janine Cochet sat at the table in the Wardroom of the *Dreadnought Arcadia* and faced her counterpart, the defeated Emperor Apportamattid XIII. In front of each Head of State lay a copy of a treaty; the Treaty of Honshu declared a formal end to hostilities between the Confederated Free Worlds and the Grugell Empire, delineated a formal border between the two races, and established full diplomatic relations, with embassies to be established on Earth, Tarbos, Grugell, and the Grugell world Gorbinia.

Behind President Cochet, Fleet Admiral Isaac Gauss smiled expansively at the Grugell Emperor. Apportamattid had been informed that Gauss was the man responsible for the destruction of his Fleet, and has reacted in a surprising manner, smiling at Gauss and placing a bony, thin, clawed hand on his arm.

"Fleet Admiral Gauss," he said in badly accented English. "You are an enemy we can respect. You are to be – appreciated?" His brow furrowed over his gleaming black eyes. "Ah – no – *congratulated* on your victory."

"Thanks," Gauss replied, trying not to flinch away from the alien's touch. "You didn't do so bad yourself."

"And so, we are now to be friends," the Emperor said. "One big happy Galaxy." He fixed Gauss carefully with an inscrutable gaze for a moment, and then turned away.

The treaty was worked out quickly, and now, on April 14TH, 2254, President Cochet and Emperor Apportamattid XIII signed the document, officially ending the First Galactic War.

## Twenty-Six
## June 2254

**Tarbos**

An endless chatter of conversation, clinking dinnerware, and the hum of traffic outside defined a meal at Mountain View's Road House Steak Emporium, but even after years of war the restaurant was still the venue of choice for fine dining in the Confederate capitol.

Senator Mike Crider Junior, soon-to-be *former* Senator Crider, stood up and waved at his sister as she walked in the door. "Over here," he called, indicating his table at a window.

Andrea Crider smiled at her brother; the Senator noted the glitter of a Medal of Honor on her dress white uniform jacket. She hugged her brother before they sat down.

"The Medal looks good on you, Andrea," the Senator grinned.

"Not as good as a flight suit. I'm ready to get back to my ship, Mike; I can't stand this headquarters crap."

"You turned down a promotion to Commodore, didn't you?"

Andrea took a sip of white wine and thought for a moment before replying. "You know, big brother, I figure a person should always have a sense of what they're best at, and then they should stick to that. I'm a hell of a good pilot, and I'm even a pretty damn good flight leader. But the moment you take that Flag rank, that means you're playing petty politics half the time, and pushing paper the other half – which means you're not flying at all. I want to keep up my flight status. I like having my office in the cockpit of a fighter."

"I can't say as I blame you."

"I figured you might say something like that," Captain Crider chided her brother. "I hear tell you won't be standing election for a fourth term."

"No, I won't. I've had enough of Mountain View. It's time to go do something else for a while."

The pilot and the Senator regarded each other for a few moments.

"I've got three months accumulated leave," Andrea said at last. "I figured on going home for a while. Will you be heading back to Forest after your term's up?"

Mike leaned back in his chair, smiling. "I'll go back to see Mom and Dad for a few weeks, but I'll be leaving again. You know, I was thinking of signing on with a privateer for a couple years. See the Galaxy, all that sort of thing, you know?"

"I have a feeling I do," Andrea replied.

## The *Arcadia*

Fleet Admiral Isaac Gauss found that the *Dreadnought* class ships made excellent flagships.

"Some coffee, sir?" Gauss looked up to see his new Chief of Staff walking towards him, a cup in each hand. His former Chief of Staff, Captain Jensen, was now in command of the *Arcadia*.

Gauss took a cup and sipped. "How far to the space buoy?"

"About three minutes, sir. Task Group has already coordinated the subspace jump. We'll jump as soon as the last screen ship clears the buoy."

"Very well."

Gauss leaned back in the leather chair, listening to the *Arcadia*'s massive drive rumbling faintly under the deck.

His Navy was taking shape. On Earth, Halifax and Tarbos, new training bases and new officer candidate programs were being planned. Most of the training curricula were being developed under the scrutiny of the first Master Chief Petty Officer of the Navy, Paul Ortega.

Something else new was happening on the planet below. The Grugell Ambassador had arrived on Tarbos the day before, strangely subdued but ready to learn the business of diplomacy – a new and strange concept for the Grugell.

Victory was won, but Gauss had no intention of allowing his ships and crews to rest on their laurels. Ignoring the President's personal request that he remain at the Tarbos Navy Base, Gauss was accompanying the Task Group to New Albion, ostensibly to 'evaluate training and readiness.' He relaxed now in a large leather chair in the *Arcadia*'s Combat Information Center, watching the main scanner tank as the Task Group prepared to jump into subspace.

"What do you think we'll see this trip, sir?"

"If we're lucky?" Gauss looked down into the black swirl of coffee in his cup. Images spun through the Admiral's mind; images of wrecked ships, of drifting bodies, of nuclear fire and shattered planets. *All that's over*, he told himself sharply. *At least for now, at least this time.*

"If we're lucky?" he repeated. "Nothing, George. If we're lucky, we'll see nothing at all." He took a sip of the dark Forestian coffee.

"Nothing, sir?"

"Well, maybe not *nothing*." The Admiral grinned and leaned forward, stabbing a contact on his chair's arm. "All ships, General Quarters, all ships, General Quarters." He looked over at the scanner tank; the trail destroyers were still a few kilometers short of the space buoy. *Close enough*, Gauss thought.

"All ships, for exercise, emergency subspace jump to coordinate-set alpha six foxtrot. Initiate!"

Gauss' laughter echoed though the CIC as the Task Group blasted into subspace and disappeared.

# Don't miss the next installment of the Galactic Confederation series
## Sky of Diamonds

*In space,*
*even the hottest blood runs cold.*

A trillionaire recluse
An eccentric old man
An Amazonian former Marine
A young, seemingly, 'innocent' girl
A racketeer's bodyguard

Driven by desire. Goaded by dark instinct. They are driven to secrecy, and hide in plain sight among the Confederacy's trillions of ordinary humans.

After the Grugell War, a tentative and fragile peace has settled over the Confederacy. During this period of peace, prosperity, and exploration, evidence of an ancient legend has surfaced.

Are the apparently immortal Elites monsters or guardians? Predators or professors? Wellsprings of evil or fonts of wisdom?

Do the Elite themselves even know the answers?

From the wards of a Confederate Navy hospital ship, to an outlaw world, to a burgeoning new colony, the Elite are slowly making their presence felt. The Confederacy and, indeed, humanity itself, will never again be the same.

# About the Author

Anderson Gentry grew up in the hills and trout streams of northeast Iowa's wooded uplands, gaining a keen interest in wildlife, camping, hunting, fishing, and the outdoors.

Gentry served in the U.S. Army in the last years of the Cold War, including service in the Persian Gulf War. Captain Gentry concluded his military career by serving on the staff of the Command Surgeon, U.S. Army, Europe. Along the way, he obtained a bachelor's degree in Biology.

Anderson Gentry's first major novel, The Crider Chronicles received a 2005 Preditors & Editors Reader's Choice Award for Top Ten Science Fiction Novel. The Galactic Confederacy series has continued with the 2008 release of Sky of Diamonds. A spin off work, Barrett's Privateers was released in 2008.

His fast-paced, hard-hitting style combines a unique blend of outdoor savvy, real-world military experience, and realistic character development.

Reaad more at https://andersongentry.com

## Also by Anderson Gentry

### *The Galactic Confederacy Series*
The Crider Chronicles
Sky of Diamonds

### *Nova Roma Series*
Nova Roma 1: De Itinere in Occasum
Coming soon -Nova Roma 2: Quaestu pro Nova Terra

Barret's Privateers

Find more about
Crimson Dragon Publishing's Books,
sign up for news, sneak peeks,
giveaways, and more!

https://crimsondragonpublishing.com

www.ingramcontent.com/pod-product-compliance
Lightning Source LLC
Chambersburg PA
CBHW010345200726
48286CB00016B/2799